MW00849250

TARGET: UNKNOWN

THE COVERT ASSET SERIES BOOK 2

BRAD LEE

Copyright © 2024 by Simply Sensible Entertainment, Inc.

ISBN: 978-1-961799-02-8

All rights reserved. No part of this publication may be reproduced, stored, or transmitted in any form or by any means known now or in the future, including electronic, photocopying, recording, or scanning, without written permission from the publisher, except for brief quotations for review purposes.

This novel is a work of fiction. Names, characters, and events depicted are from the author's imagination. Any resemblance to actual persons, living or dead, events, or locations is coincidental.

Any brand names and or product names in this book are trade names, trademarks, and registered trademarks of their respective owners. The publisher, author, and the book are not associated with any product or vendor mentioned. None of the companies referenced within the book have endorsed the work.

PART 1

THURSDAY

1

THE MISSION

Thomas "Bone" Marks stalked across the high desert terrain, green in the glow of his night vision goggles.

So far, the infiltration had gone smoothly, though a saying from his time as a SEAL came to mind: No plan survives first contact with the enemy.

He moved like a ghost, head swiveling, senses on high alert. He was miles from the nearest house and far outside his hometown two hours northwest of Phoenix, Arizona.

Another mile of slow movement—heel to toe, careful to not scatter pebbles or brush against vegetation—brought him to the target location: a 10-acre compound carved out of the desert. The area had been graded flat, leaving behind tan soil that had been packed down over the years. A few rows of bushes remained, and several mesquite trees grew, the native plants able to endure the hot, dry summers—like now.

Despite the higher elevation of the area, the night air was warm even this late, but 80 degrees felt cool compared to the baking high 90s of the afternoon.

Bone ignored the temperature and continued forward, acclimated to the heat—though the long-sleeve tan camo fatigues, plate carrier stuffed with magazines for both his recently acquired M4 and new 9mm pistol, along with the military-grade armor, had him drenched in sweat.

He stopped when the flat-roof adobe house came into view on the far side of the compound. It could be empty, guarded by a lone sentry, or filled with bad guys; Bone just didn't know. His intel was too sketchy.

He'd avoid the building and hope for the best.

His primary target would likely be a few hundred yards to the right of the house, near one of the mesquite trees on the compound.

If Bone's recent training had been good enough, the tango would soon be lying on the hard desert ground with a single bullet to the head.

If not, the night would end in disaster.

Either way, the real fun would start after Bone took that shot. Even with a suppressor on the M4, the locals would hear the sound and react.

He'd have his hands full trying to escape.

Bone continued forward, crouched low but not yet crawling. There had been no sentries during his recon two nights earlier. He should be safe for a while longer.

He snuck onto the grounds of the compound without incident, moving like his old self—a silent shadow.

All he needed now was his former Teammates around him.

As the memories of his friends intruded, Bone stopped cold and took a knee.

He couldn't let his grief for Tank, Baldy, Bossman, Sneaky, Biscuit, Iron, and Dizzy—or the image of them lying dead in the desert of Afghanistan—overcome him now.

He had to stay focused.

A breathing exercise got him back on track, and he moved more slowly now that he was closer to the enemy.

He reached a row of bushes and skirted right, guessing at the best location to set up for the shot.

It was time for extra stealth. He lowered to his stomach and crawled the rest of the way.

The ground radiated heat.

The tree where the target should be was just ahead. The earlier recon had paid off; Bone was in the perfect spot.

He sighted through the scope of his rifle, searching...

There. Standing without a care in the world.

Bone hesitated. This was the moment of truth. He'd been training for weeks. Mixed martial arts at a gym in town. Rifle and pistol at the shooting range. He'd even gone into the hellish heat of Phoenix for a few days to dust off his helicopter piloting skills at a flight school.

But was it enough?

Was he back?

Did he still have what it took to complete a mission—and survive?

If he made this shot, he faced a running gunfight as he exfilled.

If he missed… All his work, the hours of training, would have been for nothing.

He banished the concern from his mind.

He was ready.

The target hadn't moved. The time was now.

Bone lined up the shot—at the outside range of the M4, but he hadn't brought a dedicated sniper rifle—stilled his body, and fired.

The bullet slammed into the target, exactly where Bone had aimed.

As quiet as it was, the shot would draw attention. Bone jumped to his feet and ran left toward the escape route.

Ahead and to his right, clear as day in the green of the NVGs, at least a dozen tangos appeared.

Bone dropped them as he ran, barely slowing.

Targets came out of the night, more than he thought there would be.

He fired.

They fell.

He didn't have time to reload. He let the rifle dangle on its sling and drew his sidearm, angling to the side to use four large blue barrels, stacked two on two, as cover.

After dropping the latest targets, he moved farther right, conscious of the increasing distance from his planned exfil. But he was in the zone now. He'd take out all the enemy and worry about getting away later.

His heart rate had increased, but Bone was as focused as he'd been back when he'd done this sort of thing every night—and the targets had shot back.

He slipped to the next bay at the open-air desert firing range, refusing to see the compound for what it was—the best shooter's club in a hundred miles—and kept pretending that he was on a real mission with actual tangos out to kill him instead of rushing through the entire complex of obstacles and metal targets of all shapes and sizes.

His bullets *clanged* against more tangos as he darted along the courses, reloading the pistol before holstering it and moving to the next bay—a second rifle lane, similar to where he'd dropped the first ghostly white, man-shaped metal target.

Even at this distance, he nailed every shot with his reloaded M4.

Finally, the exercise was over. He'd burned through a small fortune in ammo and now had to retrace his steps to pick up the empty mags—and double-check that he'd done as good of a job as he thought.

After that, he could lower the range flag and make his way back across the desert to the car parked at a trailhead miles away. He didn't need to pretend to exfil. He'd gotten plenty of nighttime stalking practice the last few weeks. Tonight had been the final test to see if he could put together a simple approach, a long-distance, cold-bore shot, and a run-and-gun against dozens of tangos, all without losing his cool.

Bone was drenched in sweat but breathing no heavier than usual. Aside from the one brain glitch when thoughts of his old Team had briefly intruded, he had succeeded.

He was good to go.

Now all he needed was an actual mission.

2

THE REVENGE

Happy Acres Independent Living Community
Ojai, California

Patrick had been looking forward to his first murder for years.

The desire—the need—had been there for as long as he could remember.

Tonight, as the moment grew closer, it swelled inside him.

He would prove, once and for all, that he was more than just a pretty face.

He dismounted the motorcycle and pushed it another few feet off the rural road into the thin woods. The area—several miles outside town, right on the edge of suburbia—would be quiet and peaceful for another year or two before housing subdivisions encroached.

The elderly residents at the upscale retirement community on the far side of the trees wouldn't mind the development. They'd buy the pricey new homes for their adult kids to live in so they could finally see their grandchildren more often. The proximity would remove the frequent excuse of how far of a drive it was for the kids to visit.

Patrick walked just inside the tree line bordering a large pond, exactly like his two test runs. He left his black leather riding gloves on and didn't remove the full-face helmet—though he lifted the tinted face shield. At 2 a.m., it had to look strange, but he'd chosen the time carefully. Insomniacs would be fading, and the early risers—including some of the old folks who only slept a few hours a night—should still be snoring in bed.

He could not get caught. That would ruin everything. If necessary, he'd use his pistol to kill anyone who got in his way of escaping—and damn the consequences.

The sprawling independent living community was highly coveted; its wait list ran six to eight months, depending gruesomely on how healthy the current residents remained. People often moved out to transfer to an assisted living facility, usually at the insistence of their kids.

Or the residents left feet first—on a stretcher to the hospital.

Or to the funeral home, as Patrick's target would in the morning when someone discovered his cold body.

The woods wrapped around the entire community of two-story buildings connected by wide, well-lit hallways. The self-closing exterior doors that allowed residents access to the buildings from their assigned parking spots could only be opened with keycards, which Patrick didn't have. The doors were alarmed and had security cameras inside and out. There was no chance a forgetful resident wouldn't close the door. And no one would let him in. Visitors weren't allowed through the side doors—only through the front lobby, where IDs were checked, photographs taken, and visitor passes issued.

The company that owned the community, and eight others around the state, took security seriously, as did the residents.

Most of them.

Each ground-floor apartment had a screened-in patio with a simple latch-locked screen door to the grassy yard right outside.

Access to the patios was through sliding glass doors that allowed plenty of natural light to shine in.

One resident, three apartments along from his target, had left her sliding door cracked open to the night's pleasant temperature during both of his test runs.

Tonight shouldn't be any different.

Patrick left the relative security of the woods and walked purposefully across the open area bordering it, then past the luxury cars in the parking lot. He didn't slouch or sneak, nor did he hurry. Any of the old people still awake would have trouble seeing him; if they noticed, his demeanor shouldn't raise any alarms despite the motorcycle helmet.

There would be no hiding his tall, muscular frame, but it shouldn't matter. Not if everything went according to plan.

He arrived at the patio three down from his target's. The screen door was locked, but a flick of his folding knife accessed the blade. He slid it between the frame and the door and pushed up.

The hook-and-eye latch flipped open.

He folded the knife closed and returned it to his pocket. He couldn't use it for tonight's work.

The death had to look accidental.

Patrick moved across the small, enclosed patio to the sliding door, which was once again cracked open. The apartment's overhead lights were off. No one was in the small living room, crammed with a couch, two chairs, end tables, and a coffee table.

The patio door slid open smoothly and quietly.

Every outlet in the small room had a nightlight, which made avoiding the excessive furniture easy.

He crossed silently to the apartment's front door, which opened into a wide hallway. Dark green, industrial-grade carpet paired nicely with pale green walls. Just outside the door, a small shelf held framed pictures of kids and grandkids.

Patrick moved three doors up the hall. The display shelf outside this apartment also had photographs of a large family. His target featured prominently in all of them—standing with kids and grandkids, holding up an enormous fish on the end of a line, and other pictures of a life joyously lived.

There were no pictures of the man's work with the Central Intelligence Agency, and none of the pictures on display showed the depth of his cowardly disregard for doing the right thing.

Patrick tried the door—locked, as he'd suspected. Despite the community's tight exterior security, a man with his past would always lock his door.

Using a lockpick gun and tension wrench, Patrick made quick work of the lock.

The kitchen to the left and living room ahead were lit with the same type of nightlight as the first apartment, making Patrick wonder if they came pre-installed in each home.

The layout of Mr. Rutherfield's apartment was a matching image of the one three doors down, so the bedroom was down the hall to the right.

Patrick didn't hesitate. He waltzed in like he had been invited, moving quietly along the hallway and into the bedroom.

Mr. Rutherfield had a narrow, wrinkled face and pure white hair cropped short. He lay on his back, mouth partly open, snoring softly in the glow of yet another nightlight.

It saved Patrick from having to roll him over. Instead, he merely yanked the pillow from beneath the old man's head and brought it down over his face.

The abruptly awakened Mr. Rutherfield struggled immediately, though he was no match for Patrick's strength. Decades earlier, he would have given anyone a run for their money, but not now. Not at 70-something years old.

And not when Patrick held the pillow over his mouth and nose with one hand and punched him in the groin with the other. It didn't matter whether the equipment still worked well or not. A blow below the belt hurt no matter how old you were.

After less than a minute of thrashing, kicking, and flailing—along with two more punches to the man's jewels—it was over.

Patrick barely had time to enjoy it.

He held the pillow for thirty more seconds, just in case, before it went back under dead Mr. Rutherfield's head.

Patrick rearranged the sheets and blanket to appear like there hadn't been a futile struggle to live.

When everything looked like it had when he entered the room, he pulled out a burner cell phone, stood over the dead body, and took several pictures, risking the flash illuminating the room.

Satisfied all was in order, he left. The living room, the front door, the hallway.

He moved on autopilot, not yet able to process what he'd done.

Down the hall, into the other apartment, out the sliding door—leaving it cracked open exactly as he'd found it—and the screen door, which he couldn't latch from the outside. He'd have to risk the elderly resident wondering if she'd left it unlocked all night.

A steady walk across the parking lot, through the grass, and into the woods.

The magnitude of his actions hit him halfway back to the motorcycle.

He'd killed.

Certainly not an innocent person. Calvin Rutherfield was anything but that.

But Patrick had taken his first life—and enjoyed it immensely.

He'd started down a path he couldn't deviate from.

Not anymore.

It felt too good to get revenge, even though it wasn't exactly his own.

He had proven he had what it takes.

He was more than just a pretty face.

Because of tonight, he would get the recognition he deserved.

Finally.

He shivered as he mounted the motorcycle.

Not from the night air, but from the anticipation of the next murder, and the next, and the next.

PART 2

SATURDAY

3

THE OFFICE

Rahbar International Trading Partners
Surobi, Afghanistan

The past twelve months had been the most satisfying of retired Colonel Tariq's life, despite the pressure—and risk.

He rolled his shoulders to loosen the tension and shifted in his desk chair. He ignored the stack of reports in front of him, which detailed the profits and losses of the legitimate side of his new business.

After forty years of working for Pakistan's Inter-Services Intelligence agency—ISI—he'd retired with a pension, extensive connections, and mastery of the skills that were about to make him rich.

If he had allowed a window in the office, he could have seen the sun rising over the town of Surobi, halfway between Kabul and Jalalabad. The small town was on the main road straight from Peshawar and his source of plastic explosives, along with other essential bomb-making supplies.

No one would think to look for a successful international terrorism operation in the Afghanistan town.

The world had no idea Tariq was here.

Or that he had blown a hole in the wall of the American embassy in Cairo, killing ten and injuring four Americans.

That he had engineered the total destruction of a food court at a shopping mall in Turkey, killing ten.

And blown up part of the airport on the Spanish island of Mallorca, killing five but injuring sixty-two.

All practice jobs in preparation for this one in Paris—and the next, which is where Tariq would really earn his keep.

Operational security dictated the small office be isolated from the outside world. He'd had it built as a freestanding room in the far corner of a large import-export business warehouse, though as a concession to comfort, he'd had a mini-split air-conditioning unit installed in the wall to keep him cool.

It hummed quietly now as he used his phone to review the footage of his previous attacks.

4

THE ATTACKS

Nine Months Earlier

It was the third and final practice run before the bombing.

Ehab was a student, but his need of money found him driving toward the American embassy. He wiped his sweaty palms on the new khaki work pants, one at a time, as he carefully navigated the route along the tree-lined street.

He would be more nervous in two days, when he would pretend the van disguised as belonging to a local utility provider had broken down, park the vehicle, and hurry to safety before dialing a number on his mobile phone to detonate the explosives packed into the back.

He slowed as he neared the barricades on the road which forced traffic farther from the wall surrounding the embassy.

The passenger in the car following the van couldn't keep his hands from shaking, but he focused the phone's videocamera on the utility company's panel van as it slowed a half kilometer ahead.

Today was not a test run, as the student in the van in front of them believed.

Today was the day.

The driver of the car pressed a button on his mobile phone in the cradle attached to the air-conditioning vent.

In two days, Ehab would pull over just ahead. Then the job would be done. He would have the money and could return to his studies.

A loud beep came from the back of the minivan.

He had enough time to realize that he had been betrayed, but not enough to fear his imminent death.

The men in the sedan watched as the van reached the point closest to the American embassy wall.

The mobile phone completed the call, and the van exploded, obliterating nearby cars and knocking a gigantic hole in the wall surrounding the embassy.

Istanbul Central Mall
Istanbul, Turkey

Six Months Earlier

The young men had applied for jobs to work in the mall food court originally to meet people—especially the young women that also worked there.

A year later, though, they were no closer to finding the women of their dreams.

And their paychecks didn't go far.

So when they had been approached with an offer for more money than they had ever dreamed of, they agreed to do whatever was asked of them.

They would do as ordered, take the money, and go to Albania. They would live near the beach and find women who were attracted to them.

Fifteen minutes before the end of their work shift, it was time to empty the trash.

They took the stinking bags from the small bins scattered around the food court and placed them in large gray trash barrels.

They inserted a fresh bag in each trash bin as they had done countless times over the past year—except today, they'd added a sealed shoebox into the bottom of each bag first.

Thirty minutes later, they were on a bus to Albania, and didn't hear about the devastation and deaths at the mall until they were arrested at the border crossing.

Palma de Mallorca Airport
Mallorca, Spain

Three Months Earlier

It wasn't prime season yet and already the tourists had flocked to the island, lured by the prevalent sunshine and warm spring weather.

The airport was as busy as ever. Brits and Germans filled the shops, sunburnt and looking more exhausted than people going home from holiday should. Many were interested in the duty-free shops, or waited in line for coffee or a meal.

One last indulgence before returning to their ordinary lives.

Few looked through the English and German books Fernando stocked in the gift shop. People were more interested in snacks or the small, inexpensive souvenirs he sold—keychains and refrigerator magnets in the shape of the island and postcards of the beaches.

The ten boxes of books that had been delivered right before the busy afternoon rush could wait. They were stacked along the wall outside the shop, in no one's way.

Besides, he was pretty sure they had been delivered by mistake. He didn't need so many books and had no place to display them. They probably should have been split up for the other shops like his, but someone had made an error, as usual.

It was so hard to find good staff these days.

A friendly older British woman and her husband, both as red as lobsters, needed his help to find a "proper souvenir" to take home, so

Fernando ushered them to the rear of his shop where he stocked a few nicer items.

Later, when he struggled to consciousness, ears ringing, unable to hear what the frantic paramedics were saying, he realized the blood covering him was all that remained of the nice couple from London who had died when the bombs went off—and shielded him from the blast.

Rahbar International Trading Partners
Surobi, Afghanistan

Present Day

Colonel Tariq grinned in the dimness of his office as he finished reviewing the news footage he had been able to gather from the three attacks.

He should have retired years ago. Having complete control of the target selection and methods was so much better than being ordered around, despite the increased difficulty.

It had taken a great deal of effort to acquire the exact type of van used by a local utility company in Cairo, paint it to match, construct the bomb inside, and transport it undetected to the city.

But the destruction of the American embassy wall, the deaths of people in vehicles near the van, and the injury of four Americans inside the compound, had been worth the sacrifice.

As had the work spent building lightweight yet destructive bombs disguised in boxes of running shoes.

And painstakingly hollowing out hardcover books, planting the explosives, and going to great lengths to hide their scent from the airport's bomb-sniffing dogs.

Tariq had proven what could be done. The process had worked all three times.

The import-export company had successfully transported the bombs.

He had used his network to recruit and screen local men to do the necessary work.

And terrorists had paid to claim the attacks as theirs.

Everything was going to plan.

But what had he overlooked?

He had already constructed the bombs for the latest attack.

They were disguised, packed, and ready to ship.

In each of the attacks so far, he had been careful to use different explosives, methods of detonation, and vastly different targets.

However, each bombing increased the risk of discovery.

It was essential for the attacks to look and feel like they came from different sources.

For the next attack, after Paris, everything had to go perfectly. That bombing would appease his former employer and secure his freedom from them, along with their eternal gratitude.

All he needed now was the explosives—scheduled to arrive next week —and the teddy bears.

5

THE OBSESSION

Central Analysis Group Headquarters
Alexandria, Virginia

Wyatt had only worked at the Central Analysis Group for a few months, but he had found a home here.

While he put in many more hours than the other intelligence analysts, no one seemed to worry that his nearly constant presence made them look like slackers in comparison.

And Gregory—the team's manager—left him alone to pursue whatever grabbed his attention.

For the last several weeks, his obsession had been a series of bombing attacks around the world that had started nine months ago.

There had to be a connection.

Wyatt cued up the footage from the attack on the US Embassy in Cairo despite having every nuance memorized. He saw the attack in his mind while he waited for the microwave to heat his frozen burritos for dinner and breakfast in the small Central Analysis Group kitchen.

The footage played in his dreams for the few hours he slept each day.

But the idea that he may have missed a tiny detail that would help him solve his latest puzzle drove him on.

The embassy's security cameras showed the local utility company's white panel van on the street as it approached the embassy grounds.

Wyatt paused the footage to advance frame by frame, looking for anything new he could use.

The van exploded.

It had been packed with ammonium nitrate, a common ingredient used by terrorists as an explosive for bombs.

Wyatt played through the footage. Instead of stopping after the explosion, he kept watching. He wanted to note—and track—every other vehicle in the area.

Someone else must have already done this legwork, but he wanted to start fresh.

He used a stack of sticky notes to add details of each car on the road before and after the attack, one car per note.

Later tonight, he would review any security camera footage he could find of the street in the weeks prior to the attack. Maybe the terrorists had driven by to scope out the security features.

He'd watch hours of video if he had to.

Anything to catch a break.

After Cairo, he would watch the shopping mall security camera footage of the food court explosions.

The bombs had been placed in the trash bins lining the dining area.

There were cameras throughout the shopping mall.

Surely someone had conducted reconnaissance in the months prior to the bombing—and not the lowly mall workers caught and blamed for the attack. They weren't the masterminds behind the operation.

Wyatt glanced at a pile of folded, off-white paper on his desk. He would add the information he gathered tonight to his notes later, when there were fewer analysts around.

It wouldn't do to have them see how far his obsession had taken him.

After the shopping mall, if he could stomach viewing more death and destruction, he would roll right into watching video of the third attack, at the airport on the stunning island of Mallorca in Spain.

The bombs there had been disguised as boxes of books delivered to the newsstands inside the terminal.

Three attacks.

Three types of explosives.

Three distinct methods of detonation.

The only thing that tied them together was the devices being cleverly disguised.

That convinced Wyatt the same person was responsible for all three attacks.

And why would the mastermind behind the operations stop at three?

There had to be another bombing coming.

Soon.

Wyatt clicked his mouse to press play on the security camera footage and steeled himself to watch the horror of all three attacks once again.

6

THE COURSE

Every Saturday morning in the summer, Donald Everett drove ninety minutes north from his home outside Phoenix.

The Forest Cliffs Golf Club, at 4,300 feet above sea level, was at least 20 degrees cooler than any course he could play in the Phoenix area. The temperature was worth the hassle of the curvy, two-lane speedway known as Interstate 17, where semitrucks plodded along in the right lane while weekenders in cars competed to see who could drive the fastest in the left.

Last Saturday, his game had been horrible. The damn slice was back. No matter what he did, his tee shot sailed straight for a hundred yards before hooking sharply right, crashing into trees, the rough, or the long, narrow pond along the first few holes.

He'd lost four balls and stopped counting his score after the seventh hole, when his short game also went to hell.

His guys—fellow retirees in their late sixties from his neighborhood who knew nothing of his old life—gave him a healthy heaping of shit the whole time.

This week would be different. Everett had a new driver, a brush-up lesson from the best teacher in Scottsdale—who he'd never admit to hiring—and four days at the driving range hitting ball after ball.

As he pulled into the luxury golf course, he felt good. Well prepared and confident. Hell, he might even suggest they put some money on the round. Taking a hundred bucks off each of the other three would feel good and help out with his budget. They didn't rely on a government pension, and the few "off-books" investments he'd managed to get in on during his time at the Central Intelligence Agency.

The valet unloaded his clubs and strapped them onto the back of a golf cart, accepting the usual tip from Everett with a smile. After Everett hit the bathroom in the clubhouse—he wasn't getting any younger, and aside from the trees along the fairways, the nearest restroom on the course wasn't until the seventh tee—he joined the rest of the guys to warm up with a small bucket of balls on the driving range. The coaching, practice, and new driver paid off. Every shot sailed straight and long, stifling most of the razzing from the guys.

The true test came on the first hole, which was always tough. People sat on the clubhouse veranda, enjoying brunch and drinks, laughing, talking, and watching the foursomes tee off. Other groups waited to start their rounds. And though the first fairway was designed to be easy—wide open, with the pond on the right not usually in play unless he sliced it badly—being watched always ratcheted up Everett's stress level. It had been drilled into him from the first day at the Farm, the CIA training camp he'd attended as a kid straight out of college decades before: Do not attract attention. Don't be memorable. Fade into the background.

His slice here would produce more than a few whispers, giggles, and mentions later on.

It had before.

"Not today," Everett muttered as he stepped up. The guys insisted he go first on hole 1; they enjoyed watching him squirm, and since the person with the best score on the previous hole traditionally went first on the next —and he was the worst player in their group—it was usually his only chance to hit first.

As he bent to push in the tee and place his ball on it, Clyde spoke up from several paces back. "You know, you could play from the ladies' tee box. Use your 3 iron instead of the driver." He was going for helpful and reasonable, but there was no disguising the joking in his tone.

"They aren't the 'ladies' tees,'" Roy said quietly as Everett tried his best to ignore them and began his pre-swing routine. "Women play from any tees, not just the ones closer to the hole."

"We could call them 'Everett tees,'" Clyde whispered loud enough for all to hear.

Everett took a practice swing, tuned out their banter, and stepped forward. He moved his arms back slowly, loaded, and swung, head down and still.

The new driver's huge club face made contact with the ball with a solid *crack*—the sweetest sound to a golfer's ears.

The golf ball sailed straight and true, landing in the middle of the perfectly green fairway 250 yards away. It rolled, finally stopping in the center of the fairway an easy wedge from the green.

It was a great shot to start the day.

"You were saying?" he said with a grin to the boys behind him after he'd picked up his tee.

He got high fives all around, with earnest congratulations from the guys. They could talk trash, but when push came to shove, they delighted in one another's successes.

Clyde stepped forward and shoved his tee into the ground. "We'll see if you can keep that up or if you fall back into your old ways."

"Yeah," Roy chimed in. "Wait until six," he said, referencing the most difficult hole on the course. It had a narrow fairway, trees on the left, and a daunting number of pines on the right that guarded the steep drop off of a cliff with a view of the red rocks of Sedona to the west.

Hole 6 was Everett's nemesis. Something about the narrowness of the driving lane, the trees, and the cliff got into his head.

"Just wait," Everett said. "I'm a changed man. And this driver is the key."

"We've heard that before!" Dave said with a laugh.

Everett smiled and waited for Clyde's loopy yet effective swing to propel the ball straight down the fairway, like always. Busting one another's chops was part of the fun.

And it sure beat the backstabbing, politics, and life-and-death decisions he'd faced for so many years at the Agency.

7

THE PREPARATION

Before dawn, Patrick had parked the motorcycle along a quiet dirt road near the base of a cliff that ran along the edge of the sixth hole's fairway.

He had mixed water with the local soil, forming a paste, and coated the bike's small license plate to hide the numbers and letters.

The black motorcycle helmet stayed on, too.

He had to be careful.

His leather gloves had gone into the small locking storage compartment on the back of the bike. The black leather riding jacket followed, leaving him in dark tan pants that were perfect for riding, a black shirt that clung tightly to his muscular chest, and black riding boots.

He would blend in fine in the dark woods next to the fairway.

The pistol came with him, to be used only as a last resort.

He had hiked north, climbing over the large rocks that made up the cliff at the edge of the golf course. Finally, as the sky lightened, he had eased into his hiding spot in a shallow ravine, plenty wide but only a foot deep, that ran parallel to the cliff about 10 feet from the edge.

Because of the dimness provided by the trees, he'd be difficult to spot unless a golfer stood close to him—which few would. The smart ones used an iron off the tee to better control the ball and avoid losing it in the trees—or over the cliff.

Everyone besides his target, who was notorious for not only his obsession with golf but his incurable slice. Patrick had heard about it his whole life, and he was betting everything on the man's inability to change.

Well, not exactly everything. He had a solid backup plan, but murdering Everett on the golf course in a way that looked accidental—just like Mr. Rutherfield's death—appealed to him.

As Patrick lay prone in the ravine with the motorcycle helmet on but tinted visor up for now, his pulse increased with the thought of what was to come. He could picture how it would work out, and the thought made him shiver with anticipation.

It had only been four days since his first kill, but he was well and truly ready for the second.

From Patrick's vantage point, he had a narrow view through the pine trees to the tee box less than 200 yards away.

He settled in, waiting patiently for the target to slice to his death.

8

THE CHOICE

Forest Cliffs Golf Club
Hole 6

The fairway, with its perfectly trimmed grass, seemed to narrow before Everett's eyes. The trees on the left competed with the thick group of pines on right.

And lest he forget, his ball had a knack for avoiding the pine trees and sailing over the edge of the cliff.

At least, that's how it seemed. There were probably several of his golf balls, all marked with a handwritten capital "E," lost under the bushes or in the pine needles on the right side.

Surely not every ball he'd hit there last summer—and the one last week—had gone over the edge.

Only most of them.

As the guys stepped out of the carts, their silence was more telling than any joking. The air around the tee box crackled with energy as they selected their clubs.

Everett shook off the quiet. He was having a great day. The new driver worked—or the lessons and practice.

"You've got an extra ball?" Clyde, his cart partner, asked, the jibe coming at last. If Everett's ball was lost, he'd need a new one to drop. He'd take a penalty stroke and keep playing.

Dave laughed. "Or two?"

"I've never lost two balls," Everett said.

"On this hole," Roy muttered. It was true—Everett had shanked two balls into the pond last summer, one after another.

On a whim, Everett grabbed his 3 iron instead of his driver. He'd show the guys and continue his good round by not tempting fate.

"Smart," Clyde said.

"Coward," Roy said with a smile.

When it was his turn, Everett lined up his shot, ignored the narrowness of the fairway, and swung, for once not trying to drive as far as humanly possible, only hoping to avoid the loss of a ball and the penalty stroke that came with it.

Playing it safe on this hole—for once—wouldn't kill him.

Prone in the cool dirt and pine needles, hidden by shrubs, Patrick frowned as the target swung an iron, made solid contact with the ball, and let out a whoop of joy when it flew straight and true. Patrick saw a flash of white as it bounced on the grass to his right before it disappeared up the fairway.

There would be no killing today.

He controlled his disappointment.

There was always next week.

If not, he'd have to take the riskier approach. His deadline was rapidly approaching.

Donald Everett had to die. Soon.

9

FORTY-ONE DAYS

The Bar
Sands, Arizona

Thomas was forty-one days sober.

He wasn't sure he'd make it to day forty-two.

Not the way he felt tonight.

The glow of Thursday night's staged assault at the local gun range was long gone.

The thrill of knowing he was back in the game had crashed against the realization that it was all for nothing.

He was no longer a Navy SEAL. That life was behind him. He was a small-town special education teacher on summer break.

No amount of training could change that. He'd given up on a life as a warrior.

He sat in the bar, crowded with the usual locals who considered it a home away from home. Like an English pub, it was a place for a simple, inexpensive yet tasty meal while catching up with friends and watching a game on the two big-screen TVs.

It was summer, so tourists were everywhere in town—including the bar.

Thomas glanced at the front door as it swung open, praying it would be retired Admiral Nalen who entered.

Less than two months before, Thomas's world had been turned upside down. When a government computer flagged him as dead and he'd lost his job at the local elementary school, former United States Navy Admiral William Nalen had appeared out of the blue to ask Thomas to go on a covert mission for his country.

For that unexpected operation, Thomas had quit drinking, rescued a hostage, and eliminated an evil man on behalf of the United States of America.

Tonight, it was two tourists—obvious by their skinny jeans and ridiculous "cowboy" shirts, complete with pearl buttons and colorful striped print from some upscale Scottsdale store selling "authentic" Western clothes—who stepped inside.

No Admiral Nalen.

Following his previous mission, Thomas had slept well for the first time in the seven years since his SEAL Team buddies had been cut down in an ambush.

For a while, his nightmares were gone.

Since then, the school year had ended, the days had gotten hotter, he hadn't drunk alcohol—one day at a time—and Thomas had waited.

Ready and willing for his next covert assignment.

Eager for it.

Desperate, actually.

It hadn't come. Admiral Nalen never appeared to brief him on another operation for the United States.

The days passed.

Thomas trained, first getting into shape, then staying ready.

And the nightmares returned.

The desire to drown his sorrows—to avoid the traumatic memories—grew stronger, no matter how many miles he ran or the number of rounds he fired at the range.

The bar was his refuge. A welcome place to eat, chat with other veterans who were regulars, and avoid the loneliness of sitting at home, lost in his memories.

But if he didn't figure out a way to deal with the ever-intruding thoughts from his time downrange, he'd switch from nursing a few non-alcoholic beers a night to something stronger.

He sipped the fake beer and felt himself slipping away. Maybe it was the late nights the previous week, but something clicked in his brain.

The familiar faces, the tourists, and the tantalizing smells from the kitchen faded as Thomas "Bone" Marks sat in his spot at the end of the bar, stared at the baseball game on TV without seeing it, and remembered.

———

Afghanistan

Many Years Ago

"Think this is our chance?" Tank muttered next to Bone. They'd been best friends since going through BUD/S together months before and had gotten lucky enough to deploy to the same Team. Tank was handsome and charming, with light blond hair and movie-star looks in contrast to Bone's long, narrow face and dark hair.

They sat toward the back of the base's briefing room. Bossman, the team lead at the front of the room, wrapped up the mission brief.

Bone shrugged and kept quiet. He didn't want to miss a word—or get called out for not paying attention.

As the two new members of the Team, they'd been sidelined for the first few weeks in-country.

With plenty of combat experience, the rest of the men had jumped immediately back into the nightly missions. But Bossman always shook his head, face set, when Bone and Tank looked at him expectantly.

"Soon," he'd say. "We'll get a good mission for you to get your feet wet."

Tonight's op seemed perfect for the two highly trained but real-world-inexperienced SEALs. A Team would chopper into a valley, walk to a small gathering of huts, and observe the comings and goings. One of the huts may or may not house a bomb-making operation where IEDs—improvised explosive devices—were being manufactured for distribution to the Taliban so they could kill Americans.

A bomb-making instructor had been circulating in the area, teaching more sophisticated methods to make bigger, more elaborate bombs. He might—or might not—be on his way to the village.

"To sum up: We'll go to ground and observe for twenty-four hours," Bossman said. "If anything looks promising, we'll call in another Team. Together, we'll assault in a capture-or-kill mission. The priority is taking out the bomb-making teacher if he shows. He's missing three fingers on his left hand, so he should be pretty easy to spot." A blurry black-and-white

picture of a man with a long beard and dark eyes appeared on the screen from the projector. "We'll also want to gather up any of the locals who have bomb-making experience. Questions?"

"What about booby traps?" another SEAL asked. "A missile would take it all out and be safer."

"Booby traps are always a possibility, and the missile is an option," Bossman said. "But intel claims there may be women and children present. Our enemy isn't stupid, gentlemen. They've learned a lot throughout this conflict. Sure, building bombs in the spare bedroom is dangerous. They know, however, that if we find them—and they've got women and children in the same house or nearby, whether they are family, other villagers, or captives—we're not going to just blow them to hell. If there are non-combatants around, we'll bring up another Team to handle it quickly and quietly, with no loss of life to civilians."

There were nods all around. The men shifted in their seats.

"It'll be only four of us tonight for the recon," Bossman said. "Me, Outlaw, and..." He frowned as he scanned the rows of men.

Bone sensed a shift in the room's energy.

Heads turned toward the back, where Bone and Tank sat. The faces of the SEALs were serious. These were hard men who had been there and done that.

Exactly what Bone and Tank hoped to be someday.

Bone hardened his expression and met the eyes of the warriors. Beside him, he knew Tank was doing the same.

"Are you two ready?" Bossman said from the front. It was part challenge, part serious question. He wanted a no-BS answer, though there was only one acceptable response.

At this stage in their new careers, Bone and Tank had survived BUD/S —Basic Underwater Demolition/SEAL Training—the grueling program that put the candidates through hell, convinced most of them to give up, and rewarded the ones who didn't with more abuse until they eventually proved themselves worthy of being called SEALs.

Following that, they'd trained with the men of this Team before deploying to Afghanistan.

After all they'd been through, they were among America's most highly trained fighters. But the two of them weren't yet warriors.

Going on a real mission in-country was their next step.

"Ready," Bone said, his voice firm with resolve.

"Ready," Tank said.

The eyes of the Team stayed on them. No one spoke.

At the front of the room, Bossman weighed their answers for several excruciating seconds.

"Fine," he said. "Me, Outlaw, Bone, and Tank. Get your gear together. Wheels up at 2200 hours."

With that, the briefing ended. Everyone stood. Several of the men offered advice to Bone and Tank.

"Don't mess up and die," Baldy said.

"Don't shoot each other. And please don't kill Bossman," Biscuit said.

Dizzy offered more practical advice. "Just listen to Bossman and follow your training. We were all in your shoes once and made it. You wouldn't be going if we didn't think you were ready."

Bone took it in, discounting nothing. They were good suggestions, even if they were meant—mostly—in jest.

As everyone else filed out of the room, Bone and Tank fist-bumped down low, being subtle in case anyone was watching. They didn't want to seem too eager.

"You think this is a real mission or just BS to get us some real-world experience in a low-risk situation?" Tank asked as they headed to double-check their gear.

Bone hadn't considered that option. "You think they'd send us on a fake op?"

"No," Tank said. "But I wouldn't put it past them to take a low-priority request that some intel nerd wanted investigated and pretend it's an important, time-sensitive op so we'd have a sense of urgency. Pressure, but not really, you know?"

What Tank suggested made sense. That's how Bone would do it if he were in Bossman's shoes. Why send new guys into a potential meat grinder? You put the new quarterback in for a few plays in the last seconds when you were winning by two touchdowns, not on a crucial third-and-long during the big game.

"No matter what, though," Bone said quietly, "we take it seriously. This is our chance to put what we've learned into practice."

"All in, all the time," Tank said.

"All in," Bone repeated.

A few hours later, Bone was covered in blood.

And any thought of a low-pressure, moderately safe first mission was long gone.

10

THE SITUATION

Afghanistan

Many Years Ago

Bone and Tank sat on the far side of the helicopter, away from the door. The bird seemed empty with only the two of them plus Bossman and Outlaw.

"Five minutes," the pilot called over the headset.

Bossman repeated the time call, holding up one hand with his fingers wide. He was older than Bone by several years—in his early thirties. He laughed and joked with his men but was all business when it came to the mission.

"Five minutes," Bone repeated, along with Tank.

The two of them had been "swim buddies" in BUD/S—paired up to support each other through the challenges of the training course. They'd sweated through countless exercise evolutions, talked each other out of quitting, and had promised to always have each other's back.

Tonight, they were finally becoming warriors.

Bone resisted the desire to triple-check his gear. If he'd forgotten anything, it was much too late.

The insertion went smoothly, just like the training missions they'd conducted.

The helicopter landed, and they jumped out and formed a perimeter while the bird flew off.

After a long march, moving like ghosts through the night, they arrived at their overlook spot. A mountain—actually a large sand and gravel hill —rose to the west of the small village.

With their night vision goggles down, Outlaw led the way. He was a beefy man, around 5'11", with a shaggy beard and an intense air about him. He took shorter, careful steps now that they were near the village. Any bad guys in the area with half a brain would see the hill as the excellent vantage point it was.

But no guards or IEDs would get by Outlaw.

Bossman had decided to thwart conventional wisdom. They would set up in a less-than-ideal position along the side of the hill. The location would still give them a clear view of the front of the huts, but the spot wouldn't have the full field of fire that higher up on the ridge would.

The side of the hill would be less likely to be guarded or booby trapped, though, which was why they'd chosen it.

Pointing to a large boulder, Bossman gestured for Bone to set up near it.

Bone lay flat, burrowing into the loose sand and gravel, rifle out front, scope trained on "his" hut—the largest one on the far right, close to the dirt road that led to the village.

Several feet away, to the left, Outlaw slid to the ground behind his own cover.

Tank, then Bossman, took positions farther left, lower on the slope.

The village only had twelve dwellings, all built of mud and clay—adobe—in a way that reminded Bone of some of the older houses in his home state of Arizona.

These looked like they had seen better days, though. Corners crumbled, and windows were broken. The people of this village faced tough times. But the improvised explosive devices were coming from somewhere, and the intel team's information had led them here.

A wide ravine, about 4 feet deep, was halfway between their hill and the village. If they had to advance, or get closer for recon, the location would provide cover.

A lone sentry leaned against the wall of the largest home, an AK-47 slung on his shoulder. His head nodded now and then, but each time he *jerked awake and changed positions or walked a few feet in an effort to stay alert.*

He was waiting for something.

Maybe the bomb-making instructor was running behind schedule.

Bone and the rest of the Team observed. To the south—Bone's right—a narrow dirt lane twisted around low hills, terminating at the village. The place was literally at the end of the road—perfect for an out-of-the-way base to build devices to blow up American and other coalition troops.

Nothing stirred, though several of the small houses had lights on— candles or lanterns, as there were no power lines to the area and no rumble of generators came through the night air.

"Everyone okay?" Bossman's quiet voice came through Bone's headphone.

"Okay," Tank said, followed by Outlaw and Bone a second later.

So far, the operation had been remarkably similar to the countless training missions they'd been on. Ride in the helicopter, hike to the target, settle into position, and wait.

Yes, this was the first time anyone who noticed them would likely want them dead, but Bone didn't worry about that. Bossman had planned well. This was the perfect first mission. A taste of danger without any real risk.

Two hours later, they'd seen little movement. A man had emerged from one of the huts—Bone's—stretched, and checked with the guard, who had shaken his head. Then the man had gone back inside.

One by one, the lights went off in the village.

"Bone and Outlaw," Bossman said over the radio. "It looks like the high-value target is a no-show. Settle in for a nap. Tank and I have first watch."

Bone signaled by clicking his mic twice. The last thing he wanted to do was sleep, but it made sense. While they were used to being awake at night, some downtime to relax could pay off later.

"Bone and Outlaw, wake up."

Bone came to. He hadn't been asleep exactly. More like halfway between a daydream and a doze. It had only been an hour.

"Copy," Outlaw said, beating Bone by a second.

The wind had picked up while Bone rested. It felt ominous, like more than just a late-night breeze.

"We have a situation," Bossman continued. "A dust storm is forming to the west. Orders are to—"

He stopped as an ancient car led an equally old pickup truck around one of the low hills in the distance, creeping along the bumpy dirt road with their lights off. Several yards behind the truck, a larger car followed.

The only place they could be going was the little village.

"Get eyes on those vehicles while I call this in," Bossman said.

Bone centered his scope on the nicer yet still old car bringing up the rear. Tank and Outlaw would focus on the first car and the truck.

"Car number 2," Bone said. "Driver and three male passengers. No weapons visible."

"Multiple military-aged men in the back of the truck," Outlaw said. "They're alert and are all carrying AKs. There's a driver and a passenger in front."

"Car number 1," Tank said. Bone could tell he was part nervous, part excited, but didn't think the more experienced SEALs would catch it in his voice; they didn't know Tank like he did. "Driver and three passengers, all males. No weapons visible."

The first car and the truck slowed to a stop outside the village.

Bone's car hung back several hundred yards.

The village's sentry, now awake and alert, knocked hard on the door to the hut. He walked toward the car and truck, his rifle still slung, arms out in welcome.

The man wasn't a guard. He was the welcoming committee.

Six men from the back of the truck jumped out and ran to the doors of the nearest huts, AKs in hand. They rushed in without knocking, weapons up and ready. A few seconds later, each emerged and went to the rest of the huts.

Candles or lanterns were lit in all of them, glowing in the windows.

After a few minutes, the men in the cab of the truck emerged, as did the four men in car 1. All carried AKs like they knew how to use them, and were ready for a fight.

In car 2, the passengers sat tight. The sound of the engine still running carried through the clear night air.

One of the men walked purposefully toward the cars and waved his weapon in the air—an all-clear sign.

The other men gathered near the entrance to the second hut.

Car 2 crept forward and stopped when it reached the village. Its doors opened, and four men emerged. Three held AKs. One had a pistol.

The man with the pistol had only two fingers on his left hand.

"Check out…" Bone trailed off. It was too late. The men were inside. "The fourth guy—his left hand. He was missing three fingers," Bone said into the radio's mic.

11

THE SAND

Afghanistan

Many Years Ago

Bone pictured what he'd seen.

The men walked toward the open door of the hut.

The weak yellow light of a lamp spilled out and made him flip his NVGs up and out of the way.

The sentry stood by the door to welcome the guests.

The fourth man walked slower than the others. Not because he was careful—more like he'd been injured but was ignoring it, trying to be strong.

And his left hand was missing three fingers.

"How sure are you?" Bossman asked.

"One hundred percent," Bone said.

"Did you see his face? Is it our guy?"

"I didn't see his face clearly—only from the side."

"Lot of dudes out here missing fingers," Outlaw said in his Texas drawl.

Bossman didn't speak for several seconds. "Okay, here's the problem. The storm that's coming will be a big one. Lots of blowing sand. Helos will be grounded because it'll be impossible to see."

The wind gusted and the air felt wrong. Like it was angry.

"We leave now, or we're stuck out here on our own until it passes. Could be a few hours, could be a day. No matter what, being outside in the elements would really, truly suck. But if this is our target..."

"If there really are women and children, we can't just blow everything up," Outlaw said. They hadn't seen anyone besides the sentry, the man who checked on him, and the newcomers, but there easily could be families—or captives—in the rest of the huts.

"Okay, new guys," Bossman said to Bone and Tank. "What would you do if you were in charge?"

This wasn't the first time they'd been asked that question. SEALs give and take orders, but each member of the Team is expected to know the mission forward and backward—and be ready to assume a leadership role at any moment.

In the SEALs, sharing ideas and making suggestions was encouraged —within reason.

At frequent intervals during the past months of training, Bone and Tank had been asked what they would do in the situation and evaluated on their responses.

Bossman didn't give them anything more. Bone was hoping for a few options, like a multiple-choice test in high school. This was harder—a real-world challenge with life-and-death ramifications.

Bone loved it.

He didn't have to look at Tank farther down the slope to know what he was thinking. Neither one of them wanted to look like wimps.

Was Bossman looking for a gung-ho answer? Like, "Let's keep going! Screw the storm. We're Navy SEALs. We can handle it!"

Or was a level of caution the better choice?

Bone talked it out. "Couple ways to go. Hardcore would be to continue with the mission. Our equipment can handle it, and so can we. That's what I'd suggest if we were on a deadline, or in pursuit of the enemy."

Tank took over. "They'll stay put until the storm passes. We could set up on the lee side of this hill, or maybe go to ground in the wash. Wait it out and get better eyes on after the storm."

"Excellent discussion of the options, boys," Bossman said immediately. His voice was tighter than before. Talking things out took longer than giving orders, and Bone suspected Bossman was getting an earful from command on the other radio channel. "But I asked for a recommendation, not a cover-your-ass presentation."

Bone decided to go big. "We're out here for a reason. We have a probable sighting of our target. We should hang here until the front edge of the storm hits. Then we race forward, using it for cover to get closer. We hunker down in the wash and embrace the suck. Eventually, the guy with the missing fingers comes out. We ID him as the target and engage." He stopped, then added one of Bossman's favorite sayings. "Moderation is for cowards."

"I agree," Tank said. "We can't leave. If the guy is our target, we have to stay and keep eyes on. We can confirm it's him and report when he leaves. Last resort, we call in a drone strike on his convoy if there are no women and children along."

Bossman clicked his mic twice and spoke quietly on the command channel.

Bone and Tank had apparently made the right call.

The wind picked up. Grains of sand pelted Bone's face. He covered his nose and mouth with a keffiyeh—a cotton scarf.

The sandstorm came on fast.

He could no longer see the village.

Bossman gave the order to move out.

The wind raged, making Bone stagger.

He followed Outlaw, his hand on the burly man's shoulder to keep from losing him in the dust. They crept down the slope toward the shallow desert wash closer to the village.

Once they reached the wash, the blowing sand wasn't as bad, but the situation still sucked. Bone's goggles and keffiyeh couldn't protect him completely. He hadn't been this sandy since the days of BUD/S in San Diego, when they'd had to run into the frigid Pacific Ocean before rolling in the dry sand of the beach, turning themselves into "sugar cookies." It had taught them to be comfortable with being uncomfortable.

Bone "embraced the suck," as the SEAL saying went, stayed alert, and waited for the storm to pass.

Until they heard the desperate cries of women coming from the village.

12

HOLD

Many Years Ago

The screams were loud enough to cut through the wind and carry a hundred yards to the desert wash.

They pierced Bone's soul.

It took all his discipline to not rush forward and defend the innocent.

Outlaw, on his left, was an indistinct lump in the haze of the blowing sand, but the way he shifted his weight forward proved he was ready to go, too.

"Hold," Bossman's voice came in Bone's earphone. While Bone had known the older SEAL less than a year, they had spent a tremendous amount of time together. The single word told Bone that Bossman wasn't saying they wouldn't help, but they had to be smart about it.

Seconds passed. Bone guessed Bossman was calling in the latest development.

Another scream fought the storm. It sounded like it came from the second hut from the right, where several of the men from the caravan had entered after the group's leaders had gone into the first hut.

It cut off abruptly, and Bone had to bite his lip to keep from ignoring Bossman's order.

"New plan," Bossman said over the radio. "Outlaw and Bone, you hit the main hut. Weapons free. Capture or kill the target. Secure anyone else. Avoid killing the locals from the village, but everyone is fair game if they're in the fight. Remember, we're also on the lookout for the local IED maker."

"Copy," Outlaw said the instant Bossman finished, and Bone repeated it.

"Tank, you and I hit the second hut. Take out the bad guys and save the women. Then both Teams clear the rest of the huts."

Tank double-clicked his mic, followed by Outlaw. Bone did the same. There was no last-minute rah-rah pep talk from Bossman. Bone hadn't expected one. He and Tank were either ready or they weren't.

They had trained enough or not.

They would live... or die.

It took forever to work their way from the ditch to the village, though it was only a hundred yards away. The storm seemed less intense than it had before, but that could have been his adrenaline, Bone figured.

The guard at the front door of the main hut had entered along with the guests. The village hadn't posted any other lookouts; the SEALs would have the element of surprise.

Bone followed Outlaw, the two moving together seamlessly. With hours and hours of close-quarters combat training for clearing buildings, he knew exactly what Outlaw would do, and what his own role was. Tonight would be no different than the countless full-on training exercises they'd done over the previous months.

As they arrived at their target hut, Bone flipped up his NVGs. The lantern in the small home would make it easy to see once they were inside.

At Outlaw's tap on his shoulder, Bone drew back his leg and kicked.

The door was no match for Bone's heel. It flew open.

Outlaw flowed inside.

A crack of an AK firing came as Outlaw fired his suppressed M4 twice.

Knowing Outlaw's abilities, two tangos were already down.

There were two to go—plus the locals that called the hut home.

But the AK shot was unexpected—and worrisome.

Bone put it out of his mind and focused on his zone.

13

THE FIRST KILL

Afghanistan

Many Years Ago

Bone flowed into the hut on Outlaw's heels, his M4 covering his area.

The room was lit brightly compared to the darkness of the sandstorm.

Bone took in the scene.

In front of him, sitting cross-legged near the wall, two surprised men— both from the car—raised AKs from their laps.

Bone fired, pulling the trigger of his M4, killing them both without hesitation, exactly as he'd been taught.

He swung right as a man, a villager by the looks of his clothing, reached for an AK.

Bone shot him, too.

More shots came from Outlaw's side of the room, but Bone couldn't worry about him. They each had a job to do.

A fourth man on Bone's side of the room clawed for a pistol on his hip.

Bone fired, putting two shots into his body and a third into his head before continuing to turn.

Another man, shorter than the rest, fumbled with an AK he held across his lap.

He was so close, Bone barely had to aim.

Bone shot him in the head.

Bone's sector was empty except for dead men who had tipped over onto the floor or were slumped against the wall.

"Clear right," Bone called.

"Clear left," Outlaw responded a second later.

The man who had scrambled for the pistol was missing three fingers from his hand—and his face matched that of their primary target.

The short man on the far right...

Bone paused in his sweep.

The man was young.

Very young.

He couldn't have been more than 12 or 13 years old.

Bone's stomach lurched.

He had killed a kid.

14

IT IS WHAT IT IS

Afghanistan

Many Years Ago

The boy's finger was on the trigger of the AK-47. He'd been trying to raise it to shoot Bone.

"You okay?" Outlaw called from behind him.

"Okay," Bone said, forcing his eyes off the kid to sweep his side of the hut again before they returned to the dead young villager.

"I shot a kid," Bone choked out. There was a faint wisp of facial hair on the boy's upper lip. His expression was one of shock and regret.

Outlaw appeared next to him. After a second, he rested a hand on Bone's shoulder. "It was him or you. A clean kill. Harsh, I know, but it is what it is."

"It is what it is," Bone repeated automatically.

Outlaw leaned heavily against him. Bone took the weight and snapped out of his reverie. "What's wrong?"

Outlaw fought to stand straight and failed. "I'm hit."

15

THE BLOOD

Afghanistan

Many Years Ago

"Outlaw is hit," Bone said over the radio. "Not sure how bad. I'm checking."

"Copy," Bossman said. "We'll clear the rest of the huts. You help him. And stay sharp."

"Copy," Bone said, easing Outlaw to the ground along the wall close to the dead kid. It was the safest place to be if an enemy burst in.

"It hurts like hell," Outlaw said, his voice tight with pain. "But I don't think it hit anything essential." Blood soaked his fatigues at his lower abdomen, just above the groin. "At least I hope not."

It wasn't the time for modesty. Bone ripped the fabric of Outlaw's pants and checked for himself, with Outlaw desperately trying to see, too.

"Everything's fine," Bone said, before moving so Outlaw could reassure himself.

Except for the blood.

There was so much blood.

16

WHY?

Present Day

"I patched up Outlaw and kept him alive until the storm cleared enough for a bird to pick him up," Thomas said.

He didn't realize he'd spoken out loud until Henry, two stools away, responded. "Did he make it?"

Thomas blinked his way back to the present. A slow-motion instant replay on the TV showed a batter swing and connect with the ball. It soared over the center wall of the outfield for a home run.

Behind the bar, the mirror reflected Thomas's face. The dark tan from running in the desert most mornings. Bags under his eyes. A thick, bushy beard that needed a trim. The same with his dark hair.

He looked scruffy. Unprofessional.

Borderline deranged.

The bar had cleared out. It was almost closing time. Only a few diehards with no one to go home to were still there. Down the bar, Steph washed dirty glasses and pretended to ignore their conversation. She had recently dyed her short hair a hot pink after the fluorescent green color she'd had before had faded.

"What?" Thomas asked.

Had he mentioned killing the kid?

Henry didn't look as horrified as Thomas felt every time he thought of it, which was most days. Maybe Thomas had skipped that part of the story —or perhaps Henry had heard, and seen, worse.

"Did Outlaw survive?" Henry asked again. "After the chopper picked him up?"

"Yes. He lost a lot of blood, but he was fine in the end." Thomas glanced at Henry, wondering how much of the story he'd told out loud. "An alert tango got off a lucky shot as we burst into the hut. Just one of those things."

Henry raised his glass of beer. "To Outlaw."

"To Outlaw," Thomas said, and clinked his bottle of fake beer against the glass.

"And to all those who didn't make it," Henry mumbled, quiet enough that Thomas wasn't sure he heard him right.

Thomas raised his bottle again before sipping his pretend beer, picturing Bossman from a few years later, lying in the sand, face to the side, dead.

"Why did we get to come home, and they didn't?" Bone muttered, more to himself than Henry.

The words seemed to catch them both by surprise.

Henry looked over, his eyes sad, and downed the last of his beer. "If I could answer that, son, I wouldn't be here every night until closing time."

He set the glass carefully on the bar and slid off his stool, hanging onto the bar edge to steady himself.

"We can settle up tomorrow," Steph called. She'd heard the discussion and was smart enough not to butt in.

"Appreciate it. Goodnight, Steph." Henry nodded at her, put a hand gently on Thomas's shoulder for a second, and walked out the front door, his pace slow but steady.

Thomas watched him go as Steph approached to pick up Henry's glass and small white napkin. Her eyes were heavy too; she'd seen combat in Iraq and Afghanistan and had lost people close to her.

"I try to imagine what my buddies would want me to do," she said, voice low and slow. "Like, would they be happy for me, that I made it? I think they would be." She glanced around to make sure none of the few other customers could hear. "What would Tank think of you?"

After the mission several weeks ago in California, Thomas had finally told Steph the tale of the ambush where he'd died—and lost seven of his buddies. "Or," she continued, "what would you want Tank to do if it had been you who didn't come back?"

"If it had been him that survived and not me…" Thomas trailed off, picturing Tank's chiseled looks and easy smile. "I'd want him to not waste his life. To keep making a difference. And to be happy."

"Is that what he'd want for you?"

"No doubt."

"Then that's the answer—not to your original question, but it's what you're already doing. The kids at the school love you. You're making a difference."

"Not like I used to. Downrange," he said, referencing his time in combat.

"No? The kids—"

"Not like I used to," Thomas interrupted her, his voice hard and serious.

They shared a long look. Thomas had no doubt she suspected his forced "vacation" from school in the late spring—when the government computers had claimed he was dead—was anything but time off in the desert getting his head on straight as he'd told her.

When he returned from helping Zia, Lamar, and Yousuf, Steph had taken one look at him and had seemed to know he'd been on some type of mission.

"You've got to do what you've got to do," Steph whispered as she leaned close, steel in her voice.

"Do I?"

Left unspoken was how his going off on clandestine missions—and leaving her out of the loop—might impact their relationship, such as it was. Nothing had happened between them since his return from California other than two dates, as friends. They'd gone hiking one Saturday and browsed the farmers' market in town two weeks later. No holding hands, no romance, and certainly no kissing. "Friends don't kiss," she'd said during an awkward moment after the hike before giving him a bear hug fitting of a fellow vet.

"Yes," Steph said. "It's the only way to live with yourself. And the only way anyone would ever want to be around you is if you're content in your own skin."

"Okay," he said, nodding slowly.

"Okay. Now, how about you help me close up?"

Thomas stood and pushed in his stool. They were closer to some sort of arrangement. Not boyfriend-girlfriend. Not yet. But they'd crossed a line. Steph was fine with him going on missions, no questions asked. She was either an outstanding friend—or something more.

It was a start.

And thinking about Tank being happy for him, happy Thomas had made it home alive, might allow for a night of decent sleep, free of nightmares.

Tomorrow was another day.

Maybe Admiral Nalen would come along with a mission. There had to be someone out there who needed to be killed—or saved.

17

THE CONTINGENCY

Inter-Services Intelligence Headquarters
Islamabad, Pakistan

Special Projects Officer Hafiz would have worn nicer clothes if he had thought he'd be ordered to the director-general's office instead of poking around at his desk like he normally spent his days. At least the faded dark pants and wrinkled gray tunic were clean.

He sat up straight in the director-general's guest wingback chair, instead of slouching as he would at his tired, untidy desk in a far corner of the vast headquarters building, and waited for his old friend—and current leader of the agency—to finish a phone call.

Hafiz was long past his prime.

He'd been "encouraged" to retire several times.

But what else was there to do with his life?

The intelligence business was all he knew. He had never married, had no children or grandchildren to dote on, and life in an apartment watching television or doing crossword puzzles between naps held no appeal.

Coming to the office each day, reading reports, and finding ways to help out—whether welcome or not—was all he had.

Until twelve months before, when he'd landed what could be the biggest assignment of his career—or nothing to worry about.

Today, it certainly seemed the assignment was about to prove to be the former, not the latter.

The DG frowned and rolled his eyes as he continued his call, grunting occasionally. He finally handed Hafiz a one-page report from his desk.

Hafiz would have seen it later today had he been left to his usual devices. The report was classified, but only because most everything they did in the building was.

The information certainly wasn't secret.

Hafiz skimmed the first part until he landed on the important bits.

An unknown entity is offering money for information leading to the capture of the person or people responsible for the recent bombings in Egypt, Turkey, and Spain.

Efforts to trace the bounty back to a source have thus far produced no results.

The wording of the offer suggests the United States of America may be responsible.

There were references to several similar past efforts by America's Central Intelligence Agency, including phrases that matched the current word on the street.

The report listed a case file number for updates and further details.

The director-general hung up the phone. "Idiots," he muttered before turning to Hafiz. He looked more serious than normal—if that was possible—and worried. "The word is out about the bomber."

Hafiz nodded. "It sounds like what the Americans say when they are desperate."

"I agree."

"Which is the worst possible outcome."

"One of the many bad possibilities, yes," the DG said.

"Do you think they suspect Tariq?"

"Whether they do or not, it is time for you to do your job." He gestured to the report in Hafiz's hand. "That is not all the intelligence we have, of course. There is a man we have had our eyes on for a while. An Afghan businessman in Kabul named Sardar who may be more than he seems. I have arranged for you to have cash, vehicles, and weapons at your disposal, along with four operators, a field manager, and an assistant director here at headquarters. We have a room with cots and an attached bathroom downstairs, ready for you and the assistant director of the operation. Meals will be delivered for the duration of the mission. It is up to you, my old friend."

"No matter what happens, there will be fallout."

"Yes. You will make new enemies whichever way it turns out."

"Fine. So be it."

"Hafiz?" The director-general paused for a moment. "You have one priority: Protect Pakistan and the ISI. Do whatever you have to do. Watch over Tariq, warn him, or kill him. Whatever you think is best. But write no reports. Put nothing in the system. And... do not fail."

Hafiz nodded and stood with the help of his cane, a concession to maintain his balance he had to rely on more and more these days. Without another word, he made his way slowly to his desk and sat in the same chair he'd used for decades.

The job he had hoped he wouldn't be required to do had actually arrived.

One Year Earlier

Hafiz sat against the wall in the far corner of the large conference room.

He had shaved and wore a presentable outfit, reasonably clean and unwrinkled. Unlike the men sitting around the table, he wore no medals and gave off an air of unimportance, slumping instead of sitting straight and rigid like the rest of them, the ones in the prime of their careers.

Colonel Tariq sat at the foot of the table, nearest the room's locked double doors. The guards who normally stood inside had been ordered to join the ones outside. The meeting topic was too sensitive even for those supremely well-trusted men.

The director-general, at the head of the table, had long been Hafiz's friend—and a protégé in some ways, though Hafiz had gravitated to the operational side, while the DG preferred management. The DG had requested—demanded—his presence, and well past retirement age or not, Hafiz couldn't say no.

"You will listen," the DG had told him. "Remember. And if called for, you will act as you alone see fit. Do you understand?"

He was really asking if Hafiz agreed to make decisions that would brand him a coward, traitor, fool, or all three.

"Yes," he'd said. "I understand."

At the far end of the table, Colonel Tariq pushed his chair back and stood, adopting a much more formal presentation than Hafiz had thought he would.

"It has been my honor to serve my country these last forty years," Tariq began. By design and careful tradecraft, few in the organization knew the details of the incredible missions Tariq had been responsible for, along with the many students he'd trained who had added to the ISI's capabilities. They only knew him as a highly successful career employee worthy of respect.

To the men in this room, however, he was a legend.

"As you are aware, I request permission to continue my work after retirement—as a freelancer."

No one at the table spoke, but Hafiz sensed the silent dissatisfaction. The colonel's request was highly unusual.

"In exchange for your permission, I will do several things. First, I will use my own resources—not those of the ISI—to assume a new identity as an Afghan. I will leave Pakistan and never return. No phone calls, vacations, or short visits. Tariq will retire and die quietly in his sleep a month later. I will be reborn under a new name in Afghanistan."

Hafiz felt that the men around the table were far from convinced, but Tariq was off to a decent start. What he had promised was a given—the bare minimum.

"Anyone who I recruit to work with me—there will be a few people from the organization, and the military—will do the same. They will be reborn as new people in Afghanistan and never return." Tariq nodded firmly. "A clean break to protect the country."

Hafiz remained slumped in his chair, overlooked and ignored, but he felt the mood of the room change the smallest amount in Tariq's favor. Tariq and the men he took with him would make a sacrifice. They had the country's best interests at heart.

"I plan to offer my services to the highest bidder," Tariq continued. "An auction. Organizations can use me, my skills, my resources to accomplish what they could never do 'in house.' Freelance terrorism. However, I pledge to never target our country or our allies."

"Would we not still be complicit in your bombings, having approved your request here today?" one of the men at the table asked.

Tariq tilted his head. "Yes, and no. For my other promise is that I will not be detected or caught. I will vary my approaches, disguise my hand. The organizations that bid—and win the auction—will never know who they are dealing with. I will continue to use best-practice tradecraft. For forty years, I have remained hidden. This will continue. You have my word."

"And if something happens? If you are discovered?"

"One, I will never be taken alive. And two, if I am about to be revealed, I will take whatever action necessary: Go into hiding, take the fight to the enemy, what have you. You will never have to worry about me."

Here, Tariq had miscalculated. The men at this table worried about everything. Especially the director-general, which was why Hafiz sat in the corner, a long-past-his-prime nobody who could be trusted to do whatever was necessary if the time came.

Tariq hesitated, and seemed ready to sit, but he must have felt the same mood in the room as Hafiz. The men were not yet convinced.

Tariq cleared his throat. *"One other item,"* he said. *"I have long contemplated a plan to bring the region of Kashmir and Jammu back under Pakistan's full control. Of course, what I have in mind is impossible for me in my current role as an employee of the ISI, and it is too complex and sophisticated to leave to one of the militant organizations we fund unofficially. But if I am allowed to do as I have proposed, my fifth bombing attack will target India and pave the way for a negotiated settlement in which India relinquishes control of the region. And,"* Tariq said with a proud smile, *"Al Qaeda, ISIS, or another organization with no affiliation to our country will happily take credit for the attack. They will also threaten more attacks if India doesn't concede to its demands."*

The men at the table exchanged glances of approval. As with most men of power, they thought of what might be achieved and too often minimized the risks involved.

Hafiz, with his field experience, focused more on the practical.

As Tariq returned to his seat, the men at the table discussed the proposal.

The return of Kashmir and Jammu to Pakistan's control was their dream. The area had strong cultural, religious, and historical ties to Pakistan. The wound caused by dividing British India into the countries of Pakistan and India more than seven decades earlier—leading to the disputed region—had grown and festered. Finally returning Kashmir and Jammu to Pakistan would be too tempting of a prize to resist. After a time, when all had their say, they would agree to Colonel Tariq's proposal.

Hafiz would be the one to monitor the situation... And be ready to act if things went bad—but maybe it would never come to that.

PART 3

SUNDAY

18

THE WIRE

Patrick resisted the frustration welling inside him that threatened his focus. Donald Everett's lack of slice on the sixth hole of the golf course the day before had been incredibly frustrating.

And today's opportunity to kill the next man on his list was iffy at best.

On some Sunday mornings, Randall Frandren skipped church to ride his mountain bike through one of the Phoenix metropolitan area's many desert nature preserves. But despite the tracker Patrick had installed on Frandren's car during a recon trip, he couldn't discern a pattern—not in how Frandren decided on worshipping in church versus exercising in nature, nor with which nature preserve he went to.

Frandren had clear favorites, though, which was why Patrick had parked his motorcycle a mile from Frandren's most frequently chosen trailhead, walked along the road, and hiked the popular mountain biking trail with a roll of wire in his pocket.

Playing the odds.

He'd left the motorcycle helmet behind, unfortunately. It would be conspicuous, and harm more than help, but he missed it.

About a mile from the parking lot, at a downhill section of the mountain bike trail, Patrick wrapped one end of the strong, tan wire several times around a boulder off to one side, pressed it gently into the sand across the trail, and continued into the desert for several feet, where he wrapped it partway around another boulder.

He backtracked up the trail before jogging downhill, looking for evidence of the buried wire.

Nothing. It blended into the ground perfectly.

There was nowhere to hide unless he wanted to bury himself in the desert. The nearby boulders were too small to conceal him. Besides, the trail was well traveled. He wanted to kill Frandren, not every mountain biker passing by. So he perched on the rocks where he'd partly wrapped the loose end of the wire and sipped from his water bottle. Just another desert lover taking a break while out for an early morning hike.

He'd risk the exposure. No one would remember a solitary hiker.

After an hour, his water was almost gone, and he'd waved at one hiker and let two mountain bikers race down the short hill and pass without triggering the wire.

Maybe luck wasn't on his side this weekend.

He'd have to try for Everett at the golf course next Saturday and Frandren on Sunday.

The crunch of tires on gravel made him look up in time to see Frandren, 60-something years old, with a thick gut and meaty thighs crammed into a one-piece black and red spandex riding outfit, more common among road bike riders who were in much better shape. Frandren pedaled his mountain bike furiously, feet spinning fast as he crested the top of the hill.

He didn't even glance Patrick's way as he shifted gears to head downhill. Though Frandren's face was partly hidden by large, dark sunglasses, and his head was protected with a shiny red bike helmet, Patrick recognized him from the recon trip—and the stories he'd heard about the man's girth, which had changed little in the past years.

Patrick grasped the wire lying on the rock next to him.

Frandren picked up speed, zipping down the hill like a pro.

With a sharp tug, Patrick pulled the wire taut and wrapped it around the rock twice.

Frandren's bike tire hit the wire stretched across the trail several inches off the ground, stopping the bike instantly—but not checking his body's momentum. He sailed through the air before he crashed into a microwave-size rock on the right side of the trail, 5 feet past his bike.

Patrick unwound the wire from the rock, taking the tension out of the line. If anyone came by, it wouldn't be obvious what had happened.

Next, he had to be sure.

Patrick ran to Frandren's body.

There was no need to check the man's pulse. His head, twisted at an unnatural angle, was all Patrick needed to see.

Frandren was dead.

Patrick felt both lucky—and disappointed.

On one hand, there was no need for a follow-up twist of the neck to finish the man off. The plan had worked perfectly.

On the other, he didn't get a chance for another hands-on kill.

But the deed was done, and it felt good.

Very good.

Patrick quickly wrapped up the wire, and spent several seconds smoothing the ground where it had been hidden.

Hurrying now, not wanting to get caught, he used his phone to take a few pictures of Frandren's broken body.

With a last look at the dead man crumpled against the rock, Patrick walked up the hill, smiling.

A connector trail a quarter mile ahead would take him back toward his motorcycle, parked along the road.

He'd be back home in Las Vegas in time for dinner.

And as long as he killed Donald Everett next Saturday—either on the golf course or in a less subtle yet still "accidental" manner—his mission would be complete.

19

THE BUS

Rahbar International Trading Partners
Surobi, Afghanistan

Tariq held the phone screen closer. His eyes weren't what they had been in his youth.

"More to the left," he said into his American-made earbuds, connected to his burner smartphone. The encrypted communications app had turned the espionage game on its head years before, making it easy—and much safer—to have private calls.

Or in this case, a video chat.

One way only, though. His contacts never saw his face.

Onscreen, a hand moved farther to the side.

"Stop. You will attach one there," Tariq told his latest protégé. He checked the paper on the desk in front of him for the man's name, not wanting to mix it up with Jawad, the other young man who worked in a different Paris bus service depot. "You're doing well, Asad."

The screen went dark as Asad set the phone on the floor of the bus depot. It wouldn't take long to memorize where he would attach the explosive device in a few days. Then they would proceed to the next location.

"Someone is coming," Asad whispered through his own earbuds, though the screen stayed dark. He worked the night shift cleaning the buses of Paris's extensive transportation network. He wasn't supposed to be under the bus. A different crew of more highly skilled workers maintained and repaired the buses.

"Do not move or speak," Tariq whispered. His pulse increased slightly, but surely not as much as young Asad's. If caught, Asad might be merely fired, as long as he held strong and stuck with the cover story of being under the bus because he wanted to become a mechanic one day.

There was no way for the authorities to know that Asad was only a few days away from receiving Tariq's expertly disguised explosive devices designed to propel shrapnel through the thin side of the bus and obliterate crowds of tourists.

Tariq waited. The mission could continue without Asad, but the devastation would be less effective.

Less spectacular.

Less profitable.

Tariq could live with that result if he had to. He had a contingency plan ready to go—car bombs instead of buses—though the delay would be annoying. And the proposal to his potential clients had a built-in range of casualties—never a guarantee of a specific number. But if Asad's apprehension put the French on higher alert, and the authorities implemented safety measures, the entire operation would be in jeopardy.

That Tariq couldn't accept. The Paris bombing had to happen on time.

Or all the work he'd done thus far, all the preparations he'd made, would be in jeopardy.

Plus, his former superiors might be unhappy enough to revoke their support—and retire him permanently.

Tariq watched the second hand of the clock on the wall sweep past twelve and continue around again.

He thought of Asad, huddled under the bus in Paris, and Jawad, the other man like him in the second bus depot he would talk with tomorrow night. They were pawns, not like the true protégés he had trained in person over the years.

Tariq smiled at the memory of several of his past star students. His first—Zeno, with the piercing blue eyes—had a very successful career for years until he disappeared after helping to incapacitate New York City with multiple car bombs. Tariq hoped his student had retired and was enjoying his wealth in some small village in a tropical location.

Another of Tariq's pupils—a true master of improvised explosive devices after learning the hard way and blowing off three of his fingers—

had been killed years before by American Special Forces in a remote village in Afghanistan.

Tariq had long ago vowed that he would not suffer the same fate.

No in-the-field bomb making.

No need for disguises, fake passports, bribes to customs officials, or dangerous, uncomfortable, clandestine insertions into foreign countries.

He had a young man named Naveed he'd recruited from the ISI to travel and handle the sociopathic "freedom fighters"—extremists—that were ready to pay for Tariq's bombing and logistics expertise.

Tariq built the bombs and disguised them.

The legitimate import-export business he'd purchased handled their transportation.

Tariq tapped into his network to find and recommend lonely men around the world who wanted money, glory, or a sense of belonging, and he exploited those desires. They planted and, in some cases, detonated his creations.

And he could manage it all from the comfort and safety of his office in the small town of Surobi, Afghanistan.

The second hand completed another sweep. No sound meant Asad hadn't been discovered. He would never be a true bomber; he was merely a tool, a pair of hands for Tariq to operate remotely. A well-paid, highly valued temporary member of the organization—if he remained undiscovered. If he were caught, Asad would be cut loose without knowing enough to jeopardize Tariq's safety.

"They are gone," Asad whispered at last. He sounded relieved. "Where will I place the next bomb?" he asked, surprising Tariq with his dedication. The view of the underside of the bus returned.

"Move closer to the front," Tariq said. For the destruction he had planned, he had to find one more solid spot to attach a second device.

20

THE OFFER

Hard-eyed men with AK-47s tracked every step of Naveed's progress through the security checkpoints.

Other guards had initially frisked him outside the walls of the compound—in the dry, dirty street—before he could enter. The rough search of his tall, thin frame—including his short dark curly hair—didn't bother him. He had nothing to hide, and the work he'd done for his country's intelligence agency, the ISI, had thoroughly prepared him for this type of confrontation.

Naveed wore a traditional *thobe*—a loose robe that fell to the ankles—instead of a linen suit, which he preferred, but today's meeting required turning his back on Western ways and clothing.

His beard was closely trimmed, and he wore no watch, rings, or other jewelry. He carried nothing in his pockets except limited bills in the local currency—to pay for the taxi to and from the meeting—the keycard to his four-star hotel close to the airport, and a single, folded sheet of paper with handwritten contact instructions.

His perfectly forged Kuwait passport was locked in the hotel room's safe, along with a single credit card; the small overnight bag in his room held only a simple toiletry kit and a change of clothes. Should the guards have orders to confiscate his hotel keycard and search his room while he met with their leader—it had happened before—they would find nothing to alarm them. He was exactly what he claimed: an emissary from an organization in the area with a business proposition that could only be discussed in person.

A second set of guards searched Naveed once he had passed through a high-tech metal detector straight out of an international airport. Stepping into a courtyard, the already bright sun burning down on him, he spread his arms and legs wide and endured the indignity with a patient half smile.

At last, he was cleared to enter the compound's main building, a white, flat-roofed, one-story mansion with thick bars on the windows.

More armed guards stood along the walls of an ornate room, fingers extended alongside the trigger guards of their weapons, which they held at the low ready. They wore crisp, clean, desert-camouflage-patterned fatigues and polished black boots.

"Welcome," a deep voice boomed from the far end of the room. Naveed bowed his head for a second and walked along a red carpet runner leading toward a sofa sectional on a thick rug—the only furniture in the entire cavernous room. He didn't hurry. He didn't want the guards to get the wrong idea. But he sped up. It wouldn't be smart to keep the man waiting.

The leader of the Yemeni Independence Brigade sprawled across the center of one of the black sofa sectionals that formed a wide and deep "U" at the rear of the room. He sat alone, with none of the usual entourage and hangers-on that Naveed often encountered at these meetings—men he had to convince his contacts to dismiss so they could speak in absolute privacy. It was a refreshing move and showed that the former general didn't need a crowd to feel, or be, important.

There was only one personal guard, with a matte-black shotgun, standing a few steps to the side, ready to blast Naveed to pieces if he came too close.

Ali Al-Haddad had his feet on a black coffee table. He wore an outfit similar to Naveed's: off-white *thobe,* but of much higher quality. Al-Haddad might be a "man of the people" and had his followers believing he was pious, but he was clearly no stranger to the finer things in life.

The man had left the military and started a criminal enterprise, smuggling arms, shaking down aid and relief efforts in the country, imposing "taxes," and offering protection—for a price. He used a radical interpretation of religion to justify his hatred of the government, the West, and anyone not adhering to his views. But Naveed thought it was an act designed to disguise the man's ego, and his desire for power and glory.

Either way, Naveed would use those beliefs and desires to manipulate him today.

The more people bidding on the services Naveed offered on behalf of Colonel Tariq, the better.

Pleasantries took an agonizing ten minutes. Naveed sipped the strong, sweet tea that a guard had delivered. They discussed the oppressive heat of the summer and the beauty of the sea a few kilometers to the west. Common ground was established.

Naveed spoke when needed, letting Al-Haddad guide the conversation, the Yemeni Arabic he'd brushed up on coming easily the way languages always had for him.

Finally, it was time for business.

"My people tell me you have a mysterious proposal for me," Al-Haddad said after a last sip of his tea.

Naveed set his cup atop the saucer on the low table and sat up straight. "I do, sir." He outlined the broad strokes of the proposal, and ended with the final appeal. "You can punish the West for their many sins. Make them fear you. Gain power and followers. Recruit more soldiers. Make more money. Shape the region any way you see fit."

Fire burned in the former soldier's eyes. "You can make this happen?" he asked. He seemed sold on the value, but doubtful an attack the size Naveed had described could be achieved.

"Yes, sir." Naveed listed the three previous bombings he'd helped Colonel Tariq with: the "proof of concept" missions. Egypt. Turkey. Spain.

"And we take the credit?" the general asked. "Not you?"

"Correct, sir. It would mean instant worldwide notoriety, without the risks of planning and implementing the operation yourself. Publicity, however, is your responsibility. We only handle the attacks. Although…" Naveed said, leaning forward enough to be conspiratorial without getting close enough to the general for the soldier with the shotgun to become concerned. "We would provide details unavailable to anyone but the actual planners of the operation as proof you were behind the bombings. There will be no doubt that you were the mastermind of the destruction."

Al-Haddad's eyes narrowed. "And the cost for this service?"

"Ah," Naveed said with a smile, and leaned back. "It is an auction. The minimum bid is ten million American dollars," Naveed said while the former general frowned. "Cash, to be wired to a numbered account."

"Ten million…"

"The starting bid," Naveed said. He could read the man like a newspaper. Ten million was a great deal of money, but he didn't seem bothered by the amount. "There are several interested parties," Naveed said. There were three other extremist groups considering the offer, some with deeper pockets than the general.

But a man like the general would hate the idea that someone else might steal "his" glory.

Al-Haddad bit his lip in an obvious tell. "How much to ensure you will do this for me—without bidding?"

Naveed shook his head with an apologetic smile. "I'm sorry. That is not how it works. In the auction, the highest bidder will take credit for the destruction. Those who do not bid high enough, though, will have another chance for the next strike. We have several others planned, including more in Europe over the coming years."

"I do not want to bid," Al-Haddad said, his voice firm. It came out as an order.

The general flicked a finger.

The guard with the shotgun raised the weapon to his shoulder and pointed it directly at Naveed's head.

Naveed sat perfectly still, kept his breathing steady, and waited for the end to come.

21

THE MONEY

Yemeni Independence Brigade Headquarters
Aden, Yemen

When he wasn't shot immediately, Naveed held back a sigh of relief while keeping any signs of fear or frustration off his face. This was the delicate part of the assignment. Men like Al-Haddad were not used to being told they couldn't do or have what they wanted.

When Naveed refused to capitulate, the general grunted at the guard. "Not on the couch," he said.

The guard with the shotgun twitched the weapon, indicating Naveed should stand and move away from the sofa so his brains wouldn't ruin the sectional.

Naveed didn't move.

Negotiations had never gotten to this stage before.

Colonel Tariq couldn't—wouldn't—save him. As valuable as he was, Naveed was expendable. He could easily be replaced with another idiot who willingly approached extremist leaders—freedom fighters, as he had to remember to call them—and offered Colonel Tariq's terrorism-on-demand service.

The general sighed and shook his head at Naveed's stubbornness. "I will pay twelve million right now," Al-Haddad said. "Eleven million for the bombing, and you keep one million for your assistance with this matter."

Naveed bowed his head to hide how tempted he was to take the offer. Others had tried to bribe him, but never with so much money—or at gunpoint. His mother had a health condition the local doctors were unable to help with. Naveed should be with her in Kabul, not on the road negotiating with men like this.

A million dollars would allow him to get his mother the help she deserved—but would not be enough for them to disappear forever. And without more than a million dollars, he and his mother would be killed by Colonel Tariq long before his mother's condition took her.

"Or I have you shot immediately," Al-Haddad said, his voice serious but with a lightness that made it obvious that the idea of killing Naveed didn't bother him in the least. "I can get a new couch."

Time slowed down. The guard's finger tightened on the trigger. The barrel aimed at Naveed's head drew his gaze and seemed to grow larger, but Naveed dragged his eyes to Al-Haddad, who opened his mouth to speak.

Naveed couldn't watch him give the order. He closed his eyes and prepared for the end. He thought of his sick mother.

He should have taken the bribe.

"Your commitment reflects well on the people you represent," the general said, the anger in his voice tinged with reluctant respect.

Naveed kept his head bowed for three more seconds before raising it.

"I have instructions for contacting me through a secure communications app," Naveed said. In slow motion, he reached into his pocket to remove the folded paper with two fingers and placed it on the table in front of the couch. "If your bid wins, we will inform you. At that point, you will wire one quarter of the bid amount immediately. An additional one quarter is required when the strike is imminent. And the final half upon completion."

He left unspoken any threats for non-payment. Unlike Naveed's safety, getting paid was important to Colonel Tariq. The man who had planned three bombings in the past year, and the one about to occur, could target the general whenever he wanted.

"Thank you for your time and consideration," Naveed said as he stood slowly, offered a final small bow, and walked back to the door.

He counted his steps, wondering if the general would allow him to leave, and about the range of the shotgun. Not that it mattered—any of the many guards could easily shoot him before he reached the door to the street.

Naveed put one foot in front of the other, waiting for bullets to slam into him, but they never came.

Eventually, he was safely out of the compound.

He was only in his late thirties, but he was already far too old for this. He should have stayed with Pakistan's intelligence service—the ISI—instead of leaving to work for Colonel Tariq. It had seemed like a great opportunity at the time: Travel widely while working for a successful career spy going out on his own.

He recalled the meeting in the ISI's private basement room with Colonel Tariq. "A small team," the legend had said. "Me, you, and loyal guards. Maybe a student to continue my work." Tariq had shrugged an apology and waited for Naveed's answer.

Naveed had been one of Tariq's students. Naveed had wanted more than anything to leave behind the translating and advising work he did for the agency and accomplish something meaningful.

At first, it had seemed like he had an aptitude for the intricacies of bomb making, but after only a few weeks, it was obvious it wasn't his path.

He was better with people than plastic explosives, blasting caps, and timers.

"I need someone I can trust," Colonel Tariq had whispered in that little room, far from anyone who could overhear. "I will retire soon and start my own operation. Your skills are essential to me. Together, we will accomplish great things—and earn so much money."

It was the money that convinced Naveed.

His mother had started to feel constantly fatigued. Her muscles were weak, and she had lost weight.

If Naveed had more money, he could take her to better doctors.

"You will see riches beyond belief," Colonel Tariq said.

On the spot, Naveed had agreed to leave the ISI and join Tariq.

And now, a year later, the money had yet to materialize. It was always, "After the next operation," and, "There are so many expenses, my friend."

Naveed could wait no longer, especially with his mother's condition worsening and the hospitals in Kabul much less advanced than those in Islamabad.

As Naveed walked the dusty streets toward a busy intersection where he could find a taxi, he reached his decision.

He wasn't paid enough to wonder if the next meeting with extremists would be his last.

Naveed had been threatened before, but it had never been as close as today's encounter.

Maybe he should have taken the bribe offered by the general.

But to get his mother help, relocate to a country with excellent medical care, and disappear completely, he needed more than a million dollars.

He would wait no longer for Colonel Tariq's long-promised riches.

Instead, he would investigate a mysterious group in Afghanistan offering money for information. The word was all over the streets. Millions of dollars were available—or at least the rumors said. The American CIA at work, Naveed figured. They had a history of offering cash rewards in exchange for people on their most wanted list.

If the price was right, he would betray Colonel Tariq, save his mother, and start a new, safer life than this.

PART 4

THURSDAY

22

THE WATCHERS

It was a pleasant morning in Kabul, though the air was already warming. A breeze kept the worst of the heat at bay.

Latif, code-named "Lion," had worked for Pakistan's Inter-Services Intelligence for six years. Being an operational spy suited him. He traveled often—this operation in Afghanistan wasn't far from home, but still—and no two operations were alike.

Unfortunately, there never seemed to be enough staff for the missions, no matter how essential. So it was just himself and Vasim, who was also in his mid-thirties. They'd worked together before and were similar enough to get along well, but different enough to complement each other.

Vasim was spontaneous and hard charging, hence the code name "Bull," while Latif was a hunter: patient and exact.

Five days into the mission, they were both sleep-deprived from the 24/7 surveillance on Sardar, the businessman—and suspected spy—they'd been assigned to watch.

"That's him," Bull said from his vehicle on the cross street behind him.

"That is his vehicle," Lion said, correcting him. The call quality through the eight speakers in the luxury SUV was superb. It beat their usual approach of wireless earbuds in rundown cars without air conditioning. Surveillance on a rich businessman in an upscale neighborhood had its perks: the nice clothes they had been provided, the small fleet of cars, SUVs, and motorcycles at their disposal, along with the stack of bills in their pockets.

Their target left his home compound in the wealthy neighborhood each morning, always in a black SUV similar to the one Lion drove today, and always with his two long-time bodyguards in the front seat. There had been no attempts at a surveillance routine or other efforts to detect or deter being followed. Instead, the driver went straight to a local cafe. The bodyguard walked to the cafe with the target, leaving the driver with the vehicle.

Today looked to be the same.

"Watch and report," the brief had been. "Specifically," their field officer, Imran, had said, "look for indications the target is running a network of spies or informants."

Lion wondered about the intel that had them watching the man every moment of the day and night. The businessman was short and pudgy, with thinning dark hair, bushy dark eyebrows, round glasses, and a moderate beard. He dressed in the traditional long shirt and loose pants common among men of the region, though the fabric looked expensive, and he hadn't worn the same pants or top yet, hinting at an extensive wardrobe.

He looked and acted wealthy and harmless, not like a spy.

"I have him—or rather, his SUV," Bull responded, his tone light. He wasn't offended by Lion's correction.

"I'll move ahead, park, and get coffee as soon as you tell me which cafe he's headed toward this morning," Lion said. After switching watch every four hours all night, Lion welcomed a double-shot espresso, which he'd gotten addicted to during another sleep-depriving assignment the year before.

He pushed his way into the already hectic morning traffic, getting far fewer horns honking at him than he would have in a cheaper vehicle. It paid to be rich—or to look like it, especially in a neighborhood of other people driving similar SUVs. To them, he and Bull must seem like wealthy neighbors to be treated with respect.

Lion turned to drive the same direction as Bull and the target, paralleling them one street over. He signaled, waved, and changed lanes repeatedly, nodding and playing the part of a businessman running late to coax people into letting him race ahead.

"It looks like Chai Corner again," Bull said.

The cafe was the closest to the target's home and had only been open a few months, from what Lion had gathered. Although they had only been watching the man for a few days, his routine was relatively predictable, making their job much easier.

"Copy. Chai Corner," Lion said with pleasure. The cafe had excellent espresso, and a shaded bench down the street where he'd be able to sit and watch the target.

He squeezed into a parking spot along the street a half block from the cafe, unwilling to risk losing it if there wasn't a closer one. "Exiting the vehicle," he said. The phone automatically transferred the call to the white earbuds he wore.

"Enjoy the coffee for me," Bull said. He would park nearby on the businessman's likely route to his office a few kilometers away and be stuck there until Sardar was safely at work, when Lion would take over the watch to allow Bull some rest, food, and coffee before they did it all again in reverse, tailing the man to his home for the night.

"Don't worry, I will," Lion said as he hurried up the sidewalk to the cafe. It wouldn't do to end up in line behind the target.

23

THE CAFE

Chai Corner
Shahr-e Naw District
Kabul, Afghanistan

Several days a week, businessman Sardar Hotak stopped for tea and a snack on his way to work.

This morning he was near his home at a trendy new cafe with modern decor. Half of its outdoor tables were occupied already, though the sun was barely over the tops of the nearby two-story buildings of the quiet, affluent neighborhood a block from the shade trees, grass, and paved walkways of Shahr-e Naw Park. The sky was a perfect blue, and a light breeze promised to keep the temperature in a moderate range.

Sardar sipped his strong black tea, spiced with cardamom and sweetened with honey. He slathered honey onto a piece of fresh, warm naan, served by a young man who was pleasant but not talkative.

Sardar picked up the folded newspaper the bearded server had left with the tea and naan. He glanced casually at the most prominent article on the first page, allowing a single piece of paper, folded into a small square and hidden in the newspaper, to slip into his palm.

After reading a few paragraphs of the article, he set the newspaper on the table and slid the tiny square of paper into his pocket, trading it for an envelope of cash.

He smoothly slipped the envelope into the fold of the newspaper, drank more tea, and finished the naan.

After finishing the paper, Sardar drank the rest of his tea. When the server emerged from the cafe, Sardar paid him for the morning treat and left, leaving the newspaper behind.

The young man would collect the cup, plate, and newspaper. The envelope of cash would be pocketed, and the money shared with the man's network of informants—spies, really.

Sardar walked down the street, where his driver waited in the black luxury SUV. The driver opened the rear door as he approached, allowing him to climb inside the heavily tinted vehicle. Sardar's bodyguard, who had stood to the side of the cafe keeping watch, sat in the front passenger seat a moment later. The two men had been with him for years and were as close to him as his sons—and just as loyal.

"The office," Sardar said from the rear. As the driver pulled the car onto the busy road, Sardar opened the folded piece of paper.

His persistence had paid off. Offering millions of dollars as a reward for information had finally produced a result.

In careful handwriting, the message Sardar had waited for had finally arrived.

The person or people behind a slew of bombings during the last year was closer to being identified.

An insider was willing to betray them.

Ten million dollars was an enormous amount of money, but a small price to pay for what Sardar had worked toward for so many years.

As long as he could get the money, arrange a meet, and avoid a potential double-cross—and the bullet in the brain that came with it—the bomber would be stopped.

24

THE PRESIDENT

The President's Weight Room—The White House
Washington, DC

Nothing in Gregory Addison's forty-year career as an intelligence analyst had prepared him for what he discovered in the basement of the White House.

As usual, it was earlier than he preferred to be awake, but he'd gotten used to working out with the president several times a week. What had started as a back-channel way for Gregory to brief President Heringten about off-the-record missions had turned into exercise time they both enjoyed.

Stepping into the small weight room, wearing old gray gym shorts, a faded black T-shirt, and sneakers, Gregory stopped abruptly, trying to make sense of the scene in front of him.

"You've got it, Vernon," President James Heringten said to an older man struggling to bench-press the bar with no weight plates on it. "Just a little more!"

The other man, with close-cropped white hair and long, bushy sideburns, grunted and pushed the bar to the top. Heringten grabbed it and guided it to the J hooks.

"Whew," the older man said with a distinctly Southern twang. "Still got it, though, don't I?" he said as he sat up.

He wore what were obviously brand-new black workout shorts, along with a tired white T-shirt normally worn under a dress shirt. It had yellowed armpit stains.

His bony arms and legs jutting from the outfit attested to a complete lack of a recent weightlifting routine.

Still, at 89 years old, former President Vernon Westerlin had an easy smile and bright, clear dark eyes that locked onto Gregory.

The two-term president from many years earlier was the last person Gregory had thought he'd see this morning, especially in the White House basement, wearing workout clothes, lifting weights with President Heringten. Several years earlier, during James Heringten's campaign for president, Westerlin had called candidate Heringten "a clear and present danger to our country" while campaigning alongside then-Senator Heringten's presidential opponent.

"Ah, here he is now," President Heringten said, smiling at Gregory. His eyes danced at Gregory's confusion. "Vern, this is Gregory Addison, director of the Central Analysis Group." He didn't bother to return the introduction.

Gregory recovered immediately and nodded. "It's a pleasure to meet you, Mr. President."

Vernon Westerlin hadn't been a bad president—nor an exceptional one. He'd led the country reasonably well for two terms, navigated a few foreign crises and a Congress that hated him, and left the United States of America in decent shape for his successor. He wouldn't go down in the history books as anything special, but through his words and deeds, he'd proven his love of the country.

He had retired to a life of public speaking and writing nonfiction books about a variety of topics. These days, aside from a few speeches a year, he mostly stayed out of the public eye, living on a sprawling compound in northern Louisiana, where he was visited by a gaggle of grandkids and the occasional up-and-coming politician hoping for advice from a party elder.

Normally, Gregory would run a half mile on one of the two treadmills to warm up with President Heringten while they exchanged pleasantries before hitting the weights—and discussing any pressing intelligence issues Gregory needed to bring up.

This morning, he was unsure of the protocol. Were they all working out together? Or—as he suspected—was there an agenda that included something much more pressing than weights?

"Hand me a towel, would you, son?" Westerlin asked, pointing to the stack of perfectly folded towels on a small table near the door.

As Gregory handed one over, Westerlin's eyes lingered on the presidential seal embroidered in the corner before unfolding it and wiping his brow.

President Heringten waited patiently for Westerlin to take the lead, so Gregory did the same.

After several long seconds, the former president held the towel, smiled sadly at the seal, and looked up at Gregory. "I find myself in need of a favor, Mr. Addison," he said, his voice quiet and serious. "James here tells me you're the man to ask."

Gregory didn't have to glance at President Heringten to know the score. There was no way Westerlin would be in the basement of the White House if the president didn't want him there. Former presidents didn't just drop by their old home—and office—whenever they were in the neighborhood.

"How can I help, Mr. President?"

Westerlin's lips pressed together and eyebrows furrowed in anger. "Someone murdered my friend last week. I want you to find out who, why..."—he glared at Gregory and lowered his voice to a fierce, cold whisper—"and then I want you to exact revenge."

25

THE FAVOR

The President's Weight Room—The White House
Washington, DC

Gregory moved to the side of the treadmill but didn't bother starting it. There would be no working out this morning.

"Your friend was murdered and you need my help?" Gregory repeated, keeping his tone neutral. There had to be a story here for the former president to be requesting a favor of the current president instead of going to the police or an old FBI contact.

"Yes. I'm sure you'll recognize the name: Calvin Rutherfield."

Gregory stared at Westerlin, working hard not to betray his surprise. Of course he recognized the name; Calvin Rutherfield and Gregory had worked together at the CIA.

"Calvin is dead?" This was news to Gregory. For a second, he thought he should have heard, but then he realized there would have been no reason to. They'd never been close and hadn't spoken in years. Rutherfield was long retired. Gregory wasn't on social media, and Calvin would have avoided it like the plague.

The other members of their team were scattered to the wind. Gregory guessed he was the only one still in the spy business.

"Someone snuck into his independent living apartment and murdered him," President Westerlin said.

"He must have been, what, in his mid-seventies?" Gregory's implication was clear. People died, especially men of a certain age.

Westerlin glanced at President Heringten, who raised a hand to placate him.

"Look into this for us, will you, Gregory?" President Heringten asked. It came out as a mild question, but there was no doubt it was an order.

"Of course, Mr. President," Gregory said automatically.

"Thanks. I owe you one," Heringten said with a hint of a smile.

Gregory knew a dismissal when he heard it. "Mr. President," he said to Heringten, before turning to Westerlin. "Mr. President. If Rutherfield was murdered, I'll get to the bottom of it."

"Good man," Westerlin said. He lowered himself slowly onto the workout bench again. "Spot me, James. I think I can do at least one more set."

With that, Gregory moved to the door and stepped into the hallway, wondering what the hell he was getting into.

26

THE MIND MAP

Conference Room 1
Central Analysis Group Headquarters
Alexandria, Virginia

The round, four-person table in conference room 3 hadn't been big enough to hold Wyatt's creation. He'd been forced to relocate to the main conference room with its 16-foot-long rectangular table that sat twelve comfortably.

The room was rarely used; the Central Analysis Group wasn't big on meetings, and the senior analysts like Nancy and Dave, along with Haley —who enjoyed some sort of special status Wyatt didn't fully understand— met in Gregory's office or commandeered one of the smaller rooms.

Wyatt carefully unfolded the pile of wrinkled 24-by-18-inch newsprint drawing paper. He took it slow; the cheap material had been flimsy enough to start with. After daily use and frequent folding, the twenty-four off-white pages had become worn and tore easily.

He moved around the table as he progressed, wishing for the hundredth time that he could give the papers a shake or flip, like with a king-size sheet while making a bed. But the many pages, delicately held together to make what was in effect a large paper quilt, wouldn't tolerate that.

The clear tape he'd used to connect the pages had also seen better days. Several sections had multiple layers of tape, their corners peeling off. He smoothed them down when he noticed them, but they curled up again immediately.

Later this morning, depending on Gregory's reaction to the paper quilt, Wyatt could make more repairs to keep the thing from falling apart.

Assuming he still had a job in an hour.

With arms outstretched, Wyatt held the ends of the "sheet" as close to the corners as he could reach and pulled it across the full length of the conference table. It covered every inch.

The result of his obsessive research lay bare. Nearly every inch of the patchwork quilt was covered with neat, handwritten notes framed with boxes.

Each note had been written in a different color, until he'd run through all twenty-four pens in his specially bought marker collection.

Sticky notes of different colors clung to the paper, each filled with additional carefully printed ideas, explanations, and conclusions.

Lines and arrows pointed from box to box and note to note, often stretching across multiple rectangles of the drawing papers.

Certain boxes, especially along the outer border of the so-called quilt, were highlighted in orange, yellow, green, blue, or pink. He hadn't been able to find more highlighter colors than that.

The display represented everything Wyatt could discover about his latest obsession.

The players involved.

The events.

And the many things he suspected but didn't know for certain.

The greatest question of all waited like a huge, bizarre puzzle. A solitary space, the size of a sticky note, sat empty at the center of the papers.

Lines led to and from the blank area like a map of the most convoluted freeway system in the world.

The spot was ready for an answer he hadn't discovered yet.

Wyatt stepped back and pressed against the conference room wall to get an overview of his creation. He knew the work inside and out. He'd lived every nuance and detail, researched and evaluated before adding them to the massive document.

For a moment, he set aside the ramifications of his conclusion—what

Gregory would have to do if the research was even partly accurate—and did his best to look at the display from a distance, as an unattached observer seeing the multicolored boxes, lines, and notes for the first time.

Wyatt's stomach dropped.

Anyone seeing this would think he had lost his mind.

27

THE PUZZLE

Conference Room 1
Central Analysis Group Headquarters
Alexandria, Virginia

Gregory took a deep, steadying breath outside the door to the conference room and smoothed down his longer-than-regulation hair.

Wyatt—his newest hire—waited inside. The CIA, where Gregory had recruited him from, hadn't given Wyatt the free rein someone like him required. But the young man's frenetic energy—and disheveled appearance—were both an encouraging sign and a concern.

There was a fine line between hard work and compulsion.

Or brilliance and madness.

Gregory wasn't sure where exactly Wyatt fit into the calculation and struggled with the ethics of letting him work so hard. But if the kid's obsessive nature helped protect the United States of America, Gregory would happily look the other way.

It took a deft touch for Gregory to manage his team. Nancy and Dave —his senior analysts—didn't need much direction. They were solid and set a good example for the others.

Then there was Haley Albright. Her intelligence and intuition were on a level he'd never seen before—except early on in his own career. But he had allowed himself to be slowly ground down by the bureaucracy, which had left him more conventional than he'd once been.

Now, as a manager, he nudged the lazy, stuck, and slow starters to bring out the best in them.

He also corralled the wild ones, harnessed their talents, and pointed them in the right direction.

All while ensuring no one burnt out or—worse—made an intelligence analysis mistake with disastrous ramifications.

He was part team lead and part herder of cats.

When Wyatt had called yesterday to request a meeting this morning, he had sounded excited—and terrified.

But unless the new guy had discovered a plot to overthrow the government or invade America, Gregory had to pull him off whatever he was so spun up about.

Gregory needed an obsessive workaholic to tackle the death of Calvin Rutherfield.

For former president Vernon Westerlin—and for his own satisfaction.

Rutherfield, who they'd just called The Boss, had been a flawed man, but he deserved someone who wouldn't stop turning over stones until the job was done.

Gregory put a neutral expression on his face. He was ready for anything Wyatt could spring on him.

Pushing open the door to the conference room, a much bigger problem than he'd been expecting hit him in the face.

The long table was covered with taped-together pages of large, off-white paper, the cheap kind used for printing newspapers and sold at craft stores for artists to sketch on.

Three pages wide by eight long.

Twenty-four sheets of paper.

Every single one was covered with boxes, arrows, lines, and sticky notes packed with careful writing.

Gregory reached back without looking and locked the door behind him. No one else could see this until he determined whether Wyatt had gone crazy.

Or rather, how crazy he'd gone.

What was the thing on the table? Could he call it a document?

Was it a patchwork quilt of genius—or madness?

Gregory kept his face expressionless. This was a report by an experienced analyst who a few months before had discovered a puzzle that no one else had known existed—and solved it. Wyatt was responsible for providing the intel on a secret program to kill American military personnel in Iraq and Afghanistan. His insights contributed to an enemy of the United States of America being erased off the face of the earth without a trace.

But it didn't help that Wyatt had spread out his… report… so that the writing was upside down to Gregory from his position near the door.

Wyatt was as disheveled as usual. His light-blue dress shirt looked like it had been stuffed into a drawer for a few weeks before he'd slipped it on—then slept in for several days. It was tucked into his pants on the right side only; the long left front panel hung over his equally wrinkled tan chinos, which had either been purchased too short or had shrunk—they stopped a half inch above his ankles. Any effort to match socks had failed; one was black, the other navy blue.

Wyatt's ears stuck out, and his dark curls hadn't seen a comb in days, but he'd gotten a haircut in the past few weeks, which showed he was making an effort. He also didn't smell today, proving he'd made use of the building's small gym and locker room.

Wyatt radiated energy. His face slipped between hope, fear, and embarrassment.

Gregory walked around the table to stand next to him. If the kid had gone off the deep end, Gregory would get the young man the help he deserved.

And if the information on the papers spread across the conference room table represented another puzzle Wyatt had discovered—and solved—Gregory's day had taken a second dramatic turn.

28

THE COMPANY

Conference Room 1
Central Analysis Group Headquarters
Alexandria, Virginia

Gregory tried to make sense of the papers in front of him. It was a mess of lines connecting boxes, hand-printed text highlighted in various colors, and arrows.

"It's a mind map," Wyatt said into the silence, his voice apologetic.

"I know what it is."

"I couldn't make sense of the data in a spreadsheet."

They stood next to each other while Gregory took it all in.

"I know how it looks," Wyatt whispered.

Gregory glanced at him, his neutral composure slipping a bit. "Do you?" He was genuinely curious.

Wyatt nodded. "It makes me look obsessive at best. Crazy at worst."

Gregory had to give it to the kid. He'd nailed it.

"Which is it?" Gregory asked.

"Obsessive." Wyatt let out a bark of laughter somewhere between a chuckle and a sob. "I hope."

"Me too," Gregory said, more intrigued than concerned. "I had an urgent special project for you. It can't wait, but I can't pull you off this," he said, gesturing at the paper, "until you explain it to me. Before we dive in, sum this up. One sentence. Two at the most. What's going on here?"

Wyatt took a deep breath, held it, and let it out in a rush. "I believe someone is running a terrorism-for-hire company." He paused, hesitated, and continued. "They are very skilled. And shielded or hidden—possibly by a nation-state—and maybe untouchable." Wyatt shrugged. "Sorry, that was three sentences."

When Gregory didn't react, Wyatt spoke again, softer this time. "The attacks around the world the past nine months? The embassy bombing in Cairo. The explosion inside the mall food court in Turkey. The bomb at the airport on the Spanish island of Mallorca."

"All successful attacks by different terrorist groups."

"No. The same perpetrator designed, planned, and executed them. The attacks were claimed by different groups, but not executed by them. And as far as I can tell, none of our sister agencies—including our allies—know about this."

Gregory's first reaction was that his new analyst had gone off the deep end.

But...

What if he was right?

"How long have you been working on this?"

Wyatt didn't hesitate. "Since you pulled me off the Saudi Prince Rafiq Al-Najjar project."

Wyatt had researched that one and nailed the intel.

Maybe this mind map wasn't so far-fetched after all.

Gregory had a lot of questions about the intelligence spread before him, but he started with the two most obvious. "Who? And why?"

Wyatt's demeanor changed from nervous excitement to quiet dread. After a long pause, he finally spoke in a whisper. "I don't know."

29

THE POSSIBILITIES

Conference Room 1
Central Analysis Group Headquarters
Alexandria, Virginia

Wyatt held his breath, hoping Gregory wouldn't discount the endless hours of research, no matter how unlikely his findings seemed.

"You're saying what exactly?" Gregory asked, not hiding his skepticism. "Terrorist groups are outsourcing their attacks? No chance. We would have heard about it. There would be chatter."

"Not really. They wouldn't be proud of hiring someone to do their dirty work. None of them—Al Qaeda, the Taliban, ISIS, or one of the many smaller groups—would want the public or their followers to know. It wouldn't be in the best interest of the people planning and conducting the attacks, either."

Gregory pondered his argument while staring at the pages on the table. "All these attacks were outsourced?" he finally asked.

Wyatt waved at the paper. "Yes, I think at least the big ones over the past nine months have been planned and executed by the same person or group."

He pointed at sticky notes. "They start out small—the truck bombing outside the embassy in Cairo. What I would call 'proof of concept.' Like,

'Look what we can do. Now hire us to coordinate your next attack.' A demo, essentially."

He continued taking Gregory through the pages, following the lines. "Then they hit Turkey. Finally, the airport. Always bombs disguised in some way: a local utility's delivery truck, shoe boxes planted in trash bins, and boxes of books. But with different explosives, configurations, and detonators."

"Which is why everyone thinks they aren't connected."

"Exactly."

Gregory wasn't sold on it yet, but Wyatt had his attention. Most importantly, Gregory hadn't immediately discounted the possibility. "What's this?" Gregory asked, pointing at the center of the paper, where many of the winding lines converged. A blank square in the paper, just the size of a sticky note, lay bare as if waiting for the final piece of the puzzle.

"The person—or people—responsible."

"Any leads? Guesses?"

"Just that they are professionals. Not goat herders who stole some C4 or a warlord with a desire to make the big time. They have logistical experience, a network of trusted people—and a very talented bomb maker. Or several. My best guess is that it's former intelligence people or former military. And..." He paused, not wanting to get into the rest, though Gregory had likely seen the notes across the bottom of the pages.

"What?"

"I think this same person—or group—could have been responsible for many of the IEDs during the war in Afghanistan."

Gregory's eyes narrowed. "Could be former military? Could have been responsible for deaths in Afghanistan? But you have nothing concrete? No names, no proof any of this is truly connected?"

Wyatt couldn't meet Gregory's eyes, and he felt his face flush with embarrassment. "No, sir. Not yet. But... I feel it. Something is there."

Gregory didn't speak for several seconds. When Wyatt finally glanced at him, Gregory was taking in the mind map and, uncharacteristically, chewing his lip. He must have felt Wyatt's eyes on him, because he stopped, licked his lips, and frowned. "Why bring this to me now?" Gregory asked him.

"I thought you should know what I'm working on. It's all I can think about. I admit, I'm obsessed. I guess... I need you to tell me if you think I'm crazy."

Gregory glanced at Wyatt for a second before his eyes returned to the mind map.

"I can't fault you for the work," Gregory said. "There's a fine line between crazy and brilliant, and it's hard to know where that is until all is said and done. As far as I can tell, you haven't lost it. I've gone down paths searching for answers, too. We all have. You can stick with it, but if it isn't an immediate threat..." He looked at Wyatt again and held his gaze.

"Another bombing could come at any time. It's due soon, if the pattern remains the same. But I have no data about it being imminent. There's no chatter or other indications. Not that I've seen so far, at least."

"Then I have something more urgent for you and your..."

"Obsessive tendencies?" Wyatt said with a halfhearted smile to lighten the mood.

"I was going to say 'workaholism,' but that works, too."

Gregory grabbed a stack of sticky notes from a small credenza at the side of the room, took a silver pen from his suit coat pocket, and wrote several lines on the top yellow paper. He moved to the end of the table, flipped one end of the taped-together quilt, and slapped the sticky note down on the back side. "Here's a name and some details. Do a deep dive. Find out if this man was murdered, and if so, by whom."

Wyatt nodded. "Any suggestions? Parameters?"

"Leave no stone unturned. Whatever it takes for a definitive answer while staying off the radar as much as you can. But if you have to go to the cemetery in the middle of the night and dig up the body, you do it. Check that—you call me. I'll bring shovels and help. Does that explain the importance?"

Wyatt nodded quickly. Having something else to focus on besides the damn mind map would be a blessing. "Deadline?"

"It's the end of your shift, right?"

"Yes."

"Get your computer and move in here," Gregory said. "I'll bring you some coffee. You're now on the day shift." He paused and chuckled. "And the night shift. Sleep if you have to, but don't leave this building until you have an answer for me."

Adrenaline surged through Wyatt. The conversation was over, but he had to stop Gregory. "Energy drink," he blurted.

"What?"

"I don't drink coffee. But I'd take an energy drink. Or two."

Gregory nodded and unlocked the door. "I'll bring you whatever you need. Just figure this out."

30

THE NEIGHBOR LADY

Conference Room 1
Central Analysis Group Headquarters
Alexandria, Virginia

Wyatt took a long sip of go-juice from the tall, skinny can of energy drink. He sat with his laptop at the end of the large table. The paper quilt remained folded in half with Gregory's sticky note close enough for Wyatt to read.

He started by entering Calvin Rutherfield's name into a public search to see what—if any—news there had been of the man's death. Did the authorities suspect foul play?

Nothing popped.

He hit pay dirt when he entered the name into the government's primary search engine linking the country's intelligence agencies' databases. He understood immediately why Gregory had ordered a deep dive into the man's death.

Calvin Rutherfield had been a career CIA officer before retiring in his late sixties about ten years ago.

Everything else about him was classified above Wyatt's access—likely just private human resources files, anyway.

Wyatt might be able to find information about missions and threats from that time, but they wouldn't necessarily be linked to the man. It was a dead end.

He drained the rest of the energy drink, cracked his knuckles, and got busy accessing every bit of data he could get.

"Thank you again, Mrs. Pratt," Wyatt said into the office landline phone. "It's been nice to speak to someone who knew my uncle so well. I really appreciate it." It was the third time he'd tried to hang up, but the elderly woman in California loved to chat. She kept coming up with more to talk about.

Her final comment, however, had proven well worth his patience.

All the people Wyatt had spoken to who lived on the wing of the building near Rutherfield's apartment had been the same: lonely, gossipy, and very willing to talk about Wyatt's "uncle."

When Mrs. Pratt finally let him go, Wyatt eased the phone onto the cradle with a relieved sigh that turned into a gasp as he noticed Gregory standing by the conference room door.

"Sorry, I didn't hear you come in," Wyatt said to hide his surprise.

"Social engineering?" Gregory asked, referencing the technique Wyatt had employed to get information out of the elderly residents of the Happy Acres independent living facility in Ojai, California. Social engineering took many forms, but it boiled down to pretending to be someone else—someone a mark would talk to or follow orders from.

Wyatt shrugged. "I couldn't find much online." His people skills weren't the best, making social engineering challenging, but he listened well and was, as Gregory had referenced earlier that morning, obsessive. He refused to give up.

"Once I tracked down their names and numbers, it was just a matter of catching them at home. They have a ton of activities for the residents there."

"And?"

Wyatt printed the latest intel on the back of the folded pages. The area that had been blank except for Gregory's yellow sticky note several hours earlier now had scribbled notes surrounded by thick boxes of different colors from the pack of markers strewn on the table, many of the boxes connected with arrows and lines.

Several inches to the right of the first was a second yellow sticky note with another name on it.

Wyatt hesitated. He didn't want to be dramatic, but once he said this part, there was no going back.

Wyatt stood and gestured for Gregory to come around to his end of the table.

When Gregory moved close enough to read the name on the second yellow note, his normally cool exterior cracked for a moment. His eyes widened, his mouth opened, and he sucked in a sudden breath, revealing his surprise.

"What's this?" he asked, his voice rough. Gregory cleared his throat, stood straight, and turned to Wyatt. "What's going on?"

"Since last week, two retired CIA officers from the mid-2010s have died," Wyatt began. "Maybe more—it'll take time to look into it piecemeal. If you got me access to the CIA HR files, that would help."

Gregory ignored him, which wasn't a surprise. A full list of CIA employees existed somewhere, but it wouldn't be floating around for just anyone to access—even if they had a need for it, like Wyatt did.

"Frandren's dead, too?" Gregory muttered. He cleared his throat. "Were they murdered?" he asked, in his regular thoughtful, commanding tone.

Wyatt hesitated again. "Not obviously, but maybe." He nodded at the second name. "Randall Frandren lived in Scottsdale, Arizona. He had a mountain-bike-riding accident this past Sunday on a trail he'd ridden many times. The authorities have ruled it an accident. They suspect he crashed trying to avoid a rattlesnake or some other animal on the trail. Apparently, critters are pretty common this time of year, especially in the morning before the air gets too hot. He hit his head on a boulder just off the trail. He wore a helmet but unfortunately broke his neck when he landed. The police think he was going pretty fast—it was a downhill stretch of trail."

Gregory said nothing, so Wyatt pushed on.

"As for Calvin Rutherfield, he died peacefully in his sleep last Thursday. There were no signs of forced entry, struggle, or foul play. Nothing was stolen. The independent living apartment community he lived in has excellent security, and the residents know not to allow strangers in."

"Was there an autopsy?"

"No. The family saw no need for it."

"Tell me he was buried so we can—"

"No," Wyatt said, interrupting. "His body was cremated."

They stared at the paper for a second before Gregory spoke. "Any halfway decent operator could have killed these guys and made the deaths look like accidents," he muttered.

"There is one thing…"

"I thought so. Let me have it."

"The last woman I spoke with—Mrs. Pratt. She lives three apartments away from Rutherfield." He hesitated once more.

"Spit it out."

"It's pretty thin, sir. I wouldn't write it in a report."

"There's never going to be a report about this—no matter which way it goes. Just tell me."

"Mrs. Pratt and I got to talking about my 'uncle.' She's the one who pointed out the connection to Frandren—Rutherfield had mentioned his name, and it stuck in her mind because her sister is named Fran. She's obsessive about reading obituaries online, especially in Scottsdale, where several of her old friends live. She saw the story about Frandren's 'accident.' Anyway, I couldn't get her off the phone, so I mentioned I had an older friend who is like a father to me, and that he was looking to move out of his big house. She recommended the Happy Acres independent living apartments. The staff is friendly, the food is delicious, and while it's pretty expensive, 'You get what you pay for,' she said. Case in point, she complained that the latch on the screen door to her enclosed patio was broken. She always checked it right before she turned off the lights and went to bed because she leaves her sliding glass door cracked open at night so her place 'doesn't get that old lady smell.' One morning last week, she found the patio screen door unlocked. The latch had come undone by itself. She didn't forget, she swore. 'I'm not like some of those other white-hairs. I have all my marbles,'" Wyatt said, imitating Mrs. Pratt. "Within two hours, the maintenance man came by and checked it out for her. He made an adjustment on the spot, and if she had any other trouble with it, said she should let him know. 'Now that's service,' she said." Wyatt paused. "I told her I'd send my friend her way if he was interested."

Gregory slowly turned to Wyatt. "When did she have the problem with the latch?"

They stared at each other for a second before Wyatt dropped the bomb. "Last Thursday night."

"The night Rutherfield died—three apartments up from hers."

"Yes, sir."

Gregory turned back to the folded-over paper on the table and sighed. "Well, damn."

31

THE UNIT

Conference Room 1
Central Analysis Group Headquarters
Alexandria, Virginia

Gregory wanted to believe the deaths of the two CIA officers was a coincidence. The alternative was troubling, to say the least.

He leaned over the table to examine more of the scribbles, lines, boxes, and arrows on the back of the paper quilt.

His newest analyst didn't have high enough clearance to access the data and put all the pieces together.

"There's no obvious connection between Rutherfield and Frandren," Wyatt said, mostly talking to himself. "Aside from working for the CIA, obviously. But there are a lot of former CIA employees. Surely a few die every week, right? Rutherfield was in his seventies. Frandren could have easily lost control of his bike, as the police said. Aside from the screen door latch, there's no reason to think these are anything aside from normal, though unfortunate, everyday events. The CIA employs over 20,000 people, though I didn't check to see how many it had in the 2010s." His voice got excited. "I could run the numbers, see if there is a statistical—"

Gregory held up his hand. He needed to think.

After a second of quiet, he decided to give his analyst the data he needed. He pointed at the note Wyatt had already stuck to the page.

"Calvin Rutherfield was the boss of a small unit of experienced CIA officers focused on recruiting assets, gathering intel, and analyzing data during the Afghanistan war and the hunt for Bin Laden," Gregory said. "Rutherfield was much more concerned about his career than the intel, but he occasionally did some decent work over there. Made a name for himself when he got home and eventually landed himself in the then-president's orbit."

Gregory didn't explain that it was the friendship between Rutherfield and former President Westerlin that had opened this can of worms.

Pointing at the next sticky note, he explained the connection. "Randall Frandren was Rutherfield's right-hand man. He was an incompetent, self-serving jerk. The two of them were a pair: Both focused on their advancement, to the detriment of the work at times." Gregory paused. "May they rest in peace," he added quickly under his breath.

He grabbed the pad of square yellow sticky notes and one of the markers strewn on the table. He bent and wrote on the top paper.

Donald Everett

Afghanistan/Middle East

He stuck the yellow note to the big sheet of paper directly underneath Rutherfield's note. "This man—Everett—worked with them. He hated Afghanistan. It took him away from his golf game, which is all he really cared about, though he had a horrible slice. Working over there saved him a ton of money in lost golf balls. He was and—if he's alive—probably is still a lazy little weasel."

Gregory wrote another name on the next yellow sticky note and added it below Randall Frandren's note.

Mike Solermo

Afghanistan/Middle East

"Big Mike Solermo was a brave man. Spent almost all his time in the field. He recruited more assets than anyone else, came up with better intel, and nearly got himself killed every month. His efforts saved lives—of our fighters over there and of civilians in Europe and the US."

"So these four worked together?" Wyatt asked.

"Yes. In-country. The tip of the spear. Well, Mike was. Everett to some extent, but he wasn't as hard working—or effective—as Mike, though he recruited some agents, too. Rutherfield and Frandren never left the safety of the bases. They were suits. Management." Gregory smiled for a second. He'd become like those two, though hopefully much more committed and effective.

"If they're still alive, we need to warn them, right?"

"Yes, but I'll do it." Starting with Mike Solermo, whom he had a lot more respect for than Everett.

Gregory wrote one last note and stuck it off to the side of the other four.

Gregory Addison
Intelligence Analyst
Langley, Virginia—focused on Afghanistan/Middle East

Silence hung in the air as they both stared at the paper. With all the detail Gregory had provided, Wyatt had to have seen it coming, but seeing the information lined up with the other notes still hit home.

After several seconds, when Wyatt hadn't asked any more questions, Gregory walked to the door. "I'll be in my office," he said. Wyatt's eyes were glued to the notes Gregory had written. "Call me when you have something."

32

THE VAULT

Big Mike's frame filled the door to the pristine ops center in the basement of Las Vegas's most opulent high-end resort casino.

He'd been Big Mike since a growth spurt as a teenager, though as an adult he wasn't unusually large or heavy. At 14, he'd put on height and weight, topping out at 6 feet and packing on muscle. Nearly fifty years later, he was a quarter inch shorter. Getting older sucked. He still had a muscular chest and arms, but his belly was softer than ever and a few inches larger than he liked—too many rich Saturday night dinners. Plus, his back couldn't take the brutal workouts he'd done in years past. And in the last few months, he'd been too busy—and tired—to hit the gym as much as he used to.

His broad shoulders, dark wavy hair, and chiseled features should have made him a horrible spy and recruiter of assets, but he'd used the attributes to his advantage. He was strong and commanding, outgoing and loud, from his speech to his laugh. No one had ever suspected his double life filled with secrets and lies.

For several years, he'd been a successful CIA case officer. He'd recruited dozens of agents who spied for the United States, from Afghanistan and Iraq to Syria and Pakistan.

But that was the past. The present beckoned. In some ways, Las Vegas wasn't much different from those places. The sun, the baking heat, the sand and dust.

And the often desperate men and women struggling to survive.

In his operations room, six people—three men, three women, all in their twenties and thirties—sat at computer workstations. Each had been hand-selected, carefully vetted, and was completely trustworthy.

They glanced up, made eye contact with Mike, and smiled or nodded. Two of the guys gave Mike a cool chin raise in greeting.

Mike passed through the spacious, well-lit space. With his dark-wash jeans and form-fitting button-down shirt—the sleeves casually rolled up to show off his muscled forearms—and a full head of hair cut stylishly short, he was the picture of power and vitality.

On the far side of the room, he entered a ten-digit code into a keypad of the door to his inner sanctum, accessible only from the main room.

"The Vault" had a single computer desk against one wall with two large monitors.

Above them, a huge monitor filled the rest of the wall.

This room was dim, lit only by the data on the screens. Videos played, some in the crisp black and white of high-end night vision cameras, others in full high-resolution color recorded in daytime. The monitor on the right had a window displaying a list of stock ticker symbols with numbers that flickered red and green as their prices changed.

A wingback chair sat in the far corner 6 feet behind the workstation. In the near corner, closest to the door, an expensive executive leather desk chair on casters waited, ready for him to roll forward and sit closer to the screens.

Mike ignored both and stood behind the young woman at the desk with long dark hair, wearing a black pantsuit, typing on the keyboard, clicking the mouse, and running his empire.

"Mike," she said, her voice barely above a whisper. Kristine had always been the smart, quiet one. As a kid, she'd spoken so little that Mike and her mother had her tested by the best doctors, who'd all said she was fine. Extremely intelligent. "Some people are talkers," Mike's personal physician—Doctor Tracey—had said, eyeing Mike with a grin. "She's not. She's a watcher. If you try to change it, you'll lose her. Embrace it. Encourage her."

Mike had taken his advice. She'd come out of her shell over the last few years, but she was as watchful as ever.

Unlike his son, who was two years younger than Krissy and, at 31, was becoming more of a handful. He was itching for Mike to retire so he could take over the organization.

Mike put the family drama out of his mind for the moment. It was his favorite time of the day.

"How did it go?" he asked.

Every morning, Kristine took the haul from his network of spies—human and electronic—reviewed the data, and compiled it into a report.

She glanced back at him, her pale face a clue to how much time she spent in the darkness of this room, and moved an errant strand of hair away from her narrow face. She had his strong jaw and angular cheekbones, but softened—slightly—by a natural grace. Her eyes, though, were are dark and fierce as his.

"Last night, the hotel had a guest in one of the suites," she said, turning back to the computer and clicking on her mouse. "He didn't ask for a room upgrade or special treatment. No one realized who he was until I saw the video this morning."

The big screen showed a shot of a flabby middle-aged man standing in droopy tighty-whities that had seen better days. He leaned in to kiss a very young-looking woman.

"Krissy, jeez, come on," Mike said. The video paused. "I don't want to see this stuff."

The air was still for a second until Mike corrected his mistake. "Kristine—sorry." She'd been happy with Krissy until she hit 12, then had insisted on being called Kris. After going off to college, she'd refused to answer to anything besides Kristine.

"This is all I'm showing you, but we have the file," Kristine said.

"First—hell, I don't know where to start. But please tell me that the young lady in question is of legal age and that we had nothing to do with setting this up."

There weren't many lines he wouldn't cross, but this was one of them.

"We had nothing to do with it, and I had her checked out. She's a seasoned pro who is 22. One hundred percent verified." Kristine paused for a moment, and when she spoke again, her voice was filled with barely controlled rage. "She told the John she was 18—with a wink and a nudge. He likely believed her to be younger."

Mike held back bile and forced himself to maintain control.

Kristine checked her watch, a high-end dive watch with a black dial and gold bezel. He'd given it to her when she'd turned 30, along with the pistol she carried on her hip under her blazer.

Las Vegas was a dangerous place.

"She's on her way to a beach in the Caribbean by now, happily retired from the life. I saw to it that she'll never run out of money—and never return to the United States."

"Well done. Does she know who the guy was? Because I don't."

"That piece of shit is Judge Aplenkinn of the federal appeals court, one of several judges whose name has been tossed around as a likely nominee to the Supreme Court one day. Who, incidentally, is supposedly happily married to his high school sweetheart."

"Well then."

"Yes."

They sat with the magnitude of what the hidden camera in the hotel room had captured.

"An interesting dilemma," Mike said, more to himself than Kristine. They had an uneasy alliance. The older he got, the more conservative his views became. Krissy was much more liberal—at least with social issues. They avoided talking specifics about politics, though some of what they did in this room was about keeping the country moving in the direction he wanted it to go. Mike had a few politicians in his pocket and made "suggestions" when he felt strongly about a topic.

He was, for all intents and purposes, a combination gangster and behind-the-scenes extremely powerful lobbyist.

"Having a man like that in a position of power, with what we now have on him..." Mike said, thinking aloud. "On the Supreme Court someday, even. Think of that." Having a judge who would be receptive not only to voting the way Mike decided, but also highly motivated to convince a few of his colleagues to go along with his arguments, would be a power thus far beyond Mike's reach.

"He has to go, Dad." Kristine's quiet voice was matter-of-fact.

Mike knew he was in trouble when Kristine called him "Dad." They downplayed the nepotism at work. But when she played the family card, he had to be careful.

She had some of his killer instincts. He kept the proud smile off his face in case she could see it in the reflection of the monitors.

He pretended to think it over and consider her position, but it wouldn't be good to give in. Kristine had to understand he still made the final decisions, not her.

Mike could have his enforcer bump into the low-life scum of a judge and warn him to clean up his act. For all but the most degenerate, that would do the trick and keep him on the straight and narrow.

If not, there could be a second visit with a more persuasive discussion.

Or at least that's what he'd let Kristine believe. The possibility of a perverted Justice of the Supreme Court under his control was enticing. Mike had to lie to Kristine.

"A compromise. I'll have Dominic warn him off, and we'll monitor him," he said at last. He'd give the details to Dominic, his enforcer. The former SEAL would back him up with Kristine if she ever asked. "If he strays again..." He left the rest unsaid.

He'd cross that bridge if he came to it. What Krissy didn't know wouldn't hurt her.

"That's acceptable," she said. "There's more overnight intel, but nothing urgent, and you have the lunch meeting." She projected three pictures on the big screen and gave him a rundown.

"Did they click on the link this morning?" Mike asked. After much deliberation, he had hired a hacker to create a simple virus that was triggered by clicking on an emailed or texted link.

"Yes. All three have."

"Excellent."

The guests had clicked on the link to confirm their attendance at today's lunch. Each of their phones would connect to a private network when they arrived at the casino and start automatically uploading their data to the computers in the operations room next door.

"We'll see if it pays off." Mike gave one final look at the details onscreen and smiled. This was going to be interesting.

Most importantly, if all went to plan, it would be lucrative as well.

He badly needed the money the hack might provide.

33

THE FACTS

Snakeridge Trail
Outside Sands, Arizona

Thomas pushed hard on the trail. The rising sun blinded him until he slipped the sunglasses down from the top of his head.

It reminded him of flipping on his night vision goggles back in the day.

He pushed harder, running much faster on the winding trail than a long-distance runner should. To eat up mile after mile, a slow, steady pace worked best.

Not a sprint.

But he was forty-six days sober—and wanted to make it to forty-seven.

With the way he felt after waking up on the wrong side of the bed this morning, a brutal workout was the only thing he could think of that might help.

His inadvertent storytelling with Henry over the weekend had helped lighten his load for a few days, but they'd said little to each other since, and nothing approaching their toast to fallen comrades.

And there was still no Admiral Nalen.

Thomas panted from the exertion and the rising temperature. With the sun up, the heat was magnified. Eighty degrees before dawn was one thing. The same temperature in the sun felt much hotter.

He lowered his head, watching for rocks on the trail, and took stock of his situation.

He had to face facts: He was an idiot.

The previous mission weeks before from Nalen had been a onetime deal.

The man wasn't coming back.

Thomas had spent the past weeks training for a nonexistent next operation.

He wasn't the country's latest big covert asset.

He was a has-been.

A 35-year-old teacher in a Podunk western town.

Single, and firmly in the friend zone with the only woman in the area who interested him.

He was destined to work another thirty years at the elementary school. Teach the kids of the kids he had taught decades before.

What other options did he have? He could go back to war, he guessed. One of the private military companies would pick him up in a heartbeat. But what kind of life would that be?

At best, he'd be a highly paid guard or chauffeur for a rich family in some far-off land, putting his life at risk to stop a bullet for their punk kids or the parents who wouldn't bother to learn his name.

At worst, he'd be a highly paid operator in places or situations deemed too risky for American active-duty forces.

Given the stress and pressure, he wouldn't stay sober for more than a week.

No thank you.

His SEAL mantras that often kept him going didn't help today.

The only easy day was yesterday.

I will never quit.

All in, all the time.

None of them worked now.

He was no longer Bone, kick-ass Navy SEAL.

He was Thomas Marks. He lived alone, drove a hybrid hatchback car, and earned barely enough to pay his fake beer bar tab each week.

He had no prospects.

No future.

No mission.

But he had recurring nightmares, post-traumatic stress, depression, and an overwhelming desire to get drunk and drown his sorrows.

His toe caught a rock jutting from the trail and he fell. He instinctively tucked and rolled.

A second later, he was back on his feet, no worse for wear, pounding toward the parking lot, his old car, and the rest of his life.

34

THE ENCLAVE LOUNGE

The Enclave Lounge
The Fortuna Magnifico Casino and Resort
Las Vegas, Nevada

Mike loved meals. They were his favorite way to make connections, garner favors, and call in markers.

Every Saturday night, he had an exclusive dinner with invited guests where he met new people, brought marks into the fold, and asked for the occasional "favor."

They were large, boisterous affairs—ten to twelve people meeting, chatting, and enjoying one another's exclusive company.

His lunch dates were more intimate and coveted by people in the know.

In his office, just down the hall, he had changed into a dark gray suit with a form-fitting black silk shirt, unbuttoned at the neck. It may have been lunchtime, but the occasion wasn't a casual meeting. When you had lunch with Big Mike, introductions were made, relationships established, and favors traded.

Mike waited in his customary spot at the round, four-person table in the middle of the small private dining room. The thick white table linen practically glowed in the dim lighting of the most exclusive place to eat in

Las Vegas. The table was set with the finest china, the walls covered in dark wood paneling, the carpet thick.

The heavy wooden door, padded with red velvet, opened from the hallway. Mike stood, smiling for whichever guest had shown up first—twenty minutes early—hoping for a private word with him.

A young woman with a dazzling smile entered. Her fine, jet-black hair flowed to her shoulders, brushing against an elegant dark-blue, ankle-length velvet dress. She held her phone in her hand and set it in one of the ornate wooden boxes next to the door as the security guard in the hallway would have told her to.

He couldn't risk any of the marks having their phones with them when the virus started vacuuming up their private data.

"MacKenzie, it's a pleasure to meet you," Mike said, offering his hand to shake. She was a young, talented singer-songwriter just off her hit sophomore album.

Kristine's dossier said she was rebellious and impulsive, but also intelligent, business savvy, and extremely ambitious. She loved singing but wanted to be a movie star.

Specifically, MacKenzie Minrael wanted a starring role in the next blockbuster that every young woman in Hollywood was fighting for.

"Big Mike!" MacKenzie said. A brief look of pleasure at arriving first vanished from her face in an instant. She ignored his hand and greeted him like a long-lost friend, rushing over, arms wide for a bear hug. "It's such a pleasure to finally meet you."

A week ago, she'd never heard of him.

A few well-placed calls had put the idea of a lunch with Big Mike into her agent's mind. She and her agent hoped that impressing Big Mike would get her a better shot at the part than she could ever get on her own.

They were right.

Now here she was, expertly pretending to be his biggest fan.

She could certainly act, he'd give her that. Recommending her for the part would be easy.

Because as much as she needed him for the break of a lifetime, he needed her even more.

Mike hugged her gently for a second before stepping back. He had no interest in anything she might think he needed as payment for the dealmaking. "Thank you for coming. I'm interested in hearing more about—"

The door opened again, cutting Mike off. To her credit, MacKenzie's face showed only delight that another person had arrived, instead of the annoyance she likely felt at her time alone with him being interrupted.

Her eyes widened for an instant when she saw the famously reclusive older business tycoon walk in, hair ruffled as always.

He reluctantly placed his phone in another of the small wooden boxes on the table next to the door.

The plan was working.

"Mr. Norrisline," Mike said with a small bow of respect.

"Mike, what a pleasure to meet you," Sam Norrisline said, barely meeting his eyes while extending his hand for a firm but quick handshake. He wore a light gray suit, custom-made, though the fit still seemed a bit off because of the man's nerdiness. For months, he'd been uninterested in Mike's lunches or dinners. He was an introvert who, it was rumored, was uncomfortable meeting new people in person. He hated crowds and small talk.

But Mike desperately needed a meeting with him—now more than ever.

Kristine had pieced the puzzle together to discover the weakness they could use to entice Norrisline to lunch: He loved movie stars.

Young, old, up-and-coming, or fading, it didn't matter.

Meeting MacKenzie Minrael—who might be Hollywood's next big star—at Mike's exclusive lunch was perfect for him: a small gathering where he could indulge his secret desire to meet movie stars, without dealing with crowds.

"Mr. Norrisline," Mike said, "I'm very pleased to introduce you to Miss MacKenzie Minrael. I'm sure you've heard her music." He should have—Kristine would have made sure his staff had prepared him to meet MacKenzie.

Mike leaned closer to Norrisline and spoke conspiratorially without lowering his voice as McKenzie watched. "She's likely to be a movie star by this time next year."

Norrisline couldn't hide his excitement, though the man who made his competitors tremble was suddenly tongue-tied in the presence of the singer.

35

THE ACTOR

The Enclave Lounge
The Fortuna Magnifico Casino and Resort
Las Vegas, Nevada

The dining room door opened to admit the final guest.

Norrisline laughed at a witty comment from MacKenzie as Mike moved to the door. A man in his late sixties waited just inside, a frown on his face.

The aging A-list actor was past his prime but didn't know. He had one, maybe two minor hit movies left in him before his agent or someone in his entourage pulled him aside to have a tough conversation about retirement. There would be well-paid cameos in younger actors' movies, but his time had passed.

If he was lucky, he might get a few seasons as the lead in a decent TV series—if he found a person to bankroll the show.

"Gabriel, I'm a big fan," Mike said. "Pleasure to have you here."

Gabe sized up Mike and scowled, ignoring Mike's hand. He held his phone tightly. "My agent set this up. I don't know who the hell you are or why the hell I'm here. What the hell is going on?"

This had been in Kristine's dossier. The actor's people had enough pull to get the star to Las Vegas, into a room at the resort, and down to the dining room, but they clearly hadn't told him the score—why the lunch could be beneficial.

It was up to Mike.

"You've never heard of me, which is fine, but I'm Big Mike. I bring people together. I make shit happen." He leaned closer, which the actor didn't like, but he was backed up against the door. On the other side, the security guard wouldn't open it unless Mike knocked the correct sequence or Kristine, who was monitoring the entire meal via a hidden security camera attached to the room's ceiling, called and told him to.

"It looks like everyone in your world is too afraid to tell you this, so I will," Mike said. "You're a year from being a has-been. You got old. Kids today see you as ancient and terribly unhip—when they think of you at all. You have two choices. One: Retire gracefully. Sit by the pool and relive your glory days as fewer and fewer people seek you out. Two: Use your charisma and last bit of celebrity status to impress someone with a shit-ton of money who might bankroll a television series—with you in the starring role."

Mike glanced back at his two guests, chatting and studiously ignoring the obvious confrontation at the door. "Like that goofy-looking rich guy at the table. He's a huge fan of yours. Play your cards right, and you get to be famous for several more years."

The actor's face had changed little during Mike's speech, but now his eyes narrowed and the frown deepened. "Screw you. I'm out of here."

He turned and reached for the nonexistent doorknob.

Mike's fingers gripped Gabe's shoulder and pinched hard, causing the actor to gasp in pain—one of many tricks Mike had picked up from a trainer at the CIA. "You'll march your privileged ass to the table, enjoy lunch, play nice, and schmooze the hell out of everyone. Or I swear that a few hours from now, housekeeping will find your naked, dead body hanging from a towel rack in your high-roller suite upstairs, surrounded by pills and booze."

Mike released his grip and clapped the man on the shoulder. "You have three seconds. Two. One."

"Hey, everybody!" Gabriel said, transforming as he turned to face Mike and the table with a brilliant smile. He placed his phone in the last remaining wooden box. "What's for lunch? I'm starved!"

36

THE HEDGE

The Vault
Fortuna Magnifico Casino and Resort
Las Vegas, Nevada

Kristine scrolled through the contents of Sam Norrisline's phone, starting with the emails. People were always dumb about what they wrote to each other, never suspecting they'd get hacked and that their dirty laundry would be exposed for all to see.

The door behind her clicked as the lock disengaged—her father, back from the lunch meeting.

"How did it go?" Kristine asked without turning around. He lowered himself into the wingback chair in the corner. In the reflection of her monitor, he looked exhausted.

"Piece of cake," he said, a play on how easy he'd found the luncheon and the 8-inch-tall chocolate layer cake served for dessert.

She smiled at the line. It had been part of her life for years, along with the many stories he repeated—of past successes, but more so of the betrayals; lessons for her and her brother about the ways of the world that Dad had learned the hard way while living overseas for a few years when they were young.

"Don't be a Rutherfield," he'd tell her when she put herself before her duties, refused to face facts, or blamed others for her failure.

If one of her friends did something selfish or self-serving, Dad would shake his head and call them a "Frandren."

Her brother learned the hard way not to avoid his chores around the house when they were younger—emptying the trash, sweeping the garage, or taking his turn at vacuuming. "You're acting like an Everett," Dad would say during his rare visits those years, citing a lazy man he worked with. "That's not who you want to be," he'd say, then tell them stories about the work he was doing as a diplomat with the State Department.

He kept many of the details vague, and it wasn't until years later that they learned he had worked for the CIA, but the moral of the story always came through loud and clear.

Work hard.

Fight for what was right.

And don't act like some of the morons he worked with.

The unconventional approach—associating negative behaviors with a real person—did the trick for both her and her brother.

It wasn't about some vague notion of doing the right thing.

They didn't want their father to look at them the way he spoke about Rutherfield, Frandren, and Everett.

"Did it work?" Mike asked. "What's the take?"

Kristine switched the windows on the big screen to show an email inbox, small thumbnails of pictures, and electronic calendars.

"It worked perfectly. Here's an email from Norrisline's chief financial officer. Profits are up—way over Wall Street analysts' expectations. The stock should go through the roof next week when they report their numbers. But…"

"I just had lunch with the CEO. It could look like insider trading."

"Exactly. We could lay it off." She clicked her keyboard, and a window popped up. "Excelsior Trading."

A hedge fund run by one of their marks. During a visit to Las Vegas six months ago, the owner had been comped the casino's penthouse suite. For several nights, he made the mistake of living large in ways his family, employees, investors, and neighbors would find shocking.

All recorded in glorious high definition by the room's hidden cameras.

"According to their latest quarterly Form 13F, they've been buying up Norrisline's company stock the last six months anyway, seeing it as a good bet. We give them a heads-up, they buy another large chunk—larger than they might normally have—and pay us off a few weeks from now." She paused. "Or…"

"Or?"

She turned to her father and watched him like a hawk. "We let this one go. It's riskier than normal. First the phone hack, then the lunch, then a hedge fund makes an extra-large bet. It would be easy for people to get suspicious. If Norrisline's team wonders how the news got out and check his phone, or the Securities and Exchange Commission started sniffing around…"

Mike's face gave nothing away. He waited her out.

"Do we really need the money?" she asked after a few seconds. "How much is that new house costing, anyway?" she said, making a joke out of the uncomfortable topic.

They all had plenty of money. Mike paid her and her brother well; the techs in the computer room, too. And though the house in the desert Mike was having built was on a private, 5-acre lot in a new upscale subdivision, it was on the low end of the mansion scale.

Yet lately, he seemed desperate for money.

Something was going on.

She kept a close eye on her father's body language.

Dad had secrets—and it irked her to no end.

He was hiding something big.

And she wanted in.

Or at least to know what he was up to.

"Housebuilding," he said with a rueful shake of his head. "You'd be surprised by where the money goes."

She sensed he was telling the truth—she would be surprised by where the money went.

It was her father's way of being honest.

The money wasn't being spent on the house in the desert, but he wasn't going to tell her where it was going—or why he needed it.

"Reach out to Excelsior's owner via the secure comms app," Mike said. "Get him the info. Have them buy the extra shares immediately. We'll let them know when to sell and how to settle up. Make sure he knows I need…" Her father trailed off and blinked a few times as he thought. "At least two million in profit. Three would be better."

She held his gaze, hoping for more. They had never pushed this hard before. Mike's approach was that slow and steady won the race. A little here, a little there. Control and use people—but never make it too painful for them. Keep them on the line. Over time, they'd become more and more hooked.

"'Pigs get slaughtered,'" she said, quoting him.

A look crossed his face for an instant, and she chose to believe it was him being proud of her.

"Trust me, Krissy." He paused. "Sorry. Kristine. Now, what else did we get from the phones?"

There was more to the story here, and she'd get to the bottom of it, but first there was work to do.

They had to get MacKenzie Minrael the summer's most coveted role in Hollywood.

37

THE PRODUCER

The Vault
Fortuna Magnifico Casino and Resort
Las Vegas, Nevada

Mike grabbed the second desk chair and rolled it to sit next to his daughter. They had a call to make.

In the early days of setting up his Las Vegas spy network, Mike had recruited cab drivers, cocktail servers, bartenders, bouncers, street performers, and homeless people—anyone who needed a buck, a friend, or the promise of a future favor.

One Saturday night, a young and up-and-coming Hollywood director had gotten drunk and broken the arm of a dancer at a Vegas gentleman's club.

The smart club manager had locked the director into a storage room and called Mike instead of the police.

Mike had dropped everything at three in the morning to pay off the dancer for her pain, suffering, and medical bills.

He'd explained the situation to the sobering director, copied the security camera footage onto a flash drive, and waited for the man to become famous.

Corey Langfore was now a Hollywood hotshot. He'd graduated from directing movies to producing them.

Over the years, in his annual pilgrimages to Las Vegas for a few days of gambling—and Saturday dinner with Mike and the other guests—he'd been on his best behavior.

"Is everything in place?" Mike asked Krissy.

"Yes. All set."

"Make the call."

Kristine removed the room's dedicated cell phone from a special case that shielded it from being tracked and called Langfore on an open line—less than ideal from a security standpoint but the only way they had of reaching him.

"No answer," Kristine said.

"Probably thinks it's spam."

She hit redial and waited while the call rang and went to voicemail again.

"Once more," Mike said.

The third time was the charm. "Hello?" Langfore answered with a mix of concern and suspicion.

"Corey, nice to hear your voice," Mike said as Kristine held the phone between them, the speakerphone on.

"Big Mike. Hi."

"We miss you around here," Mike said, ignoring the suspicion in the producer's voice. "You have to come for the weekend soon."

"Yeah, sure. Sure. I look forward to it. It's just that I'm prepping for this next movie and I'm pretty busy—"

"Oh, I've heard all about that," Mike said. Corey Langfore was "auditioning" half of Hollywood's young female actors for the lead role in his next movie.

"I can help with that. I have your next superstar," Mike said, his voice still pleasant but firmer now. Serious.

Langfore had owed Mike for years. Now it was time to pay.

Or rather, this would be the first of many installments.

He could never pay off his debt to Big Mike. That's not how it worked.

"That's great to hear." The producer couldn't hide his lack of enthusiasm.

"The new movie sounds amazing."

"Yes," Corey said, his voice firming up. "It's going to be a huge hit. You want to come to the premiere? Next summer, we think. Maybe fall, depending on the shooting schedule. See, it's—"

"Corey." Mike's cut him off with more of an edge to his voice.

"Sorry. Got carried away. What can I do for you, um… my friend?"

"You've heard of the singer, MacKenzie Minrael? She would be perfect for the lead. She's got the looks, the singing talent, and she can act."

There were several long seconds of silence. "She can act?" was what the producer finally came back with.

Mike shook his head in exasperation at the phone while Kristine watched him and—he hoped—learned.

"Yes, she's very good. Get her in for an audition and give her a shot. For me, okay?"

Mike imagined Langfore nodding while he frantically searched for a way out of his predicament.

"And Corey," Mike added. "No casting couch bullshit, you hear me? You bring her in to sing one of the songs and act out a scene—whatever you need there, but nothing else. Understand?"

"I can do that," Langfore said. The relief in his voice was clear.

"Oh—and unless she completely whiffs the audition, which I don't expect her to, she gets the part," Mike added.

Langfore didn't hesitate. "That's harder, Mike." He sounded apologetic but honest. "I'm sorry, I'll do all I can, of course, but it's not only up to me."

Mike waited without speaking.

"See," Langfore continued, growing desperate, "the studio has to approve of her, and the male lead has a lot of say in the casting. If there's no chemistry, he can veto her." The producer took in a deep breath and cleared his throat. "And besides, Mike, while I appreciate what you did for me back then, that was a lot of years ago. Ancient history. I'm happy to give your friend a legitimate shot, but that's the end of it. Let's face facts: You no longer have any power over me."

Mike gave the man a few seconds to relish getting out the words he'd probably been rehearsing for years. Langfore was bluffing, for one. His studio would drop him in a second if they saw the security camera footage of a young, drunk Corey Langfore yanking around a half-naked dancer hard enough to break her arm, especially if the video aired on one of the many celebrity gossip shows. But Mike had an ace up his sleeve—a way to keep from destroying the man while still getting what he wanted.

"I'm sorry you feel that way—that you no longer value my friendship —but I get it. It was a long time ago. But can I ask you to do one thing for me, just for old time's sake?"

"Fine. What?" He sounded in control, like the bigshot he believed himself to be.

"Just go to your kitchen. There's something you should see."

"In my kitchen?"

"Yes. Please. Humor me."

The producer walked for several seconds. Mike pictured marble floors, tall ceilings, maybe framed movie posters on the walls of a Beverly Hills mansion.

"What the hell?" The producer was more angry than afraid—for the moment.

"What do you see?"

"There's some… asshole… in my kitchen! He's peeling an apple from a fruit basket."

"With a big knife? Yes, I gave him that. Nice, isn't it? I'd like to introduce you to my associate, Dominic," Mike said.

"What's up?" Dominic's cold, flat voice came through the speakerphone. "Your security here is for shit. You should do something about that. I can help, if you want."

"You should take him up on that," Mike said, enjoying the moment. "Assuming you and I reach an agreement. Otherwise it'll be a bit of a moot point, won't it?"

"You can't do anything to me," Langfore said, more of a plea than a statement.

Mike waited, sure that Dominic's mere presence would do what the threat of exposing a long-ago lapse in judgment hadn't.

Langfore cleared his throat. When he finally spoke, his voice was filled with Hollywood charm to hide the fear. "I've always loved MacKenzie's music. If she can act, the part is hers."

"Thank you, thank you, thank you," Mike said, completely sincere, like the producer was doing him a big favor instead of making a payment on a long-overdue bill.

"And your associate? He'll just… leave?"

"Absolutely! He wanted to drop off the fruit basket as a thank you, that's all."

"Wonderful. Yes. Yes." The smooth-talking producer was at a loss for words.

"Goodbye, Corey. Come for Saturday night dinner soon." Mike nodded, and Kristine disconnected the call, turned off the phone, and slid it back into its case.

"Get some flowers to Miss MacKenzie with a card that says…"

"'Nail the audition and the part is yours'?" Kristine suggested.

"Perfect."

Mike stood and stretched, more tired than he wanted to admit. "I'm going up to my office. Let's move this afternoon's meeting to tomorrow afternoon. I have some stuff to do." He smiled at her, and hoped she'd learned something today.

38

THE FLING

Melissa Hammund had been the first operation's room tech Big Mike hired. As Kristine's best friend since forever, she was the natural choice when they sought someone trustworthy who could work with computers.

She kept her head down as Mike walked past her workstation near the door to the Vault. A few strands of the long brown hair she'd been growing out for the last two months fell forward. Most of it was held in place by the large, ornate hair clip she'd started wearing, but some slipped free throughout her workday.

She raised her right hand to brush them back but caught herself in time, switching to her left hand to push the hair behind her ear.

The technique was called mirroring. If someone—like, say, Melissa's best friend, who sat behind the closed door a few feet away—brushed her hair back with her left hand and tucked it behind her ear, Melissa grew out her hair and learned to do it that way.

She wasn't sure it had helped yet, but she'd use every edge to get what she needed.

Melissa stared at the screen, flicking through pictures in MacKenzie Minrael's downloaded photo album, looking for anything useful.

Her concentration slipped.

How much longer could she keep up the charade?

Sooner or later, someone would catch on.

Melissa had gone from true believer, loyal worker, and Kristine's BFF to willing traitor in four days over spring break.

People from all over the country came to Vegas each spring to party, raise hell, or simply get away from the dreariness of winter.

But the first chance Melissa had, she got the hell out of the desert town and went to the ocean—the same as every year. Playa del Carmen, Mexico. Far enough south of Cancun to not be as packed with the heavy-duty partying *gringos*, but close enough to get there easily. Safe, for the most part, but things had been changing there the last few years.

She flipped through more pictures on the computer while she carefully kept the smile off her face as she remembered meeting a man in Mexico.

Shane Lopez. Tall, dark hair, easy smile, gorgeous brown eyes, muscular body without being beefy.

The harmless flirting.

Realizing they had things in common.

The day at the beach together, pulling out the same paperback novel to read on their beach chairs under the umbrella.

Wanting the same drink from the waiter who came by to take their order.

The first night together. And their second, and third.

She kept any expression off her face when she remembered his tearful confession on the fourth night.

Playa del Carmen, Mexico

One Month Earlier

"I really am an investigative journalist," Shane said, biting his lip. "You'll probably never want to see me again, but I have to come clean. Just in case we have a future. I can't start it with a lie. I... I never thought..." He used a thumb and finger to wipe his eyes. "I wasn't planning on falling for you."

Melissa was ripped apart by his words. On the one hand, yeah, she was falling for him, too. On the other, what was there to come clean about? Was he married? About to be sent off to a war zone? Unwilling to fly to Las Vegas now and then to see if they maybe had a future together?

She sat up in bed, yanking the sheet from him to wrap around her front, arms crossed, protecting herself from the emotional harm to come. Just her luck. She'd met a guy she liked, who knew his way around a woman's body for once, thank goodness, and now he had some deep, dark secret.

"What I'm going to tell you will put my life in your hands," Shane said, sitting up but moving farther to his side of the bed, covering himself with the part of the sheet she'd allowed him. "Literally," he added.

None of this made sense. They were in a four-star hotel in a small town on the coast of Mexico, ceiling fan on low but still wobbling off-kilter overhead. They'd just made love and were planning on going out for breakfast together in the morning before she flew home.

And now this.

She was going back to her room. "I don't want to hear—"

"Your boss is Big Mike," he said, stopping her. "You work in the basement of the Fortuna Magnifico Casino and Resort. You're not in human resources there like you told me; you're one of six technicians who help process Mike's blackmail, coercion, and insider trading network."

Melissa went ice-cold inside, worse than when she'd thought Shane was about to tell her that he was married with children and this had only been a vacation fling. She turned to him, shocked. At some point, she realized her mouth was hanging open—"catching flies," as her dad would have said with a laugh—and she closed it, biting her lip instead. "How...?"

"I told you, I'm an investigative reporter. I have a lot of resources. And..." Shane took a deep breath and let it out in a rush as he spoke. "Big Mike had my sister killed."

39

THE CODE

Operations Room
Fortuna Magnifico Casino and Resort
Las Vegas, Nevada

Melissa snapped back to the present as a gentle hand touched her shoulder. She jolted but held back a gasp.

"Sorry," Kristine said, whispering in her ear. "Didn't mean to startle you. Lost in your work?"

"Yes. I didn't hear you come out," Melissa said, making her tone and cadence match Kristine's and spinning to look up at her. Staying on her best friend's good side wasn't the problem; Melissa could do that without trying. But she needed more. She had to get access to the Vault, one way or another.

Shane had coached her on the mirroring technique, which she figured couldn't hurt.

Kristine brushed her hair back, which Melissa mimicked. "You wanna talk?"

Kristine hesitated a second before speaking. "Yes, I need to see that," she said in her full-voice command tone. "Come inside so I can look at it on the big screen."

Melissa nodded at the ruse and followed her to the doorway, standing back far enough to allow for privacy as Kristine entered her ten-digit code into the door's electronic lock.

4-2-7-8-6-8-5-4-1-

Melissa still hadn't caught the final digit, and wasn't convinced the 1 was correct, either.

When the time came, she'd have to waltz over to the door, confidently press the code as if she had been given instructions to enter, do her business, and walk back to her workstation, all in full view of the others in the room.

If the lock didn't open the first time, she might finagle a quick second try, but more than that would raise eyebrows, then alarms.

And then her body would end up buried in the desert like the others she suspected had come at Big Mike and missed.

The door clicked open, and Melissa followed Kristine inside. As soon as the door swung automatically closed, Kristine dropped into her desk chair and waved Melissa into the other office chair, which was still warm —it must have been where Big Mike had been sitting only a minute before.

"*If Mike finds out about me—about us,*" Shane had said that night in his hotel room in Mexico, "*he'll bury our bodies in the desert.*"

"Are you okay?" Kristine asked in her quiet tone. "Is there a flu bug going around?"

"No, I'm fine," she mirrored in the same tone. "It's just been a busy week. What's up?"

Had she covered well enough?

Kristine used the tip of her sensible flats to swivel the chair right and left, the same nervous habit she'd had when they studied together for hours in high school. "Did Big Mike seem off to you? He seemed... I don't know. Tired, maybe."

"Tired," she said, matching the tone perfectly. "Maybe." She nodded slowly. Melissa hadn't noticed a thing about the man, had been focused solely on not making eye contact in case he could somehow sense her traitorous intentions. "Now that you mention it, he seemed... off."

Men had successfully used the mirror technique on her—hell, Shane had done it for the first three days in Mexico, and she'd fallen for it all.

It might be working on Kristine, too. She'd been more talkative with Melissa lately. "I'm glad it wasn't just me who noticed it," Kristine said. "He's up to something. Probably staying up late. Thanks, girlfriend. You okay?"

Melissa smiled and stood. "I'm great. Let me know if I can help, though, okay?"

"Thanks, you're the best," Kristine said, already turning back to her jumbo monitors and huge screen on the wall. They showed little that Melissa couldn't get on her own two smaller screens, but this room was different than Melissa's workstation in one essential way.

In here, the huge computer tower on the side of the desk had high-speed ports that accepted small flash drives.

None of the workstations in the ops room had ports of any kind.

If Melissa could get ten minutes alone in this room, she could transfer a copious amount of information to a flash drive.

Certainly enough to bring the full power of the law down on Mike's head for what he'd done to Shane's sister.

Whether the data implicated Kristine, too, didn't matter. She had to get taken down, as well.

Better to be safe than sorry.

40

THE CLUE

Gregory locked the conference room door behind him again and stopped just inside.

Wyatt looked like hell. His hair was more of a disaster than usual, which was saying something. His eyes were bloodshot. There were deep, dark bags under both, and his left eyelid twitched every few seconds. Plus, whatever 24-hour deodorant he used wasn't living up to its promise.

"When was the last time you slept?" Gregory asked. Wyatt had worked the night shift as usual before presenting his terrorist-for-hire theory this morning. Gregory had put that on hold and asked him to stay and work on the potential murder of the ex-president's best friend.

That had been hours ago.

"Doesn't matter," Wyatt said, his hyped-up voice contrasting with his frazzled, death-warmed-over look. "I'm fine. I have good news and... strange news."

Before Gregory could comment, Wyatt gestured to his patchwork quilt of papers, still folded in half and taking up one end of the massive table in the center of the room. All the chairs had been pushed against the wall closest to the door, clearing the way for the paper to be accessed from every side.

Increasingly messy handwriting covered the areas near the five sticky notes with names of Gregory's former Afghanistan intelligence unit.

"First: the good news. Donald Everett is alive and well. He lives in a suburb of Phoenix, Arizona and spends all his time—"

"Golfing," Gregory guessed, cutting him off. "It's all he ever cared about. He said that when he retired, he was finally going to conquer his slice."

"Right, right. Still not so good with the whole slice thing, though. His credit card purchase history shows him buying a new driver every few months, plus every training aid, online course, and in-person coaching possible, all specializing in slice prevention."

"And the—"

"Strange news," Wyatt said, cutting him off this time. He held up a hand, asking for a second, and drained the can of energy drink. After stifling a belch, he nodded to the sticky notes. "Michael Solermo is… gone. He disappeared years ago. One day here, the next day…" He held up a fist and opened it quickly, fingers splayed. "Poof. Disappeared."

Gregory frowned. He hadn't heard this. He'd been so busy with his own career he had neglected to keep track of people.

"Well, thanks for—"

"But," Wyatt said with a grin.

Gregory gave him an icy stare. He'd had enough of the interruptions.

"Sorry," Wyatt muttered, contrite. "I'm kind of flying on caffeine and sleep deprivation right now."

"Continue. 'But…'?"

"I found a thin connection between Mike Solermo and a man named Mike Salestri. Well hidden; no one would have found it if they weren't, you know, obsessed."

"And highly caffeinated."

"Yes, that too. Definitely that. There's no actual proof Solermo is Salestri, though. And Mike Salestri has no pictures of himself online that I could find. Doesn't have a driver's license or passport. Nothing in any database. I found one picture, taken in Las Vegas at the grand opening of a new restaurant inside the Fortuna Magnifico Casino and Resort, where 'Mike Salestri' works." Wyatt turned his laptop to Gregory. An image filled the screen. Grinning men and women stood holding a thick red ribbon in front of the entrance to a restaurant. A proud older man in a sharp suit held a pair of giant golden scissors, easily 2 feet long, and prepared to cut the center of the ribbon.

Gregory scanned the picture but saw no one he knew.

"There, to the left side, in the back," Wyatt said, pointing.

A man with a powerful physique had his head turned away, as if looking at the floor behind him. All that could be seen was his ear, hair, and a muscular neck and arm.

"Is that him? He's not mentioned in the caption, but all the other company managers are there. It makes sense their vice-president of hospitality would at least be at the grand opening, even if he hung back. And who looks away while taking a picture—besides a person with something to hide?"

Gregory zoomed in on the image. He couldn't say for sure, but his gut told him that the man was the same person he'd worked with so many years ago.

"It might be him," Gregory said. "Same body type. Excellent work. What else do you have about him?"

"Not much. I called you the second I found this."

"Did you check our files?"

"Yes. Nothing there. But I haven't started with the other databases."

Gregory moved to the phone and dialed an extension. "I need you in conference room 1 right now," he said when the man on the other end picked up.

He hung up, unlocked the door, and returned to his spot on the far side of the table, looking over Wyatt's notes, though he couldn't decipher the messy penmanship.

After a moment, a sharp rap came from the door and Marcus, another of the Central Analysis Group's analysts, stepped inside. He took in the folded, taped-together paper covering half the conference room table, glanced at Wyatt, nodded to Gregory, and immediately locked the door behind him.

41

THE BRIEF

Conference Room 1
Central Analysis Group Headquarters
Alexandria, Virginia

"Tell me everything you know about a man named Mike Salestri from Las Vegas," Gregory said.

Marcus blinked for a second, like a computer accessing a hard drive. His dark-blue bow tie paired well with a light-blue dress shirt, dark-khaki chinos, and a tight-fitting navy vest. His medium-dark skin was smooth and youthful, but his eyes had new lines near them in the last few months due to the stress of the job.

"There's no file for him," Marcus started, "in part because he's a minor player. He's important in the hospitality world as a VP at the Fortuna Magnifico Casino and Resort. He's excellent at putting people together and facilitating deals, especially in the entertainment industry. There are rumors of arm-twisting on occasion: 'It would really be in your best interest to do this.' That kind of thing. He's also been known to help out people with gambling addictions. It's his pet project. He's bought up debts from loan sharks, even the markers from other casinos, all with his own money, and helped people clean up their act." Marcus gave a half shrug. "Aside from that, nothing comes to mind. He's a small fish in a huge pond."

Gregory acknowledged the analyst's assessment and stared off into space, weighing his options and obligations.

Finally, he gestured to Marcus and Wyatt. They grabbed chairs from the wall and wheeled them to the far end of the table. Gregory sat at the head, a twitchy Wyatt to his right, and the still, thoughtful Marcus farther down the table.

"For now, what you hear goes no further. No reports will be written without my explicit approval. You will not discuss it outside this room." Gregory hesitated another second, but his gut told him he had to move forward, and to do that, he'd need both Wyatt and Marcus read in.

"I believe Mike Salestri may be Mike Solermo, former CIA officer. He was part of a small unit dedicated to recruiting sources and agents to eliminate IEDs and bomb makers, cut off the flow of explosives to Afghanistan, search for weapons of mass destruction in the Iraq region, and find Osama bin Laden."

"And now someone may be killing everyone on the unit!" Wyatt said, his voice full of excitement for a moment before he bit his lip. "Sorry."

"For now, it's only two of the five people in the group, so it could be a coincidence," Gregory said, echoing what they had discussed earlier. "It's getting late, and Wyatt, you've been up for more than twenty-four hours. Take a nap—but bring Marcus up to speed before you do."

Wyatt nodded, though he looked way too wired to sleep.

"I want you two to dig deeper into Mike Solermo/Salestri," Gregory continued. "I need to know if they're the same person."

"Mike Solermo," Marcus said. "The man you knew. What was he like? How would you describe him?"

"He was dedicated and hardworking. Fiercely patriotic. Good at what he did. He recruited assets who spied for the United States in Afghanistan, Iraq, Syria—all over the region.

"Then, a few years into it, I think he saw the writing on the wall. A lot of us did, but most of us weren't brave enough to speak out. Iraq had been a huge mistake. Iran was a bigger threat than people thought. The US was getting bogged down in Afghanistan. Mission creep changed the objective from taking out actual terrorists to attempting the impossible: converting the country into a democracy. Pakistani intelligence—ISI—was playing both sides of the fence, which no one wanted to discuss. No one except Mike. He wrote reports…" Gregory trailed off. He couldn't discuss them —they'd never made it to his desk. He only knew about them from Mike.

The reports themselves, according to the spy, had been shredded, then burned, then flushed away.

"If I had to sum him up…" Gregory trailed off, remembering the fierce man he'd worked with so many years ago. "I'd say he was persistent. Like a dog with a bone."

That's why his sudden departure from the CIA had come as such a surprise. It wasn't like Mike to give up.

42

THE CALL

On the walk back to his office, Gregory debated taking matters into his own hands. There was a simple way of determining if the Mike in Las Vegas was the same Mike he'd worked with many years before.

A short phone call—hearing Mike speak—would clear this up.

If the Mike in Las Vegas disguised his voice or faked ignorance, Gregory would hear it. And if Wyatt and Marcus discovered that the two Mikes were one and the same, any attempt by Mike to hide himself in their phone call would offer another data point in the overall mystery of why former CIA officers were being murdered.

Gregory logged on to his computer and did a quick search in a public database.

Armed with a phone number, he placed the call, sat back in his desk chair, closed his eyes, and prepared.

"Fortuna Magnifico Casino and Resort, where every day is luxury! How can I direct your call?" a chipper female voice asked.

"I need to speak with Mike Salestri. It's urgent. Tell him it's Gregory Addison."

"Certainly. Please hold."

The NSA would scoop up the information; they weren't supposed to monitor calls in the United States, but other countries' security agencies did, and the NSA monitored those agencies. His name would be logged somewhere, but Gregory doubted it would raise enough red flags for an actual human to listen to the call, either live or later. Still, he'd take precautions, as would Solermo—if it was him.

Hard-learned lessons were never forgotten.

"I should have figured it would be you who found me," Mike Solermo said as a greeting. The voice sounded older, but age couldn't disguise the larger-than-life vibrancy, though it was tinged with tiredness. "You always were the smart one."

"Sorry to bother you," Gregory started. "I guess I'm feeling sentimental and wanted to reach out to you, my old friend."

Was Mike still sharp enough to see Gregory's ridiculous language for what it was: a farce for anyone who might be listening? They had been work friends, but never truly close. They'd had dinner and drinks on a few rare occasions Mike had come through DC for a debriefing or R&R. Although for a brief time, toward the end, Gregory had wondered if he was Mike's link to reality, to the truth, to the normalcy of America, far from the deceit and danger of life in Iraq, Afghanistan, or whatever country Mike worked in at the time.

Gregory had remained in the United States, tasked with supporting Mike and the rest of the unit in the field. Back then, he had Wyatt's job, taking snippets of intel and mining them for gold.

Rutherfield had been the boss—Gregory's role now. Mike had been the tip of the spear, similar to what Haley Albright had done at the Central Analysis Group: getting real-world intel while in the field and actually making things happen.

It wasn't that Gregory shouldn't be reaching out to him tonight. But the relationship between the five members of the unit was ancient history. There was no reason to dust it off—and open old wounds.

Unless someone was coming for them, all these years later.

Mike paused for a moment before responding back in kind, his voice wistful and more tired than a moment before. "We did some good back then, didn't we? All those years ago?"

"We did. Glad we both made it through. Too bad about the boss, though. And the biker," Gregory said, using descriptions Mike should recognize to avoid the names of the dead. "I'm assuming you heard?"

The brief hesitation proved the news was a surprise. "I hadn't. Sorry to hear that. But the boss was getting up there. Older than us, right?"

"Yes. It was just his time—I guess," Gregory said, conveying a lot of meaning in a few innocuous words.

"Hmm," Mike said, letting him know he got the drift, that the death was premature and possibly not an accident. "And the biker. Did he ever lose that last 10 pounds?" Frandren had always carried more weight than he'd been happy with, though he'd never let it slow him down.

"I guess not. It's tragic, really. He was out mountain biking and must have swerved to avoid a rabbit or snake or something, the authorities said. Went ass over teakettle, hit hard, broke his neck. Died instantly."

"Swerved to avoid an animal, huh? What a shame."

The man they'd known would have been more likely to try to run over the animal than swerve around it.

They paused, two old spies, having a conversation within a conversation, one that no computer algorithm listening in would ever flag as suspicious for a human to review.

"Sorry to be the bearer of bad news, but I thought you'd like to know if you hadn't heard."

"Thanks, I appreciate that. But on a lighter note, how about you? Still golfing?" Mike asked.

Gregory hadn't golfed back then and had no interest in it now. Mike was asking if Everett was still alive.

"Still golfing." That covered Everett's status. "Though I'm stuck in the office way too much," Gregory said, moving on to his own safety. "When I do play, I keep my head down." They both knew enough about golf to understand the common problem of lifting one's head while swinging and messing up the shot, using it as a convenient metaphor for being careful. "And you? Probably too hot in Las Vegas now anyway, right?"

Mike had also never been one to golf. "Yes, I'll wait until cooler weather, I think."

He would be alert to danger now.

"Smart. Well, I don't want to keep you," Gregory said. "Here's my new number, and my online contact details. Let's keep in touch." He gave Mike his cell number and encrypted communications app contact information—just in case.

Gregory had done what he could, for old time's sake—and to shake the tree.

Mike hadn't hidden who he was.

"Anyway,' Gregory said, "just wanted to say hi, catch up."

"Thanks. I appreciate it. And sorry to hear about the boss and the biker."

"Yeah. Me too. They were good guys."

"Yeah. Sure," Mike said unconvincingly and hung up without saying goodbye.

43

THE CONFRONTATION

The Office of Mike Salestri
Fortuna Magnifico Casino and Resort
Las Vegas, Nevada

Mike hung up the phone and leaned back in his chair, which no longer creaked under his weight.

Not that anyone noticed, but he'd lost 10 pounds recently—all while his workouts felt harder than ever.

He was still young, but lately he was feeling every year.

And now Rutherfield and Frandren were dead. Murdered, if Gregory Addison's hints were to be believed, which they were; Addison had been good at his job on their team, and a rock for Mike toward the end, when it all went to hell.

Mike stared into the distance and pondered the possibilities.

Could a foreign power be targeting CIA officers—including him?

Iran's Ministry of Intelligence?

Pakistan's ISI—Inter-Services Intelligence?

It had been many years since Mike had last seen Rutherfield, though he'd used the man's name and selfishness as a cautionary tale often enough to his kids. For too long, Rutherfield, Frandren, and Everett had lived rent-free in Mike's head, though thoughts of them had faded as the kids learned not to act like those guys. And eventually, he'd been too busy starting and growing his little empire to give them much thought.

With the news of the two deaths, though, all three were front and center again.

He'd been younger then, and had thought that his superiors were as focused on the truth as he was.

They weren't. Not even close.

He'd learned that lesson the hard way.

But he'd taken what the CIA had given him—a flexible morality, the skills of lying, deceit, intelligence gathering, and coercion—and run with it.

He left behind the bumbling political class firmly entrenched at the CIA, like ticks burrowed into a dog.

With cash he'd skimmed from payments to informants throughout Afghanistan and Iraq, he had abandoned the CIA, moved to Las Vegas, and went into business for himself.

At first, he recruited cocktail waitresses, blackjack dealers, strippers, prostitutes, and taxi drivers. His money flowed and secrets came his way —details that people from movie stars to politicians assumed would stay in Vegas.

It did. The information went right into Big Mike's database—as would Gregory Addison's cell phone number and encrypted comms contact information.

You never knew when you'd need to reach out to an American spy.

A few years after Mike got started, he was vice president for guest relations at a top strip hotel, a title he'd created after blackmailing the CEO of the worldwide corporation that owned the resort.

For just like the rich get richer, those who have secrets naturally collect more.

Mike closed his eyes. He was tired again, and it was barely the end of the day.

Whether Rutherfield and Frandren had been murdered or not, Mike was glad they were dead. Rutherfield had been more concerned with his precious career than winning the wars, and Frandren was a brown-nosed, bureaucratic putz.

Mike only wished he had done the deeds himself.

Afghanistan

Many Years Earlier

"I'm telling you, we're making a huge mistake," Mike said.

"Not this again," Calvin Rutherfield said in his smooth, deep political voice that would someday go over very well in the Washington, DC, halls of power. He routinely discounted Mike's intel, but Mike kept trying. He had to get the point across before the United States got itself deeper into a costly conflict against the wrong enemy.

Rutherfield's eyes narrowed as he tipped his head back and sniffed the air in Mike's direction.

"Yes, that's me," Mike admitted. He stank. He'd been in the field for a week, undercover, disguised as a local. He hadn't washed, the local cuisine had done a number on his digestive tract, and he was experiencing quite a bit of reverse culture shock sitting in a typical American-style office on the military base, complete with frigid air conditioning and—he still couldn't get over it—actual live potted plants scattered throughout the room.

In his perfectly tailored three-piece charcoal suit—and who wore a vest these days? It wasn't the 1970s, for crying out loud—Rutherfield had the air of superiority that came from an upper-level manager who was going places.

Mike hated him.

"What have I told you about cleaning up before you come see me?" Rutherfield asked, but moved on immediately. "And reports—you remember how to write a report?" Rutherfield said in his condescending way.

"I know exactly what happens to my reports," Mike said, his voice rising in anger. They ended up in a file folder in Rutherfield's safe, never entered into the system, never passed up the chain of command. Eventually, he assumed, they were shredded and burned.

"Mike," Rutherfield said as he leaned forward in his expensive leather executive chair, his face a combination of exasperation and earnestness. "I was hoping you'd snap out of this." He gestured at Mike's filthy shalwar kameez—the baggy pants covered by a long tunic common with the locals—and his dusty, sunbaked face. "You've gone native. You either identify too much with the common people or—my personal belief —they see you coming from a mile away. They know you're an American.

You're an inadvertent double agent, bringing us exactly what they want us to hear. That's why your reports go nowhere." He let out a long sigh and sat back, shaking his head. *"I'm not hindering you. I'm protecting you."*

"You're wrong," Mike told him, trying but failing to stay cool. *"What my assets report is real. Bin Laden is somewhere in Pakistan. And Iran is the real danger, not the Taliban. The Taliban are egomaniacal, religious zealot goat herders, poppy farmers, and warlords. Could they give refuge to terrorists? I'm sure they might, but we can handle that. We don't have to rebuild their country—just keep some bad-ass Navy SEALs and Delta operators nearby, drones at the ready, and intel networks like mine up and running. Will the Taliban stifle women's freedoms and take the country back to the 1600s? Yes, but that's not our responsibility or problem.*

"The real issues are taking out Bin Laden, punishing the Pakistani military and intelligence agencies who are hiding—and possibly protecting him—and making sure the West isn't hit by terrorist strikes. We can do those things relatively easily and cheaply without a huge presence here." Mike paused, then took the plunge. *"And my sources say the person responsible for training the bomb makers who have been blowing up our troops, and for providing the explosives and components for the IEDs, is a Pakistani who works in the ISI."* Mike had hinted at this revelation for the past month, but he hadn't been brave enough to put the rumors into a formal report, or to announce it so plainly.

Rutherfield shook his head sadly the entire time, while Frandren, the man's right-hand man, stood behind him with a shit-eating smirk on his fleshy face.

"Proof, Mike," Frandren said, weighing in. *"Bin Laden in Pakistan? Iran the real danger, not the Taliban? And now this theory that the ISI is killing Americans? We need proof."*

"I've given it to you!"

"You've given us whispers. Rumors. HUMIT," Rutherfield said, referencing human intelligence, which had fallen out of favor because of its potential for being unreliable. *"We need SIGINT or FININT. Get us some solid signal intelligence from your agents or financial intelligence from someone who deals with the bad guys' money. We can't rush into Pakistan after Bin Laden or some mystery bomb maker, or give up the fight against the Taliban—let alone wage war on Iran—on the word of your... sources."* He said the word like it tasted horrible in his mouth.

They glared at each other across the desk.

"This is what the Company trained me to do," Mike said, his voice going cold. *"I've done my part. Do yours."*

Rutherfield shook his head, and the heavyset putz Frandren copied his boss.

"I'm not betting my career on you or your savages," Rutherfield said.

"Dude," Mike said before he could stop himself. *"They're people. Smart. Resourceful. Crafty. Are they worldly? Sophisticated? Some are, some aren't, just like in America. But give any of them a week in New York, London, or Paris, and they'd be making money and living their lives. How well would you do if you had to live outside the wire?"*

Rutherfield glared at Mike. The seconds ticked away on the round clock on the wall. It looked exactly like the ones in the main CIA headquarters in Virginia. Maybe the government bought them in bulk.

"I know you think you're hot shit," Rutherfield said. *"You're gifted, I'll give you that. But there's a chain of command for a reason. Cooler, wiser heads at the top. We're the brains. We make the calls, not you and the many others like you at the bottom. You gather intel; we decide what it means and what to do about it. Not you. I realize it's hard to hear, but better to hear it now from me while you still have a chance to get your head on straight."*

"Wark sha." *Mike muttered, which could be roughly translated as "Go to hell" in Pashto.*

Rutherfield frowned, more sad than annoyed. *"You've got one week to clean up your act. Get your shit together, or leave now. Take a month back in the world. You've got plenty of vacation built up. See your family—it's been a while. Get your head on straight. After that, get in touch. Tell me you've learned your lesson, and I'll welcome you back with open arms. Otherwise..."* His eyes were cold. *"Get the hell out of the CIA. Go sell your bullshit somewhere else."*

Mike wanted to argue, wanted desperately to make him see the light, but with a sudden clarity, Mike knew his career in the CIA was officially over. Rutherfield might welcome him back, but Mike would always be the guy who wouldn't get on board with the mission and go with the flow.

Mike stood without a word and left Rutherfield's office.

He corralled Donald Everett hiding in his cubicle, reading a golf magazine.

"Starting next week, you take care of my network," Mike told him as Everett tried in vain to hide the magazine and pretend he'd been hard at work writing a report. *"I'll let my assets know, and leave you details about*

where and when we meet. Get out into the field once a week, listen to them, and pass along whatever you feel you can. But keep paying them. They're good people risking their lives to help us out."

Everett nodded but said nothing. At best, the guy would slowly let the network fade away. At worst, he'd bumble his way around the city at night with a truckload of SEALs for protection and get the locals burned.

Mike leaned close and whispered so no one nearby would hear the danger in his voice. "If you mess with my people, I'll find you someday." Their faces were so close that Mike's nose brushed against the other man's nose.

Mike stood, his eyes still locked on Everett's, then spun away.

For the next several nights, Mike took a SEAL who didn't mind playing fast and loose—Dominic—along for security, climbed into a busted-up local car, and met his assets to break the news to them.

A week later, he was on a plane home.

He was done with the CIA, and that was that.

44

THE REAL CONSPIRACY

Conference Room 1
Central Analysis Group Headquarters
Alexandria, Virginia

Gregory slipped into the conference room to find Wyatt on his back under the conference room table, snoring.

Marcus had unfolded Wyatt's quilt of papers. He stood back from the table, hands on his hips, frowning.

They locked eyes. Gregory's concern doubled instantly.

"Wyatt, wake up," Marcus called. He tapped the younger man lightly with the toe of his shiny black dress shoes.

"I'm awake," Wyatt mumbled. He sat up, slamming his head on the underside of the table. "Ow."

"Gregory's here. Let's take him through this," Marcus said, and folded the long paper back upon itself, revealing the three new sticky notes Gregory had added, along with the ones with the names Rutherfield and Frandren on them.

There were many more arrows, lines, and written details than an hour before, when Gregory had gone to his office.

"Yeah. Yeah, right." Wyatt crawled on his hands and knees toward Gregory, stopped, turned, and crawled the other way to stand next to

Marcus on the far side of the table. He grabbed an open can of energy drink, chugged it, and rubbed his eyes.

"While you wake up," Gregory said as he joined them on their side of the table, so he could see the paper from the correct angle, "I can save us some time. Mike Salestri is Mike Solermo, former CIA case officer."

"How…?" Wyatt asked.

"I called him. We had a nice chat. Caught up on old times."

There was a long silence before Marcus spoke. "That might have been a mistake," he said quietly.

Gregory was expecting the comment. "Yes. I have my reasons, but run it down for me. What have you learned?"

Wyatt finished the can, tossed it toward a recycling container near the door, missed, cursed under his breath, hurried over to throw the can away properly, and returned.

"Okay," Wyatt said with a deep breath. "Here goes. Mike Salestri is, as you said, former CIA case officer Mike Solermo. The more we looked into him, the less we found. He's exactly who Marcus said he was earlier—a small-time dealmaker, fixer, and matchmaker, mostly for Las Vegas and Hollywood, though he has the ear of some mid-tier politicians. He's affable and very smart, but everyone clams up if pushed to talk about him. People owe him favors, he calls them in, and he does favors for others. He's basically a one-man Las Vegas mafia don, though he's not in the mafia. It's just him, though we think his grown kids help out in some capacity."

Wyatt and Marcus both looked at him expectantly. "I'm sensing a 'but' here."

"Yes. Well." Wyatt seemed suddenly nervous.

"Do it," Marcus whispered.

Wyatt peeled the sticky note with Mike Solermo's name and details from the back of the folded paper quilt.

Marcus took the paper and flipped it so the entire original mind map came into view.

Gregory had a bad feeling.

Wyatt's shaking hands—whether from caffeine or nerves, Gregory didn't want to guess—placed the sticky note onto the paper in the small open space at the exact center, where all the lines and arrows ended. Pointing at the person behind the bombings in Egypt, Turkey, and Spain.

"This is only a working theory," Wyatt said, practically whispering.

"What did you find, exactly?" Gregory asked, though in his gut he knew.

Wyatt looked at Marcus and nodded for him to go ahead. "Mike Salestri earns a reasonable wage at his position at a Las Vegas resort and casino. His side hustle as a dealmaker and fixer undoubtably earns extra money. But he's building a multi-million-dollar house in Henderson—a suburb of Las Vegas. He's getting a lot of extra money from somewhere—and he started putting it into a numbered account based in the Cayman Islands a few months ago, after the first bombing—at the embassy in Cairo."

Gregory frowned. It didn't sound like the Mike he'd known.

"Also," Marcus said, "we found indications that he's running some sort of clandestine operation in the basement of the casino. He has several people working down there doing something hush-hush."

"You think Mike Salestri is planning terrorist attacks from the basement of a Las Vegas casino?"

The man Gregory had known wouldn't be involved in killing innocent civilians.

"That's one possibility," Wyatt said. "He was in a position to make connections with countless people in the Middle East and Southwest Asia back in the day. He has the training and skills to plan the attacks we've seen in the last year. Reading between the lines of the files we have access to, he left the CIA abruptly, without adequate explanation."

"There's also a chance he was working with Calvin Rutherfield and Randall Frandren," Marcus said. "Or that they were eliminated because they suspected him."

"Both were living beyond their means. Maybe they were blackmailing him—or in on it," Wyatt added.

"Could Salestri have killed Rutherfield and Frandren?" Gregory asked. Big Mike had sounded genuinely surprised when Gregory had called, but he could have been faking it. Professional-level acting was a basic requirement of a good field agent.

"Maybe," Marcus answered. "He would have had to drive, not fly, unless he has fake documents we are unaware of or he had a chartered jet at his disposal. Given the distances to where the two victims lived, and the times we can confirm Salestri was at the casino working, it's possible but unlikely."

"So who killed them?"

"Unknown, sir," Wyatt said.

"We need more time," Marcus said. "More people, too, if you're willing to read them in. Boots-on-the-ground intel would help. But sir, my gut tells me there's a connection between Salestri and the three worldwide attacks. I admit the intel is nearly nonexistent, but… I think Wyatt's theory bears looking into."

Gregory looked at Marcus, the more senior and careful of the two analysts. Marcus had several years of rock-solid analysis to show at the CAG. And Wyatt had done a ton of investigative work into the attacks.

Gregory leaned over the table to examine the sticky notes, scribbles, lines, boxes, and arrows.

His intellect told him that his newest analyst—and Marcus—were grasping at straws.

His gut told him they were onto something. Maybe they didn't quite have it yet, but…

It was something that couldn't be ignored—as much as he would have preferred.

Whether it pertained to the ex-president's friend Calvin Rutherfield being murdered, along with Randall Frandren, and how—or if—Mike was involved, remained to be seen.

But in trying to do the right thing by calling Mike, had Gregory inadvertently given the actual culprit a warning they were onto him?

Mike had been an expert in reading people; field agents had to be.

There was a good chance Gregory's lack of knowledge—calling before getting fully briefed by Wyatt and Marcus—had saved the day. Gregory would have come across as sincere and concerned for his former colleague.

Mike would know he was on Gregory's radar—but only out of friendship, not under suspicion.

"Okay," Gregory said as a plan formed in his mind. "Keep digging. Let's get to the bottom of this."

45

THE PLAN

Central Analysis Group Headquarters
Alexandria, Virginia

Gregory sat at his desk, computer off, staring into space, working through his options.

Two of the four other men he worked with on a small intelligence unit many years before were dead. At least one—Rutherfield—had likely been murdered.

A third member of the group—Mike Solermo—had vanished and reappeared with a new name in Las Vegas. Mike "Salestri" seemed to be using the skills of manipulation that the CIA had taught him to act as a local fixer and Hollywood dealmaker.

He was also conducting some sort of top-secret business from the basement of the casino.

And two of Gregory's analysts thought it might pertain to a wave of bombings around the world over the past year.

That left Donald Everett...

And himself.

Gregory was no closer to the promise he'd made former President Vernon Westerlin to find out the truth of Rutherfield's death—and dispense justice if the man had been murdered.

If Wyatt and Marcus were right and Big Mike Salestri was up to no good, President Heringten and former President Westerlin needed to be kept as far from it as possible.

There was more to this than met the eye, and Gregory wouldn't get to the bottom of it sitting in an office building thousands of miles away.

He had a plan. It was risky—and somewhat unethical—but necessary.

Besides, as a former CIA case officer, if Everett ever found out, he would understand—though definitely not appreciate the idea of being bait to catch a killer.

Gregory picked up his phone and opened the secure communications app.

It was time to make a call to former Admiral Nalen.

The SEAL that had handled the situation with Saudi Prince Rafiq Al-Najjar would be perfect for this.

They had to get Thomas "Bone" Marks involved.

46

THE DRILLS

301 North Ellison Street
Arlington, Virginia

Shari Addison took one look at her husband's face and knew the night would be unlike any other in their thirty-two years of marriage.

Gregory smiled at her as he always did when he arrived home, keys jangling as he removed them from the high-grade lock on the reinforced door to the garage. He insisted they keep the door locked, claiming that it was too easy for a home invader to use a simple device to open the electronic garage door and gain entry into the house.

He took their security seriously.

Shari wasn't naïve or stupid. They lived near Washington, DC. Gregory was a smart, even brilliant, man who worked for the government. He refused to discuss his work, but over the years had dropped enough hints—on purpose, she believed—for her to figure out he was in management at an intelligence agency. Whether it was the CIA, NSA, or another clandestine organization didn't matter.

She had seen him stressed to the max and called in at all hours. He'd also come home with the satisfied look of someone who had done a good job at the office—but with another emotion there, too. Pride, she figured, tinged with a heavy dose of relief.

While he didn't mention specifics, he would occasionally talk about having a stressful situation, a rough day, trouble with his employees, or a work success. She understood his ups and downs. And he was an excellent conversationalist; they never lacked topics to discuss, even if questions about his job were off-limits.

She laughingly fantasized that her man was a hero who somehow helped save the country from all sorts of danger.

They'd often spoken seriously about the importance of personal security: not believing anything people might say about him, never accepting rides or packages from strangers—or even casual acquaintances.

And every six months for the last several years, they had practiced an emergency readiness drill. Gregory would announce—with a wink—that they were in danger and had to leave the house immediately. She played along, donning the ballistic vest kept on a hanger in the coat closet by the garage, grabbing the black go-bag with spare clothes, toiletries, a burner cell phone, food, water, and other essentials, and off they'd go. Sometimes they'd take their own car. Other times, Gregory had a car waiting for them. Once, he had put her into a vehicle, kissed her goodbye, and sent her to a nearby resort for a surprise spa weekend with her girlfriends.

The drills were strange and likely unnecessary, but whatever. She loved him, he loved her, and they had a wonderful life together.

Now, here he was, locking the garage door and moving a kitchen chair in front of it. He hid his feelings well, but she hadn't seen him look this scared since she joined him at the front of the church on their wedding day so many years before.

"Has it been six months already?" she asked, hoping he was acting terrified to make the scenario more realistic.

Gregory turned to face her after double-checking the chair propped under the door's knob. His eyes were dark and serious. "It's the real thing this time, darling."

She reached back, gathered her long dark hair into a high ponytail, and slid an elastic band from her back pocket around it. It would be much better to have the hair out of her face for whatever came next.

Gregory unzipped a thin, baggy nylon jacket he must have put on at the office; it wasn't one he normally wore.

Underneath, a short-barrel, matte-black, scary-looking weapon hung from a sling. It wasn't a rifle or a pistol.

A distant part of her brain informed her that the term for it was "carbine."

Beneath the carbine, Gregory had a black vest like the police and Special Forces soldiers wore.

A "plate carrier," the now concerned part of her mind told her.

Its front pockets were stuffed with extra magazines for the weapon.

They had a gun safe in the den. Most months, she'd have a day with her girlfriends and Gregory would go to a gun range. He said he enjoyed the challenge of target shooting.

But she'd never seen a weapon like that in the house, nor him all kitted up like he was now.

He opened the closet door, pulled out her ballistic vest, and handed it over.

As he grabbed the go-bag from the shelf, she slipped into the vest, calmed herself, and focused. She could handle this.

47

THE SCENARIO

301 North Ellison Street
Arlington, Virginia

Gregory hated scaring his wife, but until he had a better grasp of the overall situation, he needed Shari to be safely tucked away.

He wouldn't let anything happen to her.

He checked the tightness of Shari's thin ballistic vest, kicking himself for not investing in a full-plate carrier with military-grade armor. This vest wouldn't stop a bullet from a rifle or a high-caliber pistol round from close range.

While Rutherfield and Frandren hadn't been shot, they had been easy, unsuspecting targets.

Assuming the two former CIA officers had actually been murdered, that is.

If they had, there was no telling the lengths their killer would go to if his victims were prepared and expecting him.

"You're good," he said after tightening the Velcro strap on the bottom.

"What's happened?" Shari asked. She was afraid but under control.

"I'm not sure yet, but it's not safe for you here."

They'd been over this in their biannual readiness drills. They'd practice leaving the house, then would go out for dinner and laugh about how seriously he took it all.

Over time, they came up with silly names for the various options—whether they had to go to ground together, hole up in a hotel, or get "off the grid" by going camping. He'd never taken it that far—he'd only needed to prepare her for the possibility of danger, for leaving the house quickly without arguing or freaking out.

He hadn't expected to ever need more than that.

"Which scenario is it?" Shari asked. "'Second honeymoon?' 'Love nest?' 'Yosemite?'" Just mentioning the ridiculously named options lightened the tension. "Where am I going?"

"Not far."

"How bad is it?" she whispered.

They had a 1-10 scale of danger they used during the drills, but he'd never had to answer the question with the truth.

"This was a lot more fun during practice," he joked, failing to keep the tension from his voice. He was probably overreacting, but he couldn't live with himself if his actions, his career, brought Shari pain and harm.

"Gregory, you're scaring me more by being evasive than you would by answering my questions."

"I can't say much," he finally offered, "but it's an 8. Maybe a 9."

Her face lost some color.

"People are already dead," he admitted.

"How many?"

She'd always been perceptive and seemed to know exactly the question to ask—the one he didn't want to answer.

"Two of five."

She blinked hard, processing his words. "A coincidence?"

"Maybe."

"Just the principals, or their families too?"

A smart question, and one he didn't mind answering. "Just the principals. But one was a widower."

His answer didn't relieve her as much as he'd hoped.

"Where are we going?"

"I'll be locked in my office. The security is excellent. I'll sleep on the couch and see this through."

"And me? You didn't answer my question."

"Take the go-bag, but you need to pack more clothes. Nicer ones. We can spare the time."

"Gregory Addison, answer my question right now." Her commanding voice, tinged with fear, allowed for no more evasion.

"How do you feel about Pennsylvania this time of year?"

"Pennsylvania isn't one of our scenarios."

"It's not exactly Pennsylvania the state. Let's call this scenario… '1600.'"

It only took her a second to catch up with him. "1600 Pennsylvania Avenue?"

He nodded and offered what he hoped was the same disarming smile he'd used the first time they met.

"You're saying I'm staying at the White House?" Sheri asked.

"The Lincoln bedroom. But only for a few days."

She searched his face, waiting for him to break character and admit it was one of their drills taken to the extreme.

He shrugged apologetically. "I, um, called in a favor. And we need to get moving."

"There's a lot you haven't been able to tell me the last few years, isn't there?"

"Yes. There still is. I'm sorry. But we can deal with that when this is over. Come on, let's grab you some clothes and get you to safety so I can do my job."

They walked hand in hand down the hallway to their bedroom and its walk-in closet, both lost in thought.

PART 5

FRIDAY

48

YOGA

71 Ocotillo Street
Sands, Arizona

Thomas waited outside his house, feeling like a fool. Yesterday's deep depression while out for a run had lifted as quickly as it had descended on him.

There was no longer need for today's extreme plan.

Steph's compact car coasted down his street and came to a stop in front of him. He opened the passenger door but didn't get in. "We don't have to do this. I'm fine now."

Steph wore tight black yoga pants and a black cotton T-shirt with a white tree spreading its branches and roots. She wore no makeup, yet her tanned face was as beautiful as ever.

She raised an eyebrow at him. "Get in the car."

His brain responded to the commanding tone she used from her time as both an Army NCO and MP.

He suppressed a sigh, climbed in, and buckled the seat belt as Steph made an expert three-point turn to head back into town.

Namaste Yoga and Healing Center
Sands, Arizona

They didn't speak again until they had parked and walked to the yoga studio on a side street downtown. "Desperate times called for desperate measures," Steph said as she opened the door to the studio for him.

She had a point.

Although he felt fine today, if he didn't get a handle on the depression, hopelessness, and other emotions dragging him down, his next step would be a call to the Department of Veterans Affairs—the VA. They'd set him up with a tele-med psychologist, probably someone who had never seen his buddies bleed, hadn't pulled a trigger and watched a living, breathing enemy drop, his life extinguished in an instant. A person who had never smelled the stench of rotting corpses or wondered if he'd live to see the dawn.

But they could help him deal with his demons?

Right. Sure.

It would be better than nothing—a start—but if there was another option, he'd take it.

Yoga might not be the way—it probably wasn't—but he had to do something. He wouldn't stay sober much longer if he had many more days like yesterday.

If Admiral Nalen wasn't going to drop in and give him a mission, Thomas had to take matters into his own hands. Something had to give.

As crazy as it sounded, he'd agreed to Steph's request. He was here, and he'd go through with it.

He stepped inside a small room, took off his shoes near another doorway, and prepared himself.

Thomas was the only guy in the yoga studio. A long mirrored wall made the space look bigger than its 30 feet. The reflection doubled the eleven women—plus him—as they rolled out thin rubber mats on the wood floor.

His face in the mirror surprised him. The thick beard needed another trim. The normally short dark hair did, too, especially now that summer had arrived. His long, narrow face had always seemed a little sad, even as a kid. This morning, his eyes looked more haunted than usual.

"This is ridiculous," he muttered to Steph. Aside from her, these women were not his tribe. The only thing they had ever killed was the occasional spider inside the house.

On the thin purple mat next to him, Steph looked at him with a fierce expression, which softened when she saw how uncomfortable he was.

"Big bad SEAL afraid of a little stretching?" she asked, quietly mocking him.

The jibe hit close to home but also helped him lighten up. How hard could this be?

"I've never been big, rarely bad, and I'm a teacher now, not a SEAL," he said, cracking his knuckles. "And I'm not afraid of stretching."

The last part sounded like a lie even to him.

"You want to heal?" Steph whispered, her voice mild. "To feel better? Then be here now. And remember," Steph continued as a young woman facing them at the front of the room—the yoga teacher—fiddled with her phone until soft, relaxing instrumental music played from a small portable speaker next to her. "It's not a competition. Do your best."

"Don't worry, I think I can handle ninety minutes of bending."

His can-do attitude lasted only ten minutes, through the initial warm-up sequences, when the class began in earnest.

He was much tighter and stiffer than he'd thought.

And his focus kept wandering. First, it went to Steph's flexibility, so different from his own. A minute later he was back in combat for a moment, which left him reeling. Shortly after that, he obsessed over what he needed at the grocery store until his thoughts turned to why Admiral Nalen hadn't approached him for another mission.

His mind was like a caged animal, rushing around, desperate for escape.

Through it all, he drew on his experience as a candidate at BUD/S, dragging his attention back, working on each pose as best he could, trying to bumble along without making a fool of himself.

"And fold forward," the instructor said, drawing Thomas once again back to the moment. He bent at the waist, his back popping loud enough for him to wonder if the other students heard.

"Now, fit your fingers under your toes and use the placement to stretch your entire back body."

Thomas did as he was told, feeling the stretch for a second before leaning a bit too far forward. As he started to topple, his weight trapped his fingers underfoot. He grunted in surprise and kept himself from falling only at the last moment.

Steph, obviously trying to stifle a laugh, snorted—an honest-to-goodness pig snort at his expense.

"Everybody okay?" the instructor asked, biting her lip to keep from laughing as Thomas resumed the position. The other ladies in the room tried to hold back their laughter, but it didn't work. There were chuckles all around.

"Good to go," Thomas said with a laugh. Instead of being embarrassed, the stumble had helped his spirits. He was actually having fun.

"Okay, everyone, now we roll up, one vertebra at a time," the yoga teacher called.

Thomas stood, his back popping again as it aligned. He locked eyes with Steph in the mirror and smiled.

This had been a good idea.

For the first time in a while, his heart felt lighter.

49

THE LONG RUN

Snakeridge Trail
Outside Sands, Arizona

Yoga had been better than expected, and Thomas certainly needed to stay flexible, but nothing could stop him from his daily run.

Although it was later and hotter than he normally preferred, he parked at the trailhead of his favorite running area. There was nothing wrong with sweating more than usual—combat rarely waited for ideal conditions.

The lot was hard-packed dirt. He shrugged into his running vest with a water bladder in the large back pocket and jogged to the start of the trail on the right.

The area was crowded with tan boulders, the trail dipping and rising around them. It twisted and turned, making for a fun, challenging run. There were few straightaways and only one flat section. The 6-mile trail started to the right, curved around to the left in a large circle, and ended back at the trailhead a few feet from the start—right by his hatchback.

Thomas ran easy. He'd been averaging 50 miles a week, working to keep his demons at bay.

The morning's yoga class had limbered him up, and he felt loose and free. Quail shot out of the bushes ahead of him and ran across the trail. A hawk hung in the sky, hunting.

Life was good. He'd take a short break at the 4-mile mark—a large, flat rock that had an incredible view to the northeast and the mountains far in the distance—and decide whether to take a connector trail and add extra miles before heading back to the car.

As he approached the 4-mile mark, the trail dipped and twisted, but there were enough gaps in the rocks to show that another person had had the same idea; a solitary figure was in the middle of the huge flat rock that marked the spot. He stood ramrod straight in a blindingly white T-shirt that showed off his lean physique, and unfashionably small olive-green running shorts. He ignored Thomas's approach and stared at the view.

Admiral Nalen had finally returned.

Thomas slowed, walking the last 50 feet. He took a long drink from the water bladder's hose hanging over his shoulder. He didn't let any of his relief, excitement, or the hint of trepidation lurking in the back of his mind show on his face.

"Yoga?" Admiral Nalen said as Thomas stopped next to him.

"Yes, sir," Thomas said, refusing to be surprised that Nalen knew how he'd spent the morning.

"I do a little myself," the admiral admitted, turning to Thomas. "Nothing formal. Stretching in the morning. Sometimes I stream a video to follow. Helps to stay limber."

"Yes, sir." While the SEALs weren't exactly known for their formality, and neither he nor Nalen were still in the Navy, old habits died hard. With a superior officer of Nalen's rank, Thomas would speak only when spoken to.

But Thomas had so much he wanted to report. Should he confess that the previous mission, though it had ended well, had been a series of rookie mistakes on his part? That he'd been rusty and had nearly blown everything multiple times?

And that he'd worked his ass off since then to prepare for whatever Nalen wanted to throw at him next?

He mustered the courage to speak, but Nalen held up a hand to stop him. "I don't want a single detail, Bone. The less I know, the better. This isn't the old days. This is off the books. What happened, happened."

"Yes, sir." Bone had to find something else to say—he sounded like a damn parrot.

He pulled himself together, stuffing down the feeling of intimidation the man brought up in him.

"There you go," Nalen muttered with a nod of approval at Bone's change of demeanor.

"It's good to see you, sir," Bone said. "I'm ready for another mission." He hesitated. "Assuming that's why you're here."

Nalen nodded. "It is indeed. And that's good to hear, because your country needs you again."

The running, the nights at the gun range, and even the yoga, all were about to pay off.

"Who—or what—is my target?"

Nalen frowned. "Unknown."

"Okay. Then how can I help?"

Admiral Nalen turned to take in the view. As at their previous meeting, he didn't seem to be in much of a hurry, though this time Bone sensed something he hadn't before. Frustration, maybe, well hidden but present.

"A man died last week. He was a former CIA officer. A few days later, another man died; he and the first one had worked closely together at the Company."

"Murdered?"

Nalen frowned. "Not according to the authorities." He turned away from the view and hit Bone with the full weight of his stare. "Remember, none of this gets discussed, mentioned, et cetera. Not to the police or anyone else. Including your... friend," he said with the hint of a smile.

The bastard knew about Steph—and their not-at-all-romantic relationship.

Bone nodded and said nothing.

"The men were part of a five-man CIA unit in the early to mid days of the war in Afghanistan, focused on intelligence gathering in the region."

"You want me to protect the three who are still alive?"

"No. Two are aware of the danger—one of them is the source of this intel. He's in DC and very safe. No, I have something different in mind for you." Nalen's head tilted to the side in a silent question: Could Bone figure it out?

"The other one is a tethered goat—and I'm the hunter of the wolf?"

Nalen smiled, clearly pleased. Bone felt vindicated. He was doing a lot better than the last time he'd met Nalen, when his life had been falling apart and he hadn't been able to figure his way out of a word-search puzzle.

"You got it. Find out if he's being targeted—and why. Protect him if you can. Capture or kill the person or persons responsible."

"Rules of engagement?"

"Anyone murdering or targeting former CIA officials needs to die. Full stop."

Bone considered for a second. "Sorry, sir, but I have to ask. We're 100 percent sure the CIA people are the good guys, right? There's not another team out there like you and me that had a conversation a few weeks ago, saying, 'These guys are traitors, but we can't publicly take them down, so let's do it privately—and very quietly. Make it look accidental.'"

Nalen raised his eyebrows, and a tight smile appeared. "Your head is definitely much more in the game than it was last time."

"I'm getting there."

"It's funny you should ask that…"

Bone loved that his mind and gut intuition were back, but he didn't like the idea that there was more to this operation than met the eye.

"There's always the chance one of them is responsible for the deaths of the others. Not the guy in DC. I can vouch for him; he's solid. But…"

Nalen looked like he was at war with himself, trying to decide how much to tell Bone. "We're still working out the details, but there's a pretty decent chance that one of the other two guys—the one in Las Vegas—is doing something underhanded. It may be related to this situation, or not. We can't be sure. But if there's more going on than we realize…"

"Handle it?"

"Exactly. Quickly and very quietly, to the best of your ability. No matter where it takes you."

Bone waited for Nalen to break character, crack a smile, and give him real orders.

Instead, the older man turned to take in the desert baking in the heat and the mountains shimmering 50 miles away.

"Pardon me again, sir, but what the hell? I'm expected to go into a situation cold, investigate with no official authority, and do… something, all without knowing if it's what you would want?"

Nalen barked out a quick laugh. "Yeah, I know. Less than ideal. But there are good reasons you're being asked to do this instead of bringing in the FBI. Some things need to be done on the down-low and kept quiet." He shrugged. "Embrace the suck. If you didn't want another mission, you shouldn't have done such a good job in San Diego. You're more capable than you realize. Act like it."

The rebuke had been said with a smile, but it hit home. Bone had succeeded by handling the problem with Prince Rafiq Al-Najjar.

He could get to the bottom of whatever this situation was.

"Yes, sir."

"That's more like it. I'll fill you in as we run back. Just remember: Make good choices, and whatever you do, don't get caught."

50

THE AFGHAN

The Office of Mike Salestri
Fortuna Magnifico Casino and Resort
Las Vegas, Nevada

Mike unlocked the large wall safe and removed all the equipment he needed. His hotel operations office had a solid door, soundproof walls, and no window. Only he had the ten-digit code for the keypad on the door. Still, old habits died hard.

First, he unplugged the casino phone from the wall.

The room had no television, computer, or other electronics that could be hacked to hear or see what happened in the office.

Next, Mike swept for listening devices, looked for hidden cameras, and conducted a physical search for anything unusual.

He could have used the Vault downstairs, but Kristine spent most of her time there. It wasn't that he didn't trust her—but he couldn't.

Not with this.

There was only one person in the world he could rely on for this project, and he was due to call in four minutes sharp.

Satisfied the room was safe, Mike sat heavily in his old leather desk chair with a tired sigh. He'd skipped his morning workout again today. He just didn't have his usual strength. He'd taken a nap at his desk after the conversation with Gregory Addison the previous night, entered his old

CIA colleague's contact information into the database on the Vault's computer, then went home, had gone to bed early, and had slept like a dead man until well after his normal wakeup time.

And he still felt tired.

He shrugged it off. It was likely just stress. The project of his life was always on his mind, and the ramifications of success—or failure—were beyond calculating.

He had to pull this off. It would be the culmination of his life's work.

A chance at redemption.

And revenge.

Having politicians and celebrities in his back pocket paled in comparison to what he and Sardar—his oldest and last remaining source in Afghanistan—had taken to simply calling "the mission."

Mike powered on the last item from the safe: a high-end burner smartphone. He never carried one on a day-to-day basis. They were too easy to hack, too easy to use to keep track of a person's location and movements. This one was used once a week, on Friday mornings—Friday night in Kabul, Afghanistan.

Mike waited motionless in his chair. After all these years, he could still wait patiently—no matter how anxious he felt.

He checked his watch. Sardar was one minute late.

If it had been anyone else, or any other year, Mike wouldn't have been worried. Sardar had moved up in the crazy world of Afghan business and alliances, eventually taking over his father's company when the older man stepped down to live a life of quiet luxury in Bamiyan, a beautiful part of Afghanistan.

Sardar was a well-known, widely respected, and thoroughly corrupt businessman, a die-hard Afghan who quietly supported the Taliban, a resurgent Al Qaeda, and other lesser-known insurgents in their efforts to destroy the West—along with any other opponents who stood in their way.

Or so people thought.

For the past twenty years, though, Sardar and Mike had been a team focused on thwarting the extremists.

Mike provided the money for Sardar's spy network.

Sardar risked his life to bribe people for intel.

Together, they passed along tips to people they trusted: mostly to an old contact of Mike's in the Mossad—Israel's intelligence organization—who then shared it with the CIA or other appropriate parties interested in the region.

The system had worked all these years, but their most recent efforts would top everything else they'd done so far.

They were going to stop a terrorist attack, and bring to justice the people responsible.

They had hit a dead end in their search for the person behind the attacks, but their last-ditch effort to produce leads had to pay off.

Someone would betray their boss, friend, or relative for the millions of dollars he and Sardar were offering.

Mike checked the smartphone. It had a full charge and was connected to both cellular data and the internet network used by the operations room in the basement below him.

Sardar should have called by now.

The age of smartphones combined with secure communications apps made his life so much easier. If he'd have had this back in the day, he'd have been even more successful in recruiting and managing assets.

So why was Sardar late?

Would today be the day no message came?

Had his last source finally been uncovered?

Was he being tortured by the Taliban, Al Qaeda, ISIS, or any number of other zealots who would extract their pound of flesh if they discovered his treachery?

If so, Mike would have yet more blood on his hands.

Kabul, Afghanistan

Many Years Ago

Mike wore the traditional baggy pants, knee-length tunic, and scarf common to the area as he walked along the dark, silent streets of the city just past midnight. He took care to not move like an American, but adopted the slower, more world-weary gait of an Afghan returning home after a trying day.

Every time he left the confines of the nearby military base, he was in danger—doubly so when he abandoned his Navy SEAL escorts and slipped off on his own.

But with his deeply tanned skin, thick beard, and flawless Pashto, he was fine as long as he stayed in character.

He took a breath, resting his hand against the still-warm wall of a home—a ruse to check the deserted street behind him while listening for the scuff of a footfall.

There were only the normal nighttime sounds of the crowded city: a few televisions, a baby fussing, a dog barking, and cars on a larger road to the east.

Two blocks ahead and one over was tonight's house for meeting Sardar, his best source. Mike would rather lose his own life than risk leading the wrong people to Sardar's door.

Or rather, whoever's door tonight's meeting would be held at. Sardar was the son of a wealthy businessman. He had many contacts in the city, and people respected him; they would gladly provide a place to meet for the opportunity to do the man a favor—and for the cash he offered.

Under his tunic, Mike's pants pocket bulged with money.

Most of it would be passed along to Sardar for his assistance. America was very grateful for every intelligence tip it could get.

Some of the money would stay in Mike's pocket. Skimming off the top wasn't officially taught to new CIA case officers—and he would be punished if caught—but he'd learned from his instructors: Life was uncertain, money made the world go 'round, and you could never have enough. Plan ahead. Have contingencies.

Contingencies were expensive.

Satisfied that no one followed him, and hoping Sardar was being as careful, Mike continued up the road, turned right after one block, and found the proper door—marked with a small scrap of fabric by the handle.

Acting as if it were his home, Mike opened the door without knocking and entered the dark room, his heart pounding.

If Sardar had betrayed him—or had been captured and interrogated—this was the moment Mike would be taken.

He coughed once, then quickly twice more, covering his mouth with his right hand—one final code for, "All is well."

A light on the far side of the one-room home came on—the city's electricity was working tonight.

Sardar stepped into the light. He was a short, round man in his forties—Mike's age—with thick dark hair, thicker, darker eyebrows, a trimmed beard, and round, black-frame glasses that made him look both smart and wealthy. He smiled as he shook his head at Mike. "You even smell like us! How do your people feel about that?"

Mike chuckled, taking the remark as a compliment. It made no sense to *dress, walk, and speak like an Afghan if he smelled of American deodorant and dandruff shampoo.*

"They don't know what to think of me," he replied, also in Pashto. They sat in two old chairs near the light. The small home was clean, neat, and smelled like meat slow-cooked in aromatic spices—cinnamon and cardamom, maybe.

Mike moved immediately to the business at hand, risking being too pushy, too American. But he had to warn his asset. "You weren't followed?" he asked.

Sardar's friendly smile faded, replaced by the sharp, focused look of a man used to thinking through—and solving—problems. "No, I was very careful. I heard of a man accused of helping the Americans, but I don't have any details. People use 'working with the Americans' as a pretense to blame those they owe money or want eliminated for whatever reason."

Mike nodded, and Sardar continued immediately. "I cannot stay long, but I have information. There is a rumor of an attack on an outpost in Marjah, Helmand Province," Sardar said. As he provided details, Mike memorized them, nodding when he was ready for the next piece of information.

After that came more intel: the movement of bomb makers, where and when explosives would be transported across the border from Pakistan, and what areas improvised explosive devices—IEDs—were to be planted in the next few days.

Mike took it all in, expertly filing it away.

Finally, Sardar stopped.

Mike removed the wad of American money from his pocket and peeled off several bills, which he set on his left knee. He passed the rest to Sardar, who nodded in understanding. The Afghan surely kept a portion of the money himself before disbursing it to his own network of informants.

"And how are you, my friend?" Mike asked, pocketing the bills he'd skimmed. "It is a dangerous game you play."

"Do not worry. The Taliban are easily fooled. They believe I support them."

"If you are ever in trouble…"

"I know. You will be there." Sardar gestured his thanks and offered a raised eyebrow. "And cannot the same be said of you and your dangerous game?"

From the start, Mike had kept Sardar's name and details from his superiors. Things were happening at the CIA, and he'd seen other case officers' assets get killed. Although the fault likely came from the Afghan side, Mike couldn't rule out American incompetence, stupidity, or a callous disregard for the safety of the Afghan people working hard to assist the USA in defeating Al Qaeda and the Taliban.

"I collect information from many sources, though you are, of course, the best. I give the credit to others to protect you. Should I be found out, I will admit my deception, be reprimanded—and still not give them your information."

"These games…" Sardar shook his head and frowned. "We should not have to play them."

"And yet we do."

They sat with their shared risks and motives: the desire for a safe and prosperous Afghanistan, the elimination of the Taliban and other terrorist groups using Afghanistan as a safe harbor, and an end to the killing of innocent civilians everywhere in the world.

Mike stood, followed by Sardar. It was time to go. They'd spent too much time together already. Every minute increased the risk.

"Thank you, as always, for tonight," Mike said. "Your information will save many American lives. I'm grateful, and I count you as a friend." Mike didn't need to lie. He'd grown closer to the man over the past months than was prudent. Sardar felt like the brother he'd never had. "I will see you next week."

He put his hand on his heart, which was mirrored by Sardar.

"Go in peace," Sardar said.

51

THE TAIL

Kabul, Afghanistan

Present Day

Sardar refused to look at his watch. He was late for his weekly call with the American, but it couldn't be helped.

"There may be two cars, sir," his driver said. "It could be nothing, but..."

Sardar resisted the urge to turn and look.

Had the hunter become the hunted? Sardar had recently put the word out far and wide that he was looking for information about those behind the bombings of the past nine months. The word shouldn't have been traced directly back to him, but mistakes were made—and people on his payroll might have been offered more money to tell what they knew about him.

"One has turned off," the driver said.

"Continue to the house," Sardar said. In the passenger seat, his trusted bodyguard—Abdul—glanced back at him but said nothing. Instead, he checked the chamber of his small submachine gun—the best money could buy—and sat up straighter.

"Permission to detour instead of heading directly home?" the driver asked.

Sardar nodded, and the man turned the SUV sharply down a side street.

It wasn't the first time they'd thought they were being followed, but each instance had proven a false alarm in the end.

Even without the current "project," as he and Mike called it, there were plenty of reasons people might track him.

Many of his business competitors would relish killing him and taking over.

Criminals would be happy to kidnap a wealthy businessman and hold him for ransom.

And of course, the Taliban, Al Qaeda, ISIS, or one of the other, smaller but often more volatile groups that used Afghanistan and Pakistan as staging and training grounds could have finally discovered his years of treachery, giving money to support them while gleaning information about their goals and activities to pass along to Mike.

He'd been careful, but in this business, someone was bound to talk, change sides, or do something to raise suspicions.

Sardar entered a long passcode on his smartphone, opened the secure communications app—which required a second passcode—and scrolled until he found *Janana*—"My beloved." He would risk his wife discovering the contact, as he couldn't very well have an entry of "Mike Salestri, former CIA officer" in his phone. If he was ever taken and tortured to unlock the phone, it was better for his abductors to believe he cheated on his wife than to know he was still in touch with his old CIA handler.

His wife knew enough about his side business that she wouldn't fear he had a mistress.

I'm sorry, my darling, but I'm running late.

A check on the front seat showed that the attention of the guard and the driver remained on the traffic surrounding them and the potential for being followed, but he still didn't dare type anything specific. Not here. He trusted the men, but the less they knew, the better.

Please keep your phone with you. I want to not only speak with you, but see you soon.

That would give Mike a clue that the moment they had been working toward might finally be here. The note Sardar had received at breakfast yesterday seemed authentic. A person had the information they were looking for.

I will contact you when I can.

Sardar didn't wait for a reply but logged out of the app and swiped it from the phone's memory before returning the device to his pocket and relaxing into the comfortable leather seat. For all the danger, he kept his cool. He was at peace.

It wasn't yet his time to die.

By this time next week, the best-case scenario would be that he remained a free man and had helped eliminate terrorists who had killed and injured hundreds around the world.

In the worst case, he would be captured by the extremists he was about to betray—who, to make an example of him, would torture him for years before they finally let him die.

52

THE KNOCK

The Office of Mike Salestri
Fortuna Magnifico Casino and Resort
Las Vegas, Nevada

Mike read the texts on the secure comms app and frowned.

First Gregory Addison—a man Mike had trusted and had considered... not a friend exactly, but a steady, reliable partner in the intelligence business—had reached out to warn him about an unknown assailant.

Now Sardar was in danger. There was nothing else that would prevent him from calling on time.

Plus, he wanted Mike to break protocol and carry the phone with him so they could communicate at any time instead of during pre-arranged windows.

Something was happening.

After all the effort he and Sardar had put into the hunt for the terrorists who had planted the three bombs this year—the planning, the money, the secrecy—was it all coming apart at the last minute?

It might be merely the endgame. The time had come for the final steps. In a few days, maybe a week, the identity and location of the extremists would be in their hands.

Or maybe they had been discovered.

Mike had a jet at the ready, millions of dollars in an account waiting to be wire-transferred at a moment's notice, and a few million more coming once the insider trading of shares in Sam Norrisline's company paid off.

He was as ready as he could be.

A knock from the door startled Mike. No one disturbed him on Friday mornings unless it was an emergency.

He slipped the phone into the front pocket of his pants, checked the office to make sure he'd replaced the electronic detection devices and closed the safe, and opened the door, ready to chew someone out or deal with a disaster.

Kristine put on a concerned but contrite look and prepared for her father's wrath. On Friday mornings, he didn't want to be bothered. It must be when he worked on his secret... whatever it was. He always played things close to his chest and wasn't ready to turn over the reins of his empire yet —far from it.

But she had to know what he was doing.

She'd risk sticking her nose where it didn't belong and hope to be given access to whatever his plans were.

And if he wouldn't tell her, she'd find out on her own.

The door opened. Dad looked drawn. Stressed.

It was more proof he was up to something.

"Sorry to bother you, but I have concerns," she said. "Can I come in?"

His eyes flicked left and right, searching the hallway behind her. He hid it well, but there was a split second where her father's expression changed. A narrowing of the eyes, maybe—she couldn't put her finger on what it had been, exactly.

Anger? Guilt? Or...

She had it. He was on alert.

"Sure, Krissy—Kristine," he said, correcting himself. "Come in."

She noticed it right away: He had a cell phone in his front pocket.

He hated phones and refused to carry one. They were too easy to hack and track. Plus, he was fond of saying, "Power is partly who you can get ahold of—and partly how few people can get ahold of you."

It was another piece of the puzzle. He was in communication with someone important enough to him to break one of his cardinal rules.

What did that mean?

What kind of deal would he make—and with whom—that didn't

involve her, the database of secrets and blackmail material, and their normal process?

It had to be huge.

"What are your concerns?" Mike asked as he settled back into his chair. He seemed to deflate, like he was exhausted at just after nine in the morning.

"The insider trading with Norrisline's company," she said after taking a second to get herself on track. "It's too much money. It might trigger an investigation." Her excuse to interrupt his special Friday morning time was legitimate. They'd never risked so much before—or done it so blatantly. "You taught me well. 'Never go for a big score. Be smart. Play the long game.' This flies in the face of that rule. It's an unnecessary risk."

Kristine stood before Mike's desk, arms crossed over yet another one of her black pantsuits, waited, and watched.

No matter what Dad said or how he reacted, she'd learn more about his secret.

53

THE DESIGNATED SURVIVOR

The Office of Mike Salestri
Fortuna Magnifico Casino and Resort
Las Vegas, Nevada

Mike knew without a doubt that Kristine was onto him. She was smart, using a valid concern as an excuse to investigate what he was up to.

After all these years of hiding his true feelings, it was easy to keep the proud smile off his face.

He'd taught her well.

In his frequent, ongoing evaluation of which child would be better at taking over from him when he eventually—reluctantly—retired, Krissy had jumped forward several steps this morning.

He had an opportunity here to tell her why he needed as much money as possible—quickly.

Mike wanted to say, "I may have to pay off an informant to give me information on a terrorist organization, get that intelligence to the Mossad or the CIA, and stop the next bombing somewhere in the world."

If he and Sardar got scammed or double-crossed, they needed extra money to offer the next informant. And the next. The terrorists had to be stopped, and if the world's intelligence agencies weren't getting it done, Mike wouldn't stop hunting. They'd work every contact they had to find and eliminate what he and Sardar believed to be the group behind the three recent bombings in Egypt, Turkey, and Spain.

One, because it was the right thing to do.

Two, because it was what he'd been trained for.

And three, because eventually the terrorists would no longer be content to bomb those countries.

The terrorists would set their sights on the United States of America.

Mike had kept this secret from Kristine since he'd realized the various attacks around the world had to be linked; they were likely the result of one mastermind...

The man he'd been after all those years ago while stationed in Afghanistan.

A man who had trained bomb makers and supplied everything they needed to kill Americans with IEDs.

Kristine's face hardened as Mike considered what—and how—to tell her about the operation he had kept secret.

She tried another approach. "What do we need all that money for?" she asked him. It came out as a joke, but he knew she meant it seriously. "How much are you spending on that mansion, anyway?"

"Everything costs more than you'd expect," he said, letting the opportunity to confide in her slip away. He trusted her, but this wasn't the time. He and Sardar had worked for years to get where they were today. They had passed along important intel that had resulted in the capture or killing of several very bad men. Sardar had spent hundreds of thousands of dollars in bribes cultivating informants and gathering tips.

And nine months ago, the bombing in Cairo had the feel of an operation by the mastermind they'd hunted all these years.

It was all coming to a head, and the last thing he needed was his smart and opinionated daughter butting in. Wanting to "help."

Besides, he'd need someone to manage the organization while he went to Afghanistan to meet the informant in person, look them in the eyes, and guess if they had the intel he needed—or if they were trying to scam him.

Or if the mastermind had sent the informant to take the money...

And kill him.

If the deal went south, Mike could be dead soon.

Who would pick up the pieces and take over?

Krissy's brother?

No. Over the past few years, Kristine had become a smart, capable woman—and devious in her own way. Her brother would be pissed that he wasn't chosen to take charge, but he'd get over it. He contributed to the organization in other ways. It would likely be her who took over.

"We stick with the plan," Mike said. "Excelsior Trading makes big bets all the time. I'm fine with the risk." He paused as he considered returning to Afghanistan, meeting a member of a terrorist organization, and wiring millions of dollars to them in hopes they betrayed their leader —and weren't double-crossing him to steal his money before eliminating him.

"If anything ever happens to me unexpectedly," he said, the words coming out without much thought, "I'll need you to handle things here." He gestured toward the floor—the operations center in the basement below them.

"Why would something happen to you, Dad?" Kristine asked, and nearly broke his heart. Wasn't it bad enough her mother had died much too young? Now he was moving forward with an operation that might see him gone, too?

He waved her off without answering. "Don't worry. That's not going to happen."

She didn't believe him, but the discussion was over.

Kristine wouldn't get any more out of her father. Not today. He'd shut down.

At least she'd confirmed that the excessive bet on the stock was important for some secret reason.

He had to be running a large operation—and excluding her.

At least he trusted her enough to name her his designated survivor if the mission went bad.

That was more than she'd had before coming to his office this morning.

She nodded and turned to leave when the phone in his pocket buzzed.

If she turned and asked about the phone, would he let her in or order her to leave?

Kristine hesitated for a moment, hoping her father would change his mind and bring her into the fold, give her a glimpse of the operation, but he said nothing.

The phone buzzed again with another text message—she recognized the generic angry sound their preferred secure communications app made —but she only walked to the door, stepped out, and closed it securely behind her, leaving Big Mike to his secrets.

There were other ways to find out what was going on.

54

THE RISKS

The Office of Mike Salestri
Fortuna Magnifico Casino and Resort
Las Vegas, Nevada

With Kristine gone, Mike slipped the phone from his pocket, entered the code to unlock it, then entered the secondary code to access the secure comms app. There were two messages from Sardar.

I'm sorry I was delayed.

Can you talk?

Yes, Mike replied. *Call anytime.*

The secure communications app buzzed like an angry bee a moment later as the call came in.

Mike answered but said nothing. From the other end of the line, there were three quick raps of a finger against the phone.

Mike responded with two finger snaps, two silent beats, and two more snaps.

With the security protocol complete, Mike spoke in Pashto. "Hello, my brother."

"I have news," Sardar said, skipping the usual niceties. "A source has information—for a price. Ten million. We can handle that amount?"

"Yes," Mike answered. "Barely."

"Then it won't be long now."

Finally, after all this time, the plan was coming together.

"Where and when?"

"I do not know yet. Only that it must be soon."

"Another attack is imminent?"

"They didn't say, but that is my guess."

"Or they may be concerned they are compromised."

"Exactly. It could also be that we are about to be betrayed. But it feels legitimate."

"I agree. Only a source with accurate information would ask for so much money. Should I come now?"

"Not yet," Sardar said after a short hesitation. "I am to receive further details soon. And..."

"Yes, my friend. I am sure I want to come," Mike said, answering the unspoken question. "I must be there to transfer the funds—and I would rather my life be in danger than yours in case of a double cross."

Mike knew Sardar would be shaking his head. "Without you, there is little money to continue," Sardar pointed out. "Without me, you could—"

"There is no one else I trust. Without either of us, the work stops. The CIA and other intelligence agencies of the world would have to manage without us."

"Let us hope it does not come to that."

"Agreed."

There was a pause. When Sardar spoke again, he sounded worried. "I was followed tonight. Two cars. We lost them and I returned to my home. I am safe here."

"Is it the mastermind? Or could it be the informant who somehow traced you and is vetting the offer?"

"I don't know."

Mike confessed his own concerns. "I received a call from a reliable old friend. In the business. He helped when we worked together in Kabul."

"The—what did you call him?"

"The intel nerd," Mike said in English. There wasn't an exact translation in Pashto. "Two of the other men from that time have died in the past week. I've had no connection to them in years."

Sardar didn't respond immediately, so Mike spoke again. "It could be a coincidence."

"Who could have such a large operation to conduct direct action missions in Kabul—to follow me—and to kill former CIA officers in America?"

"Only the man we have suspected all these years. Perhaps we have been right this whole time—he was, and still may be, connected to Pakistan Intelligence."

"Or his organization is larger than we understood."

Mike shared his biggest concern. "What if the target knows about us and has directed the source to steal our money and then kill us?"

"But why kill the other two men and not you or 'the nerd'?"

"There is also another man. He is still alive as well."

"Strange. Perhaps it is a coincidence. People die."

"Yes, but not you and me. Not yet."

"Not yet. And there is nothing different for us to do anyway except be careful."

"Yes—the results will be worth the risk."

"Any risk," Sardar agreed.

They sat with the dangers a moment before Mike spoke again. "It is around sixteen hours to Kabul on the plane I have secured, so I would prefer 20—or 24—hours' notice if possible."

"Can you keep your phone with you? In case there are any changes? And perhaps you should plan on leaving Monday morning your time—to be ready. You would arrive early Tuesday morning in Kabul. I will handle the bribes at the airport—I have already made the arrangements. The cover story is that you and your associate are part of a humanitarian mission. There will be no problems."

"Money opens every door," Mike said, quoting the popular Pashto saying.

"That it does, my friend. And thanks to your ongoing support, I look forward to finally eliminating our enemy."

"*Da khuday khwahish,*" Mike said. If God wills it. They had different faiths, but the sentiment was the same.

"*Da khuday khwahish,*" Sardar repeated, and after a second, they both hung up.

55

THE ROCK

Melissa's heart pounded at her workstation in the operations room. She wiped her palms on her khaki pants as she'd done countless times in the past few minutes.

Kristine always arrived to work early, went home late, and rarely left the Vault while at the casino. Yet at a few minutes before nine this morning, she had appeared in the Vault's doorway with a determined look on her face, firmly closed the door behind her, and stalked across and out of the ops room without a word.

There were two unisex bathrooms off the back of the main room for the exclusive use of the team—but that's not where she went.

This wasn't like her.

Had she left for the day?

This was Melissa's chance.

She was going to do it.

All she had to do was march to the door, enter the code—and hope she guessed right.

Once inside the room, she'd reach into her hair and remove the large, ornate hair clip that hid the mini flash drive, shove the device into the computer's USB slot, and let the software do its thing. After about five minutes, the data would be transferred.

She could then leave the Vault, walk across the ops room like the trusted employee she was, have Leo the security guard scan her with the handheld metal detector wand as he did to everyone who entered and left, explain that she wasn't feeling well, and get out of the building.

All before Kristine returned.

Would anyone tell Krissy that she had entered the Vault?

Maybe. Maybe not. But if Melissa could get out of the casino, she was free.

She and Shane would have all they needed to expose Big Mike's operation, and then she and Shane would be together forever.

As she pushed the chair back to finally take the risk, one wheel caught on a tiny rock on the linoleum floor, stopping for a second before rolling over it.

Melissa froze. She had a bad feeling. The pebble might be an omen. A sign that now was not the time.

She wiped her sweaty palms on her pants again and tried to make up her mind. Her nerves were frayed. She couldn't keep up the charade of trusted employee in this evil organization much longer.

But knowing what Big Mike had done to Shane's sister didn't make it easy to do what she had to do.

Melissa slid her chair forward, avoiding the rock.

Now wasn't the time.

She focused on her screen, but her mind returned to her last night in Mexico with Shane the month before.

Playa del Carmen, Mexico

Melissa lay in Shane's arms, her head on his chest, listening to his heartbeat as Shane whispered in the darkness.

"Big Mike had my sister killed," Shane said. "She was a reporter like me..." He trailed off. "Well, okay, she had a large following on social media and wanted to break into journalism. People opened up to her, telling her things they'd never mention to others."

Shane went silent for several seconds. His heart rate picked up noticeably.

"You can tell me," she whispered, and held him tight. He needed an anchor, and she was here for him.

"Long story short, she stumbled upon a man whose life had been ruined by Big Mike. He'd done some bad things, yes, but nothing that warranted what Mike did to him. He told my sister about others in his situation, and she got them, reluctantly and off the record, to give her more details."

Shane paused again, his heart hammering. Melissa held him tight and waited for him to continue.

"Mike found out about it." He choked back a sob. "He lured her to a building under construction and shot her. Or had one of his goons do it—a retired soldier. I still don't know."

"Did you tell the police?"

Shane shook his head in the dark. "What could I say? I had no proof. They would have laughed at me. Or worse: gone to Mike and asked him about it. Then he would have had me killed, too."

"So what did you do?"

"I took her notes—she'd left a copy with me, 'just in case,' she'd said with a laugh. I went back to some of the people she'd interviewed, but they wouldn't speak to me. Not after they heard what happened to her."

Melissa thought it through. "Wasn't that... I don't mean to be critical, given all that happened, but..."

"Was what I did—going to speak with them—stupid? Dangerous?" Shane asked.

Melissa nodded against his chest.

"Yes, it absolutely was. But I was out of my mind with grief, and I thought..."

"What?"

"If I could expose Mike..."

Melissa understood. "You thought he'd find out, come after you, and..."

"End it. Yes. Put me out of my misery. End my guilt." He choked back another sob. "I encouraged her. She wanted to do what I did. Do you understand? I got her killed."

The tears came—along with the sobs, deep and desperate.

She held him as he let it out, then propped herself on an elbow and soothed him by running her other hand through his hair until he lay still, spent, eyes closed but still awake.

"I want to help you get revenge," she said.

She was falling for him.
Besides, he needed her, and she could help.

Operations Room
Fortuna Magnifico Casino and Resort
Las Vegas, Nevada

When a sound came from the door to the ops room, Melissa's eyes darted to the clock on her computer. She'd been lost in thought for only a few minutes. The door *beeped* quietly, and Kristine pushed her way inside.

If Melissa had tried to steal the data, Kristine would have caught her red-handed.

Krissy nodded at her briefly as she walked past, looking pensive and focused.

The pebble on the floor had been an omen. It had saved Melissa's life.

She took a deep breath, let it out slowly, and wiped her damp palms on her pants once again. Instead of risking a midday operation, she vowed to wait until Saturday night. Kristine wasn't likely to leave her father's weekly dinner in the middle of the meal.

Melissa subtly turned her head toward Kristine at the control room door and watched for the last digit of the entry code.

56

THE NECESSITY

The Vault
Fortuna Magnifico Casino and Resort
Las Vegas, Nevada

Kristine cursed silently as the door to the Vault buzzed. Her fingers had moved too fast and must have landed on the wrong buttons for the entry code. She forced herself to go slowly and pressed each number carefully.

The door *beeped* and unlocked, allowing her inside the comfortably small room she called her own.

She slid into the desk chair, entered the password for the computer, and smiled as the screens flickered to life, already filled with data.

One monitor showed a list of potential targets that would help their efforts. CEOs of up-and-coming tech companies were a priority. Their stock prices leapt upward on good news and plummeted on bad. Once Kristine had insider data prior to their upcoming quarterly earnings reports, it was easy to place bets and make money whether the stock went up or down.

Politicians were a close secondary priority, but harder to target. They were reluctant to spend much time in Las Vegas and usually careful about living it up, even in their hotel rooms. She had spoken to Mike about expanding their reach, taking over a hotel in DC they could wire for surveillance, but somehow they never had the cash.

It was finally time for her to find out where their money went.

Because when she was in charge, things would be different.

When she controlled a hotel in the nation's capital, every room would be wired for sound and video. Politicians would be courted and encouraged to stay there.

Everyone who visited would fall into her spider web.

Emails confirming reservations would hide the virus they'd used successfully Wednesday. She'd have spy software installed on the politicians' phones, allowing them to be turned on remotely and used as portable listening devices.

After a few months, she would have the inside track on every meeting, discussion, and off-the-books deal made behind the scenes.

Kristine would learn foibles, vices, fears, vulnerabilities, and hot buttons—of the politicians and their staff.

Eventually, she could begin to remake the country the way she wanted it to be.

As long as she had her father out of the way.

Or under her control.

Kristine stretched her arms, fingers interlaced, and cracked her knuckles—a bad habit she didn't allow herself to indulge in when her father or others were around.

It revealed her true self: ambitious, driven, and ruthless, not the soft-spoken professional some people believed her to be.

The pistol at her waist, hidden by her pantsuit jacket, weighed heavily. The extra ounces of the small USB flash drive hidden in the holster shouldn't make a noticeable difference, but she felt it somehow. When she entered the operations room, she was "wanded" with the metal detector just like everyone else—even Big Mike. Only she and her brother were allowed weapons, but no one, including her, was allowed electronics. Phones stayed in employee lockers upstairs or were left in vehicles, and any type of computer or flash drive was obviously off limits. None of the organization's data left the rooms.

Thankfully, she carried the pistol every day. When Lou the guard found it this morning, he hadn't looked closer to find the illicit flash drive in the holster.

She checked her watch. Dad wasn't due for their afternoon meeting for a few hours.

What was her father up to? It had to be big; he wouldn't hold back unless he thought she wasn't ready for it—or wouldn't like it.

Finding out his plans would be risky. Mike wasn't an expert in computers like she was, but he kept up with technology.

He trusted her. He wouldn't suspect she'd spy on him.

Probably.

What choice did she have, though? Her dad's time had come and gone. He'd lived his life, had his adventures, made his mark.

It was her turn—and he was holding her back. While he could be protecting her from danger or unsavory business he thought she was too delicate of a flower to handle, she was ready, willing, and able to take the reins of his empire.

Preferably by his choosing. But if not…

Well, she could blow up that bridge if she came to it.

She hesitated. If he came down early, if she went through with her plan and got caught…

Kristine bit her lip and shook her head, not willing to go there.

What she had planned wasn't a betrayal. Not really. It was insurance. A safety measure—that's how she had to think of it.

What if Mike was unavailable and there was an emergency?

A car accident.

A heart attack.

Long shots, certainly, but shit happened.

As he'd said earlier, if anything were to happen to him, where would she be?

She wasn't snooping or betraying her father's trust.

Capturing his login information was an absolute necessity.

Once she had the passwords, she didn't have to access his side of the computer. Not unless there was a real emergency.

It just made sense.

Kristine drew the pistol her father had given her, set it next to the keyboard, and dug the micro-flash drive from the holster, peeling off the black gaffer's tape holding it in place.

This was the perfect time.

Without hesitating to consider the ramifications if her father discovered her treachery, she inserted the thumb drive into the computer.

57

THE NAP

The Office of Mike Salestri
Fortuna Magnifico Casino and Resort
Las Vegas, Nevada

Mike awakened to a noise in the office. His eyes popped open, searching the room for threats as he swung his feet off the desk.

No one was there.

He processed the sound he'd heard.

He had been snoring.

According to his watch, only ten minutes had passed.

He was no less fatigued.

His body felt like he had gained 20 pounds over the last month instead of losing 10.

He and Kristine had a standing Friday afternoon meeting to review the week and make last-minute preparations for the traditional Saturday dinner party.

The mundane tasks of the casino and resort, which he usually handled on Friday after his call with Sardar, didn't interest him today. Nor did the opportunity to cultivate new marks at Saturday's dinner. Not with the coming mission to Afghanistan and what he'd long considered his real work.

Perhaps he needed some time off away from the office. He'd knock off early and go visit the house he was having built. See what the builder had accomplished this week. The countertops in the kitchen should be in by now, and the pool should have at least been dug. The trip would help clear his head, give him some time to think through the angles, see if he and Sardar had missed anything in their planning.

Kristine wouldn't mind moving up their meeting time. And it would be a good test of her team. Did they wait until the last minute to prepare the weekly report, or were they ahead of the game?

He'd pop into the control room hours early. A surprise inspection.

If Kristine was as good as he thought, she'd be ready and waiting for him.

Maybe they could take a drive to the new house together. That would be nice. Some father-daughter time away from the grind of running the empire.

He slipped on his sport coat and moved to the door, lost in thought.

Maybe he should have confided in her earlier this morning. It might be time to let her in on some of the details about the upcoming operation.

Why he was taking such a risk with the insider stock trading of Sam Norrisline's company.

Where all the money had been going over the past several years.

A broad overview, perhaps.

Just in case Rutherfield's and Frandren's deaths weren't accidents... and he was next.

He could trust her.

58

THE SOFTWARE

The Vault
Fortuna Magnifico Casino and Resort
Las Vegas, Nevada

Kristine navigated the computer's file structure to find the small tracking program on the thumb drive. With a click, she activated the file.

Install keyboard logging software?

She clicked a button.

Warning: ALL keystrokes and mouse clicks will be logged until the program is halted. Continue?

She hesitated once again.

After this, there would be no going back.

Ninety percent of the time, Kristine sat at the desk and ran the computer, on her own or with her father directing her. About once a week, often on Saturdays, her father took over, kicked her out of the room, and did... something.

The computer had two logins—Kristine's and her father's. He had his passwords, and knew hers as well, but she could only log into her side.

What he did was a mystery—until the next time he kicked her out of the room, logged in, and did whatever he kept from her. The tiny software program she'd installed would record his passwords, the websites he visited, and everything he typed for her to review at her leisure.

She could sneak away tomorrow night during Saturday dinner.

He'd be schmoozing.

Her team would be hard at work accessing the guests' cell phone data with the new email confirmation link that installed the virus.

It would be the perfect time to snoop.

Still, if Mike found out...

What could he do? She was his daughter. Arguably his favorite child. She could say that he'd taught her well. That she looked at his side of the computer as a test from him, and she had passed by proving her abilities.

He might be proud of her.

She stared at the screen, trying to convince herself to betray her father.

Mike breezed through the outer security station with a nod to Leo, the daytime security guard, who stood from his padded stool by the entrance and picked up the security wand to check for weapons and electronics. Mike didn't have to submit to the ordeal—he was the boss, and could do what he wanted—but it looked good to the staff if everyone was scanned.

The wand beeped for the small pistol in a holster at his waist, hidden by his shirt and sport coat, along with the phone in his pocket, which got a raised eyebrow from Leo.

Years ago, he had asked Krissy to carry a weapon every day, even at work. Las Vegas brought out the worst in people, and he didn't like the idea of his daughter unarmed in the parking garage or while stuck in traffic on Las Vegas Boulevard.

He hadn't carried in far too long, but after Gregory Addison's warning last night, he'd impulsively brought the weapon with him from home this morning.

"You never know," Mike told Leo, explaining both the pistol and the phone.

Leo said nothing. Big Mike made the rules.

Mike moved on. The interior door opened with his passcode.

He offered nods to the room of techs as they glanced up from their workstations.

He had good people here. Dedicated. Reliable. Each recruited for their trustworthiness.

Kristine ran a tight ship.

He was proud of her.

Kristine didn't reach a conscious decision so much as she grew tired of staring at the screen, undecided.

She clicked the *Yes* button.

The software immediately burrowed inside the machine and hid itself. It was active immediately, though she could shut it down with a keyboard sequence.

On the screen, a popup:

Program installed and running.

Beneath were keyboard control sequences to stop logging keystrokes, pull up the program for review, or uninstall the software. She'd already committed them to memory, but it didn't hurt to review the instructions one final time. Without the proper keys pressed, the program would remain hidden, doing its job, until accessed.

She had done it.

Whether a betrayal or insurance, she was committed.

Mike entered a passcode on the door to the Vault, pausing to turn his body to better hide his hand from Kristine's friend Melissa, who sat closest to the door.

Everyone in the room could be trusted.

But he'd survived this long because he was careful.

Kristine pulled the tiny flash drive from the computer tower and returned it to its hiding place, smoothing the tape over it.

A faint sound from the door made her heart race. Aside from her, the only person with a passcode was her father.

She grabbed the pistol off the desk and holstered it as Mike opened the door.

Out of the corner of her eye, the monitor still showed the software's keyboard shortcut control sequences.

She tapped the space bar with her left hand, praying the instructions would disappear, and turned to face her father.

"You're early," she said, hoping her tone didn't betray her terror.

Dad was an expert at reading people: the micro tells of a face, a pounding pulse on the side of a neck.

Would he see her terror now? Her guilt? Her betrayal?

"What are you working on?" he asked as he swung the door shut and stared at her screens. He didn't sound suspicious, but had the operating instructions vanished as she thought, or were they displayed on her monitor, revealing her treachery?

"Reviewing for our afternoon meeting." She covered well—she hoped.

He said nothing as he moved to the wingback chair in the corner and sat with what looked like relief.

She had done the right thing. Dad was young yet—only in his mid-sixties—but you never knew.

"Let's get started now, if you're ready," Mike said. "What's first?"

Kristine spun her chair around and checked the monitor.

The secret software had vanished.

Instead, the screen showed the spreadsheet she'd been reviewing earlier. At the top were the names of the three top technology firms whose stock prices fluctuated wildly based on their earnings reports. She had invited their CEOs to Big Mike's Saturday night dinner next week.

"Where's your brother? He usually wants to be in on this," Mike asked.

He sounded exhausted. That wasn't like him at all.

When she turned, though, he looked awake and alert.

"He's still out of the office."

"I thought he was due back today."

Kristine shrugged. That had been the original plan, but he hadn't showed. No call, either. She was torn between covering for him and letting him take a hit to prove she was more dedicated to the organization.

"People take vacations, Dad," she said. Keeping peace in the family wasn't a bad thing. She might need her brother's support someday. "Okay, not you, but people in general need time off." A look from her father made her smile. "Yes, not me, either. But he has his motorcycle. We have this," she said, gesturing to the videos on the big monitor.

"His loss," Mike said.

"I'll show you what we got this week," she said, pulling up video recordings from the wired resort suites. "And who I've invited for next week's Saturday night dinner guests—just in case you wanted to make more money."

59

THE SHORT GOODBYE

71 Ocotillo Street
Sands, Arizona

Bone had been prepping for the day he finally received a new mission, so packing took only an hour.

He'd replaced the hatchback's spare tire with a gun safe bolted into place. The new M4 and 9mm pistol went inside, along with suppressors for each, spare ammo, night vision goggles, a plate carrier, a thin ballistic vest he could wear secretly under a shirt, a lock pick gun, and an extra knife, along with a waist pack to carry the smaller items in the field.

Once the space's plastic cover was in place, and the thin carpet placed on top of that, no one would guess Bone had an arsenal at his disposal.

A duffel bag with clothes—from tactical to everyday—and another with bottles of water, MREs, snack bars, and miscellaneous gear, went in the back.

He'd learned on the last mission. If he was going to be some sort of super spy or government assassin—whatever Admiral Nalen happened to need—he had to be able to blend in better. This time, he had generic light-gray workman's coveralls in another bag, along with hats and other simple disguises.

With a smaller pistol in a concealed carry holster under his loose-fitting button-down shirt, and a wicked sharp folding knife in his pocket, he was as ready as he could be.

Online research took the rest of the morning and part of the afternoon. Bone used a virtual private network—VPN—on his laptop and a browser specializing in anonymity that he'd chosen specifically for the day he got a new mission. He memorized maps, investigated the people Admiral Nalen had briefed him on, and came up with an initial game plan for the next few days.

It took time, but eventually, he had what he needed—or at least enough to get the mission started. He cleared the browser history and put the computer and his phone in the safe after pocketing a burner phone without turning it on.

Finally, he left the house and backed the car out of the driveway.

He had a couple of miles and a few minutes to figure out how to tell Steph he was leaving and why—without lying to her or disobeying Admiral Nalen's orders about mission secrecy.

* * *

The Bar
Sands, Arizona

Bone arrived a few minutes after the bar opened.

The interior was dark and cool. The background smell of stale beer was mostly masked by the crisp, clean scent of the cleaning product Steph used to mop the floor.

Bone glanced at Henry, but the man was too engrossed in his "medicine" to pay any attention to what he had to say to Steph. The other men of the "Breakfast Club," as Stephanie called her regulars who showed up like clockwork at 4:00 each afternoon, were the same. They settled into their spots with their usual drinks ready in front of them. Greetings were short and muted for now; they would be more talkative when the day's first taste of alcohol hit.

Steph's face faltered for a moment when Bone stood behind his stool. He didn't usually come in so early.

At least, not since he'd gotten sober.

"No," he said. "I don't need a drink."

Her relief was obvious, but she had to know something was up.

"I, um…" Bone said, losing the smooth line he'd practiced on the way over.

Steph shook her head a fraction, just enough for him to see. "You decided to go visit your buddy in California?" she asked, helping him out. Could she see it in his face, or did his excitement—and relief—at getting a new mission from Admiral Nalen show that clearly?

"Yeah," Bone said, continuing the act in case the regulars were paying more attention than he thought. "Just got off the phone with him. He could use the support, and it's summer, so…"

Steph nodded. "Got it. Have fun. I'll—" She cut herself off, and he could swear she blushed, though the bar was dark and maybe it was just wishful thinking. "We'll miss you, and… I'll miss your help around here."

They locked eyes for a second. There was so much to unpack that Bone didn't know where or how to begin, nor what to say.

"I'll be back soon," was the best he could get out.

One of the regulars was ready for another drink. Steph nodded at Bone, he nodded back, and she turned to pour, listen, relate, and be the big sister/sounding board/therapist/entertainer that her job required.

As Bone turned to leave, Henry mumbled to him from a few stools down. "Get some, kid."

Bone kept walking. He didn't—couldn't—acknowledge the old veteran's rallying cry for going into combat, but he certainly took it to heart.

60

THE HOUSE

Mike's under-construction house sat on a 5-acre plot of desert about twenty-five minutes from the casino and a mile from the nearest neighbor. By this time next year, there would be other lots sold and more mansions being built, but for now, he had the area to himself.

The purchase had originally been the kids' idea. Mike figured they wanted a mansion to fight over once he was dead.

Or more likely, they both wanted him in a luxury oasis far from the casino so they could take over more and more of the organization.

Designing the home with the architect, however, had turned out to be a surprisingly enjoyable distraction from running the empire.

Besides, after all he'd done and the uncomfortable hell holes he'd slept in, didn't he deserve to spend the rest of his time on the planet in luxury?

Assuming he made it back from Afghanistan alive, that is.

The builders had left for the day, and Kristine had begged off driving out with him, claiming she had too much on her plate.

Probably just proving she was a hard worker and angling for his approval. He didn't mind. He had called his fixer, Dominic. Dom was happy to come over for a talk.

The house looked odd sitting nearly finished in the middle of raw desert. A single-story, modern take on an adobe style, with sharp, clean lines, a light taupe stucco exterior, and a three-car garage.

For now, the long driveway was packed dirt, but eventually, artisans would place pavers in an intricate pattern.

At night, Mike would have an incredible view of the Las Vegas Strip to the west, especially from the rooftop observation deck accessible via a black spiral staircase off the back patio. To the east, the ground rose gently, providing a natural view of the "mountains"—low hills, actually— to admire at dawn.

The rest of the area wasn't flat like lower-priced subdivisions whose dips, hills, and other terrain got razed to make cookie-cutter homes easier and quicker to build. His acres were crisscrossed with desert washes that ranged from 1 to 4 feet deep. The next lot, to the south, had a decent-sized hill between his home and where the neighbor's would be. He wouldn't be able to see their house, and they wouldn't see his. It would be like living in the middle of nowhere.

He didn't want to like it, but the house had grown on him. He'd scoff and deny, but he was looking forward to living here. After the trip to Afghanistan, maybe he could wind down his involvement in the organization. Krissy could manage the spying, insider trading, and deal brokering. She was quiet, but she had his killer instincts, though he had to figure a way to convince her to use them. Her brother would handle the people side, which he did so well.

Would they work together without him? Or be at each other's throats and blow up the business vying for position?

The questions had kept him from stepping away thus far, but after the upcoming mission with Sardar, he had to have a clear succession plan in place, more than the informal conversation he'd had with Krissy the day before.

Mike walked the perimeter of the home, admiring the workmanship. The grounds were clean, with no pieces of wood or trash lying around. The workers took care of all that before they locked their tools in the garage at the end of the day.

There was no landscaping—the bushes and desert trees would be the last step in a few weeks.

In back, the enormous pool had been dug but not yet poured. Stacks of rebar sat ready, though the bottom still needed final shaping, smoothing, and packing.

Mike picked the lock on the front door to let himself into the house.

There was no certificate of occupancy, and he hadn't been given a key yet. But locked doors had never stopped Mike before, and they weren't going to on his own damn house, no matter what the builder said about security and liability.

He toured the home from room to room, shaking his head at the luxury. He'd slept in fields. Under bridges. Up against the walls of mud huts, praying the sun's warmth radiated off them long into the cold nights.

His steps echoed on the oversized marble tiles. Rugs—he had to remember to find some rugs to soften the noise.

A low whistle came from behind him. "Nice place you have here," Dominic called from the front door. "You have a guest house for your favorite bodyguard/door kicker/trigger puller/hatchet man?"

"I drew the line at including a casita," Mike called with a smile. Dom always lightened his mood, despite the seriousness of the business the former SEAL conducted for him. "Kids move into guest houses."

"And the hired help," Dominic said, joining him in the great room.

The tiredness Mike had valiantly ignored all afternoon hit him hard, but he didn't let it show. He wanted to get home, grab a beer, and sleep. Maybe that would kick whatever was dragging him down.

"Any word from my son?" Mike asked, to ease into the important conversation they had to have. The kid had gone to Dominic behind his back.

Dominic walked the huge room, checking the views out the back windows. "No, nothing since last time. Why, have you had a change of heart?"

"No. I don't want him operational."

"I get it, but it's not the worst idea in the world, him working with me. I could show him the ropes. If he's determined, he's likely to do it on his own. That could get… messy."

Mike waved him off. "It would never work, and you know it."

"Yeah. You're right. Too bad, though. I could use a protégé. Not getting any younger."

"Neither of us are. Which brings me to my next point."

"I didn't realize there was a formal agenda," Dom said with a chuckle. "Should I be taking notes?"

Mike ignored the banter. Dominic and his partner had provided security for Mike in Afghanistan years ago. They'd grown extremely close, as only people who risked their lives for each other did.

"Actually, before we get to that, how did it go with Mr. Corey

Langfore, movie producer extraordinaire?" Mike asked. "I didn't want Krissy to hear about any of the hard stuff."

Dominic laughed. "Guy wet his pants all over his fancy marble tile." He looked down at the expensive flooring below their feet and shrugged. "No offense."

"None taken. Did you deliver the message?"

"Of course, just like you asked," Dom said with a chuckle. "I told him not to move, cut off his stinky silk PJs, and gave him my crazy face." Dominic's face changed into the look of a wide-eyed madman. "Told him that the only thing holding me back from having fun with him was that I was afraid of what you'd do to me."

It was Mike's turn to chuckle. Dominic could easily slit Mike's throat, break his neck, or beat the life out of him. Mike had training—the CIA didn't send its people out into the world without the basics of how to take care of themselves. Mike had been in tough situations before and knew how to handle himself, but against Dominic, it would all be over in seconds—unless Dom wanted to make it last.

"Did you tell him?" Mike asked.

"Yep. I explained exactly what you had in mind if he ever crossed you again."

"Well done."

Mike moved to the front of the house. The high-priced windows kept the heat from entering. It could have been winter outside instead of the height of summer.

The sun slid behind the Vegas skyline. The lights of the casinos shone.

Dom joined him, standing on the right. "You want to talk about what's really going on?"

Mike stayed silent for several seconds. Without turning to look at the former SEAL, he finally spoke. "It looks like I'll have a trip back to the Sandbox in the next few days. I need backup. How would you feel about returning?"

"I live to serve," Dom said with a laugh. "It would be nice to get out of this desert heat and into... oh wait, the desert heat. But yeah, whatever. I'm down."

Mike gave it a few seconds for the man's naturally easygoing nature to catch up with the situation. "It might be dangerous. Check that. It will be dangerous."

"Like, 'Watch my back, the world is an uncertain place'? Or, 'Bring as much ammo as you can carry'?"

"Riskier than the first, probably not quite as bad as the second." Another pause while he ran through the likely scenarios. "But closer to the second."

The admission made the usually gung-ho Dominic pause. "Backup?" he asked, his tone finally serious.

"Not much. Maybe another person. I'm considering taking my son—his liability might not be so bad over there. I haven't decided yet. But we'll have a local we can trust as a one-man quick reaction force."

"A one-man QRF? That's new."

"Yes. Less than ideal, but it is what it is," Mike said, quoting one of Dom's favorite sayings.

"It is what it is."

They watched the sun sink lower by the second.

"Is that a yes?" Mike eventually asked.

"You really have to ask?"

"For this, yes."

"I'm all in. After that night…"

Mike remembered the dark night, the dirty streets of the Kabul neighborhood that were supposed to have been safe enough for his meet.

As he'd returned to the beat-up car for the ride back to the base, two men had been closing in on it, AKs up and ready to fire.

Dominic and his partner would have likely seen them in time to defend themselves, but Mike had risked his life to sneak up behind the attackers and kill them.

Plunging his small knife repeatedly into their necks from behind.

Then slitting both of their throats as they bled in the dirt.

His first kills.

"I owe you," Dom finished.

"No, you don't." Dom and his partner—since killed in a training accident—had saved his life at least once as well.

"Nice of you to say, but whatever. If you need me, I'm there. When are we on the move?"

"Monday morning, probably. Private jet straight there, a day or two on the ground, then home. More details to come."

"Copy that."

Mike considered for a moment, then pulled a sealed envelope from his sport coat pocket. A serious document he'd composed while sitting in his driveway with the air-conditioning blasting.

"Notes?" Dom asked.

"Yes." He passed the envelope over, *I.C.E.* printed on the front. "In case of emergency."

"A contingency?"

"Two of our former colleagues are dead." He told Dom about Rutherfield and Frandren. "What's coming is too big to not have a clear backup plan. Don't let this fall into anyone else's hands. Seriously—protect it with your life."

Dom held it reverently for a second, then nodded. "Can I at least fold it? Not all of us wear fancy sport coats."

Mike chuckled, grateful for the moment of levity. "Go ahead."

Dominic folded the envelope and shoved it into his back pocket.

"When should I open it?"

"You'll know."

Dom nodded and let it go.

With the important business concluded, Mike returned to Dom's meeting with the movie director in Los Angeles. "With Langfore, what did you decide on? For him to remember the repercussions for refusing me?"

"I broke a few of his toes. Took my time, made it last."

Mike nodded, pleased. "Perfect. Easy to hide, no visit to a doctor necessary."

"And painful as hell." Dom looked over. "Did Kristine suspect?"

"No, she bought that I was letting him off the hook."

"She's softer than I thought," Dom said. "I sense a streak in her—a killer instinct—but she's reluctant to tap into it. Holding herself back, maybe?"

"Yes. It's there, but I don't know what she's waiting for. I'll work on it. But LA—good job."

"Anything for you, boss."

"I might hold you to that. This mission is important."

"I'll be ready."

61

THE RECON

Saguaro Ranch Estates
Cave Creek, Arizona

Depending on traffic, the Phoenix metro area was about ninety minutes from the bar in Sands—and 30 degrees hotter.

What came next for Bone was going to suck.

But at least he had a mission, as strange and undefined as it was.

The digital thermometer on the dash of the hatchback said the early evening air outside was 115 degrees. A dry heat, people joked about the area—the same as in many parts of Iraq and Afghanistan where he'd spent time.

Dry or not, lying in the baking-hot desert watching some guy's house because Admiral Nalen thought he might get murdered would be unpleasant, but at least it would be dark soon. That would make the stakeout slightly easier.

And if Nalen was right, Bone would be there to save Donald Everett.

The admiral's term for Everett had been "the little weasel," though it had sounded more like he was repeating someone else's words than speaking from personal familiarity.

Why Everett had been selected as the tethered goat to lure the bad guy —or guys—Bone hadn't been told, which was annoying. Bone was supposed to be an anonymous, one-man personal protection detail, but he also had to get to the bottom of the problem.

If he caught or killed the people trying to murder Everett, would that be the end?

Maybe whoever was pulling Admiral Nalen's strings would understand what was going on if they had a culprit caught in the act.

Bone just had to stop the murder to solve the mystery.

He didn't believe for a second that it would be that simple.

Bone turned off the main road into a newer subdivision of expensive homes, which were packed much too closely together for his tastes. Single level, though, which meant that neighbors weren't looking down on each other's backyards. The houses were typical upscale Phoenix homes with stucco exteriors, tasteful shrubs and small cacti in the desert-landscape front yards, and block fences enclosing the backyards.

The sunset painted the sky as Bone slowly drove the winding roads of the neighborhood. No one was out; the pavement would be too hot to walk dogs until long after dark. This time of year in Phoenix was like winter in colder climates. People hibernated, watched television in their air-conditioned homes, or lounged in and around pools in backyards, especially after dark. Many of them—people who could afford houses like these—took extended summer vacations to cooler places like San Diego or Boulder. Those who couldn't go far escaped to Sands, Flagstaff, or other high-elevation small towns north of Phoenix for day trips, or at least enjoyed outdoor activities as early in the morning or as late at night as possible. When the temperature hit triple digits, it made sense to be indoors.

Bone resisted driving right up to Everett's home, located in a small, four-house cul-de-sac, but from the subdivision's winding road, it looked similar to many others. A flat roof in typical southwestern style. It was classy and well kept.

Because of its location in the subdivision, the house backed to a small desert preserve that locals used for hiking and biking when it was cooler.

Bone left the neighborhood behind and followed the main road to a five-car dirt parking area: the trailhead for the local nature preserve. Dust filled the air around the car as he parked.

Everett's house was about a mile away. This might be where an attacker would park and use the hiking trails to access the back of the house.

It didn't make sense to park here. Bone's car could scare away the culprit.

Bone backed out and drove a short way to a large shopping center anchored by a big-box hardware store. His hatchback blended in perfectly in the parking lot for the 24-hour urgent care center near the corner.

With a desert sun hat, durable but lightweight tan chinos, black trail running shoes, and a black long-sleeve shirt, he was ready. Bone slung a small pack with plenty of water and snacks—along with his new short-barrel M4, binoculars, and night vision goggles—on his back and walked across the parking lot.

Behind a large block wall on the side of the shopping area, another affluent subdivision would give him access to the desert trails that he could take to Everett's house.

The smell of burgers and fries beckoned from a fast-food place, but he kept walking. The less he appeared on surveillance footage, the better.

By morning, there might be a dead body he wouldn't want to be associated with.

62

THE PUTTS

The Cave Creek Sonoran Preserve
Behind the Saguaro Ranch Estates
Cave Creek, Arizona

In Arizona, while most houses had block walls surrounding their backyards, homes that backed to nature preserves, green spaces, or golf courses often had decorative black iron bars instead. They allowed the feel of an extended backyard.

It worked out for Bone. He rested prone under a stubby mesquite tree 50 yards from Everett's home, with a clear view of the entire backyard through the fence, along with the north side of the house and the entrance to the short cul-de-sac beyond the driveway.

He'd see anyone approaching by car or on foot through the neighborhood, and the only trail through this section of the nature preserve passed 10 feet in front of him.

The tree had kept the ground cooler than the open desert, making the evening more comfortable than Bone had thought it would be.

As the sun set and the sky darkened, lights came on in Everett's backyard, and he emerged from the house. Instead of a pool like most of the area's homes, his yard had an extensive putting green, with slopes, hills, and multiple holes.

Bone focused his binoculars on him as the man practiced putting, carefully lining up shot after shot.

Everett stood over a ball, slowly pulled back his putter, and swung.

The ball missed, 2 inches to the right of the hole.

The man's frustration was obvious. Everett hurried to the patio, took scissors from a table, and returned to the green to trim an errant blade of grass.

Bone was impressed—the grass was all natural. No easily maintained fake lawn for Everett.

He took his golf seriously.

Which meant that if a killer didn't appear tonight, Bone would follow Everett north to his exclusive golf club tomorrow to continue the role as the man's secret guardian angel.

Everett eventually picked up six balls from the putting green and placed them in a metal basket on the patio table. He lovingly wiped down the putter with a clean, white cloth before snapping a leather cover over the head of the club and taking it inside with him.

After locking the sliding glass door, he bent to slip a long, thick dowel in the door track as a backup, making the door impossible to slide open if the lock was breached. But he didn't draw any blinds.

None of the other homes backing to the preserve had their curtains or blinds closed, either, to not spoil the view. It made Bone's job easier—he had a clear line of sight to the entire back of Everett's house.

For a few minutes, the golfer disappeared into what Bone guessed was the garage. When he returned, he wore flip-flops instead of his golf shoes, and the putter was gone. He must have put everything in the car for tomorrow.

Everett kicked off the sandals, put his feet on a coffee table, and settled onto a leather sectional. He used an elaborate remote control to turn on a huge wall-mounted TV, but didn't change the channel. A golf tournament recap was on.

Bone barely needed the binoculars to watch the TV, but he used them to scan the street in front of the house and the neighbors' yards. He gave the desert around him one final sweep as the sky faded fully to black.

He kept the binoculars out but added the night vision goggles to his head for later.

He focused on Everett, watched the golf news that came on next, and scanned the area every few minutes.

No assaulters parachuted into the backyard, cut a small hole in the patio door, and released an odorless gas into the house.

No lone gunman slipped through the dark neighborhood, jimmied open a window, and smothered Everett before he could fight back.

Bone frowned. Was this a stupid, cover-your-ass mission to prove to a person in power that someone was looking out for poor-old-weasel Everett?

Or an essential operation to save a person who might be next on a hit list, and golf-obsessed Everett had been deemed a potentially expendable early warning signal?

None of it made much sense, but Bone didn't care. This was a lot better than sitting in the bar and sipping fake beer that would never get him drunk.

63

TWO OR THREE

The Cave Creek Sonoran Preserve
Cave Creek, Arizona

Patrick eased the motorcycle off the four-lane asphalt street onto the gravel of the small, deserted trailhead parking lot.

It wasn't a good night for what he had planned. Despite the abundant palo verde and mesquite trees, prickly bushes, and a few washes, the desert preserve was mostly flat. At 2:00 in the morning, no one should be out, but the heat made people crazy—at least in Las Vegas. Patrick figured those who enjoyed the outdoors in Phoenix were the same. A handful would be up at 3 or 4 in the morning to get in a hike or their daily run while the air was a "cool" 95 degrees, or walk the dog before the sun made the ground too hot for their paws.

The odds were slim of him encountering anyone, but in a moment of clarity, Patrick had to admit this wasn't the best idea.

He should wait until the morning. Everett would be at the golf course as usual. This week might be when he sliced the ball into the pine trees off the sixth hole—where Patrick could lie in wait and push him off the cliff.

A terrible, unfortunate "accident."

Not a home invasion gone wrong, which was tonight's less-than-brilliant plan.

It would be easy, though. Everett didn't seem the type to have a home alarm system. And if he did, how many people went to the trouble to arm them before going to bed? People felt safe in their sprawling homes in their fancy subdivisions.

Patrick turned off the bike, lowered the kickstand, and stepped off.

He'd stretch his legs.

There was no need to hike across the desert, smash a window to Everett's bedroom, and beat his head in with whatever small, blunt object was handy.

A clock radio, maybe.

Or a lamp.

But it would feel so good.

Patrick's time was running out. Saturday night's deadline loomed, a heavy presence in his mind.

If the golf course didn't work in the morning, he wouldn't have another chance.

He'd have to settle for two deaths instead of the three.

Two would be enough, right?

Patrick rolled his shoulders to loosen his back, trying hard to convince himself—but failing.

No, it had to be all three.

For his entire life, the three names had been lumped together.

Killing only two made him look incompetent, not like the determined, capable person he needed to prove he was.

Was getting caught killing the third target worth the risk, though?

No. Definitely not.

Then again, he wouldn't get caught, would he? Across the desert, over the wrought-iron fence, and into the house.

Patrick could wear the motorcycle helmet for the last part. It wouldn't matter whether there were security cameras or if a neighbor happened to look out and see him running away afterward. He'd be back at the bike and long gone before any police arrived.

Patrick had walked a few hundred yards into the desert before he realized what he was doing. Against his better instincts, he kept moving along the trail, pretending to himself he was still working out the kinks of the long ride from Las Vegas instead of succumbing to the overwhelming need he had to kill someone.

Tonight.

He couldn't wait until morning.

For now, he removed the helmet and breathed in the smell of the desert.

It was a good night for killing.

64

THE DESERT

The Cave Creek Sonoran Preserve
Behind the Saguaro Ranch Estates
Cave Creek, Arizona

Patrick took his time, partly to move as quietly as possible, but mostly to savor the delicious sense of anticipation building inside him.

The trail had led from the small parking area along the center of the long, narrow preserve, avoiding the subdivisions bordering the east and west.

After twenty minutes of careful walking, the trail bent toward the neighborhood to the west—Patrick's right.

The houses were dark inside, but each had an excessive amount of exterior lighting. Pools were lit up, decorative sconces threw weak light every few feet along the perimeter of the backyards, and brighter lights shone on the sides of several of the houses. Didn't people understand light pollution? What were they so afraid of—a random stranger approaching the house from the preserve, sneaking into their homes, and attacking them while they slept?

Patrick smiled at the irony. That's exactly what he intended to do.

It was time.

The motorcycle helmet in his hand was a comfortable presence that he had missed when he'd watched Frandren fly off his mountain bike and crash into the rock.

He shivered with delight.

What had started out as a necessary evil, a project to earn the recognition he deserved, had turned into something much more.

He had found his calling.

And wearing the helmet so far from the bike meant it was time to kill. He raised the helmet to his head, savoring the moment.

Bone sat up to give his body a break from lying prone in the cooling sand. The new night vision goggles didn't work as well here as he'd hoped. Too many people had lights outside their homes, which flared the optics, rendering them useless.

Still, they were helpful for scanning the desert once his eyes readjusted. He flipped them down over his eyes and turned north, toward the small parking lot.

Patrick froze with the helmet partly on his head. A faint sound had come from ahead on the left. It might have been an animal, but Patrick's instincts told him it was a person.

He squatted low and kept the helmet where it was—leaving his ears uncovered but ready to jam it down to hide his face if necessary.

Was there a kid sneaking beers in the middle of a Friday night, away from unsuspecting parents but close enough to home to be in bed by dawn?

Or could there be a stargazer? A nighttime hiker?

It didn't matter. Someone was out there, close to Everett's house. It would be impossible to sneak in and bludgeon Everett to death.

Patrick fought with himself, struggling between his need to kill and the danger of being seen or caught.

He had to wait until the golf course.

He could last a few more hours.

Couldn't he?

Or…

Was it better to eliminate whoever was nearby in the desert, then slip into Everett's house and kill him, too?

Patrick let the energy of the idea flood his system before he reluctantly forced self-preservation to take over.

He had to return to the bike, ride north to the golf course, and get into position.

A person dead in the desert outside the target's house would arouse too much suspicion.

And the extra kill would ruin the entire plan. Patrick wouldn't be seen as a careful, skilled operator, but as a psychopath.

He removed the helmet, turned, and headed back to the motorcycle, more slowly, carefully, and quietly than he'd approached.

Better safe than sorry—and caught.

He'd get his third kill in less than six hours, anyway.

65

THE DATA

Wyatt hadn't slept in what felt like years. His eyes burned, his stomach churned, and he stank of body odor and desperation.

The data refused to come together.

He kept going around in circles.

Mike Salestri. Potential target of a plot to kill former CIA officers? Or the person responsible for the deaths of Rutherfield and Frandren?

Was Salestri running a terrorist organization from the basement of a Las Vegas casino? Or merely playing the role of a fixer for hire, making small-time deals behind the scenes?

A truck bomb had exploded in Egypt nine months before. Six months ago, a shopping mall in Turkey had been bombed. And an airport on a Spanish island had been decimated by bombs three months ago.

Was another attack coming any day?

Was Salestri somehow involved, or were the extremist groups who had claimed credit for each bombing really to blame?

Wyatt didn't have the data to make informed decisions—or even guesses.

He'd come so far, gathered so much intel, but was still stuck.

Marcus had left the room at some point. Wyatt had a vague memory of him mentioning home, or sleep, or food. Something like that—he hadn't been paying much attention.

All that Wyatt had was the mind map, a growing stack of empty energy drink cans, and brain fog.

The sticky notes, lines, circles, and squares on his mind map overwhelmed him. He had an almost overpowering desire to rip the papers to shreds.

He grunted in frustration, which turned to a gasp of surprise followed by a groan of embarrassment when Gregory cleared his throat from near the door.

"Sorry," Gregory said. "I thought you heard me come in."

Wyatt shook his head, too tired and frustrated to do more.

"When was the last time you slept?" Gregory asked.

"Um…" The big white analog clock on the wall was no help. It could be morning or evening, and Wyatt couldn't guess what day it was.

"I know exactly what it's like to get caught up in the data," Gregory said, his voice kind and more than a little concerned. "And what happens when the flow stops. It's time for a reboot. Take a nap. Eat. Shower. You can do all that here if you don't want to go home. But getting away from this room will help. Your mind will continue to work while you recharge, and you'll come back fresh."

"But the next bomb attack could come any day. And Everett and Salestri—"

"Are handled for now. A few hours off will only help your focus. Go. It's an order."

The fight left Wyatt in a rush. Gregory had barely finished speaking when Wyatt sank to the floor and crawled under the table. "Maybe just a short nap," he mumbled as he closed his eyes, and then he was out.

PART 6

SATURDAY

66

THE CLUB

Forest Cliffs Golf Club
East of Sedona, Arizona

Bone pulled into the golf course a few minutes behind Everett, hoping the guy wouldn't get ambushed on the way to the clubhouse. It was a risk Bone had to take—it would have been too obvious to tail him from Phoenix and follow him all the way in.

The grounds were exquisite—much nicer than the municipal courses Bone and his Team buddies had hacked their way around while stationed in San Diego.

He figured Everett was safe on his own for a short time. After all, at a fancy place like this, he'd be dropping his clubs off and having his car valet parked. How much trouble could he get into?

No one was likely to kill him in the busy parking lot or clubhouse, "accidentally" or otherwise.

Bone's night in the desert on guard duty has passed without incident. No ninjas had attacked, the Russians hadn't blown up the house with a missile shot from a drone, and the mailman hadn't delivered an early-morning pipe bomb. Bone fought to stay awake until dawn, and watched Everett try on three different golf outfits before he made himself a sensible breakfast and left the house.

Bone had run back to his car and hightailed it to the interstate, where he'd quickly caught up to Everett, who drove 5 miles per hour over the speed limit in the right lane.

Now, Bone passed the front of the clubhouse—an impressive structure. There was an extensive veranda overlooking the course, with wicker chairs and low tables for drinks before or after golf, or for the non-golfing spouses to relax and enjoy the views of the red cliffs of Sedona to the west.

The employee parking lot was hidden around back, and Bone's hatchback fit in perfectly. After parking, he changed clothes and slipped into the gray generic coveralls from one of his bags.

With the baggy work clothes hiding khaki chinos and a black polo shirt, he was ready. The high-end black trail running shoes looked slightly out of place for both a worker and a golfer, but if people noticed his shoes, he'd deal with it.

The beauty of the tall trees scattered around the parking area—ponderosa pine, Arizona pine, and Douglas fir—competed with the stunning green of the fairways and the red dirt common to the area.

Surprisingly, there were only two groups of homes near the course, both near the clubhouse. One had a few dozen villas while the other was a matching pair of long two-story buildings—high-end condos. The rest of the golf course appeared mercifully free of mini mansions backing to the fairways, a rarity these days when everyone seemed to dream of having a home on the golf course. The wildness and lack of development was likely part of the course's appeal for the players.

The sun had warmth, but this early in the morning, the high desert was still pleasantly cool. It was going to be another spectacular day.

Bone walked at the medium pace of a dedicated worker—a man putting in his hours. He avoided checking out the view, as if he'd seen it all before and the beauty had grown mundane; it was just another day at the office.

Although the course was far fancier than any Bone had played, golf courses were golf courses. There would be a double row of electric golf carts lined up, facing out, ready for the valet attendants to attach the bags to the back with wide belts to keep them from jostling as the players drove like maniacs around the course. Something about a little electric cart brought out the speed demon in everyone.

The keys were always left in the carts. They were ready to go. All someone had to do was walk up and drive one away.

Bone loitered at the back of the line of carts, bent forward inspecting a tire, as Everett and three other men checked their bags and drove their two carts to the first tee.

Bone sauntered forward, kicking a tire here and there, until he reached the front of the two rows.

A glance confirmed that while there were people around, no one was paying attention to him. He was just another worker in the coveralls.

Bone slid into the driver's seat, turned the key to the ON position, and pressed the accelerator. With a lurch common to the carts, he was off.

He skirted the first tee box, nodding to four older men waiting for the players on the fairway in front of them.

Everett and his group would follow these guys.

Bone's plan was to stay ahead of Everett's group, checking sand traps and the greens, moving around the course as needed to hide in plain sight. There was a minor risk the club already had a worker like him doing the same job, but Bone bet the place was fancy enough to keep the on-course help to a minimum, especially in the morning. He should be fine. If questioned, he had a cover story ready, along with the names of the big bosses of the course uncovered during his research the day before; he'd name-drop and dare another worker to make a call questioning Bone's right to be there.

And if it all went to hell, he could strip off the coveralls and be a golfer who had forgotten his lucky club the day before and had come back to look for it this morning.

Easy.

Bone wasn't sure exactly how he could stop someone from murdering Everett without being close enough to protect him. But aside from clubbing the man to death or drowning Everett in the water hazard, how many ways—and places—were there to kill a person on a golf course?

67

THE NEED

Forest Cliffs Golf Club
East of Sedona, Arizona

Bone identified the thick woods and the secluded location of hole 6 as perfect for an ambush—or a murder. There weren't any other places on the course as private. If a player went into the trees to the right of the green, he'd be out of sight of his friends.

He skirted the right side of the fairway, just before the green for hole 5, as Everett and his companions walked to the fifth hole's tee box a few hundred yards behind him.

Bone left the cart out of the way and behind a hill near the fifth hole's putting green.

No one paid attention to him.

He hustled forward, balancing urgency with his desire to not give himself away as anyone other than a busy groundskeeper.

Bone slipped inside the trees behind a low rise to the far right of the course, near a cliff. The woods stretched off in front of him, dim and moody.

He let his eyes adjust to the shade of the tall pines and walked along the cliff edge, going from tree to tree, keeping them in between him and the fairway, moving like the ghost he had been back in the day.

The odds were slim that anyone would be brave or crazy enough to use the woods as a hiding place from which to ambush Everett, but two men were already dead.

If Bone had to kill Everett on the golf course, this was where he'd do it. A suppressed rifle shot from within the woods and a rappel over the cliff for the escape would be easy to set up. The murder wouldn't look accidental, but after the first two deaths, maybe the assailant didn't plan on being subtle.

Once again, Patrick lay prone in the cool red dirt of the shallow ravine that ran parallel to the cliff about 10 feet to his left. His motorcycle helmet was hot, but he didn't remove it. He was well hidden, but he had no reason to be here. If anyone happened to come upon him, Patrick had to remain anonymous. Let them describe his body—as long as they didn't see his face, he was fine.

Besides, he liked the helmet. It made him feel powerful. Invincible.

Deadly.

As he waited, he was forced to reconsider his choices. Pushing Everett off the cliff while the man searched for his errant tee shot appealed to Patrick's sense of style.

But that mattered less today. The desire inside of him had grown. Since late last night, outside Everett's house, it had become a need so strong he could taste it. It had a pleasant spice on his tongue, like the aftermath of eating a hot pepper.

He had to kill again.

Everett's death would be so much better if it looked like an accident— for Patrick's personal sense of accomplishment and to keep the authorities at bay. Accidents happened all the time and weren't given much thought.

Murders, on the other hand, were investigated.

And if someone connected Everett's death to those of Rutherfield and Frandren, that could be bad.

But given half the chance, Patrick would kill Everett any way necessary.

From the ravine, he had a narrow view through the trees to the golf course's hole 6 tee box. Barely moving, he brought his focus back to the moment and checked his watch, hidden under the long sleeve of his black shirt. If the group had started on time, Everett and his friends should soon park their stupid golf carts where he could see…

They arrived right on time.

Patrick froze, barely blinking, his entire being focused on Everett. He willed him to choose the longer club and try to hit the ball onto the green instead of using a shorter club—the iron—as he had last week.

The four men looked happy and relaxed, though Everett had a more determined, focused look as he moved to the back of his cart and the golf bag attached there.

This had to be the day.

Patrick held his breath, hoping.

68

THE TREES

Hole 6
Forest Cliffs Golf Club
East of Sedona, Arizona

Everett was in the zone and having a great round. The new club—and the secret lessons, he supposed, though he hated to admit it—had paid off. Golf was all he'd ever cared about. And this summer, at last, it looked like things were coming together.

He'd gotten lucky on the previous hole—number 5—sinking a 20-yard putt for par.

Hole 6 had a narrow fairway lined with trees, but it was shorter. He had a chance to drive the green and maybe get a birdie—one under par.

If he didn't slice.

He slid the new club from his bag and spoke before he could talk himself out of what was probably a stupid idea. "Want to make it interesting?" Everett asked the guys.

"We're just in this for the fun," Clyde said with a chuckle, shaking his head.

"Yeah, come on," Roy said. "Just hit it. We're all impressed with how you're playing. It's not a competition."

It was easy for them to be so casual. They didn't have to watch their budgets like Everett did. They probably had millions in investments. His government pension kept him comfortable, and the little extra on the side that he'd scammed along the way made his current lifestyle possible, but it was a stretch.

"I tell you what," Dave said. It wasn't even 9 in the morning and he was already on his third beer. "I'm happy to make it interesting—just for this hole. We know it's your favorite," he joked. "I bet you one thousand dollars you slice it into the woods and you lose your ball. But we're checking your pockets so you can't cheat, and I saw you write that big 'E' on the ball this morning, so unless you find another ball you've lost there—"

"One of the many!" Roy said, jumping in. "Watch out, Dave, he might get lucky and come back with one from a few weeks ago!"

"I'm willing to risk it. So what do you say?"

Everett didn't have a spare thousand to lose. His big mouth had gotten him into trouble once again. All he'd really wanted was to have the guys refuse to take his bet because he was on fire. He didn't want to risk serious money, but he couldn't back down now. Besides, the slice was gone. All he had to do was swing easy and collect a thousand dollars. Even if he sliced it, the way Dave had called the bet, as long as he found the ball and hacked it out of the rough, no matter how many strokes it took, he'd have a grand.

"You're on."

He waited his turn—he'd go third this hole.

Dave swung his long iron and connected well. His ball flew straight down the middle of the fairway, as usual. Not as far as he could have hit with a driver, but a nice, safe play.

Clyde did the same. His ball rolled to a stop about 10 yards short of Dave's.

"You've got this," Clyde whispered as Everett stepped forward. "Just don't try to kill it."

Everett planted the tee in the ground, set the ball on top, and stepped back. He relaxed and pictured sweeping the grass with the overside club head, letting the club do the work.

His practice swing was perfect, exactly as the golf pro had worked with him on.

Everett stepped closer to the ball, settled the club head on the ground behind it, loosened his shoulders, and relaxed. He had this.

He drew the club back slowly, coiling, and swung with all his might.

The head of the club connected with the ball, which sailed straight, straight… and veered sharply right, slicing at the woods.

It could still hit a tree and bounce into the fairway…

The ball sailed into the trees, crashing against at least one branch and disappearing from view.

There was only a second of silence before the guys cracked up. Dave laughed so hard he could barely breathe.

Worse, Clyde chuckled and shook his head, looking at Everett with a pity that hurt almost as much as the shock of watching his ball vanish into the woods. "You'll find it. It couldn't have gone far."

Roy laughed so hard he had tears in his eyes. "That baby is gone, gone, gone. Good luck finding it in that rough. Or over the cliff! Now, stand back. Let me show you how it's done."

As Everett stumbled out of the way, Roy teed up. After one relaxed practice swing, Roy stepped forward, wound up, and smacked the ball straight down the fairway. It bounced once, and again, and rolled to a stop just off the green.

They headed back to the carts. "You need help finding your ball?" Dave asked Everett with a shit-eating grin.

"No. I saw exactly where it went," Everett lied with false bravado. "No problem. Don't count your money yet."

He headed back to the cart, shoved the driver into his bag, and sat on the bench seat next to Clyde while suppressing a dejected sigh.

"I'll drop you off to look for the ball," Clyde said. "You'll find it. It can't have gotten too far. If you can't find it right away, yell and we'll come help you."

Everett nodded with a tight smile while he prayed the ball hadn't careened through the trees and over the edge of the cliff that hugged the course along this hole.

69

HOLE 6

Hole 6
Forest Cliffs Golf Club
East of Sedona, Arizona

The shade under the canopy of the pine trees was a welcome respite from the warming day, especially with Bone's coveralls adding a second—hot —layer over the chinos and polo shirt. But the gray one-piece had been an excellent choice; he didn't exactly blend in, but at least he didn't stand out too much.

He hid behind a tree, resisting the temptation to move closer to Everett, who was oblivious to the world. Everett's sole focus was on the ground in front of him as he swept his foot back and forth. The golf shoes knocked down the dry grass and moved the layer of pine needles in what so far had been a futile attempt to find his ball. Bone had heard it crash into the woods but had been too far away to see where it came to rest before moving up to be near the spot Everett would investigate.

Bone's senses tingled.

If the killer was nearby, this could be it.

Everett was separated from his group. The shade made it hard to see until one's eyes adjusted. It would take patience to ambush him on the course, but if Admiral Nalen had discovered the man golfed here every Saturday in the summer, an enemy could, too. Sooner or later, given the narrow fairway, Everett might slice into these woods. And with the cliff nearby…

Bone chuckled silently. The idea was crazy. Was he seriously entertaining the extremely unlikely chance someone would lie in wait week after week, hoping for a shot at a hack golfer?

No one was that patient—or desperate.

Bone would chalk up today to another part of the training process, a chance to stalk prey in the woods and reclaim his old skills. No one was going to kill Everett. Nalen—and the former CIA intelligence analyst he had mentioned—were grasping at straws. The two previous deaths were a coincidence. Bone was wasting his time. In a few days, when nothing happened, he'd drive to Las Vegas to check out the other potential target—Mike Salestri, who rarely left his resort and casino so was better protected.

Still, it was a nice day. Being on a fruitless mission based on someone's paranoia beat counting the hours until the bar opened and he could hang out with Steph while she worked.

Everett moved toward the cliff. Some of the rock in this area was brittle. The ledge could give way and collapse if he wasn't careful.

He'd lost more than one ball over this edge, and the damn things were expensive. He wasn't poor by any measure, but the idea of whacking six dollars over a 50-foot cliff once a week pissed him off. And that was assuming he only lost one ball per round.

The laughter from the guys when his ball sailed into the trees…

The penalty stroke he'd have to add if he couldn't find it…

The thousand dollars it looked like he owed Dave…

He hated everything about this miserable game.

He peered over the edge. Fifty feet below and twenty feet out from the base of the cliff, a ball rested between two small boulders. Was it his or another poor sucker's?

It didn't matter. The cliff was too steep to climb, not even to save a thousand dollars on the bet.

He looked left and right, wondering about an easier way down.

Next summer, he'd talk to the guys about joining a different club, one with wider fairways, fewer trees, and certainly no damn cliffs.

Patrick pressed himself closer to a tree. Fifteen feet away, Everett stood by the edge of the cliff, probably trying to figure out a way down to pick up a ball that wasn't his.

This was it.

Patrick had already snagged the ball with the big printed "E" on it, which would make a great souvenir—and proof, since he wasn't going to risk running along the cliff, climbing down the boulders farther south, and running back to take close-up pictures of the guy's broken body on the rocks, no matter how cool it would be to have those shots.

He would have to be content with just one or two images from the top of the cliff. If the dude's head got twisted around like Frandren's had, it would be perfect for his growing collection.

If not, at least looking down from way above at a dead man on the rocks below would make a great picture.

Patrick savored the now-familiar feeling sweeping through him. He had the power of life and death. His pulse quickened. Behind the motorcycle helmet, he was grinning like a madman.

Bone caught movement out of the corner of his eye. A figure dressed in a black shirt, wearing a motorcycle helmet of all things, emerged from behind a tree and ran straight toward Everett, still leaning over the cliff edge to look for his ball.

Bone reacted instantly. He sprinted, his powerful legs propelling him forward.

The other man had a head start.

Could Bone make it in time?

He was a long-distance runner, not a sprinter. People who ran ultramarathons—any distance over 26 miles—were often slow but persistent. Their motto was relentless forward progress. But he ran miles and miles every day. He could push when needed.

It was going to be close.

"Hey!" Bone called. Better to give himself away and save Everett than have the man pushed over the edge if Bone didn't make it in time.

The guy in the helmet turned his head enough to note Bone—but didn't slow. He was committed.

Everett turned to look at Bone instead of the threat coming from the other direction.

Bone was a second too late. The motorcycle guy shoved Everett as the golfer stared wide-eyed at Bone.

A second later, Bone slammed into the helmeted man, taking him down.

Behind them, Everett cried out as he crashed to the ground. "Help!" he yelled at the top of his lungs.

Bone slammed his fist into the attacker's stomach. A surprised grunt of pain came from the tango, muffled by the motorcycle helmet.

As Bone pressed the attack, pebbles and rocks skittered behind them.

"No!" Everett cried. He was going over the edge, clawing for a handhold.

Bone could capture the man in the motorcycle gear or save Everett, but not both.

Bone rolled off the biker, desperate to protect Everett.

If the man in the helmet had attacked, Bone would have defended himself and hoped for the best with Everett. But the man in black jumped to his feet and ran into the woods, parallel to the cliff.

Bone had no time to worry about him.

He had to save Everett—if he hadn't already fallen to his death.

70

THE WEASEL

Hole 6
Forest Cliffs Golf Club
East of Sedona, Arizona

Everett's fingers slipped on the rock he clung to, a solid chunk that hadn't given way.

He scrambled for purchase with his feet on the vertical rock face.

Someone had tried to kill him.

He was going to die.

After all he'd been through in Afghanistan, Iraq, and Syria, the greedy, desperate, and dangerous men he'd cajoled into spying for America, he was going to fall to his death off a golf course's cliff.

A groundskeeper had distracted him from whoever had shoved him toward the edge of the cliff. They must be working together.

Would Dave be so petty over not wanting to lose a thousand dollars?

Or had it been a joke gone wrong? Someone meant to scare him but pushed too hard, throwing him off-balance more than intended?

Trying to find a foothold on the rocks shifted his weight. The fingers of his left hand—in the golf glove—slipped.

He lost his grip.

This was the end.

Bone slid along the edge of the cliff face-first, like a baseball player stealing home plate in a playoff game. He extended his hand and slammed his toes into the ground, praying for traction as his right hand snagged Everett's wrist.

The man's weight nearly pulled Bone's arm out of the socket. He was yanked forward, closer to the edge.

Bone's left arm frantically clawed at the rocks, desperate for a handhold.

His feet stopped his momentum. Bone's stomach stretched over the cliff's edge. Staring up at him, Everett's eyes were wide. "Please don't kill me!"

Bone held firm as the man dangled in midair. "I'm saving you, not killing you!"

The shocked look made it plain Everett didn't believe him.

"Yes, someone's trying to kill you. A guy just ran south—he's the one who pushed you."

Inch by inch, Bone muscled his body backward, pulling the dead weight of the golfer. After several excruciating seconds, Everett found footholds and helped. A moment later, they both lay on the edge of the cliff, panting with exertion and adrenaline.

"Finish your round of golf, Everett," Bone said as he caught his breath. "He won't try again here, and probably not anywhere now that you know he's after you. Lock yourself in your house for a few weeks until this thing blows over."

Bone had done what he could. He pushed himself up—he had to catch the motorcycle rider.

"Is this some kind of joke?" Everett demanded as he sat up. "Hey, I'm talking to you. What's going on?"

Bone couldn't explain more of the situation without breaking Admiral Nalen's rules. His paper-thin excuse for being on the golf course wouldn't stand up to scrutiny. He'd be held for questioning at least and possibly accused of attempted murder.

Bone had to run, even if it confused the situation or made him look guilty—but he didn't care. He now had solid intel. The well-built man in the motorcycle helmet had clearly tried to kill Everett.

Bone ran south along the cliff. The assailant had a good head start, but Bone would catch him and get to the bottom of this.

"Help!" Everett called from behind him. "Help! Some guy pushed me off the cliff!"

Bone dashed between trees. Nalen had been right. The man was a weasel.

Everett staggered to his feet as the groundskeeper disappeared into the woods.

Dave yelled from his left. "Everett? Where are you? What's going on?"

For a moment, Everett was touched by the genuine concern in his friend's voice.

Until he realized that none of them would believe his story. It was preposterous. Some golf course employee pushes him off the edge of the cliff, but saves him the instant he's falling? While claiming someone else had tried to kill him?

Then the guy disappears into the woods?

Everett had no proof except for the scrapes on his hands and forearms from the rocks, torn knees on his favorite golf pants, and scuffed shoes.

He'd almost died, the damn slice was back, he had lost his ball, and he was out a thousand dollars.

He was giving up this stupid game.

His neighbor played pickleball—maybe he'd give that a try.

71

THE COINCIDENCE

Forest Service Road 26
East of Sedona, Arizona

Patrick's heart pounded harder than ever as he pushed the motorcycle onto the dirt back road. Running all the way from the golf course in the helmet hadn't been fun, but he hadn't dared remove it. The man he had fought in the woods could be right behind him.

He started the bike and gunned it, fishtailing on the red dirt. Pushing the bike as hard as he could without losing control around the curves, he considered his options.

Cellular service on the golf course was hit or miss near hole 6, so reaching 911 from there wasn't a sure thing.

As Patrick skidded around a corner, almost dumping the bike, he eased off a touch. It would take time for the situation back there to get sorted out.

Had Everett plummeted to his death? Or had the man who'd suddenly appeared caught him before he fell?

That man—he'd been a golf course worker. Where the hell had he come from?

One minute, Patrick would have sworn there was no one else in the woods except for him and Everett. The next, the guy had just... appeared, like he'd teleported there. And the way he moved—so fast and smooth. Like a ninja or something.

Patrick's stomach throbbed with pain. He'd be sore for days. The ninja packed a serious punch. The guy was someone who could move silently through the woods, spring into action instantly, run like the wind, tackle like an all-star linebacker, and punch like a champion boxer.

Had Everett heard the news about Rutherfield and Frandren and hired a bodyguard? Or was it a pesky golf course groundskeeper who just happened to be in the right place at the right time?

Patrick didn't believe in coincidences.

Something was off.

And his gut told him Everett was still alive.

He shivered at the implications.

His whole plan might be going up in flames.

The ninja had seen the motorcycle helmet, and the sound of the bike could have carried. Anyone coming after him would be on the lookout for a motorcycle.

Patrick could be seconds away from being caught.

He slowed at the bump where the forest road transitioned to pavement, then accelerated slowly to the 35 mph speed limit of the town road as he passed upscale houses.

The freeway onramp was a mile ahead. He could turn north toward Flagstaff, then west on I-40—but that was more than 40 miles away.

To the south, Phoenix was a ninety-minute ride—or 15 miles to a major exit of the interstate with gas stations and fast-food restaurants.

On the other hand, there was an interstate exit only 2 miles south without any facilities. It led to a winding, dusty back road. It would be a slow ride, but eventually, he'd be in Sedona, which would lead to a scenic drive to Jerome, Prescott, and, if he wanted to be extra careful, all the way down to Quartzsite before turning north to Lake Havasu City and eventually home.

Avoiding the direct, obvious route to Vegas would add hours to his trip. But for much of the journey, from at least Sedona to Prescott, he could tuck in with other motorcycle riders—either a single or a group—and hide in plain sight.

He swung onto the interstate southbound and forced himself to keep from rocketing forward. Blending in right now was essential. Only a few minutes had passed. Even if Everett or the ninja had reported an attempted murder by someone wearing a motorcycle helmet, there was no reason to suspect him. He was a tourist on vacation from Nevada, exploring the beautiful high desert scenery of the area. If he didn't panic, he'd be fine.

The thought brought a smile to his face behind the helmet. Although not killing Everett was frustrating, fending off the ninja and escaping had been strangely fun.

A new challenge.

A rush.

After 2 miles, he signaled and slowed, pulling off the interstate onto the lonely exit. It was less than a mile on a poorly maintained asphalt road before it changed to the red dirt common to the area. He'd made it. No one would be looking for him here.

Patrick relaxed into the ride. He had a lot of hours to think about the situation, its ramifications, and how to spin the fact that he'd failed to kill the final person on his list.

72

THE BET

Forest Cliffs Golf Club
East of Sedona, Arizona

The sound of the motorcycle faded long before Bone could find a way to climb down the rocks to the dirt road that ran near the golf course.

He'd lost his only lead.

By now, Everett's friends would have heard the whole story—and might have called the police.

It was time to exfil.

Bone stripped off the gray coveralls to reveal the khaki chinos and black polo shirt underneath. He put on a black ball cap from his pocket, changing his appearance. There was no hiding his long face, overgrown beard, and dark eyes, but anyone on the hunt for a golf course groundskeeper would ignore him.

Everett had looked right at him, but the guy had been dangling above a 50-foot drop to rocks below. Would he describe Bone's face, or tell the authorities that a groundskeeper had pushed him over the edge of the cliff only to save him seconds later?

Bone had to count on the description focusing on the outfit.

He stuffed the coveralls just below the cliff face in a long horizontal crack hidden from above.

Now, risk walking all the way back to the clubhouse and his car along the cart path, like a golfer looking for a lost club, or slip back through the woods to the golf cart he'd left near the hole 5 green farther north?

It was a tough call, but he felt more comfortable in the woods. If seen, he'd be in trouble, but a lone golfer walking back to the clubhouse would stick out more.

Everett's CIA training finally kicked in.

He had been targeted.

Which was more likely—that someone had attacked a random golfer —or a former CIA case officer?

Both were far-fetched, but the guy who had saved him—after pushing him?—had said that someone was trying to kill him.

"What happened?" Dave said, panting as he rushed into the woods.

"I lost my ball," Everett said. The old habit of lying convincingly came back easily. He walked toward the fairway with Dave. "I thought it went over the edge of the cliff. When I looked down, the ground crumbled, and I fell. I… I saved myself at the last second."

Dave looked like he wasn't sure whether to believe him or not, but Everett was in no mood to answer questions. He swallowed his pride.

There was something happening that was much more important than a lost golf ball.

"Just as you predicted," Everett added with a reasonably sincere laugh. Dave would take any residual fear or deceit in his voice as embarrassment and regret. "I owe you a grand."

The CIA had taught him that the best defense was often a good offense. Don't leave time for people to think about your words and ask questions. Control the conversation. So this time, the offer of a wager was a calculated move. "Double or nothing I can still get… bogey." He had to be realistic. Par was out of the question. Bogey would take a minor miracle—but anything to move on, finish this round, and get home where he could lock the door, and try to figure out what the hell was going on.

"Double or nothing? You sure?" As they emerged onto the fairway, Clyde and Roy had pulled the carts nearby and sat with knowing smiles on their faces. It was obvious Everett had lost his ball.

Dave still looked like he wanted to question Everett's story, but his greed won. "You're on," he said. "This I gotta see."

After several minutes of moving carefully through the woods, Bone emerged near the cart he'd left behind, hopped in, and drove toward the clubhouse.

There were no police cars or commotion.

Only the distant sound of a few cheers and one loud curse from behind him on the sixth hole.

He parked the cart near the side entrance to the clubhouse, hopped out, and walked away, just another young, rich golfer.

The motorcycle rider had a big head start, but there were only two directions he could go—north to Flagstaff, which led toward California or New Mexico—or south to Phoenix, Tucson, and eventually Mexico.

Bone drove out of the parking lot and through the small town beyond the course.

If he'd had a way to call Admiral Nalen, maybe he could have had access to satellite imagery of the roads, or put out an All-Points Bulletin with the highway patrol and local police.

But Everett was a retired CIA case officer long out of the business, and Bone had nothing to go on aside from someone trying to kill the guy—and no way to contact Nalen, anyway.

Bone was on his own.

He could no longer use Everett as a tethered goat to catch the predator.

There was only one move left. Bone had to stake out—and try to protect—Mike Salestri, who according to Nalen may or may not be up to something no good himself.

He might even be the person responsible for the first two murders, and the latest one Bone had just thwarted.

Bone turned onto the interstate heading north, his eyes searching for a motorcycle rider with a shiny black helmet. It was a long shot, but miracles happened. And already, he'd had better luck on this operation than his last one.

He pushed the little car, settling on 10 miles per hour over the speed limit. Bone had a pistol under his shirt and multiple weapons locked in the trunk area of the hatchback. A speeding ticket would be fine, as long as he and the car weren't searched, but avoiding a traffic stop would be best.

The guy on the motorcycle wouldn't want to attract police attention by going too fast, either.

Bone would push on and hope for the best.

He smiled as he drove. The day was sunny, he was on an operation, and he'd already saved one life. Things were looking up.

And his next stop: Vegas, baby.

73

THE RED ROCKS

The Red Rocks Grille
Sedona, Arizona

The breakfast and lunch place had a long row of motorcycles parked along the side—at least thirty. Patrick pulled around and slotted his in at the far end, kicked the stand down, and took stock.

The escape from the golf course had gone as planned, aside from the dusty, potholed dirt road, which had taken longer to travel than he'd thought.

If he continued with his original plan, he'd be late for work tonight, which would prompt uncomfortable questions and put him in a bind.

He had to risk a more direct route.

The restaurant had a small take-out area at the front, like a general store, with fresh, pre-made sandwiches and bottled drinks for patrons who didn't want to wait around for a table. It wasn't unusual for bikers on a quick stop to not remove their helmets, so Patrick flipped up the tinted visor, made his selection, and used the restroom before walking back to the side parking lot. The snack went into his tail bag for later.

He scoped out the scene, biding his time.

A few solo motorcyclists had pulled in as he shopped, backing into the line of bikes next to him. Other riders up and down the row gathered to chat, or leaned against the shady side of the building, eating, drinking, or stretching their muscles. Toward the front of the line of bikes, a group of four—two couples—stood with helmets in hand, preparing to leave. One of the men pointed north, likely explaining their route to the others.

Patrick ambled over, like he didn't have a care in the world, and nodded to them as he stopped. "Nice bike!" he said. He asked a question about the model. The second man answered with a brief explanation.

"Thanks—have a great ride," Patrick said, preparing to turn away.

"You too," the man said as he turned back to his group.

"Say," Patrick said as if he'd just had the thought. "You guys heading toward Flagstaff by any chance? Is the highway worth taking, or should I go back to I-17?"

The group was happy to tell Patrick about the exciting highway, from the switchbacks to the views, and encouraged him to stick with the scenic route.

"Thanks, that's just what I was looking for. I might tuck in behind you, if you don't mind? It would be nice to not have to fight with the cars for an hour or two."

"You're more than welcome," the first man said, who seemed to be the leader of the group. "Safety in numbers."

"Amen," Patrick said.

"But once we get to Flagstaff, we're high-tailing it to Kingman, then Laughlin. We'll probably leave you in the dust."

Patrick laughed and waved. "No problem. Drop me anytime."

If anyone was on the lookout for a motorcycle, they might focus on solo riders, not a group. These chumps were Patrick's ticket out of here. He was going to stick to them like glue.

And just that simply, he had a disguise. He was home free and would make it back in time to go to work.

Exhausted and frustrated, but unrecognized and free.

74

THE PIÑATA

Henderson, Nevada

Mike groaned and forced his eyes open against the glare of the sun shining through the bedroom windows.

He was sprawled diagonally across the king-size bed, lying on his back.

It felt like he'd gotten hit by a truck, or like kids had taken turns pretending he was a giant piñata.

It was after 10. He'd slept thirteen hours and still felt like shit.

Dragging himself out of bed, he stumbled through brushing his teeth. He skipped the robe hanging on a hook in the bathroom and walked in his boxer briefs and T-shirt to the kitchen. He needed coffee.

After breakfast, he was more tired than when he woke up.

Sardar hadn't messaged him on the phone. There was nothing Mike could do for the operation in Afghanistan now.

And he wasn't due at the casino until this afternoon to prep for the weekly dinner.

He hated the idea, but he needed to get checked out by his doctor.

There was too much at stake to get a cold or the flu right now.

He made a call and got an emergency appointment with Doctor Tracey, who he'd saved from a bad situation years before.

Mike would get the full VIP treatment. Doc, like half of Las Vegas, owed him. He would come into his office on a Saturday to give Mike an IV to rehydrate him, or some antibiotics. Maybe a shot.

Whatever he needed to be good to go for tonight's dinner and Monday's flight to Afghanistan.

75

VEGAS

By the time Bone arrived in Las Vegas, the elation of being on a mission had faded.

Exhaustion had taken its place.

He desperately needed a nap, but there was work to do. Whoever had tried to kill Everett on the golf course wouldn't try for Everett again right away, since the man was now on high alert. And the attacker would be stupid to drive straight to Las Vegas and go after Mike Salestri at the casino, but it couldn't be ruled out. The motorcycle rider had the patience to lie in wait and ambush Everett on the golf course—a long shot. He might go to the other extreme and rush to Salestri's workplace and strangle him to death in an office or the bathroom.

In the car on level B3, Bone quickly changed into black jeans, a black T-shirt, and a black button-down short-sleeve shirt to better hide the concealed pistol tucked inside his waistband. The polo shirt and chinos he'd worn on the golf course were fine, but that shirt didn't hide the weapon well enough to walk around a casino.

And there was no telling when he'd get back to the car. If he needed to blend into the shadows in the parking garage or elsewhere, a stealthy black outfit was best.

He dragged himself up the parking garage stairs, ready to check out the casino and resort, get the lay of the land, and see Mike Salestri in the flesh to make sure he was safe.

After that, if everything looked good, maybe he could return to the car. The parking garage was cool, and an hour of sleep might be enough to keep him going for now.

Unfortunately, he wasn't 25 any longer.

And exhaustion created mistakes.

If he could locate the man's vehicle, he'd follow Salestri home later tonight.

Otherwise, he'd go straight to Salestri's house. Nalen had given him the address.

Either way, he'd watch it all night as he had with Everett's, on guard for the muscular mystery killer from the golf course.

76

LEVEL B1

Parking Garage Level B1
Fortuna Magnifico Casino and Resort
Las Vegas, Nevada

Patrick eased the motorcycle to a stop in his reserved spot, next to his father's SUV and his sister's expensive yet practical sedan. He'd made great time from Sedona. The motorcycle group had been true to their word, ramping up their speed once they turned onto Interstate 40 westbound. With Patrick tucked in behind them, they flew down the freeway in the left lane, only occasionally slowing for a highway patrol speed trap, which the lead rider seemed to have a nose for.

Patrick waved goodbye to go north to Las Vegas. Riding with them had made up for the slow, dusty back road to Sedona. Overall, the trip had taken the same number of hours as if he'd killed Everett, escaped without detection, and ridden straight here.

He was back in time for work, though worn out from a lack of sleep and the many miles he'd covered over the past forty-eight hours. He'd have time to clean up in his office's bathroom, change into a suit, and have an energy drink.

After dismounting, he stretched for a second before locking the helmet to the bike with a cable. The gloves and riding jacket went into the bike's locking tail bag. While the employees of the casino knew his bike and wouldn't dare mess with his stuff, there were always tourists and gamblers wandering around the parking garage who might snag the gear to pawn for a few bucks.

Anything for another roll of the dice or spin of the slot machine wheels.

Patrick pushed back his disappointment as he walked to the staircase, but it was all he'd thought of the entire ride back. Over and over again, he'd reviewed the trip, starting with standing in the dark behind Everett's house with another person nearby, frustrating his plans.

Patrick had chosen the safe play.

He'd stuffed down the all-consuming need to kill with the assurance that the deed would only be delayed a few hours.

Finally, there had been the thrill of pushing Everett toward the edge of the cliff...

Followed by the shock of being tackled by the groundskeeper.

The punch to his stomach and the certainty that he was caught, only to escape when his attacker abandoned him to save Everett.

And the relief of fleeing—tinged with the rage and grief of not completing his mission.

He trudged up the stairs, head down, physically exhausted from lack of sleep, and emotionally spent from fighting his inner demons.

In a few minutes, he'd have to hide his true self once again, put on the mask he wore, and be the handsome, outgoing, charming guy his father never appreciated.

77

THE ODDS

Fortuna Magnifico Casino and Resort
Las Vegas, Nevada

Bone stopped at the door between the underground parking garage and the casino.

He was making a tactical mistake. There had been plenty on his previous mission for Nalen, and he'd resolved to think things through better this time around.

He considered the situation, his exhaustion, and weighed his decision, fighting for focus.

No one would take a shot at Salestri in the casino. The first two murders—and the attempt on Everett's life—had been made to look accidental. In a crowded casino with guards and cameras, Salestri should be safe for now. Admiral Nalen had said Salestri hosted a combination high roller/VIP Saturday night dinner each week. That type of event surely had an extra layer of security.

In a way, the casino security staff could be considered part of Bone's team.

It made more sense for Bone to take a nap immediately and be fresh when he might be called on to act.

He'd return to the car and sleep for an hour or two, then scout the casino.

Heavy, slow footsteps came from the stairwell below him as Bone started down to B3 and his car, happy with the decision. He'd chow down on one of the Meals Ready-to-Eat he'd ordered for exactly this type of situation and get some rest on a full stomach.

A man trudged up the stairs, eyes on the ground in front of him. He looked to be about Bone's age, broader across the chest, with more muscles than Bone's lean runner's body. Unlike Bone's bushy dark beard, the tired guy had a few day's worth of stubble—which only enhanced his handsomeness. From what Bone could see, he could easily be a male model or a movie star with a leading-man jawline. Bone wondered if he was an up-and-coming movie star in Las Vegas for some R&R; he was way too good looking to be an employee going to work as a bartender or blackjack dealer.

Bone continued down the stairs, ready for food and a nap. Just like in BUD/S, he'd pushed himself through a rotation. Now it was time to rest and prep for the next part of the mission.

The heavy metal door leading from the parking garage to the casino slammed shut with a *clang* above him as Bone made it to the B2 landing.

Something nagged at him.

What had he missed?

Between the yoga class, the long run in the heat of the desert, prepping for the mission, saying goodbye to Steph, driving to Phoenix, the all-night stakeout, sneaking around the golf course, saving the ungrateful Everett's life, and finally the drive to Las Vegas, he'd been awake more than thirty-six very eventful hours. He wasn't thinking as quickly as usual.

There's a reason front-line SEALs accepted promotions as they aged: Direct action was a younger man's game.

He stopped at the door to the B3 parking area. The comfort of his car was less than 50 feet away.

Was his gut telling him Salestri wasn't as safe in the casino and hotel as Bone thought?

No, that wasn't it.

What else could it be?

The guy on the stairs? He was handsome, fit, and tired.

A model checking into the resort to recover from a busy schedule of posing for money.

A ladies' man turned degenerate gambler, exhausted yet showing up to find an attractive hookup and whatever rush he could eke out at a blackjack or craps table on a Saturday night.

Or a good-looking employee who had chosen Vegas over LA, ready to change clothes and start his shift, turning on the charm only when he clocked in.

Bone stared at the door to the parking garage, reviewing the brief encounter.

The guy had worn sturdy black boots.

Dark tan pants, more like work clothes than chinos.

The black boots triggered a thought.

Hadn't the guy in the pine trees on the golf course worn black shoes?

It had all happened so fast…

The man on the stairs had the same build as the one in the helmet Bone had fought for a second before saving Everett's life at the cliff.

Bone closed his eyes and pictured the scene in the woods, but he couldn't remember what shoes the assailant had been wearing. Just the black motorcycle helmet, a dark long-sleeve shirt, and dark tan pants.

A motorcycle rider—and those boots would be perfect for a multi-hour ride on a bike.

He turned and looked up the stairs. The odds were ridiculously long that he'd run into the person he'd fought on the golf course.

And that Everett's attacker would have movie-star-caliber looks.

Still…

Wasn't Vegas built on the hope of long odds coming around?

People won big here. Not most people, certainly, and the rare winners lost most of the money back instead of going home with cash in their pockets, but it happened.

Bone had thrown off the assailant's plan to kill Everett, who would likely barricade himself at home and not leave for weeks.

If Salestri was next on the hit list, the killer might head directly for the casino, just like Bone.

They could have been on the same roads, a few miles apart, for the past several hours.

The timing worked out. It wasn't as far-fetched as it had at first seemed.

At least, in theory.

Adrenaline flooded Bone's system. There was no way he could sleep now. He resisted the urge to race up the stairs to find and confront the man.

Salestri had to be safe in the casino. The murderer was doing the same thing Bone had planned: casing the joint, looking for an opening—a weak point to attack—or preparing to tail the guy from the casino.

Ambush him on the way home.

A hit-and-run, maybe.

For the moment, Bone had an edge—if the guy from the stairs really was the assailant, and if he hadn't recognized Bone.

The first step was to try to find the motorcycle and determine if this was a big coincidence, or if the killer was actually in the building.

78

THE TARGET

Fortuna Magnifico Casino and Resort
Las Vegas, Nevada

Patrick walked through the casino on autopilot—and nearly slammed into a cocktail server with a full tray of drinks for the many slot machine players on the casino floor.

He was exhausted and not paying attention. He had to pull himself together.

It was another busy Saturday night, and he had a job to do.

Once he got through his father's latest stupid dinner party, he could spring his surprise.

Finally, he'd be shown the respect he deserved.

He'd be able to leave behind the schmoozing. The gregarious facade.

And prove he could be much more than a pretty face.

He could help with the hard stuff. Kick things up a notch. His father played it far too safe.

If the marks had the fear of sudden death on their minds, the organization could be so much more powerful—and prosperous.

He unlocked the door to his office and went directly to the attached bathroom for a much-needed shower.

In a few hours, his life would completely change.

New doors would open.

He'd no longer have to be something he wasn't: a personable performing monkey to amuse his father's guests—and sucker the targets.

———

It didn't take long for Bone to find what he was looking for. There was only one motorcycle in the entire parking garage.

But what a bike. A black high-performance Italian-brand motorcycle was parked diagonally in a reserved space near the B1 staircase door.

A black helmet was locked to the bike.

Although the rest of the helmet was smooth and pristine, the back had several light scratches—exactly where someone falling onto the ground would hit their head on tiny pebbles near the edge of a cliff on a golf course in Arizona.

The scratches were far from conclusive, but in his gut, Bone knew the truth: Despite the long distance involved, Everett's assailant and Bone had ended up at the same place, at roughly the same time.

And if the markings on the parking spot were to be believed, the owner of the bike was also an employee of the casino—and high enough up the food chain to warrant a reserved parking spot a few steps from the stairs to the entrance.

79

THE CASINO

Fortuna Magnifico Casino and Resort
Las Vegas, Nevada

The night had barely started, and the casino floor was already busy with gamblers. Cheers came from a craps table surrounded by ten young men. Two rows of blackjack tables, with most of the seats filled with people—young and old, dressed in everything from jeans to suits—lined a wide, carpeted walkway from the valet parking entrance to the rear of the casino.

Well-dressed couples walked by on their way to a high-end steakhouse along the back wall.

As much as Bone hated the idea of his face being recorded by the hundreds of security cameras in the casino, he had to gather intel. And the quickest, safest way he could think of was at the bar near the front entrance.

"Non-alcoholic beer, please," he called to the bartender. She was a few years older than him and had the looks of a former showgirl.

When the woman brought his beer, he paid—he wasn't gambling, or it might have been free—and leaned in to ask a question over the noise of the casino next to the bar area. "I ran into a guy who works here—he has that really nice Italian motorcycle? He told me to look him up tonight, but for the life of me I can't remember his name. Can you help me out?"

The bartender nodded "That'd be Mr. Salestri. He loves that bike."

Bone nodded while hiding his confusion. Admiral Nalen hadn't said anything about Salestri riding a motorcycle—not that it was an essential piece of information.

"Salestri, that's right," Bone said to cover while he thought through the potential ramifications. Nalen had mentioned that Salestri was up to something, and might be behind the deaths of the other two CIA officers for some reason.

Maybe that's why Nalen—and whoever was pulling his strings—wanted someone like Bone to get to the bottom of this. The only thing worse than a stranger killing former CIA employees was one of their own doing it.

But it didn't add up. Salestri was supposed to be Admiral Nalen's age. The man Bone had fought on the golf course—and the man walking up the stairs—had been much younger than mid-to-late sixties.

"Michael? Mike?" Bone asked. "Which does he go by?"

The bartender shook her head. "No, Mike's the father. He works here too, but you're looking for Patrick. He'll be over at the steakhouse soon. They both will," she said as she gave him a little wave and hurried down the bar to help another patron.

Of course. If Bone hadn't been so tired, it would have clicked earlier. Mike—the father—was the one Bone had to protect. Bone must have fought the son, Patrick.

80

THE SALESTRIS

Fortuna Magnifico Casino and Resort
Las Vegas, Nevada

Bone posted up at a bank of slot machines with a view of the entrance to the steakhouse, fed a twenty-dollar bill into the machine, and pressed the button as infrequently as he could while still looking like he was a gambler lost in the lights and sounds of the machine.

A few minutes before the top of the hour, several women in black dresses and men in suits gathered near the entrance to the restaurant. A taller man in his mid-sixties—around 6 feet, with plenty of muscles but a soft belly—emerged from the steakhouse's front door with a big smile for the waiting crowd. He had chiseled features and dark, wavy, slicked-back hair.

Mike Salestri, Bone guessed.

Right behind him, a younger man followed. He was equally muscular —but without the belly—clean shaven, with a strong jaw, nicely styled short dark hair, and a wide smile with perfect white teeth.

Model-quality looks.

The man from the stairs, cleaned up and radiating charm.

Patrick Salestri, the son, motorcycle rider—and possible killer.

The women received kisses on the cheeks from Mike Salestri while Patrick shook the men's hands, then the two switched.

Other restaurant diners who weren't as richly dressed waited to enter, watching enviously as the group adjourned to the restaurant's private back room.

As Bone pushed the slot machine's button and lost his money, he puzzled out the situation.

Patrick Salestri had the build to be the man in the woods by the golf course.

He rode a high-end motorcycle and wore a plain black helmet with scratches on the rear consistent with being tackled by Bone and landing on the rocks near the edge of the cliff.

Was Salestri senior—Mike—behind the killings of his former CIA colleagues Rutherfield and Frandren, having outsourced the murders to his son?

Or could Patrick be acting on his own—and keeping a dark secret from his father?

81

THE CAKE

Fortuna Magnifico Casino and Resort
Las Vegas, Nevada

Bone had a feeling the rest of the night was going to be long and eventful. A packaged meal—one of the MREs in the car—wasn't going to cut it. Best to fuel up well now, rest while the Salestris were hosting the party, and figure out the rest as he went along.

He ordered takeout from a fancy sports bar off the casino floor, paying an eye-watering amount for a burger, fries, and a large soda.

While he waited, he marveled at a refrigerated vending machine where he bought a large slice of chocolate cake. The sugar might come in handy later.

With supplies in hand, Bone returned to the parking garage stairs. He snacked on fries while waiting at the level B1 door.

Soon, the fries were gone, and he'd started on the burger when the door banged open. The young men who had been playing craps emerged, loud and boisterous.

Bone wrapped the remains of the burger, ran down the stairs to B3, and sprinted to his car.

He backed out and sped up the ramps to B1, arriving in time to back into one of the two spaces vacated by the craps players.

He had a partial view of the motorcycle, the SUV, and the luxury sedan parked next to it.

The rush to snag the parking spot had his blood pumping. Bone slotted the tall soda into the car's cup holder and put the cake package on the passenger seat. By his guess, he had at least an hour—maybe two—until the Saturday night VIP party broke up.

He tipped the seat back, set an alarm on his sport watch, and gave in to the food hitting his stomach.

82

THE KIDS

In the luxurious back room of the restaurant, Patrick shoved aside his tiredness and frustration. Instead, he smiled and laughed, joked and gossiped, mixed and mingled.

He was the life of the party.

Big Mike sat at the table and chatted.

Patrick did all the hard work while everyone kissed his father's ass and treated him like royalty.

Kristine stood as quiet as ever by the door in a boring black pantsuit. The cut of it was all wrong—it showed the bulge of the small pistol she carried.

She could never do what he did. Krissy didn't have the looks, sense of style, or charisma.

It wasn't fair. Patrick did all the work, yet she was their father's favorite.

This would be the last Saturday night party he worked. Let them find someone trustworthy to replace him. Or make Krissy step up.

If Mike didn't promote him after what Patrick showed him tonight, he'd leave the organization and strike out on his own.

The impulsive decision almost made the evening bearable.

Kristine plastered a smile on her face and watched the men and women around the long table eat, laugh, and lie. Their cell phones rested in individual ornate wooden boxes on a long shelf just inside the doorway. Each of the guests had clicked the link confirming their attendance—and installing the virus on their phones.

Right now, the phones were uploading their contents to the private computer server downstairs for the ops team to examine for anything juicy or actionable.

Kristine would rather be downstairs, but her father liked her nearby, and someone needed to prevent the guests from accessing their phones while the virus did its work.

She was out of her element in social situations like this. One-on-one, she'd be fine, but in a room full of people, with conversations ebbing and flowing, she would flounder.

Thankfully, her brother had returned on time from his motorcycle-riding vacation. She'd never seen the fun of riding for hours on end, but whatever floated his boat and put him in the outgoing frame of mind to keep the Saturday night parties fun was fine with her.

When he hadn't showed until right before the dinner, she'd had a minor panic attack at the thought of being enlisted to help her father mingle, tell stories and ask exactly the right questions of the guests.

That was Patrick, not her.

Mike could do it on his own, but he looked more tired today than he had all week, which was saying a lot. He was young—still in his sixties—but slowing down. She'd noticed it the last few months but chalked it up to stress or his punishing workout routine.

Tonight, though, she had to face the facts: At some point soon, she and Patrick would take over. Maybe sooner than she'd hoped, even.

She'd never had the looks or personality for the social side of the organization—the lunches or dinners, and recruiting assets. Manipulating people, stroking egos, or soothing nerves the way her father did so well with countless targets, along with the cocktail servers, cab drivers, valets, butlers, hustlers, blackjack dealers, strippers, and bouncers he'd recruited over the years. She was socially awkward with people she didn't know well and came across as quiet and mousy with many she did.

Plain, bookish, and passive.

Behind all that, though, she was a wolf in sheep's clothing. She had a sharp mind and clear ideas on how to make her father's organization—and the country—much better.

If her father wasn't up to the job, she'd be happy to take over.

Patrick wanted to work with Dominic, her father's "fixer."

But another fact she'd have to face—and convince Patrick of—was that she couldn't run the operation without him. If Dad retired, Patrick would have to step up and fully embrace being the face of the operation, not just Dad's outgoing righthand man.

Maybe they could find some safe "projects" for Patrick to do from time to time. Visit the occasional malcontent mark who thought they could push back. Break a few bones.

Whatever it took to keep him happy.

She'd talk about it with him in the morning. See if he'd noticed the change in their father.

The way Dad looked tonight: pale, tired—almost deflated—meant they might have to encourage him to retire to his almost-completed mansion sooner rather than later.

83

THE TIME

Operations Room
Fortuna Magnifico Casino and Resort
Las Vegas, Nevada

Melissa came in at 3 p.m. on Saturdays so she could work late.

Saturday night dinners started promptly at 7:00 when the guests were greeted in the lobby of the restaurant by Big Mike and Patrick.

Tonight, the new virus was already working its magic, uploading the contents of the attendees' phones so Melissa and the others could flip through pictures, read emails, and mine for gold.

This was the safest time for Melissa to access the Vault. Neither Patrick nor Mike would leave the party, and Kristine had to guard the phones to prevent guests from accessing them in the middle of the data dump. Krissy also watched the party for her father, a set of eyes to take in the big picture and note any action items for Big Mike.

It was now or never.

Melissa lifted the phone receiver next to her monitor, though it hadn't rung. People often set their ringer on low. If anyone questioned the call, they would hopefully think they'd just not heard it.

"Yes," she said into the dial tone, pretending Kristine was on the other end of the line. "You're sure? I guess. Hold on."

Paper and pens weren't allowed in the room, so Melissa played to that. "Okay, go ahead, but slowly."

"Mm-hmm, got it. Yes. Okay. Yes. Mm-hmm."

She paused, reviewing the door access code she'd worked so hard to see and memorize. "Once more, okay?"

Faking the call from Kristine was essential but obvious. It was taking up valuable time but had to be done.

"I have it, I think. I'll call you back if it doesn't work." She hung up the phone and rolled the chair back.

This time it didn't catch on any pebbles.

Melissa walked straight to the door to the Vault without looking around to see if any of her colleagues were watching. She was on a mission from Kristine—she wouldn't be worried about what anyone thought.

She pressed the door's keypad, entering the first nine digits, paused for a second, and entered the tenth, praying she had it right.

The door *beeped*, and the lock clicked open.

She walked confidently inside and shut the door behind her.

So far, so good.

84

THE RED LIGHT

The Vault
Fortuna Magnifico Casino and Resort
Las Vegas, Nevada

Melissa wanted to collapse into the comfortable chair in the corner and take a moment to calm down, but she couldn't risk it.

With shaking fingers, she released the clasp of the vintage metal hair clip. Her hair tumbled free while she tried to push the small sliver of metal on the inside of the ornate barrette.

Her hand shook too much.

On the fourth try, her fingernail found purchase and pressed, springing the back of the clip free.

Inside, the small, high-capacity flash drive waited.

It took two tries for her shaking hands to line up the device with the computer tower's USB port.

Finally, she slid it in. A tiny red LED blinked steadily on the end of the drive—the only indication that anything was happening.

The hacking software was self-executing: It started immediately when the drive was plugged into a computer. It would worm its way into the operating system, embed itself, and start a countdown timer. Later tonight, a virus would go live.

The virus would encrypt the computer's hard drives—the system ones in the tower and all the larger, external hard drives connected to it on the server. All data would be inaccessible without a passcode.

But first, the virus searched the drive for what its algorithm deemed important data.

Spreadsheets—which the team used as an overview to keep track of blackmail material on individuals and groups.

Financial records.

Frequently accessed files.

The customer relationship management software used by the team: a vast database of every tidbit of information about each person, from business details to use for insider trading to indecent, sensitive, or incriminating pictures and embarrassing text messages. There were login passwords for social media accounts, financial institutions, contact phone numbers, and more.

And finally, as many video files as the flash drive would hold.

It would be a tiny fraction of the contents of the blackmail material available on the hard drives. But the small flash drive could only hold so much, and there hadn't been a way to smuggle a larger, portable hard drive into the room.

This would have to do.

By now, only a few seconds into the process, the virus had spread to all the hard drives and the workstations in the next room.

The file transfer had also begun. There was no telling exactly how long it would take to fill the drive. Smaller spreadsheet and word processing files would be moved almost instantaneously. Larger video files took longer.

Melissa wouldn't know what she'd stolen until she got to a laptop and investigated the haul. If the hacking software Shane had purchased worked to his specifications, they would get plenty, including enough material to expose Big Mike's insider trading, blackmail, and whatever other illegal activities he did that she didn't know about.

They would avenge Shane's sister's murder, then live happily ever after.

Melissa settled into the wingback chair, which was as comfortable as it looked, and kept her eyes fixed on the blinking red light of the flash drive.

All she could do was wait—and hope none of her colleagues wondered about her sudden access to the room.

85

THE STEPS

The Enclave Lounge
Las Vegas, Nevada

The dinner party was going well, as usual. Kristine watched from near the door, pressed against the wall, blending in.

Mike had rallied with the energy in the room and laughed at a story Patrick told.

The guests were happy and well on their way to being drunk.

Their phones had been hacked and infected with the computer virus.

By now, the downloaded files were being given an initial examination by the team downstairs.

Photo albums were being scanned for incriminating or embarrassing pictures.

Saved passwords were being extracted and added to the organization's CRM—customer relationship management database.

Confidential emails were being read for insider trading ideas.

Given tonight's guests—two CEOs of hot technology companies, a famous actor known for his excessive lifestyle, an extremely wealthy woman who had been living it up since her recent divorce, and two female singers from America's top pop band—there was sure to be juicy material to work with.

Patrick and Mike had the group well under control.

If Kristine was going to take over someday soon, she wouldn't stand around like a wallflower for these dinners.

Why not start tonight?

She could check on the team and see for herself what the initial pass through the data showed.

She'd be back in time to shake hands and smile at the guests as they left.

Kristine blended in so well, she doubted anyone noticed as she opened the door and left the room.

The Vault
Fortuna Magnifico Casino and Resort
Las Vegas, Nevada

Melissa abandoned the wingback chair to pace the small room. Three steps in one direction. Three steps back.

Each time she turned toward the computer tower, her eyes locked onto the flash drive's blinking red LED, praying it stopped so she could snatch it out of the port, fit it back into her barrette, and return to her desk.

She didn't want to think about what Big Mike would do to her if she were caught in his ultra-secure vault, stealing his files and encrypting them so he could no longer have access.

Betraying the trust of both him and his daughter.

86

THE DOCTOR

The Enclave Lounge
Las Vegas, Nevada

Kristine emerged from the laughter and revelry of the private dining room at the back of the restaurant to the subdued elegance of the steakhouse. Tourists, high-rollers, businesspeople, and a C-list celebrity—none wealthy or important enough to be invited to dinner with Big Mike—enjoyed some of the best food on the Las Vegas Strip.

The maître d' raised his hand, stopping her from heading to the back hallway and down to the computer room in the basement.

An older gentleman stood near the restaurant's entrance, dressed in a black suit with an unfashionably wide tie. She had known him all her life. As the family's private physician, Doctor Tracey had tended to her, her brother, and their father for decades.

Seeing his face out of context, here in the upscale restaurant instead of in his nice but dated private offices, stopped her in her tracks.

There were very few reasons he would travel the half hour from Henderson on a Saturday night, fight the always crazy Las Vegas Strip traffic, and make his way through the noise and cigarette smoke of the casino.

None of them were good.

With Mom long passed, and Kristine feeling fine, it could only be about Mike or Patrick.

Patrick looked tired, but her father had been out of sorts for weeks.

Their eyes locked. Doc Tracey couldn't even muster a smile.

Her stomach dropped.

"Doc?" she asked, trying to keep the terror from her voice.

"Krissy," he greeted her. His lips finally smiled, but not his eyes.

She let the use of her childish nickname go uncorrected. "Is it Dad?" she asked in a whisper as the maître d' stepped away to give them privacy.

"No, no, of course not. But I do need to speak with him about another matter," Doc said. He'd lied to her plenty—about how the routine vaccination shots wouldn't hurt—and each time she had believed him.

Until now.

It suddenly all made sense.

Her father was sick.

"Come with me," she said. She took him by the hand to lead him—much more slowly than she preferred, but he had to be in his eighties at this point—and brought him to the private room in the back of the restaurant.

"Stay here. I'll be right back with Dad." Kristine wasn't sure how her father would react to the dinner being interrupted, but Patrick could handle everyone for a few minutes.

Kristine opened the heavy, padded door and eased into the room. A second after she entered, Mike looked up and made eye contact with her. She gave a subtle tilt of her head. He nodded, chuckled at a comment from one of the young CEOs, and excused himself quietly. Patrick noticed but covered smoothly.

They were a well-oiled machine—but one part might be failing.

For all her bluster earlier about getting Mike to retire so she could run things her way, she regretted the thoughts now.

But it was far too late to take them back.

87

THE QUESTIONS

The Vault
Fortuna Magnifico Casino and Resort
Las Vegas, Nevada

The file transfer was taking too much time. Melissa had been in the control room far longer than she'd planned.

She had to wait it out. There would be no second chances.

But what if the hack hadn't worked?

Or the virus was stuck in a loop of some sort?

The stupid red LED continued to flash, but could the process have already finished?

Would it ruin everything if she yanked the flash drive out of the port in the middle of the process?

If she was caught in here…

She refused to let her mind consider what would happen. There was no going back now—she was committed.

Later tonight, the ransomware virus on the flash drive would lock the main computer, the workstations in the next room attached to the network, and the backup hard drives.

Without the passcode, the data wouldn't be accessible.

And while Shane had tried to memorize the long, complicated password before giving up and writing it on a piece of paper for each of them, she hadn't wanted to know it. It was a calculated risk. If Kristine or Big Mike caught her and demanded the key to unlock the encryption, she wanted to be able to say she didn't know it. No matter what they did to her, she couldn't give them what they needed.

The passcode was sealed in an envelope and locked in a safe deposit box at her bank.

If Mike wouldn't simply release her, he might take her to the bank to retrieve the code. That would give her a chance to make a scene and either escape or get the police involved.

The data kept transferring, and the damn red LED kept blinking.

88

THE NEWS

The Office of Mike Salestri
Fortuna Magnifico Casino and Resort
Las Vegas, Nevada

Mike didn't bother unplugging the phone or sweeping the room for bugs. He could tell from Doc's face that none of that mattered now. What was said here in the next few minutes wouldn't be a secret long.

Mike stood behind his desk. Doc stopped in front of it. Neither of them sat.

"Don't sugarcoat it or beat around the bush," Mike said. "Give it to me straight."

Doc nodded and swallowed. He couldn't speak for a few excruciating seconds.

"Do you need water? A drink?" Mike asked.

Doc shook his head, took a deep breath, and spoke. "A full diagnosis is required to be sure—imaging and biopsies—but I believe you have stage 4 cancer. It's likely spread throughout your body."

Mike reeled at the news, but he kept the emotion off his face. On some deep level, buried in denial, he'd suspected it all along. "That's why I've been so tired?"

Doc nodded. "I'm sorry," he said, in a voice barely above a whisper.

"So I'm not just getting old?" Mike asked, using humor to keep his emotions from overwhelming him.

"No."

"I can beat this, right?" Mike asked, desperately hopeful.

From the look on Doc's face, he knew the answer.

"You can try," Doc said. "You might get a few extra weeks. Maybe a month. But if it doesn't work, as I suspect, your final days will have been filled with misery. If it were me—and a lot of other doctors I know feel the same—I'd opt for palliative care only."

They regarded each other across the desk.

Mike instinctively switched to work mode. If this was a problem to solve, he might be able to focus on the practicalities and avoid the fear, anger, and sorrow he barely held in check.

"How long?" he asked, proud that his voice was steady and strong.

Doc hesitated. "It's hard to say."

"Doc." They'd known each other for decades. Now wasn't the time for bullshit.

"As long as three, maybe four months at the outside."

"And on the short end?"

"I'm not lying when I tell you it's hard to say," the doctor told him. "I consulted with a colleague at the hospital—a specialist. One patient in a similar situation lasted six months. He passed peacefully surrounded by his family. That could be you." Doc paused, glanced away, licked his lips, and finally met Mike's eyes again. "Another patient... He was gone within a week."

"A week?" It came out more shocked and desperate than he'd wanted.

Mike wasn't ready to go yet. A week wasn't enough time to eliminate the terrorist mastermind hiding in Afghanistan, or Pakistan... hell, he could be anywhere.

"What will the progression look like? How long do I have—up and physically able?"

"You will feel worse as the days—weeks, if you're lucky—go by," Doc said. "But again, it's impossible to be sure. Do yourself a favor. Turn your... business... over to one of your kids. Do it quietly or with a big blowout party, whatever. Then sit by the pool. Drink. Eat. Find someone nice to fool around with. Savor the moments while you can. Reminisce. Make amends—or settle scores if you must. But appreciate every second."

Mike's emotions welled up.

Seven days?

A month?

Longer?

What would he do with that little time?

Accept the end, as Doc suggested?

Say goodbye to his kids as they watched him reduced to nothing?

That was not how he wanted to die.

He'd rather go out fighting than fade away in Las Vegas.

"What are the odds you're wrong?" Mike asked, covering all the bases.

"Zero. I'm sorry, my friend."

Mike nodded and offered his hand. "Thank you for letting me know so quickly. I'll be in touch," he said, shook, and left Doc standing in his office before the older man could offer useless platitudes.

Mike had a lot of thinking to do—and plans to make.

At this point, every minute counted.

89

THE ACCOMPLISHMENT

The Vault
Fortuna Magnifico Casino and Resort
Las Vegas, Nevada

Melissa paced. When her steps brought her close to the wall, she turned back toward the computer.

The tiny flash drive's red LED had stopped blinking.

It was done. She had installed the virus and transferred the files.

The clock was ticking.

Her shift was almost over.

Later tonight, the ransomware hack would disable the computers.

Melissa's fingers continued to shake, but she managed to fit the small flash drive into her barrette's hidden recess. She clipped it into her hair and straightened it.

With a deep, steadying breath, she put on a serious, capable expression, stood straight, and exited the vault.

Moving at an unhurried pace, striving to act normal and not at all guilty, she closed the door behind her, checked to be sure it had latched properly, and returned to her workstation only a few steps away.

No one looked up or asked why she had gone into the off-limits room.

Her close friendship with Kristine made what she had done seem reasonable.

Her fingers still shook so badly that it took her three tries to log back into her system.

But she'd accomplished her goal.

In an hour, she could exit the room with her prize—if the security guard didn't inspect her overly large hair clip...

And neither Kristine nor Mike discovered that she had entered their precious vault.

90

THE SUV

Mike had too much on his mind to return to the dinner. Patrick and Kristine would have to handle the rest of the night.

Mike left a message with the security guard outside the door to the Enclave Lounge before leaving the restaurant and hurrying across the casino floor.

It was the same as every night.

The flashing lights.

The sounds of slot machine bells ringing. Men and women cheering—and swearing—at the blackjack and craps tables.

In the past, the casino had invigorated him. Tonight, as he made his way to the door to the parking garage, it felt fake. A false front. A veneer of fun and excitement hiding desperation and sadness.

He had to get away from here.

Think things through.

Decide once and for all if Krissy should lead the organization when he was gone.

And how quickly he and Sardar could handle the mission in Afghanistan.

The new house awaited. There were no nearby neighbors. He, Krissy, and Patrick would be alone to work things out with no one to overhear.

Parking Garage Level B1
Fortuna Magnifico Casino and Resort
Las Vegas, Nevada

Bone didn't sleep. He didn't want to snooze and miss Patrick leaving.

Instead, he tilted the seat back and relaxed his body and mind. It was the next best thing to getting some shuteye.

The slam of the metal door to the stairs brought him out of the restful state, but he didn't sit up. With the driver's seat tipped back, he could barely see over the dashboard, but it was enough.

Mike Salestri hurried past Patrick's motorcycle and the expensive sedan, toward the large black SUV. His face was whiter than earlier inside the casino—Salestri looked shell-shocked.

Bone knew the expression well.

He'd seen it on the faces of men in the Teams when they'd heard a brother had died or been badly injured.

Something big had happened in the restaurant.

Had Patrick told him that he'd failed in the killings Mike had assigned him?

Or had Salestri learned what his son had been up to recently?

Who was the one calling the shots—the father or the son?

The SUV's engine started. The truck raced backward out of the parking spot.

Bone faced a dilemma. Salestri had gotten bad news and was about to speed away.

Patrick was nowhere to be seen.

Should Bone follow the father or wait for the son?

The SUV's engine roared as it flew past Bone's hatchback.

The primary target won out. Wherever Salestri senior was going, Bone would follow.

He tipped the seat up, pushed the button to start the car, and pulled out slowly.

The black SUV sped up the ramp with Bone several car lengths behind, once again grateful for his boring, nondescript vehicle.

91

THE SHEEP

The Enclave Lounge
Las Vegas, Nevada

Kristine checked her watch. Mike had been gone too long for a simple meeting with Doc. Either they had a lot to discuss, or Dad wasn't coming back.

She stood inside the private dining room, disappearing into the woodwork as Patrick joked and laughed with the dinner guests. He was a master of conversation, able to play whatever part was needed, from the life of the party to a quiet, appreciative listener when a celebrity's ego required them to be the center of attention.

The organization was lucky to have him.

He would be fine on his own for the rest of the evening.

She would check on Mike. If he was still in his office with Doc, she'd pop down to the operations room and check on the evening's "take" from the dinner party guests' cell phones.

Melissa might have a quick update for her.

As soon as Kristine slipped from the room, the guard stationed outside the door stopped her. "Mike left a message for you. He said for you and Patrick to meet him at the new house when dinner is over."

She nodded and turned for the main room of the restaurant and the casino beyond. If she left now, she could have time alone with her father before Patrick arrived, learn what was happening... and if it was as bad as she thought, make her case for taking over the organization.

———————

Patrick fought to keep his anger from boiling over and showing on his face when Kristine left the party for a second time.

Mike had disappeared several minutes before, leaving him to shoulder the burden of entertaining these idiotic sheep who laughed, drank, and ate as if those pleasures were all there were to the world.

They would never know the pure joy of taking another person's life.

As he listened to one CEO's boastful story about his most recent vacation, the urge to strangle the life out of the man while the other guests watched in shock nearly overwhelmed him.

Or he could draw his pistol and shoot them all, one after another.

Patrick should have made sure Everett had gone over the cliff and was dead—and killed the groundskeeper who had interrupted the morning's fun.

He smiled and pretended to listen as the businessman droned on and on.

Killing two people in one go—that would have been something.

So would taking the lives of all six dinner guests. Although he'd never risk it, the idea was fun to consider.

One of the women in the group made what she thought was a witty comment. Patrick was forced to drag his attention back to the room and laugh along with the rest of them.

At last, the businessman's story ended.

Kristine hadn't returned.

Patrick had been abandoned to the boring work while they obviously had something better to do.

His smile vanished.

Patrick got himself together and coughed, pretending he'd swallowed wrong, but not before the businessman's eyes widened in fear at Patrick's expression.

92

THE TRUTH

Bone crawled along a shallow wash, hurrying toward where Mike Salestri had parked his SUV.

Down in the desert rocks and sand, the way illuminated in the familiar green glow of the night vision goggles, it felt like the good old days.

He had no team backing him up, but he'd successfully tailed Salestri from the casino to the freeway, then on progressively narrower roads until he'd been forced to turn off the headlights and rely on the NVGs to avoid being discovered.

When Mike had taken an unpaved driveway toward a nearly completed house in the desert, Bone had parked the car out of the way behind a small hill, run forward until he found the protection of the wash, and used it to approach the house.

Bone faced the side of the garage, and the SUV parked in front of it. The shallow ravine curved to the left, which gave him a berm high enough to hide behind yet low enough to see over by raising his head a few inches.

Mike sat in the darkened SUV 75 yards away, hands on the steering wheel, not moving.

Bone didn't know what was going on, but he was in an excellent position to observe whatever came next, and he had his primary target in sight.

It felt like the night of his first mission, all those years ago, with incomplete intelligence and the ever-present desert sand.

He settled in to watch and wait.

Desert Valley Foothills
Henderson, Nevada

Mike sat in the SUV, lost in thought.

A week to live—or a few months.

As tired as he'd been lately, he guessed the shorter end of the timeframe.

He ignored his emotions.

There were important decisions to make.

He'd deal with his feelings later.

At the end.

Most importantly, he had to help Sardar find and eliminate the man responsible for the recent terror attacks around the world. The man they both believed to be the mastermind behind the majority of the IEDs that had killed Americans in the region during the Afghan and Iraq wars.

He used the secure communications app to send a message to Sardar.

Must talk. Urgent.

He waited, hoping for an immediate response, but nothing came. He set the phone on the dash where he could grab it quickly if Sardar called.

Next was the organization. Should he turn it over to Kristine, as he'd been leaning toward, Patrick, both of them…?

Or take his legacy with him? Go out with a bang?

The unfairness of Doc's diagnosis ripped through him. He was young. He should have much more time. Although the kids wanted to take over someday, he had plenty of good years left in him. Retirement held no appeal and, obviously, neither did death.

Yet here he was.

The tiredness hit like he'd gained a hundred pounds in a moment, weighing him down inside and out. The day before, he would have blamed it on stress or the flu. After tonight's meeting with Doc, though, he knew it was the cancer invading his body.

It gave him an idea of what the next days and weeks, if he was lucky, would feel like.

Mike shrugged off the self-pity and returned to the problem at hand.

Instead of leaving the kids in charge, he could take everyone down with him.

He could assemble all the dirt he'd gathered over the years.

Use the pictures, emails, texts, recordings.

Share everything with the world.

Burn everyone to the ground.

When it came out, some of the country's top businesspeople would be exposed as corrupt, morally bankrupt hypocrites.

Several big-name celebrities would have their true colors revealed.

A few politicians would be forced to resign for their depravity. Others would be hauled off to jail for bribery and other crimes.

The world would finally see the truth.

A few of the people might escape to private islands or luxurious retreats in far-off countries. With what he had on them, though, nowhere on earth would be far enough away for long.

The celebrities would cower in their mansions, never to perform on stage or appear onscreen again.

Mike smiled. For a moment, the tiredness was gone.

He could do his duty as a spy, reveal the truth to the world, and let the chips fall where they may.

The grin faltered as the exhaustion returned, but it didn't matter.

In a few weeks, when he faded away to nothing, he could laugh his ass off at the destruction.

If that's what he wanted.

His reverie was broken by a car's headlights approaching on the blacktop road behind him, slowing to turn up his driveway. Kristine had arrived early.

It was decision time.

93

THE TAIL

Kabul Naan & Chai Cafe
Wazir Akbar Khan
Kabul, Afghanistan

Sardar finished his tea at the small table just inside the cafe, near the open door, which let in the hot morning air. There was no breeze this morning; the city would bake today.

He ate a last bite of naan, which wasn't as fresh as at the cafe nearest his house. But the server at this cafe had a large family. The brothers worked in a variety of industries, from retail to car repair. They kept their eyes and ears open for him, and had been valued members of his spy network for years.

They needed to be paid for their efforts.

Sardar slipped the envelope filled with money from his pocket into the folded newspaper, and prepared to pay for breakfast.

His phone buzzed in his pocket, a distinct vibration that indicated a message from the secure communications app.

It could be Mike or a small number of his most trusted agents, but none of them would be reaching out now unless it was important.

Still…

Sardar resisted reaching for the phone. All morning, he'd felt like he was being watched. It was likely just paranoia. But he would wait to check the phone until he was in the privacy of the SUV with its tinted windows and his trusted guards.

The waiter took the money for the meal, along with the envelope stuffed with money in the folded newspaper, and Sardar walked without hurrying to the SUV, his bodyguard pacing him along the way.

Sardar slid inside, welcoming the cold from the air conditioner running at full blast. The driver made eye contact, but waited until the door closed to speak. "We may have been followed again, sir. Don't look yet, but there is a black SUV 100 meters back. Different license plates, but it has a minor dent—the same as the one that followed us last night."

Sardar nodded. "Do nothing unusual—do not go faster or slower, or use different roads. Go straight to the office. Pretend they are not there."

It seemed that offering the reward for information leading to the bombing mastermind may have gotten around too far.

Someone had traced the interest back to him, which meant there was an informant in his pipeline.

But with such an extensive network, there were bound to be leaks.

He could only mitigate the damage, plan around the possibility of watchers, and manage the situation long enough to make the deal with the informant and have the mastermind captured or killed.

The phone waited in his pocket with a message he dared not look at yet. Technology was a marvel, but he didn't know its full capacities—or limitations. The communications app was secure, but could viewing it in a public setting—the back of his SUV—be picked up by the people following him?

The driver pulled into the increasingly heavy morning traffic.

Sardar decided to wait until he reached the safety and security of his office before looking at the phone.

He hoped whoever it was could wait fifteen minutes for a reply.

94

THE SPEED

Patrick swung the bike into the fast lane on the freeway doing 130 mph, flying past the boring people and their pitiful little lives.

The speed exhilarated him. Not like killing a person, but damn close.

Kristine had a head start on him, but he would make up the time. He had to hurry—she and Mike were plotting something. Probably how they would continue running the organization and leave the boring work to him.

Mike would be pissed when he learned that Patrick had left the surprised dinner guests to entertain themselves the rest of the evening, but Patrick didn't care. He wasn't going back to that life. Being abandoned to babysit the rich sheep tonight was the final straw.

With his new skills and experience with Rutherfield, Frandren, and—almost—Everett, he'd make his own way in the world.

Barely slowing, he exited the freeway onto the two-lane road leading into the desert and Mike's new house.

The anger returned, along with the hunger he'd been fighting off since the night before in the desert outside Everett's home, on the golf course this morning, and even in the Enclave Lounge after dinner.

Having the motorcycle helmet on didn't help. The feel and smell of it reminded him of the prelude to a kill.

Once he confronted Mike and Kristine—and got a few hours of sleep —he would ride back to Phoenix.

By this time tomorrow night, he'd be at Everett's house, ready to climb the fence, break in, and kill the man in his sleep.

But first, he had to make his case to Mike, put his sister in her place, and transform from flunky to—what?

Enforcer? That sounded fun.

But if he could convince his father to take things up a notch, he would get the role he truly wanted: killer.

95

THE DECISION

Desert Valley Foothills
Henderson, Nevada

Mike stepped out of the SUV to greet Krissy.

The dark house loomed in the night.

Between the mission in Afghanistan and the cancer, would he be able to move into the home?

The pool was supposed to be poured this coming week.

But he might not have enough time to enjoy it.

Krissy parked next to his SUV in front of the garage and left her lights on. She'd never been comfortable in the dark, even as a child. To him, the darkness meant safety. To her, it held danger.

He walked slowly, his right hand on the SUV to steady him. The diagnosis weighed heavily.

He met Krissy at the front of the SUV with a tired smile. "How are the guests?"

She brushed him off with a wave, her voice louder and more forceful than he'd heard it before. "You're sick, aren't you? How bad is it?"

Mike shook his head. "Patrick will be here soon. I'll tell you both then. Before he gets here, though, you and I have to talk."

He hadn't made up his mind until that moment, but he was now sure. He didn't need to blow up the world and take everyone with him. It made more sense to leave the organization in Krissy's hands. She'd surely change the direction in some ways, take more risks in certain areas and less in others, but it was what it was. "I'm formally choosing you to take over the organization," he told her.

Kristine had looked ready to push him on Doc's news, but his words set her back. Her eyes widened in the light reflecting off the garage door. She started to speak, then stopped, as if unsure what to say.

"But when Patrick comes, I have to say you're both in charge," Mike continued. "Really, it'll be all your show. He's sensitive, though, and will rebel if I say you're the boss. So you'll have to manage him. Play like you're doing it alongside him, working together, but it's you I trust with the work. You will need to step up at the dinners. No more being a wallflower. It's not fair to put it all on him. Having a wingman, a backup, is important." He stared at her through his tiredness. "I know you're not used to lying or manipulating, but I need you to learn. Quickly. Can you handle all that?"

Kristine stood straighter. "I can. Thank you."

A motorcycle, moving fast, was coming their way.

They turned to watch the headlight of Patrick's bike slow on the street before turning up the driveway. "One more thing," Mike said. "I'm working on something big and will have to go away for a few days. I'll be back before..." He glanced at Krissy, his little girl, now all grown up, who blinked back tears as she seemed to know what he meant.

"Dominic and I have one last thing to do," he said. "Don't worry. It's all going to be fine. You'll see." He took her hand, squeezed, and let go as Patrick rode up and parked his fancy motorcycle next to Krissy's car.

Bone low-crawled closer to the house while Salestri senior and someone who had to be his daughter—there was a clear resemblance—were distracted by the approaching motorcycle. It must've been Patrick on the bike, and the three of them were using this out-of-the-way location for an important meeting.

Had Salestri senior ordered the deaths of Rutherfield, Frandren, and Everett? If Bone could get close enough to overhear their conversation, it might give him all the answers he needed.

He'd been too far away to hear the discussion between the father and daughter, but it had been emotional. Salestri had at first brushed her off, then confided in her. Something serious—he'd taken her hand briefly.

Had he given her bad news? That could explain Salestri senior's shell-shocked look in the parking garage.

Bone continued creeping forward until he was 20 yards from the driveway.

He couldn't risk getting closer, given the open ground with only a few bushes and cacti. He'd have to stay here and hope for the best.

96

THE DEMAND

Desert Valley Foothills
Henderson, Nevada

The fire burning within Patrick had only intensified on the rest of the drive. Between the missed opportunities to kill Everett, being abandoned at dinner, and the thrill of having the helmet on, he was hot, ready to blow off some steam, and focused on getting what he wanted.

Nothing less was acceptable.

He hated to admit it, but he wanted to kill again.

Needed to.

Soon.

First, he'd deal with whatever bullshit his father and Krissy had deserted him over.

Then he'd drive back to Phoenix—tonight, not tomorrow—and finish the job with Everett.

That would feel good. His arms tingled at the thought.

And then?

Who could he kill after that?

The need threatened to overwhelm him, but he pushed it to the back of his mind.

One target at a time.

There would always be people that had to be eliminated.

And he couldn't wait to see the look on Mike's face when he showed Dad the pictures of Rutherfield and Frandren.

He left the helmet on the seat of the motorcycle and stomped past Krissy's car to meet her and Mike next to the SUV, lit up like idiots in her headlights bouncing off the garage.

"What the hell was that?" he asked. "Leaving me alone with those marks?"

Mike shook his head in a way Patrick found particularly condescending. It stopped him cold, but made the fire burn hotter.

"My call," Mike said. "Sorry. I have news for the two of you."

Patrick held up his hand. "Before you get started, can I say something?" He had to head off whatever Krissy and Mike had cooked up. If they meant for him to do more boring, bullshit work, he'd preempt them with his demand.

Krissy sighed quietly and Mike's face flickered in anger, but he nodded. "Go ahead."

"I'm tired of being the glad handler. Your handsome backbench guy," he said, working hard to sound firm and not like a whiny little kid.

"You are so much more than that, and you know it," Mike said, his voice surprisingly kind. "You smooth ruffled feathers. Say the right thing at the right time. You are integral to the operation."

"It's true," Krissy said. "Tonight, right before you came in, I was freaking out at having to do your job."

The sincerity of their words set Patrick back. He'd been expecting more of a fight.

"Thank you," he mumbled, looking down, before finding his backbone again. "But I still want more. I want to be operational. I want to get my hands dirty. Work with Dominic. Learn that side of the business." He paused, then blurted out the rest. "There's so much more the organization could do with another enforcer. Someone not afraid to take things up a notch when needed."

There, he'd said it.

Now, would his father deny him again?

Or was tonight the beginning of a new life, where he could be his authentic self?

97

THE SON

Desert Valley Foothills
Henderson, Nevada

Yesterday, Mike might have considered Patrick's argument. He was tall, well built, and sharp. Aside from his movie-star handsomeness, he would make a good enforcer.

It made sense in other ways, too. Dominic was a few years older than Mike—he had to be closing in on 70. He was a tough guy, but at some point it was sad for a man of a certain age to break some idiot's toes.

Having a younger man—a hothead, or at least someone like Patrick, who could convincingly play the part—might instill more fear than an aging warrior. No matter how scary Dom had been back in the day, did he really terrify people the way a young man would?

It would be handy to have a person with certain skills—and the willingness to use them. It made sense for Dom to train Patrick before retiring.

But not now—not after the shocking diagnosis from Doc.

Patrick had to help Kristine at Saturday night dinners, and he'd be essential at managing the network of spies in Las Vegas, LA, Phoenix, and countless small towns in the region, who kept their eyes open and collected tidbits for the organization. Kristine wouldn't do well with them —but Patrick would.

Patrick must have taken Mike's moment of reflection as a rejection, not the careful consideration it was. Before Mike could make a final decision, Pat jumped in. "You think I'm not ready?" he asked, hurt and anger blatant on his face as he pulled out his phone and entered a passcode. "Not skilled enough? Well, could an unskilled newbie do this?"

Patrick held the phone up, facing Mike, a mix of fear and pride on his face.

Mike squinted. He fumbled his reading glasses from his pocket to make out the picture. "What's this?" he asked as he slipped the glasses on.

Next to him, Kristine gasped. "Oh, Pat. No."

Mike peered at the screen. It showed a man's sleeping face, lit up in the flash of the camera. He looked familiar.

"Is that... Rutherfield?" He had aged well in the many years since Mike had last seen him in his office on the base in Afghanistan. Mike glanced at Patrick, who had a crazed look in his eyes. "How did you find him—and why do you have a picture of him sleeping...?"

Mike took in the screen again for a moment before it clicked.

"What did you do?" he whispered.

Patrick's smile said it all. Instead of answering, Patrick swiped the screen to show a different picture of Rutherfield dead, a full-length shot of the man lying in bed.

Patrick swiped to another picture. A heavy-set mountain bike rider in Lycra shorts and top lay next to a desert trail. His head rested against a rock at an unnatural angle.

Mike leaned closer to the phone. It was hard to tell, but the man's build and his face...

"Frandren?"

His son had murdered Rutherfield and Frandren.

Mike sagged against the SUV. It was all too much. The mission to finally catch the mystery bomber. The tiredness from the cancer spreading throughout his body. His impending death. The monumental decisions to be made about turning his life's work over to his children.

And now this.

"Patrick, no," he muttered.

He'd raised a meek, wallflower daughter in Krissy, and what? Patrick —a murderer?

Yes, Mike made threats, blackmailed people, and committed countless insider trading crimes. On rare occasions, he'd ordered Dominic to break bones or scare people half to death. He'd allowed people to believe he'd killed others who crossed him.

But he'd never murdered anyone. And the rest of it hadn't been done for something as simple, as base, as revenge, and never for pleasure. Only to further his real work of protecting the country, to get the money needed for him and Sardar to track down terrorists.

His work, he realized with sudden clarity, that had taken the majority of his focus, leaving little time or energy to nurture relationships with Krissy or Patrick. To see them for who they truly were. To be a father—a dad—instead of a boss committed to growing an empire so he could play hero and save the world.

What a fool he'd been.

Patrick put the phone in his pocket and reached into another one. With a dramatic flourish, he presented a golf ball. He turned it slowly with his fingers until Mike could see a large E, written across the dimples in black permanent marker.

"Rutherfield, Frandren, and... Everett?" Mike asked.

The three names he'd used as examples of the type of people Krissy and Pat shouldn't grow up to be.

Mike's best attempt at parenting.

"Someone intervened today," Patrick said, calm, but his voice was filled with disappointment. "I almost had him. Don't worry. I'll take care of him soon. Later tonight, maybe."

Mike looked at Patrick like he'd never seen him before, this handsome, charming kid who was so good with people.

The son he'd trusted with such a large part of his business.

The man he apparently barely knew.

"And no one saw me," Patrick said, proud and excited now. "The first two: Rutherfield and Frandren. The police are convinced they were accidents." Patrick smiled. "Dad, I know what I'm doing. I'm good at this! We can take the organization to the next level. No more small-time blackmail or insider trading. The sky is the limit. We can do whatever we want. And if anyone stands in our way... I'll take care of them."

98

MALICE

Bone had a bad feeling about the confrontation taking place directly in front of him, but he was too far away to clearly hear the fierce words being exchanged.

Patrick had held up his phone for Salestri senior, who had peered at the screen before recoiling in shock.

It made sense to Bone once the phone was put away and the golf ball came out.

Patrick was showing his father proof of his actions. Pictures from killing Rutherfield and Frandren. And Everett's golf ball from this morning in Arizona.

At least Bone had stopped him there.

Judging by Mike's reaction, he hadn't been the one to order the killings.

Patrick had done it on his own—and Dad wasn't pleased.

Bone had to risk getting closer.

The group stood next to the front of the SUV. The car's headlights shone off the garage door, illuminating the area. Between their intense discussion and the bright lights, they wouldn't be able to see far into the desert.

Bone crawled slowly from behind a bush that hadn't provided much cover, but at least it had broken up the outline of his body in the dirt. His hands, forearms, and legs propelled him forward at a turtle's pace. He had to hear what they were saying—and be closer in the event of the confrontation spiraling out of control.

Mike processed the news slower than usual. The fatigue made him want to return to the SUV, tip the seat back, and sleep for a few hours, not deal with his son, who had learned well—but the wrong lessons.

Instead of not turning into the power-hungry, ass-covering Rutherfield, the incompetent jerk Frandren, or the lazy weasel Everett, Patrick had decided it made sense to kill them.

Where had Mike gone wrong as a father?

That question would have to wait. It would be an excellent one to contemplate on his death bed.

More urgently, he needed to manage the current situation.

What could he say or do to get a handle on Patrick, deal with his murderous actions—and move onto the night's pressing business of telling his kids he didn't have long to live?

Patrick noted the mental calculations all over his father's normally unreadable poker face. Tonight, Patrick saw him more clearly than he ever had. The man was a manipulator.

A user.

A liar.

Whatever he had to say, whatever the excuse for leaving the dinner early, for talking with Krissy before Patrick arrived, for the clandestine meeting in the driveway of Mike's expensive new home, it would be yet another of his father's harebrained schemes.

Like what company to infiltrate so they could make money with insider trading.

Or which movie star to help get a role that would make the actor millions of dollars—while Mike collected a small finder's fee and a favor for a later date.

Schemes and machinations.

So pointless.

So trivial.

If Mike was willing to use Patrick's newfound talent, he could control whatever he wanted.

But Patrick could see the truth in his father's eyes: He wouldn't allow that to happen.

Mike had to say something—fast. Patrick's handsome face was twisted into an unusual expression, a smile filled with malice—and madness. Mike had seen it before in Afghanistan. It came when a person went over the edge, when they'd seen or done too much and could never go back.

"Good job, Patrick," he forced himself to choke out, hoping his exhaustion didn't make the lie too obvious.

Patrick read the deceit on his father's face. "You've never appreciated what I do," he muttered. "Who I am."

"That's not—"

Patrick cut him off before he could spew more of his lies. "You've only used me. Us," he said, nodding at Krissy. "Two more of your assets."

The solution was obvious.

His father had to go.

It was the only way Patrick could get what he wanted.

What he needed.

The hunger surged within him. His skin tingled, his heart pounded, and the need took over.

He drew the pistol, savoring its weight...

The feel of the grip on his palm...

And the surprised expression on his father's face...

Which turned to panic as Patrick pulled the trigger and shot him.

99

THE GUN

Desert Valley Foothills
Henderson, Nevada

It all happened so fast. Kristine had wanted to puke after seeing the dead men on Patrick's phone.

Then Dad lied poorly and Patrick had the gun in his hand.

He fired it once… and again… and Dad grabbed his chest, stood there for a second, then collapsed to the ground.

Kristine's ears rang as the gunshots faded in the still desert air.

Her eyes met Patrick's. He looked crazed, and proud, and happy, and not at all like the sweet, handsome little brother she'd thought she knew.

She reached under her pantsuit coat for her pistol, the one Dad had given her and trained her on. The one she carried because he wanted her to be safe in a dangerous world.

The gun cleared the leather holster smoothly, exactly like Dad had taught her.

There was no need to aim. Patrick was right in front of her with the pistol at his side, his eyes now on their dying father.

Kristine shot Patrick once in the chest.

And as his expression changed from crazed pleasure to shocked pain, she shot him again, right between the eyes.

100

THE QUESTIONS

Desert Valley Foothills
Henderson, Nevada

"Dad!" Kristine said, holstering the pistol out of habit as she dropped to the ground. Mike had both hands pressed against his chest, trying to hold back the blood.

Her hand reached for her phone, but she'd left it in the car out of long habit. They were too easy to hack and use as listening devices.

Her father's eyes flicked from her face to over her shoulder, looking behind her.

Kristine swung around to see a man dressed in black, night vision goggles flipped up on his head, skid to a stop next to her.

She reached for the pistol, but her father's hand, wet with blood, stopped her.

"Do you have a first aid kit in the car?" the stranger asked as he dropped to his knees by her father.

"No, I don't think so."

He used a knife to cut her father's shirt, revealing two holes with blood —way too much blood—flowing from them.

Bone knew the moment he saw the wounds. There was no time for bandages or clotting agents. No time to call 911 and wait for an ambulance. This much blood meant the man would be dead soon.

"You did good, Krissy," Salestri told his daughter. His voice was weak and face white. Blood trickled from the corner of his mouth. "Don't worry about this," he said, glancing at his chest. "I was already dead. Doc said cancer—a few months, tops."

Krissy held her father's hands, eyes wide, breathing fast—she was in shock. Tears streamed down her face.

Salestri turned toward Bone. "Did Gregory Addison send you?"

The question caught Bone off-guard. His face must have betrayed his confusion—and uncertainty.

"You don't know," Mike said, his voice fading. "Smart. A totally black mission, even for the operator."

Mike's next words also took Bone by surprise. "Do you speak Pashto?" Mike asked in that language.

Bone nodded. "Some," he said back.

The answer pleased Salestri. He turned back to his daughter. "Take him to Dominic. Tell Dom what happened." Mike glanced at Patrick lying nearby as his breathing grew labored. "Don't put the organization in jeopardy. There would be too many questions, too much scrutiny. Make up an excuse for our absence. Bury us under the pool. The ground is already loosened. There's a shovel in the garage." He coughed up blood and his eyes went wide with pain.

His eyes fixed on Bone with the desperation only a dying man could have. "Help Sardar," he said. He didn't have the strength to say more.

He sagged. With a last look at his daughter, Salestri silently mouthed the words, "I love you."

And then he was gone.

101

THE CHOICES

Desert Valley Foothills
Henderson, Nevada

Bone was in over his head with no clue what was going on.

In front of him, Mike Salestri lay dead, blood seeping into the packed dirt driveway.

His son's crumpled body did the same a few feet away.

All lit in the glow of the sedan's headlights.

Salestri's daughter held her father's hand, sobbing quietly.

The clock was ticking. Either the police were on their way, alerted to the gunfire by a concerned neighbor in one of the distant houses, or dawn would come. Whichever way the next hours went, Bone had to get on top of the situation.

He couldn't let himself get tied up in an investigation and its uncomfortable questions. How had he happened to be here with night vision goggles, knives, guns, and everything needed to go to war in his car on the other side of the small desert hill? What was his connection to the victims? Who was he working for?

He wouldn't answer those or any others.

Hell, he couldn't allow himself to be asked in the first place.

"I'm sorry, I don't know your name," Bone said to the daughter, his voice quiet and respectful. "Is it Krissy?"

She didn't stop staring at her father's still face. "Kristine." With a remarkable show of resolve, she took a deep breath and seemed to pull herself together enough to look at him. "Who are you, and what the hell is going on?"

"I could ask you the same question—about what's going on."

"I don't know. And why should I trust you?"

Bone had an answer for that one. "Because your father did."

He stood to look down the driveway.

There were no flashing lights or sirens from police cars. "Listen, it doesn't look like the police are on their way, at least not yet."

"The nearest neighbor is too far away—and people are private out here. I doubt anyone called 911," Kristine said.

"Still…" Bone knelt next to her. "Who's Sardar?"

She again tore her gaze away from her father's body to look at Bone.

"You don't know," he said, when she didn't answer.

Kristine shook her head, still holding herself together—barely.

"Okay," Bone said. Admiral Nalen trusted him to follow his gut and do what needed to be done. His intuition was telling him to listen to the dying man's words. "I know this is a horrible situation, but I'm here to help. I can't get into how or why. But I saved Everett's life this morning in Arizona. Your brother tried to push him off the edge of a cliff on a golf course."

Bone paused. He'd had only a few orders from Nalen—one being to prevent the deaths of Everett—and Mike Salestri. "I wasn't close enough to save your father just now—I didn't see it coming," he said, half to himself.

"Neither did we," Kristine mumbled.

This mission hadn't gone at all the way Bone had thought it would. He'd saved Everett, and had been almost close enough to help Mike.

But he had a feeling the operation was far from over.

In fact, it was probably just getting started.

Kristine gently set her father's hand on his chest. "Dad mentioned the name Addison a few times, years ago. They worked together. I don't know the details, but Dad respected him. One of the good guys, he said. Could he have sent you?"

Bone shrugged. "I don't know, and I'd lie if I did. Now, who's Dominic?"

"Dad's fixer. A former Navy SEAL."

Kristine tried to stand and nearly fell over. Bone held her arm to steady her.

There were still no sirens. Maybe they had time. He was flying blind, but it felt like he was doing the right thing.

"You have some big decisions to make," he said. He held up his fingers and counted off her choices. "Trust me or not. Do as your dad said and bury the two of them under the pool, or call the police. Finally, take me to Dominic and tell him what happened, or tell me to get lost. Your call —all of it."

Bone could walk away right now. The puzzle had been solved. Patrick Salestri had killed Rutherfield, Frandren, and tried to murder Everett. And he'd shot his father—then been killed by his sister. The threat to Everett and the last person of the team—who might be Gregory Addison—had been eliminated.

The mission from Admiral Nalen was technically over.

But a dying man had requested Bone's help.

If there was a larger problem that had to be handled, was Bone's work truly done here?

Kristine was slow to respond, but she finally spoke. "My father had something big in the works. I know nothing about it except that it was expensive and extremely important to him. I guess Dom will have more." She looked at the bodies. "Going to the police makes the most sense to me, but it would bring a lot of unwelcome attention to our operation. And it might hinder whatever Dad needs us to do." She glanced up at Bone. "You're on board with this?" Kristine asked, her voice filled with doubt and suspicion.

"I am." What else could he say—or do?

Kristine searched his face and must have liked what she saw. "Then I'll trust Dad's plan. Let's get them buried. And I'll take you to see Dominic. Maybe he'll have some answers—for both of us."

102

THE PATTERN

Conference Room 1
Central Analysis Group Headquarters
Alexandria, Virginia

Gregory entered the conference room to find a relatively clear-eyed Wyatt and Marcus poring over the mind map. Wyatt made notes along the far edge with a red marker.

The square at the center of the mind map where the many lines pointed was empty. Mike Salestri's sticky note had been removed.

"Where are we?" Gregory asked as he walked to the table.

"We went back to the beginning," Marcus said. "After sleeping and eating—"

"And showering," Wyatt chimed in. He looked like his old self: wrinkled and disheveled, but awake and focused. And, thankfully, he no longer stank.

"Yes, and showering," Marcus continued. "The data makes more sense now, but we still don't understand how—or if—the CIA officers: Rutherfield, Frandren, Everett, Solermo/Salestri…"

"And me. It's okay, you can say it."

"Yes, and you. We don't see how the CIA officers and the bombings could be connected. But we've dug more into Salestri's history and you were right: There is nothing that leads us to believe he is planning the bombings. He worked too hard at the CIA to be anything but loyal to the country and dedicated to fighting terrorism. Something is going on with him, but we don't know how it fits in with the worldwide bombing attacks —if at all."

"That's a relief," Gregory said. "I couldn't see Mike involved. When I knew him, he would move heaven and earth to protect the innocent, not take their lives."

"So we're back to the beginning on that problem," Wyatt said. He gestured to the empty spot at the center of the mind map where Salestri's sticky note had been.

"Donald Everett is alive and well," Marcus continued. "He spent the day golfing a course near Sedona, Arizona before returning to his home in Cave Creek, a suburb of Phoenix."

"No one has tried to kill him?" Gregory asked.

"Not that we can tell. No police response or report. All quiet."

"And Salestri?"

"As of a few hours ago, also still alive," Wyatt said. "He is much harder to pin down—he doesn't have a cell phone, so we can't access location data. But we confirmed that he hosted his normal weekly VIP dinner at the casino earlier tonight."

"On another note…" Marcus said.

"What else?" Gregory asked. "Let me have it."

"The bombing attacks have definitely followed a very clear pattern," Wyatt said. "The first was nine months ago. The second, six months ago. And the latest was three months ago, almost to the day."

"You think another attack is coming?"

"After looking over the data," Marcus said, "I agree with Wyatt: The next attack is imminent."

"In that case, prioritize stopping the next bombing," Gregory ordered. "We can deal with Everett and Salestri later."

Preventing a terrorist attack was much more important than Gregory's former colleagues.

Wyatt and Marcus didn't need to know that Gregory had Thomas "Bone" Marks working on the situation with Everett and Big Mike.

The two analysts returned to their laptops to work the puzzle.

Gregory eyed the mind map, looking for a clue that would help reassure him. He couldn't shake the feeling that something was already very wrong—and that the worst was yet to come.

PART 7

SUNDAY

103

THE BURIAL

Desert Valley Foothills
Henderson, Nevada

A shovel was in the garage, just as Salestri had said. Bone had to pick the lock on the side door, but once in, they had all they needed.

He wore work gloves from the garage and wrapped the bodies in large black trash bags—one from the head, one from the feet, and more around the middle, sealing the edges with duct tape.

A wheelbarrow made moving the dead weight to the backyard easier.

Digging a deep enough hole for the two men took time. The soil had been loosened, but it was still hard work. The excavation crew had stopped for the weekend with the rough size and depth of the pool, but the ground hadn't yet been perfectly shaped.

When the workers returned Monday morning, they would finish the shaping, then smooth and compact the soil before placing rebar within the pool area. Soon after, concrete would be sprayed on the framework. The pool shell would be set—and the bodies hidden forever. The process should go quickly enough that the smell of death never reached the surface.

Bone's tiredness threatened to overwhelm him, but he kept going through sheer force of will and the knowledge that he could keep pushing long past when his mind and body told him he had to stop.

Kristine was a strong, hard worker through the tears. She hauled away the extra dirt remaining after the bodies went into the hole Bone dug under the deep end of the pool, scattering it in the desert at the edge of the yard.

They finished as the sky lightened in the hour before dawn.

The pool looked the same as it had earlier. No one would suspect there were two bodies buried there.

Bone scooped up the blood-soaked dirt of the driveway, flinging it into the desert and replacing it with clean fill.

When they finished, the only indication of the evening's confrontation was Salestri's SUV and Patrick's motorcycle. Both went into the garage—they'd have until Monday morning to dispose of them.

Kristine emerged from the SUV with a phone. "Dad didn't use cell phones, but he had this in his pocket Friday and had left it in the SUV last night." There were alerts showing three missed calls on a secure comms app, but they didn't show a contact, and Kristine couldn't unlock the phone. They'd bring it along in case Dominic could provide answers.

Bone jogged across the desert to his car and drove it back to a waiting Kristine in her sedan, the window rolled down.

"Is this your car?" she called, eyeing his hatchback.

"Yes," he said without further explanation. Why did everyone seem surprised with his vehicle choice? It was practical, got great gas mileage, and blended in everywhere—the perfect car for a spy, operator, assassin, or whatever he was now.

Bone followed her car as they escaped the empty roads of the future upscale housing development and onto a wider local road. His stomach rumbled as he fought off overwhelming fatigue.

The chocolate cake beckoned, and while he disliked celebrating the evening's deaths with cake, he couldn't wait. He shoveled it into his mouth and washed it down with the watery mix of soda and melted ice in the to-go cup from the casino the previous evening, which seemed like a lifetime ago.

104

THE HELP

Bone parked next to Kristine's car in the driveway of a two-story home in a decent neighborhood about 10 miles from Salestri's place. The landscaped desert yard was well maintained, and the home looked freshly painted. An American flag hung in the early morning air.

Someone had put work into the house, and it showed.

The cake had helped his energy, but Bone was still running on fumes. He'd need to sleep soon, but the hope of finding out what the mission might bring kept him going for the moment.

Kristine rang the doorbell without hesitating, though the sun had just come up.

Several seconds later, the security hole darkened for a moment before the door was unlocked. A muscular man in his late sixties, wearing small workout shorts and no shirt, opened the door. His close-cropped white crewcut matched his pure white chest hair. Despite his age, he was the picture of a Navy SEAL: strong, focused, determined.

And sweaty. They'd interrupted his workout.

He held his right hand next to and slightly behind his leg, concealing the pistol he'd brought to the door. "Krissy?" he asked. His eyes flicked to Bone, assessed him, and returned to the woman. He frowned and sighed, like he hadn't been expecting them but wasn't completely surprised they were there. "Come in." His eyes scanned the driveway and the neighborhood as he let them inside. He locked the door behind them. "Dominic," he said to Bone, the weapon now in his left hand and his right stretched out.

They shook. "Thomas," Bone said. The man's grip was firm but not overbearing; he had nothing to prove. Bone's was the same.

Dominic led them through a nicely furnished, spotless living room to a large, eat-in kitchen and family room, picking up a shirt from the back of the great room's sofa and slipping it on. He passed around bottles of water from the refrigerator.

Kristine slumped onto a stool at the kitchen island with her head down.

When she said nothing, Dominic glanced at Bone. Since Kristine didn't seem to be willing or able to report, Bone jumped in. "Mike Salestri is dead." He paused, wondering how much to offer, but stopped there. "He said to come to you for details, asked me if I spoke Pashto, told me to 'Help Sardar,' and died."

Dominic had the pistol in his waistband, and Bone sensed the tension building. "Did you kill him?" Dom asked. His eyes bore into Bone's. It had been a lot of years since anyone had looked at Bone like that, and he felt his guts tighten. The man might've been older, but he was as dangerous as a coiled snake.

"No." Bone hesitated, and checked with Kristine.

"Patrick did," she muttered.

Dominic's face flickered in disbelief for a moment before changing to sadness. "And Patrick?" he asked.

Bone shook his head, one warrior to another, and that was enough.

"Well, shit," Dominic muttered. "And what's your story?" he asked Bone.

Bone shrugged and offered a grim smile. "I'm here to help."

"Why?"

That was an excellent question. Bone could answer several ways, but he stuck with the truth. "Because I'm qualified—and it's what Salestri wanted."

105

COFFEE

1270 Dove Court
Henderson, Nevada

"Do you have anything to eat?" Kristine asked. The water had helped, but she was famished. It felt wrong to eat at a time like this, but Dad would have insisted she take care of herself.

The organization—and the operation—always came first, but if she didn't eat, she'd crash.

That wouldn't serve anyone, least of all her dead father.

So while Dominic made eggs and bacon, Kristine processed her feelings and filled him in, all while acutely aware of the stranger—Thomas, as he'd introduced himself—standing in the kitchen with them.

"Dad hadn't been feeling well," she said.

"Yes, I saw that," Dom said. "He met me yesterday, and we had a chat."

"What did he say?"

"You first," he said. The bacon sizzled in one frying pan while he used a spatula to make scrambled eggs in another. As everything cooked, Dom poured them coffee from a drip machine at the end of the counter.

Kristine drank the coffee and continued. "He was working on something big, but kept it from me. I'm hoping you can fill me in."

Dominic said nothing, only kept cooking with his back to her.

"Anyway, the family doctor showed up at Saturday night dinner. They went into Dad's office and spoke for only a few minutes. Dad left and drove out to his new house. I followed a while later. Patrick…" Her voice broke, and she faltered, the images of the night overwhelming her.

The pistol had been in her hand before she'd consciously thought about it.

Patrick's eyes had looked wild. Crazed.

Her father had dropped to the ground.

Patrick had shot him.

Patrick had to die.

Preferably before he shot her, too.

She hadn't hesitated, had felt no uncertainty. She had raised the weapon as she'd practiced countless times at the range, shot Patrick once in the chest, found her brother's face as it lined up in the front and rear sights, and pulled the trigger again, shooting him between the eyes.

The memory—combined with the smells of breakfast—overpowered her senses. She dropped the mug, breaking it and spilling coffee on the kitchen island, but she didn't have time for that. She had to get to a bathroom. The house was a typical one for the area, not unlike her friend Melissa's, and there should be a small bathroom right off the kitchen.

She made it in time to bend over the toilet and empty her stomach as the tears returned.

106

BREAKFAST

1270 Dove Court
Henderson, Nevada

The sounds from the bathroom were unmistakable, but Dominic ignored them. He'd comfort Krissy later if necessary. She was a strong kid, but from the story so far, the night had been a real shit show.

Thomas, the mystery man, cleaned up the spilled coffee and pieces of broken mug, saying nothing. The guy looked like he could handle himself —and watching two people die a few hours ago hadn't shaken him.

He had seen death—and killed—before.

Dom used the moment to size him up again. "If I asked around, what would people tell me about you?"

Thomas took a sip from his cup like a man dying of thirst before replying. "That I'm solid. All in, all the time." He offered a tired shake of his head. "I don't know what's going on, and I can understand why you would be hesitant to trust me, but we're cut from the same cloth."

Dom took that for what he suspected the man meant—Thomas was a fellow SEAL. He certainly had the vibe.

"What did Mike say—exactly—before he died?" Dom asked. He'd circle back to the circumstances behind how Thomas had happened to be near Mike's house at exactly the right time to rush in and help Kristine, but too late to save Mike's life.

After another sip of coffee, Thomas walked around the kitchen island and refilled his cup.

"He said that he was already dead. 'Doc' told him he had cancer with only a few months to live."

Dom nodded slowly. "Better to go the way he did," he muttered.

"Agreed," Thomas said just as quietly. "He asked if a man sent me."

"What man?"

"Gregory Addison," Krissy said as she returned from the bathroom. She seemed better than before. "Dad mentioned him a few times over the years. Not as often as the others—Rutherfield, Frandren, and Everett. His name wasn't used as an example of who not to be."

"Addison..." Dom said. It rang a bell. "Analyst?" he asked.

Thomas shrugged, but Krissy answered. "Yes, I think so. A good guy, Dad said."

"Did he send you?" Dominic asked Thomas.

"No," he said, followed a second later with the truth. "I don't know."

"Who did?"

Thomas ignored the question. Once again, Krissy jumped in. "Dad said it was smart of whoever sent him—that it was a black mission even for him."

"Then he spoke Pashto to me," Thomas said quickly, "asking me if I spoke the language."

Dom noted that Thomas was eager to get away from the topic of who sent him.

Another thing to circle back to before he could be trusted.

"You can?" Dom asked.

Thomas nodded. "Not fluently, but yes, decent. He told Kristine to take me to you and tell you what happened."

"We buried him under the hole for the pool," Kristine said, her voice barely a whisper. "He told us to. And Patrick..." She started sobbing again, hands covering her face, standing at his kitchen island.

He shared a look with Thomas, neither of them sure whether to give her space or console her. Dominic vividly remembered the first time he'd killed, and he bet Thomas did as well.

"Breakfast is ready," Dom said, putting the bacon and eggs onto plates and serving his guests. Krissy ignored hers, but at least didn't run back to the bathroom. Thomas dug in immediately.

Dominic took a bite of bacon and chewed, thinking through the angles.

He had a lot of questions, but he started with the biggest one. "Who is Sardar?"

Bone frowned, and Kristine looked up from her tears. "We hoped you'd know," she said. "You don't?"

Dom shook his head. He'd never heard the name before.

107

THE LETTER

1270 Dove Court
Henderson, Nevada

Dominic made them go over the story again, but the only thing he got was more information on what Patrick had done before shooting Mike.

Two days before, at Mike's new house, Dom had vouched for the kid. Argued it might be good to teach him a thing or two, so he didn't go off on his own and get into trouble.

He had been both right and wrong—and much too late.

At least he hadn't gotten dragged onto the kid's crazy train.

Dom still wasn't sure about Thomas, but Mike had vouched for him, and Krissy trusted him. And it sure seemed like Gregory Addison, the intel nerd Mike had mentioned a few times when they'd worked together in Afghanistan, had a hand in getting Thomas involved in this mess.

Dom shook his head while putting the dirty plates and forks in the dishwasher. Big Mike had been a great guy. Morally flexible, but he always did the right thing—from a big picture standpoint, at least.

"If you don't have any insights into the situation," Kristine said, "I don't know what to do next."

Dominic closed the dishwasher door.

"We have to do something about the SUV and the motorcycle before tomorrow morning, when the contractor returns to the house," Thomas said.

"And come up with a plausible excuse for Mike and Patrick's disappearance," Kristine said in a quiet voice.

They both turned to him for guidance, and he knew he couldn't hold back any longer. "I have some thoughts," he said. "Give me a minute."

He left them in the kitchen, went to his wall safe in the den, and returned with the sealed envelope Mike had given him Friday. It was still folded from when he'd stuffed it in his pocket, thinking Mike was being paranoid.

"When I met Mike at the house on Friday, he gave me this. Said he was going to Afghanistan Monday—tomorrow. I was to come along as backup, and maybe Patrick, but he hadn't decided yet." He let the news sit for a few seconds before continuing. "A local we could trust would meet us there and act as a quick reaction force for our mission."

"One man?" Thomas asked.

Dom smiled. "Exactly what I said. My guess is he's this 'Sardar' character. Anyway, Mike handed me this and told me to open it in case of emergency." He unfolded the plain white business envelope and showed the letters written on the front: *I.C.E.*

"He was worried about his safety after Rutherfield and Frandren had being killed," Dom told them. "Rightly so, it turns out."

The three of them shared a look.

"He said I'd know when to open it." Dominic took a paring knife out of the wooden knife block on the counter and used it to slit the top of the envelope. "I guess that would be now."

Dominic scanned the first sentence, ready to read it aloud, but stopped himself. He didn't need to get choked up in front of Krissy and some guy he'd never met.

Dominic—my brother in arms. We've seen some shit together, haven't we? Thank you for having my back, not only in Afghanistan but here in the USA. I couldn't have built the organization without your help.

I hope you know how much I appreciate you.

And while money doesn't fix everything, if you need more than I've given you in the past, please tell Kristine to give you whatever you want. Seriously—pick a number higher than you think is reasonable, have her wire it to your account, and go live the rest of your life on a beach, in the mountains, or wherever will make you happiest.

"What does it say?" Kristine asked, interrupting his reading.

"Personal greetings to start, then this." He read her the part about the money.

When he glanced up, she nodded firmly. "Whatever you need."

Dominic read the rest of it aloud.

Not to be melodramatic, but if you're reading this, the same person or people that got Rutherfield and Frandren got me.

Or whatever is going on with my health was more serious than I thought.

I hope you'll do one last mission for me. It's the most important thing I've ever worked on. I trust you to get the job done.

Back in Afghanistan, I had a source I never told the bosses about. I attributed his intel to others to protect him.

His name is Sardar.

He and I were convinced a person in Pakistan's army or their intelligence organization—the ISI—was actively working against America. This mastermind was behind the IEDs smuggled into Afghanistan, and he taught others how to make bombs. Because of him, hundreds of our forces were injured and killed.

The higher-ups didn't want to hear about it. We had rumors, and some leads, but no actionable intel.

My last week in country, when I knew I was done with the CIA, Sardar and I made a pact. We agreed to continue the search for the person or people behind the bombings, no matter how long it took. He would run the assets in Afghanistan and Pakistan; I would supply the money to pay for intel, bribes, equipment, and whatever else was needed. We would be a two-person CIA network, answering to no one but ourselves.

When we eventually caught up to the bad guy, we'd tip off someone we could trust to take him out.

If it took a while, fine. We would have our revenge—someday.

The target went dark as our forces drew down over there.

But we believe he's back and responsible for the recent bombings around the world.

Someone in his organization is willing to betray him for money.

My money.

The plan was for me to go to Afghanistan with you Monday morning. Sardar will meet the plane at the airport. I was to meet the informant, ensure the deal was legit, transfer the money, and call in the cavalry on the bomber's location.

It's all on you now.

Trust Kristine—she knows nothing about this, but she'll be able to help. (Under no circumstances is she allowed to go to Afghanistan, though.)

Details below.

Wheels up at zero dark thirty on Monday.

Please don't let me down.

No one spoke in the kitchen.

Dominic scanned the bottom of the page but didn't bother reading it out loud. "There's a ten-digit code at the bottom, along with what are probably other passwords—for a phone, maybe. One set of numbers is probably the combination for a safe. And the last ones look like login details to a computer."

"He has a separate login on our computer system," Kristine said, her voice filled with emotion. "That's where he handles the banking for the organization." She choked up. "Used to handle, I mean."

Dominic looked at Thomas. With his experience as a warrior and Pashto language skills, he would be an asset in Afghanistan—if he was up for it.

And if they could trust him.

"You and I need to talk," Dom said, digging deep to find his most commanding voice.

Thomas nodded. "Definitely."

They both looked at Kristine, who had once again rallied and pulled herself together. "If Mike trusted him—even from the short encounter—so do I. We," she added, looking at Dom.

Dominic stared back, ready to argue, or at least discuss the situation, when a buzz came from Mike's phone.

Onscreen, a notification showed two messages from a secure comms app Dominic knew well, but there were no other details.

Kristine gestured for the paper, and Dominic handed it over.

A few seconds later, the phone was unlocked with one of the passwords from the bottom of the letter. Kristine used a second to unlock the comms app.

The message wasn't in English, though the Latin alphabet was being used.

"It's in Pashto," Thomas said as he came around the kitchen island to stand next to Dom and Kristine. It says, 'I tried to call. What is happening? Are you able to talk?'"

Thomas looked at Dominic for permission, but he turned to Kristine. "It's your call, kid," Dom said.

Kristine handed the phone to Thomas. "Type this: 'Mike is dead. This is a friend typing for his daughter. Can you talk now?'"

Thomas hesitated, thought for a second, and typed slowly at the keyboard. He either didn't text much, or his Pashto wasn't as good as he claimed.

"I'm better at speaking the language," Thomas muttered as he finished and hit send.

A few seconds later, the phone rang.

108

THE DAUGHTER

Shahr-e-Naw District
Kabul, Afghanistan

Sardar stared at the message on the phone, wanting to be surprised.

Mike had been concerned about his former colleagues at the CIA being targeted.

Now he was dead.

The communications app meant that only someone with Mike's phone —or login credentials—could have answered. With the poor spelling and basic syntax of the message, Sardar's gut told him this wasn't a scam or con.

After all they'd been through, the dangerous situations Mike had navigated in Afghanistan, he had been killed in America.

But by whom? Their unidentified terrorist mastermind?

If so, it meant Sardar wasn't safe.

The concern of being tailed wasn't mere paranoia.

There was only one way to find out what was happening.

Sardar pressed a button, and the phone handled the encrypted person-to-person call.

The phone buzzed in Bone's hand with a voice call coming through.

With Kristine by his side and Dominic nearby, Bone felt the pressure of being a translator.

The last time he'd thought he could handle the job, his entire Team had been killed.

The kitchen faded.

Rounds zipped past his head.

Tank's dead body appeared on the ground.

There was so much blood.

"Answer it," Kristine said.

Bone blinked back to the present. For a second, he'd been back in Afghanistan in the middle of the ambush.

He pressed the button on the app, making sure the speakerphone button was selected. "*Salam alaikum*," he said as he answered the call in Pashto. It was the way Zia had taught him.

"*Wa alaikum salam*," the caller—Sardar, most likely—replied. His voice was that of a man in his sixties or early seventies; not old, but no longer middle-aged. He sounded intelligent—and grief stricken.

"My name is Thomas," he said in Pashto. So far, so good.

"I am Sardar," the man replied. "Who is there with you?" Bone translated quickly.

"I'm here," Kristine said in English. "Mike's daughter."

"Krissy?" Sardar asked.

"Yes," Kristine said after a moment's hesitation.

Sardar said a sentence, speaking quickly. Bone didn't catch it all, but he caught the apology and Kristine's full name. "I think he apologized for calling you by your... nickname? Childhood name, maybe?" Bone told her. Bone directed his words to the phone. "Please speak slowly and use easy words. I am not fluent in Pashto."

"I understand," Sardar said.

Bone got that. He translated what he said next, the words coming easily to him thanks to long calls he'd had with Zia over the past several weeks. "He says he has heard much about you. Many stories. He..." Bone paused to make sure he had the translation correct. "He said, 'You are like the daughter I never had.'"

After the translation, Sardar continued speaking and Bone kept translating. "He wants to know who killed Mike." Bone had learned from

Zia: Out in the field, the interpreter didn't answer questions. He translated and waited for the answer, even when he thought he knew what to say. This was Kristine's gig. Bone had to let her answer however she thought best.

Kristine hesitated for a moment, but finally told the truth. "Patrick."

"Patrick?" Sardar repeated. "His son?" he asked Bone.

"Yes," Bone answered.

"Not those who killed Rutherfield and Frandren?" Bone said, continuing to translate. He looked at Kristine to see what she wanted him to say.

"Patrick killed them, too."

Bone translated. "He asks why."

Kristine shrugged at him. "He was insane?"

"I don't know that word. I'll use 'crazy,'" Bone said, and translated when Kristine gave her permission.

After a second of processing the words, Sardar spoke again.

"He said their expression for, 'I'm sorry for your loss,'" Bone said.

"Thank you," Kristine said.

They shared several seconds of silence.

Kristine was the one to break it. "My father's dying words were, 'Help Sardar.'" After Bone translated, she continued. "How can we help you?"

───────

Sardar summed up the situation as simply as he could.

"Mike left the CIA, but we never stopped working together," Sardar told the Americans. "He provided money. I handled the spies." Thomas wouldn't understand the word for "network."

He waited for the English translation. The American male—Thomas—was far from fluent, and his accent needed a lot of work, but his pronunciation was decent.

But it was far from Mike's abilities—Mike could have passed as a native speaker even after all these years.

Thomas was doing a decent job—and the group had passed Sardar's test. The woman actually was Krissy. The hesitation when he purposefully used her childhood name as Mike often did, knowing from Mike that she despised it, confirmed that. And her grief was obvious.

But Mike had never mentioned a man named Thomas, including on their last call.

While Americans who spoke Pashto were relatively rare, the terrorist mastermind might have a long reach. It was a long shot that the bomber could have a man infiltrate Sardar and Mike's organization—but not impossible. Sardar wasn't worried about providing his real name. It was common enough in the region.

For the moment, though, Sardar would keep his English fluency to himself.

He continued using the simplest Pashto words and phrases he could, checking Thomas's translation all along. "We hunt a terrorist. The man with bombs in the Middle East, South Asia, and Europe the past year. We called him the mastermind."

After another translation, he summed up the situation. "A man will take money to give the location of the mastermind and where the next attack will be. Mike was to meet him soon in Kabul. He would decide if the information could be trusted, give the man the money, stop the attack, and have the mastermind killed using his intelligence contacts."

Thomas translated reasonably well after Sardar offered a few clarifications.

"Without Mike, what can we do?" Sardar asked.

Thomas translated. In the background, there was a whisper from possibly a second man. "I'll go," it sounded like.

"I have someone I can send," Kristine said. "Someone Mike trusted."

Thomas translated, the desire to come to Afghanistan barely hidden in his tone.

"My English. Bad," Sardar said, feeling like a fool at the ruse. But he had to warn Kristine. "Talk Kristine only."

The phone was picked up, and the sound quality changed. He'd been taken off speakerphone. "Wait, please," Kristine said.

"Yes," he replied. She was walking out of the room where the two men were.

"Okay. I am alone," Kristine said, speaking slowly and clearly for him.

"I speak English fluently," Sardar admitted. "But don't give any sign, please. Let it be our secret for now. If you understand and are alone, please say, 'I understand' slowly, the way you spoke a moment ago."

"I understand."

"I am sorry for your father's death. He has been my friend—my brother—for so long." Sardar fought to keep from choking up. There was too much to say and do. "Do you mean you can send Dominic to

Afghanistan? Can we continue Mike's and my work? Just answer yes or no for now."

"Yes."

"Thank you. I spoke with Mike Friday. He was concerned about the situation with Rutherfield and Frandren but didn't mention Patrick—or Thomas. Is Patrick alive?"

"No."

The way she said it…

"Did Mike kill him?"

"No."

No, of course not. Sardar got it. He could see it in his mind. Patrick and Mike having an argument. Patrick killing Mike. And Kristine killing Patrick, probably with the pistol Mike had given her for her birthday a few years before.

"Krissy—Kristine—I am so sorry."

"Thank you," she said, fighting back tears. Trying to be strong—the way her father had taught her to be.

"How well do you know Thomas?"

"Zero," she answered, helping to maintain the ruse.

"Do you trust him?" That was the most important question.

"I don't know."

"Before we make any plans, or speak more in front of him, you must find out who he is and why he is there, even though your father may have thought trusting him was fine. Can you learn more about him?"

A few seconds passed while Kristine considered his question.

"Maybe," she said. "Yes. I have to make a call."

109

THE CURSOR

Kristine smiled patiently as Lou the security guard used the metal detector wand on her. It beeped as usual at the gun tucked into her waistband—the one she had used to kill Patrick. It still had two rounds missing from the magazine.

She'd have to replace them. And it would be smart to "lose" the gun—or break her car window, call the police, and claim it had been stolen from the glove box. If Patrick's body was found—maybe tomorrow, if Thomas's efforts to bag and bury the bodies deep under the pool weren't good enough—it would be much better to not have the murder weapon.

Thankfully, she'd had her wits enough about her to leave the keys to Patrick's motorcycle and her father's SUV with Dominic, and their cell phones in her car when she'd changed into a spare outfit in her office—khakis, a T-shirt, and a light blazer.

The operations room was dark until she flipped the switch to turn on the fluorescent overhead lights. No one worked on Sunday unless Kristine asked them to, which was rare. Mike had instilled in her the importance of treating workers well. They kept the organization's secrets. They deserved to be paid well and given ample time off.

Which reminded her. She still hadn't asked about Melissa's recent vacation to... where did she go? Cancun, maybe, or somewhere nearby. She'd ask on Monday. Like nothing was wrong. Like Kristine hadn't watched her brother kill their father—before she shot Patrick twice.

She stopped in the middle of the room amid the darkened computer monitors, holding back the need to vomit again.

She couldn't get Patrick's expression out of her head, how shocked he'd looked when she'd shot him in the chest.

And the hole in his forehead after the second bullet...

She blinked the image away and continued to the door to the Vault.

Her fingers entered the code without her conscious thought.

There was too much to do. If she kept thinking about last night—and needing to vomit every time the images came into her head—she would never find out if Thomas could be trusted, cover up Mike's and Patrick's deaths, and help Sardar find and kill a terrorist.

She made it inside the Vault and collapsed into the desk chair.

Her sanctuary soothed her. In here, she was in control. Safe.

The monitor came to life when she moved the mouse. She would log in and access the database for the material she needed to send—a video of a congressman in one of the resort's suites, surrounded by naked escorts, with drugs on the coffee table next to the briefcase full of cash he'd received an hour before from a businessman in his district. With it, she could get exactly what she wanted.

The monitor displayed a login prompt different than normal.

PASSWORD:_

The cursor blinked, waiting. All in green, like an old-fashioned computer from years ago.

Normally, there would be a place to enter her user ID and her password—white text on a black background.

Something had changed—but how?

Accessing the computer in here was impossible. First, someone would have to get past Lou or whichever guard was on duty, 24/7.

They'd then have to get into the ops room, which took a ten-digit code, and past the door to the Vault with a different ten-digit code.

And then log in using either her or Dad's ID and password.

The system was accessible over the internet, but that route was well protected, first behind the casino's highly guarded system, then with its own safeguards.

What she saw on her screen was impossible.

Unless the software she'd installed to capture her father's password and keystrokes had infected the system.

The thought turned her blood cold.

Had she ruined everything?

If she couldn't access the computer, would she be able to transfer the money required to pay off the informant?

The banking information was locked in her father's part of the computer. The letter he'd left with Dominic had a username and passcode but no banking institution or website address. All of that should've been easily found once she logged in as him—which she couldn't do.

She had until Dominic's meeting with the informant to figure out a way around this, or all of her father and Sardar's work over the past years would be for nothing.

And if the mastermind wasn't stopped, innocent civilians would soon die in more terrorist attacks.

Kristine shook off the fear that she had caused this situation by betraying her father when she installed the software. This wasn't the time for recriminations.

If the software was to blame, the system might still accept her password.

Kristine hesitated, hating to risk it—a virus might be waiting for her to enter her password so it could be stolen—but she had to try.

The prompt disappeared for an instant before reappearing, looking exactly the same, with the damn green cursor blinking patiently.

She dug her father's letter to Dominic out of her small pocket.

Her father's password didn't work, either.

She was locked out.

110

THE FAVOR

Kristine removed the Vault's cell phone from its frequency-blocking case and called Melissa's number from memory. If anyone could figure out what had happened to the system, it would be her.

The call went directly to voicemail.

After a few choice swear words, she sent a text, expecting a reply immediately.

Nothing.

Melissa was likely following protocol by not replying to a text from an unknown number, despite Kristine having identified herself. She'd have to try from her personal cell when she was back in the car.

For now, she had a mission. And while the blackmail material was inaccessible on the computer for the moment, her father had taught her well.

Time was of the essence. She would improvise.

Kristine used the cell to look up Congressman Nathan Treblen's contact information and dialed.

A recording welcomed her to leave a message for the congressman.

She disconnected and tried the next number, and the next.

In the end, she got through to an emergency answering service and put on her most frantic young mother voice. "This is Jennifer, Kelsey's mom. I need to speak with Nate immediately. It's about his son and my daughter. Please ask him to call me right away! It's an emergency!" She gave the number and waited.

After ten minutes, she called again, sounding more frantic.

Five minutes after that, a concerned but obviously suspicious Nathan Treblen was on the line.

"Oh my gosh, thank you for calling me back!" Kristine said, still in full panic mode.

"My son doesn't know a Kelsey, but I'm calling out of an abundance of—"

"Listen carefully," she said, her voice now cold and all business. "I have a videotape of you accepting a bribe from a local businessman, followed by copious drug use and other behavior with several women in a Las Vegas hotel room. Tell me you understand and move away from your wife, son, or whoever else is with you."

It took a second, but the congressman's answer finally came. "I understand."

It had worked. Like always. She hadn't needed to send a screenshot from the video.

She could do this.

"When we're done, you'll tell your family this call was from a constituent who has mental health issues. You had to talk me down, and you'll put a stop to it tomorrow at the office. Tell me you understand."

"I understand," he repeated, sounding like he was about to start arguing. The marks often did that when confronted. "Listen," Treblen started.

"No. Be quiet," Kristine said, cutting him off. "I will only expose you if you refuse to help me. And don't worry, this is easy. I need the phone number for a man named Gregory Addison. He works for the CIA or another American intelligence agency."

The congressman would try to bargain now, and while she'd always found it amusing when listening to her father's calls like this, she didn't have the time today. She had to preempt him and speed the process along.

"What would your wife say if she saw that video, Congressman? Your son? Your constituents? Or should I start with the FBI? They'd certainly be interested in the briefcase full of cash. As would the IRS."

After a short pause, the congressman spoke. "Gregory Addison, with one of our intelligence agencies." The words were filled with resignation, along with a hint of desperate hope.

"Do this and you'll never hear from me again," she said, knowing he'd latch on to the promise like a drowning man to a life preserver.

She glanced at her watch—the one her father had given her—which made her nearly choke up. A long, deep breath helped. "I'll give you thirty minutes, since it's a Sunday. You can call me back at this number."

The congressman said nothing, though he was still there. She could hear him breathing—or maybe crying.

"Congressman, I have no interest in getting you in trouble. Your secrets are safe with me. Do we have an understanding?"

"Yes… Yes, Miss…?"

"Twenty-nine minutes, Congressman. Goodbye."

Twenty minutes later, the cell phone rang. No number displayed.

"Hello," she said in her calm, cold voice. The congressman would try to buy her silence and demand the video. They always tried to make a deal.

The voice that spoke was unfamiliar.

"I was told you needed to speak to me," the man said. He sounded around her father's age—in his sixties, maybe—and gave nothing away, except for the slightest bit of curiosity beneath the words, but that could have been her imagination.

Before she could answer, he jumped in. "No names," he said, apparently anticipating that she was about to ask if he was Gregory Addison.

Kristine thought for a second. "You worked with my father," she said, hoping she didn't sound as choked up as she felt.

The man—Addison, she hoped—said nothing for a moment, though she thought she heard a sigh.

"He's gone?" Addison asked after a few seconds.

"Yes." She didn't trust herself to say more.

"Do you know who did it?"

"Yes. The same one who… did the other two."

"And has the situation—the threat—been handled?"

"Yes. Definitely."

"Thank you for letting me know. I'm sorry for your loss."

Kristine panicked—he was dismissing her. The call was over. "Wait. I need your help."

Once again Addison said nothing.

"My father spoke highly of you—unlike the other two, or three, I guess. I can't say much, but my father left some unfinished business. I have instructions, and I have help, but he's just one man, and he must be seventy years old." She stopped blabbering, hoping he'd take up the conversation, but there was only silence.

"We have someone who was there when my father…" She cleared her throat. "My father asked if you sent him. He denied it, but the truth is he didn't know. He'd never heard your name. He helped then, and he's offered to help now. I just need to know if I can trust him."

In other words, did Gregory send Thomas—or was Thomas running some kind of scam on her and the organization, the same way she and her father—and Patrick—had taken their marks over the years?

The silence stretched on for several seconds. Finally, Addison spoke. "I'm sorry, I don't have any information on your specific situation, but a saying that has always helped me decide on a person's character is, 'Actions speak louder than words.' I hope that helps. And once again, I'm so sorry for your loss. Your father was a good man. Goodbye."

The call ended.

Kristine stared at the blinking cursor on her computer screen, considering Addison's words.

Thomas had obviously been watching her father and Patrick's confrontation.

He claimed he had saved Everett's life that morning.

Thomas didn't stumble upon that by himself. Someone had sent him. Reading between the lines in her conversation with Gregory Addison, Kristine put her money on Addison working behind the scenes but keeping everyone—including Thomas—in the dark.

Addison couldn't get involved. This way, he had more than mere plausible deniability. He was completely separated from it all.

It's what her father had believed at the end.

She had to trust Dad's expert judgment, Addison's veiled hint, plus her own gut feeling, and get Dominic and Thomas to Kabul as soon as possible.

And somehow figure out a way into the computer server so she could wire the money and stop a terrorist—and the next attack.

111

THE CONFRONTATION

1270 Dove Court
Henderson, Nevada

"You're sure?" Dominic asked Krissy on his cell phone. He stared across the kitchen island at Thomas.

Kristine, not Krissy. Now that Big Mike was gone, she was the boss. The least Dom could do was call the kid by her chosen name instead of what he'd called her when she was an adorable little girl looking up to her big bad "Uncle Dominic."

"I can't check him out the way I'd like—computer issues," Kristine said.

In the kitchen, Thomas sipped coffee. He had to know the call was about him, but he didn't seem nervous or edgy. If anything, he looked exhausted.

"But I made a call and got an answer I'm satisfied with," Kristine continued. "Are you good with him?"

"I don't know yet," Dominic said.

"Decide. Quickly. My next call is to Dad's pilot. I'd like you—both of you, if you're cool with it—wheels up as soon as possible. Best to get you on your way."

"You got it, boss. Talk soon."

Dominic hung up before he heard her reaction to being called the boss.

Across the kitchen island, Thomas set his coffee cup down. "What's the verdict?" he asked.

Dominic didn't believe in beating around the bush—especially not with so much at stake. "She says you're in. Sounds like someone vouched for you—in a way."

"But?"

"But it's my call. I'm not going to war with someone I don't know."

"I feel the same."

They stared at each other. The mysterious Thomas didn't flinch or look away, but he didn't come across as aggressive. Dominic nodded. The kid had himself under control. He'd seen some shit along the way and knew it would show to a fellow warrior.

"I'm Thomas Marks. Former SEAL, like you." He rattled off a few details of his service.

Dominic nodded, neither impressed nor sold yet. Lots of SEALs had gone to war in the past two decades. Most were solid. Some were top-notch. Few were liabilities—they never lasted. It was rare, but there had been a bad apple now and then—and a couple of guys who just weren't quite as dialed in as the others.

Which kind of man was Thomas?

"You've been there and done that, huh? What else should I know about you?"

Dom had thought it through. Instead of asking specific questions, which could be danced around—or outright lied about—the open-ended question would reveal a lot, both in how it was answered and what was said.

Thomas sat silently for a moment. It seemed less of a hesitation and more like he was steeling himself.

"I'm Thomas Marks, as I said. 'Bone.' I was on Operation Clear Water."

Dominic didn't bother to hide his surprise. Both "Bone" and "Clear Water" were familiar.

It clicked. The man in front of him was the only survivor of one of the deadliest ambushes in SEAL history.

"You're 'The Dead Man.'"

"No one really calls me that, do they? And I was only dead for a while," Bone said with a haunted smile.

Dominic took a moment before speaking again. "Sorry about your guys."

"Thanks."

Dominic only knew what he'd read in the news and heard from people who'd heard it from others—third- or fourth-hand. The men had gone down fighting, taking five or six times their number with them.

One guy—Bone—had been pronounced "barely dead" by a frantic medic bent on saving him.

On the medevac chopper, the medic had brought Bone back to life.

Somewhere deep in his soul, Bone hadn't given up, even when dead.

Dominic was happy to go into battle with a warrior like that.

He nodded. The matter was closed.

"What do you need to know about me?" he asked.

"You're Dominic Dawburn?"

Dom nodded, impressed but not too surprised the kid knew his name. The warrior community was pretty small, and he had an unusual name. "What have you heard—and is that a problem?"

Dom knew he had an "interesting" reputation.

Bone shook his head. "You're a hell of a person to go to war with."

"But?"

"But off the battlefield... you can be a little much."

"Yeah. It's not all true, but most of it is."

"Good thing we're going to war then, right?" Bone said with a chuckle.

"You're ready to go back to the Sandbox?"

"All in," Bone said.

"All the time," Dominic said, finishing the phrase.

112

INFORMATION TECHNOLOGY

The Vault
Fortuna Magnifico Casino and Resort
Las Vegas, Nevada

Kristine unlocked the door to the Vault and held it open for the casino's IT manager. "I've never been in here before," he said, half in wonder at the high-tech layout and half accusingly, like Kristine should have invited him down into their secret, illegal operation for lunch a few times a week.

"If you don't mind my asking," he said, his voice low as he stared at the large computer monitors on the desk and the massive one attached to the wall, "what do you do down here?" His bright purple casino polo shirt strained across his ample belly, and he spoke exactly like the chief nerd he was.

"We assist the CEO and the rest of the executives," Kristine said. It was the standard lie Mike, the techs, and she used if any of the casino or hotel staff asked. "That's probably as much as they'd want you to know, but you can call them and ask if you like."

If the IT chief called her bluff, the CEO would go along with anything Kristine said. Mike's file on him was extensive—or would be if she could access the system to view it.

"Gotcha," the man said. "What's the problem?" he asked, angling his head at the computer chair for permission to sit.

She nodded, and he slid into the chair. "The login display changed—and it doesn't accept my password," she said as he moved the mouse and the screen came on. "It used to ask for the username on one line, then password directly beneath. Both in white text on a black background." She pointed to the main screen. "Now it's that."

PASSWORD:__

The cursor blinked next to the word in a bright green, old-fashioned font. "That font has to be from the early days of computing, right?"

The IT guy said nothing as he stared at the screen.

"What?" Kristine asked. "You've seen this before?"

"Um, yeah. Online in a cybersecurity article."

Kristine stared down at him. "That doesn't sound good," she said.

"No. It's very not good. It's a ransomware virus. Hackers used it successfully to steal money a year ago, then offered it for sale on the dark web. But..."

"What?"

"Your system should have been immune to it. You update your security whenever necessary, right? You get our memos? And never click on unknown links?"

"Of course."

"And you're behind our firewall..." he said, mostly talking to himself. He looked up at her. "Who has access to this computer? Here—this server, not the workstations in the next room."

"Only Big Mike and me."

He stared at her like he was giving her a chance to confess.

"Me? No."

Kristine wouldn't mention installing the hidden software to log every keystroke and website. She'd purchased it from a reputable corporate software company specializing in employee monitoring. Her gut told her what she'd done wasn't to blame.

"And Big Mike," the IT chief said, as delicately as possible, in the voice one used when accusing one of Las Vegas's most connected men.

"Never," Kristine said.

The silence stretched for several seconds before he spoke again. "If the hack had come in over the internet, they would have taken us out first. No matter what you're doing down here for the executive committee, no matter how sensitive or secret, the casino's system handles millions of dollars a day on the gaming floor and hundreds of thousands in revenue from the overall company. If they could shut us down, they would—and we would gladly, very quietly, pay whatever they asked. I'm saying we're a bigger, better target. No, whoever hit you did it right here at this keyboard."

"That's impossible," Kristine said. "Literally impossible. Only Mike and I have the passcode. If we both died, you'd be here with a blowtorch cutting the door open. No one gets in."

Damn. Maybe the software she'd installed was to blame.

He gave her a patient smile. "Someone did." He rolled the chair back and stood. "I'm sorry, I can't help you. No one can, probably. You need to wait until you're contacted by whoever hacked you. Be prepared to pay a ransom. Know what it would cost to replace the information or run things without this system. That'll help you decide whether to pay or not. You can always try negotiating, too. That might work and save you some money. Hackers can be manipulated if you figure out what buttons to push."

Kristine thanked the man as she escorted him out of the Vault, through the operations room, and into the small security station.

Once he left, she turned to the guard. "I want to see the log of every single person who came into this room for the past seventy-two hours."

She didn't wait for his reply before turning to unlock the door, pass through the ops room again, and press the code for the Vault.

As she opened the door, she turned to look at the six workstations in the room behind her.

Besides the security guards, the techs were the only people with access to the ops room.

Five of the workstations were too far away or at the wrong angle to see the door's security code keypad.

But the nearest workstation…

Depending on how she and Mike stood in front of the door, there was a small chance the code could have been seen as they entered it.

If the only way the virus could have been introduced into her computer server was through this door, it had to be the software she'd installed—or one of the techs.

She had purchased the software the same way hundreds or thousands of other businesses had. If she was having this issue, others would be too —and the IT tech would have heard and mentioned the problem going around.

No, as impossible as it sounded, the logical conclusion was that one of the techs had snuck into the Vault when she was away and installed the ransomware virus.

Maybe they were all in it together.

But the nearest workstation belonged to her best friend forever: Melissa.

113

THE RISK

58 Desert Song Lane
Henderson, Nevada

For Melissa, remaining in Las Vegas until the first flight to Mexico—leaving in the early afternoon—was a risk.

Staying at her house overnight was problematic as well. If Krissy guessed she had entered the Vault and tampered with the computer server, her home in Henderson would be the first place Krissy and Mike looked.

Booking a hotel in town or anywhere nearby would have been risky, though, too. Once Krissy looked at the house and didn't find her, Mike would put out the word to his extensive list of contacts, from hotel front desk clerks to security guards, homeless people to bell hops. Someone would talk; people would relish Mike's money or—better still—being owed a favor.

And while she could have driven to Los Angeles or Phoenix, they would probably have found her there, too. Mike had a ton of connections in both cities. Besides, leaving town would have aroused immediate suspicion, if anyone had noticed. And she wouldn't put it past Big Mike to not have a way to track her phone or car, too.

She had only one real hope—that neither Kristine nor Mike would attempt to access the computer server before she left for the airport.

No one came into the operations room on Sundays, so the odds were in her favor.

It would work.

Dawn came and went with her sitting on the couch in her living room, curtains drawn, nervously twisting the tiny flash drive in her fingers. Her small green backpack with only the essentials waited by the front door. Her flight was on time, but she had ninety minutes until she ordered a rideshare for the airport.

She could see the light at the end of the tunnel.

Shane's daring plan was working exactly as they'd hoped.

They had spoken when she got home. He had been proud of her, and reassuring, but she couldn't wait to be back in his arms. She would be safe and secure. They'd avenge his sister's murder, then live the rest of their lives together.

She hadn't wanted to risk looking at the contents of the flash drive. Big Mike wasn't a hacker, and neither were her colleagues, but she feared that merely inspecting the data on the miniature drive would trigger a hidden spyware program and reveal her treachery.

But as the time drew closer for her to leave, her curiosity won out. She had to know whether what she'd done—or at least this part of it—had gone as planned.

Melissa risked inserting the flash drive into her laptop.

File names filled the screen. She sorted by size, largest to smallest, and randomly clicked on one—a video file. It showed a nationally known senator in a hotel suite with long lines of white powder on the coffee table. He wore what looked like silk boxer shorts and danced around the room with a naked young woman.

There were dozens of other videos labeled with names she recognized.

Aside from the videos, one of the largest files had an extension she recognized as the database program that kept track of contacts. She had limited access to it at work; only Krissy and Mike could view all of it. And since she didn't have the software installed on her laptop, she couldn't open it now. But she guessed it was the entire database. As long as it wasn't encrypted or password protected, the authorities would be able to open it and access all of Big Mike's information.

The virus had done its job.

Melissa took a minute to password-protect the entire drive. If Krissy or Mike got to her, it wouldn't be accessible to them.

Maybe it would buy her some time, or she could use it as a last-ditch bargaining chip.

She had to tell Shane that the hack had worked. They only communicated via a burner phone she'd bought at a kiosk at the airport on the way home from Cancun.

I couldn't wait. I had to check the flash drive and... it worked! I have it all. Videos, database, etc. It's all here!

I knew you could do it! You're still good?

Yes, she replied. *Counting the seconds. Nervous. More like freaking out.*

Stay strong. You'll be in my arms soon! You're home free.

She wanted to tell him to take it back, to not jinx it, but she didn't. It was fine.

See you very soon, she typed instead. *I'll text you before I board the plane.*

The clock on the phone showed there were only seventy-five minutes until she left for the airport.

114

THE PREPARATION

1270 Dove Court
Henderson, Nevada

Bone stood next to Dominic in the man's primary bedroom, a tidy room with a king-size bed, matching nightstands and dresser—and a walk-in closet with a gun safe bigger than Bone's back home.

"Are you sure about this?" Bone asked, his phone, pistol with spare magazines, and knife in hand.

He didn't mind leaving the burner cell phone behind—he had all his important phone numbers memorized, and the cheap thing likely wouldn't work in Afghanistan without a new SIM card, anyway. But going to war without a weapon was stupid.

"Orders," Dom replied. "Nothing that could be traced back. We'll get clothes and shoes from there when we arrive, too." Dom placed a phone on the top shelf next to two pistols—one larger, plus a smaller, easily concealed gun—and a small knife he'd had clipped to his shorts all morning.

Bone placed his items on the right side of the shelf. They could pick up weapons once they arrived—there was no shortage of guns in the region.

If the mysterious Sardar could smuggle him and Dominic through immigration with no questions asked, along with providing local clothes, a few weapons shouldn't be difficult.

Dom shut and locked the door, sealing their fate.

Bone was going back to Afghanistan.

He had no memory of the final hours of his time in the country, barely clinging to life on a base as the doctors stabilized him before a flight to Germany for surgery.

The last thing he remembered of Afghanistan was coming back to life in the helicopter after the ambush to the medic's surprised words: "Holy shit, it worked!"

And before that…

Bone pictured Tank bleeding into the sand.

Farther away, Bossman, his team lead, slumped over his M4 with a bullet to his face.

The others were scattered across the area, bodies unmoving in the green glow of Bone's night vision goggles.

While the enemy advanced, sensing victory.

"You with me?" Dominic said at the doorway to the hall. His eyes were narrowed, tracking Bone as he came back from the memory of the ambush where his buddies had died one by one.

"Yeah, no problem," Bone said as he joined Dom. "Just thinking through the angles. Wondering about the meet with the informant and how much firepower we can request."

Dom nodded, but Bone didn't think he bought the story meant to cover Bone's slip into the past.

"I'm sure Sardar will work it all out." He held out his hands as they reached the kitchen. "Car keys."

The way he emphasized it made Bone self-conscious about the little hatchback.

Bone handed them over for Dominic to hang on a key holder screwed to the wall next to the door to the garage—stained wood in the shape of a large skeleton key, like the one Bone's family had growing up.

He and Dom had spent the morning moving Patrick's motorcycle and Mike's SUV from Mike's new house to Dominic's garage. It wasn't a permanent solution, but it had to do for now.

"If something's going on with you," Dominic said, "post-traumatic stress or whatever, anything that could affect our mission—I have to know about it now." The older man glared at him, but Bone had years of honing his ability to lie about the pain and trauma buried inside. He had to fake normalcy every day in front of the staff at school, plus the kids—who were often more tuned in to the secrets of adults than anyone realized.

"I'm good to go," Bone said.

After all, it wasn't a lie if he believed it, right?

115

THE PRESSURE

58 Desert Song Lane
Henderson, Nevada

The pressure was unbearable for Melissa. Each minute seemed like an hour. When she wasn't obsessively playing with the flash drive, she was nodding off—both from exhaustion and to escape the stress.

She stared at the bright sun peeking around the blinds at the front window and shook her head.

What was she doing?

She'd been best friends with Krissy since kindergarten.

And she had just met Shane. The intimacy they'd shared had been wonderful, but what did she know about him?

Melissa had researched him when she'd returned from Mexico, of course. Before she'd bought the flash drive and the barrette to smuggle it in and out of the control room.

Shane was exactly who and what he claimed: a reporter from Las Vegas, currently living in Los Angeles. He wrote for a major paper there and had broken some big stories over the past few years, but nothing recently.

His sister had been brutally murdered in Las Vegas in what the police considered an open case. They had no leads.

Shane hadn't written about the investigation—which made sense. He'd told her how the paper wouldn't allow him to report on it—not with him being so close to the story.

Overall, everything checked out.

But what if he was another one of the many losers she managed to attract?

What if she was being scammed?

No. She shook her head in the shaded living room. That was the exhaustion talking. The guilt. The shame. Shane loved her, and she loved him.

They were doing this together to expose Mike's illegal activities. To bring him to justice.

Her eyes closed. She could rest for a while—her phone's alarm would go off when it was time to order the rideshare.

116

ONE MINUTE

The Vault
Fortuna Magnifico Casino and Resort
Las Vegas, Nevada

Sitting in front of the locked computer server, thinking about everything that had happened since last night's dinner, Kristine gave herself one minute to mourn.

When the sweep of the second hand on her watch reached twelve, she shoved the feelings of loss away, as she'd heard Dominic and her father talking about how to do when she was younger.

She was in charge of the organization now.

The weight of responsibility rested on her.

Along with the genuine threat of jail for killing her brother.

But her situation paled in comparison to the mission her father and Sardar had planned. She had to help her father's old friend—who Dad had kept secret for all these years.

She had been ready, eager even, to take over the organization—but figured her father would help her transition to being in charge, or at least be available to advise her.

And Patrick would be her right-hand man, handling the web of informants and schmoozing the marks and the VIPs.

It wasn't supposed to be like this.

Her, all alone, making the crucial decisions without input or advice.

Kristine had figured she'd be a small fish in a big pond as she expanded the operation to target more politicians, to take on more important matters than who would star in a movie or which company's top-secret information she could exploit for massive financial gains.

She'd had no idea of her father's true efforts.

No inkling that the Las Vegas scams and Hollywood deals were window dressing, a disguise to hide the real work.

She was shocked to learn that all the money they'd made from insider trading hadn't gone into investments or greater luxury for her father's new home in the desert, but that he had spent it on an extensive spy network in Afghanistan, Pakistan, and beyond.

Her father: a one-man CIA.

Now what?

She organized the priorities.

Big picture: She had to help stop a terrorist mastermind.

Dom and Thomas had to fly to Afghanistan.

She could handle that—Dad's pilot was an old friend. Mike had made the arrangements. All she needed was to change the timeline to whatever Sardar recommended.

Most pressingly, she had to get into the computer to wire the money once Dom and Thomas met with the informant and felt like the deal could be done, and that the money was in fact buying the details of an upcoming terrorist attack, along with the secret of who and where the terrorist mastermind was.

She'd then have to pass along the information to people who could do something about it immediately.

Her father probably had details in his side of the computer—contact information for old friends in the intelligence business.

She would have to cross that bridge when she came to it.

Because first, she had to find her best friend Melissa and discover if—along with how and why—Melissa had betrayed her.

And last but certainly not least, Mike and Patrick had to disappear in a way that didn't raise questions—especially from the authorities.

Assuming their bodies weren't discovered Monday or Tuesday by the people building the pool in Mike's backyard.

Among all of the rest of it, she had to somehow grieve…

And process the magnitude of killing her brother.
She fought back tears.
That would have to wait.
Right now, she had calls to make…
And a former friend to find.

117

EMPTY

58 Desert Song Lane
Henderson, Nevada

Melissa woke with a start. The alarm hadn't gone off yet—she still had a while before she needed to leave for the airport—but something had disturbed her.

The burner phone was silent. There were no new texts from Shane.

Her real phone was waiting on her nightstand until she could safely return to Las Vegas after Mike and Kristine were in jail.

What had woken her?

Her hands were empty.

That was it.

The tiny flash drive she'd been fidgeting with to manage the stress was gone.

118

THE ESCAPE

58 Desert Song Lane
Henderson, Nevada

After a frantic few minutes, Melissa found the flash drive in between the couch cushions. With a relieved sigh that came out more like a sob, she undid her hair and slipped the mini thumb drive into the safety of the ornate silver hair clip, clipped the barrette into place, and tried to calm down.

There were still forty-five minutes until the plan called for ordering the ride, but she couldn't wait any longer.

She'd risk being seen by one of Mike's spies at the airport.

Anything to move, to get out of the too-quiet home, to escape.

She used the burner phone to order the ride, knowing that if Mike or Krissy were monitoring their staff's credit cards or tracking the rideshare apps, the burner phone would be worthless. The app still used her account and was linked to her credit card.

But it was a risk she had to take.

119

DESERT SONG LANE

58 Desert Song Lane
Henderson, Nevada

Kristine coasted past Melissa's house. The blinds were drawn, and there was no car in the driveway. The home felt deserted. But it was late morning on a scorching-hot summer Sunday; Melissa might be at the grocery store. Or she could be inside working out, or on the back patio.

There was no way to know without knocking on the door and confronting her best friend, which she wasn't looking forward to.

Being in charge of the organization wasn't turning out to be at all like she'd thought it would.

Kristine pulled to a stop along the curb, her instincts telling her not to park in the driveway. After the night she'd had, and not knowing how this meeting would go down, she wanted to be able to jump in the car and drive away fast without reversing into the street.

Before she could turn off the car, Melissa barged out the front door, looking frazzled. Several strands of the brown hair she'd been growing out had come undone from her favorite silver barrette she had worn every day for a month now. She had a green backpack slung on one shoulder. After locking the door, Melissa took two steps along the walkway toward Kristine's car before turning back to double-check the door was securely locked.

What the hell was going on? Had Melissa been expecting her? That made no sense. If she was guilty, she should have been on the first flight out of the city last night.

She wouldn't wait for Kristine to pull up to her house—and then rush to the car.

The rideshare car was nicer than usual, but Melissa wasn't going to complain. The app had said a black sedan, and here it was, ten minutes earlier than promised.

She resisted checking the front door lock for a third time. Although she wasn't usually obsessive like that, the stress of the past month, and especially the last twenty-four hours, had her on edge like never before.

All she wanted to do was get to the airport and go through security. Once she was there, it would be much harder for Mike or anyone in his pocket—except for the police—to get to her.

If she made it that far, she'd be home free—like Shane had said.

The flash drive was in her barrette, and she had enough clothes in her backpack to get by for a while. By then, Mike and Kristine would be in custody, their empire in tatters, and she could come back home—with Shane—and start over.

Or sell the house and live in Mexico, where Shane still was. Start fresh. They could settle in a tourist town, get jobs, and put the past behind them.

The fantasy calmed her nerves and got her to the curb. She was always uncertain what to do in this situation. It was someone's private car—their side hustle. Yes, she was paying for the ride, but it wasn't a taxi or limo. Where should she sit? If it was similar to a ride from a friend, shouldn't she sit in the front? Or since she was a customer, should she ride in the back?

Melissa shook off the concern, opened the rear passenger door of the upscale car, and slid in the back.

"Thanks for coming early," she said, setting her backpack carefully on the expensive-looking leather of the backseat. She touched the hair barrette to check it was still firmly attached and absently brushed loose strands of hair behind her ears, proud she had remembered to do it with her left hand.

The car didn't move.

"Is there a problem?" Melissa asked, finally meeting the driver's eyes in the rearview mirror.

The eyes not of a stranger, but of her best friend, boss, and one of the two people in Las Vegas she'd hoped to never see again.

120

THE GAMBIT

58 Desert Song Lane
Henderson, Nevada

There was nowhere for Melissa to run. She sat paralyzed in the back seat of Krissy's car, eyes locked on her friend, knowing her face gave away her guilt, stress, and shame.

At least Big Mike wasn't here.

Yet.

Images of the torture she was about to endure threatened to overwhelm her, but she thought of Shane—and the ransomware virus password locked in her bank's safe deposit box.

She could make it out of this alive…

Maybe.

Melissa pressed her lips together and steeled herself for what was to come.

If they didn't kill her right away, all she had to do was hold out until they forced her to the bank in the morning.

Once there, she could cause a scene. Scream. Cry for help.

The people in the bank couldn't be part of Mike's organization.

Not everyone in the city was on his payroll.

Someone would help her.

If she could last until tomorrow morning.

Kristine took one look at Melissa's face in the mirror and knew her best friend had betrayed her.

Acting on instinct, she slammed the car into gear and floored the accelerator. The car roared forward, leaving tire marks on the pavement.

The doors locked automatically. There was no way Melissa could open the back doors until the car was parked.

Her father's new house—isolated at the edge of the new, mostly deserted housing development—wasn't far away.

It would make a great place to have a private "chat" with Melissa, find out what was going on—along with how to fix the computer server in the Vault—and then decide what came next.

The shovel was still in the garage, and there was plenty more room in the dirt at the deep end of the pool.

121

THE U-TURN

Kristine barely slowed for the stop sign at the exit from the housing development. No cars were coming from either direction, so she rolled through the intersection and sped up as she turned toward her father's new house.

In the back passenger seat, Melissa sat with her lips pressed tightly together and arms crossed, defiant. She refused to meet Kristine's eyes in the mirror.

Kristine had less than fifteen minutes to decide.

How far was she willing to take things with her oldest friend?

If Melissa wouldn't tell her what happened...

Kristine wasn't naïve. Many of the men and women her father had used or blackmailed were terrified of him—and Dominic. There must have been at least the occasional threat of violence. Threats that happened when she wasn't around.

Or more than mere threats.

But Dominic was prepping for the trip to Afghanistan.

And her father was gone.

She ran the organization now.

The choice was hers.

Violence.

Or threats—but without follow-through if Melissa called her bluff.

There had to be another way.

Kristine took another look at her friend in the back seat and made her decision.

There was a break in traffic. She slowed, cranked the wheel, and hung an illegal mid-block U-turn.

"We're going back to your house," Kristine said. "I need your help."

Melissa glanced at her friend in surprise, but Kristine was focused on driving back the way they'd come.

It had to be a ploy.

Yet another one of Mike and Krissy's cons.

Melissa wouldn't fall for it.

She wasn't one of their marks.

"Mike's dead," Kristine blurted out as she signaled and turned into the housing subdivision she'd left a minute before. She could sense Melissa's suspicion and defiance. If she didn't get to the heart of the matter immediately, Melissa might jump out of the car and run into the house once the car stopped.

"You're one of two people who know," she said, purposefully omitting Thomas from the equation, along with her father's old intelligence friends.

Even that felt wrong. She didn't want to start this discussion—or negotiation, or whatever it was—with a lie. "Sorry, that's not completely true. You're the fifth person besides me who knows. I won't talk about who, but I'm going to tell you the truth and hope I can earn your trust. Because whatever happened—and happens—I really do need your help."

Kristine fought back tears. The feelings of losing her father—and shooting Patrick—weren't staying buried the way she'd hoped.

In the mirror, Melissa looked shocked, but her arms remained crossed.

"Patrick shot him," Kristine said. She took a breath and added the kicker. "Then I shot Patrick. I buried their bodies in the backyard of Mike's new home."

She pulled the car into Melissa's driveway and put the car in park. The automatic door locks clicked open. Melissa could now escape if she wanted.

"You could call the police," Kristine said. "I'd be in trouble for not reporting the incident and for hiding the bodies, but eventually I'd get off. It was self-defense, and I have a witness. But you'd win—if it's you behind the ransomware virus, like I think it is. The police would look into the organization, grant you immunity from prosecution to testify, and I'd be ruined."

Melissa stared at her, eyes wide. She hadn't run yet, but she still wasn't convinced enough to help.

"Or we can go inside, I can tell you what else is going on…" Kristine trailed off.

How far down this new road was she prepared to go? It went against every strategic impulse in her to trust the person who had likely gotten her into this mess with the computer server, but radical honesty might be the only way to reach Melissa. "I need to get back into the computer to catch an international terrorist," she said. It sounded far-fetched to her ears, but the truth was the truth. "If you help with that, I'll be able to stop a bomb attack and turn the intelligence over to the good guys to capture or kill the terrorist. After that…"

She hated to make this bargain, but if that's what it took, so be it.

"I'll give you money. Or turn myself in and pay for the crimes Mike and I have committed. Whatever you want."

Kristine turned to face her friend—and waited.

The seconds ticked by as Melissa processed the offer.

Finally, Melissa sighed. "You better come inside. We have a lot to talk about—and some big decisions to make."

122

THE DEAL

58 Desert Song Lane
Henderson, Nevada

Melissa had only been gone a few minutes, but the house already felt hot and stuffy. She and Krissy sat in the kitchen, unopened bottles of water from the refrigerator in front of each of them, dripping condensation onto the dark, polished wood of the kitchen table.

Melissa canceled the rideshare moments before it arrived—paying a fee, but that didn't matter. Right now, she had to give her old friend a chance to explain herself, and figure out what to do after that.

She listened intently to Krissy's story, waiting for the lies, justifications, and bullshit, but they never came.

Instead, her friend poured her heart out, telling the story of the past eighteen hours: the doctor's private meeting with Big Mike; Patrick's proud, demented confession; him shooting Mike; Krissy shooting him; and the stranger who appeared to help bury the bodies.

And the incredible reality behind Mike's illegal empire—this whole time, he'd been channeling money into a two-man version of the Central Intelligence Agency in a secret pursuit of a mysterious man who coordinated the bombings of soldiers during the war in Afghanistan, along with, more recently, innocent men, women, and children around the world.

It was all too wild to not be true.

But as good as Krissy's motives were, it still didn't explain—or justify —what Big Mike had done to Shane's sister.

"I haven't convinced you," Krissy said in the soft, quiet way she used to speak when they were younger, before she'd blossomed while working at Mike's organization. "Why not? All I need is for you to undo the ransomware virus. I'll fund the informant, stop the terrorist, and then you can lock the computer server again until I give you what you want. Money. Or call the police, as I said. I'll cooperate. Why won't you help?"

"Because of what you did to Shane's sister," Melissa blurted out, the first words she'd spoken since they came into the house.

"Who's Shane?" Kristine asked, entirely at a loss.

"My boyfriend," Melissa answered with a combination of pride and... what? Surprise, it sounded like. But her poorly hidden glow of pleasure faded immediately. "Big Mike murdered his sister—or had Dominic do it for him. Same difference." Melissa's face once again had a fierce, angry glare.

Kristine opened her mouth to deny that Mike would ever do anything like that, but closed it before speaking. So far, telling the truth had worked. She had convinced Melissa of the importance of the mission, and she wasn't going to blow it now by pretending Mike had been a saint.

He'd kept so much from her.

The hunt for the mastermind.

Sardar in Afghanistan.

The years of sending their insider trading money overseas to keep an intelligence network alive.

She'd had no idea. Not a clue.

It was entirely possible Dad had ordered Dominic to kill people.

"I..." she said before trailing off. She nodded. "It could have happened, but I never heard about it, and I'd remember the names 'Shane' or 'Lopez.' Do you have any other details?"

Melissa told the story. To Kristine's ears, it sounded like total BS.

"It might be true—you can check the database yourself, though if there was a murder involved, it might not be in there. But I'm sorry, my friend," Kristine said as gently as she could. "To me, it sounds like a story made up to pull you in. There could be kernels of truth—Shane's sister might have been murdered, but I doubt it was by us. It sounds like something Dad,

Patrick, and I would come up with to manipulate a mark and get her to do exactly what we wanted."

They were at an impasse, but...

"There's an easy way to resolve this," Kristine said. "Let's go to the Vault. There has to be some record of Shane's sister—or someone she was connected to. We can search by name, city, dates, whatever. We'll find it if it's there. If not..." She trailed off, desperately reaching for a solution that would allow her to access the computer server to transfer the money to the informant when it was time. "We'll figure something out, okay?"

Melissa didn't hesitate. "We can't. I don't have the password. It's locked in a safe deposit box, and the bank doesn't open until tomorrow."

Kristine did the math. It would be Monday morning when they could go to the bank for the password, then get to the Vault. That would be fine. If Dominic and Thomas left later tonight, they wouldn't arrive until tomorrow afternoon Las Vegas time, which would be Tuesday night in Kabul. The meet could happen right away or several days later—Sardar would be finding out soon: Monday morning in Kabul.

"That will work," Kristine said. "You help me with this, and in exchange, I promise to figure out what happened with Shane's sister and..." She hesitated, then plunged forward. "And make it right— whatever the cost."

Melissa didn't hesitate. She stuck out her hand. "Deal."

"Deal," Kristine said as they shook. "But with you about to fly somewhere—to meet Shane, I'd imagine—I'm going to have Lou, the security guard from work, come over and hang out here until tomorrow morning, okay?"

Melissa shrugged. "I'm not going to run. I'll see this through at least until tomorrow night."

This time, Kristine stuck out her hand for Melissa to shake. "Until at least tomorrow night," Kristine said, and she hoped it would be that simple.

123

THE RESCUE

58 Desert Song Lane
Henderson, Nevada

Melissa sat at the kitchen table, the barrette with the mini flash drive safely tucked inside holding back her hair. Kristine had no idea there was more to the plan than merely the ransomware virus.

Lou, the security guard from outside the operations room, was engrossed in his cell phone in the living room with a clear view of her. If she stood, he'd put down his phone and pay attention. He had already followed her to the bathroom once, standing near the door to make sure she didn't crawl out the window next to the toilet.

Kristine had confiscated her burner and personal cell phones, leaving her with no way to contact Shane. But when she didn't text from the Las Vegas airport, or arrive in Mexico as planned, he'd know something had gone horribly wrong.

Shane would come for her.

He had to.

Together, they'd help Kristine catch the terrorist—Melissa believed her friend's story. She couldn't allow the next attack to happen or the people responsible to escape.

Then she and Shane could make a new plan, maybe go to the police together with the data from the flash drive, the story of Shane's sister, and whatever Melissa found on the computer server.

If Kristine went to jail willingly, fine.

If not, they'd have all they needed to make sure Krissy paid for what she and Mike had done—no matter what else Big Mike had been doing over the years to save the world.

124

THE JET

Bone sat in the back passenger seat of Kristine's car, directly behind Dominic. Kristine parked near a private jet on the tarmac of the executive airport, with the car running and the air conditioner on full blast. Even in the evening, the heat was ferocious. They had delayed their departure to arrive around 10 p.m. Kabul time, when Sardar could guarantee they wouldn't have to deal with customs and immigration personnel.

On the drive from Dominic's house, they'd had as detailed a mission brief as they could—which wasn't much.

They were flying to Kabul.

They'd leave their IDs with the pilots for safekeeping.

Upon landing, they would theoretically be allowed off the airplane without any questions.

A car would meet them.

They'd get local clothes, weapons, and phones, along with instructions about what was next, all courtesy of Sardar, Mike Salestri's fellow spy.

At some point in the next few days, they would meet with the informant who was willing to betray the mastermind.

Assuming it wasn't a setup—a pretty big assumption—and that the guy seemed legit, Dominic would contact Kristine, who would wire the money to a numbered account accessible from anywhere in the world, or to the informant's account if he had his own.

The source would then give them details about the next terrorist attack, along with the name and location of the mastermind.

After that, Bone and Dominic's work would be done. Kristine would send the plane back, and they'd fly home.

Meanwhile, Salestri's former CIA, Mossad, or other intelligence agency contacts would stop the attack and capture or kill the mastermind.

Easy.

In theory.

Bone kept his discomfort at the lack of proper planning to himself, but he bet Dominic felt the same way he did.

They were traveling to a dangerous country on a secret, unsanctioned mission to bribe a foreigner with funds procured illegally.

Not an ideal situation.

"Dad's phone should work over there as a backup form of communication," Kristine said as she handed Mike's cell phone to Dom. "The password, phone number, and secure app username and password are on a sticky note on the back. Memorize them, then destroy the note."

"Got it," Dom said. He looked at the note for several seconds before showing it to Bone, who also committed the information to memory.

Next, Kristine asked Bone to hand her the backpack on the seat next to him. It looked like a standard large laptop bag. When he passed it to her, she unzipped the main compartment and removed two stacks of hundred-dollar bills.

"Here's ten thousand dollars each—pocket money courtesy of Big Mike," she said, handing each of them one packet. "That leaves eighty thousand in the bag. It should be more than enough to get you out of any jam you find yourself in."

Bone and Dom pocketed the money. Dom zipped the bag and held it in his lap.

"One last time—everyone clear on the plan?" Kristine asked.

"Yes," Bone said.

Dominic nodded. "We meet the guy, somehow confirm he has the goods on the mastermind and that we're not being set up or scammed, and call you. You give him access to the money. He gives up the bad guy. We call you again with the details."

"I'll handle it from there with Dad's old colleagues," she said.

Kristine was a good liar, but Bone caught a hint of deception.

"What aren't you telling us?" he asked.

She shook her head, but didn't deny his accusation. "Nothing to worry about."

"That just makes me more worried," he said.

"Fine. Then let's say it's nothing you can help with. It's something I have to handle here, but everything's fine." She held his gaze, and he believed her.

There was nothing more to say. After a second, Bone and Dom reached for the door handles at the same time and stepped out of the car.

"Good luck," Kristine called.

"Luck is for amateurs," Dominic said under his breath, only loud enough for Bone to hear, while he gave a thumbs-up to Kristine.

Bone would normally agree, but for this mission, they'd need all the help they could get.

125

THE CITIES

Conference Room 1
Central Analysis Group Headquarters
Alexandria, Virginia

Gregory eased the door closed and locked it behind him.

The taped-together papers still covered the conference table.

The room once again stank of body odor, smelly feet, and bad breath.

Gregory moved to the mind map.

A few notes had been added, but the box at the center was still empty.

Wyatt looked strung out again. His curly dark hair stuck out in every direction. He shifted his weight from foot to foot, and his body twitched with excitement.

"I've finally got it!" Wyatt said. "See, at first the pieces didn't fit together, but then I—"

"Just take it step by step," Gregory said. Marcus caught his eye and gave Gregory a nod.

If Marcus was on board, this might be the real deal.

"Right. Right. Okay," he started, gesturing to the patchwork of papers taped together on the table. "I know how this sounds, but I believe a former Pakistan intelligence officer is the man behind the bombings. What I need is..." Wyatt hesitated and stepped close to whisper in his ear so

Marcus wouldn't hear. "Remember how I needed access to a computer a while back, and the next day you had a login and password?"

Gregory said nothing. Marcus looked away, minding his own business.

"I know it's a big ask, but I need access to the ISI's human resources computer. Is that…?"

"Impossible," Gregory said. He had a hacker at his disposal—in a roundabout way, via Haley—but Gregory wouldn't ask for what Wyatt wanted. If the ISI caught the hacker or suspected the Central Analysis Group was involved, there would be hell to pay.

"Without access," Wyatt said, no longer whispering, "this is only a theory. I don't have a name, a location, nothing. But the patterns clearly suggest the same person who made IEDs during the war in Afghanistan— or taught the people who did—is behind the bombings around the world."

He pointed at a new sticky note off to the side of the mind map. On it, Wyatt had carefully printed: ***Pakistan ISI officer? Retired?***

"Take me through why you believe that," Gregory said. Maybe he could find a way to help.

What they had was thin.

"It's a decent hypothesis, but it's not enough," Gregory said. "Certainly not for what you requested," he told Wyatt. Gregory wasn't worried about Marcus guessing that Wyatt had wanted access to the ISI's computers. "Here's what I want you to do. Focus on when and where the next attack could be. What if you were right and the terrorist groups that claimed credit were not the ones who planned and perpetrated the attacks? If it's a Pakistani ISI officer behind it all? And whether it's a terrorism-for-hire organization or not, where would they target next? When?"

"That's easy," Wyatt said. "We've already looked at some of that. They've been working closer and closer to targeting the West."

"The United States?"

No," Wyatt said, shaking his head as he stared at the mind map. "I doubt they have the capacity for that yet. My bet would be Europe. A capital city. London, Paris, Barcelona—"

"They already hit Spain," Marcus pointed out. "The airport on the island of Mallorca."

"Good point. Not Spain again. Vienna? Prague?" Wyatt asked.

"Nothing against them, but they aren't high profile enough," Marcus said.

"Okay, then Rome, Berlin, Amsterdam, Milan…"

Marcus bit his lip. "London, Paris, Rome, Berlin, Zurich. Maybe Amsterdam."

"What about the Middle East?" Wyatt asked. "They could be targeting oil wells, shipping… They could attack Dubai, anywhere in Israel…"

"Or Jedda, leading to Mecca and Medina…"

Gregory shook his head. "That's too many to do full workups. Focus on the highest probabilities. Put yourself in their shoes. If you weren't capable of attacking the United States, what would be your top three cities?"

"London, Paris, and Rome," Wyatt answered immediately.

"I'd swap out Rome and choose Berlin," Marcus said. "It's bigger, has more people, and feels closer to America than Rome. Just a gut feeling. Though Rome has more tourists."

"Fine," Gregory said. "Prep an assessment of the most likely targets of a bombing in London, Paris, and Berlin—in that order. And Rome if you have extra time. Where are the weaknesses? Where do people congregate, from the average citizen to the top people in government? Assuming you're correct about a terrorism-for-hire scheme, what would make the most appealing targets to sell to extremists? But worry less about who and more about where—and when."

"Yes, sir."

"Get busy. Come find me when you have something," Gregory said as he moved to the door. They were on the right track now. As they worked the problem, something would come up.

126

THE PATIO

58 Desert Song Lane
Henderson, Nevada

The stress and anxiety of the past several days hit Melissa hard. She dozed on the couch all afternoon and well into the evening, not sure if Lou took cat naps, too, or stayed awake watching her sleep.

As the sun set, she woke up hungry—with a certainty that Shane was coming. While Lou kept an eye on her, she went to the kitchen to find something for dinner.

She was committed to helping Krissy with the plan they'd agreed to, but she longed to see Shane and explain the situation. Between the two of them, they'd make sure they didn't get conned...

As long as Krissy was right, and Shane wasn't the one conning her.

Krissy had never lied to her.

Even this morning, Kristine had told her about Mike and Patrick, including where their bodies were buried.

Why did Melissa believe Shane over her oldest friend?

Maybe Shane was the one she had to watch out for, not Krissy.

Melissa's doubts grew. Shane had targeted her from the start. Could he be lying about everything?

She fought back the urge to vomit.

Only one of them could be trusted—her best friend, or the love of her life.

She wasn't sure which one to hope was telling the truth.

Hot soup wasn't exactly the ideal dinner on a summer night, but it was what Melissa had in her pantry. She heated up a can for herself and one for Lou.

"Let's get some fresh air. It should be cooler with the sun down," she said, following her gut. If Shane had acted as soon as she hadn't texted him from the airport, he could be in Las Vegas by now. Lou would never let him into the house, which meant she had to get outside to have a chance at communicating with him.

Lou stood well back from her, perhaps wary of the bowls of hot soup in her hand. She could have told him not to worry, she wouldn't hurt him, but he wouldn't believe that. Instead, she balanced the second bowl on her wrist and arm as she unlocked the sliding door to the back patio, slid it open, and stepped out. Lou followed a few seconds later.

The air was still hot, but it felt good after being stuck in the air conditioning all day. And the 20-degree change between the hottest part of the day and the evening made all the difference. Desert dwellers enjoyed being outside after dark; the lack of sunshine made the nights feel relatively cooler.

A gasp came from behind her as the air crackled with energy. She cried out in surprise and dropped the bowls, which shattered on the concrete patio. As she turned, Lou dropped to the ground, still convulsing. Thin silver wires trailed from his chest to a black and yellow gun held by a grinning Shane standing against the wall, close to the door. His dark hair perfectly in place, his big, beautiful brown eyes gorgeous in the glow of the overhead patio light.

"Are there more inside?" he whispered.

Melissa shook her head.

Shane hurried forward, rolled Lou onto his stomach, and slipped black zip ties around each of the guard's wrists before using two more to connect them. He did the same with the man's feet, and finally connected his wrists and ankles together, hog-tying him. Lou groaned as Shane grabbed an ankle and used it to drag him back into the house, frantically gesturing for her to follow.

"What happened?" he asked, sliding the door shut and locking it. "They figured it out?"

Melissa rushed to him, holding tight, relishing the feel of his arms around her. "Kristine showed up and... She just knew." She couldn't bring herself to admit that she'd willingly confessed immediately.

Shane gently pulled back, but he kept hold of her arms. "Did she get the flash drive, or just guess you were behind the ransomware?"

Her hand went subconsciously to the hair clip with the tiny thumb drive. "Only the computer server virus. She doesn't know about the rest of it. We can still use the data on the flash drive to take them down. But Big Mike is dead. Krissy wouldn't give me details," she said, lying without thinking. She fought back tears. "I know it doesn't bring your sister back, but the man responsible is gone. Murdered, I think."

For an instant, Shane looked confused. His eyes narrowed, and he tilted his head. The next moment, he pulled her close in a tight hug. "That is a huge relief," he said with his face buried in her hair.

Between the look when she mentioned his sister, the feel of his arms around her, and the way he spoke, she knew.

Shane had played her.

Kristine was right.

There was no dead sister. Big Mike hadn't ordered her killed—because she didn't exist. A woman with Shane's last name had been murdered. There had been stories about her in the Las Vegas news. But now that Melissa thought about it, they had never mentioned a brother who was a reporter. And the last name was so common...

Once again, she'd been a sucker and had fallen for a loser.

Melissa realized too late that their closeness was a double-edged sword. While she'd felt his lie, he must have sensed her revelation.

And revulsion at his touch.

Shane pushed her away, and they locked eyes.

Her body froze as her nerve endings burned with excruciating pain.

From a distance, she heard the crackle of the stun gun.

Then she was falling, unable to control her body as electricity coursed through her.

She wished she had never gone on vacation to Mexico.

PART 8

MONDAY

127

THE CHANGE

Chai Corner
Shahr-e-Naw District
Kabul, Afghanistan

Monday Morning (Afghanistan Time)

Sardar couldn't shake the feeling of being watched, though there had been no more suspicious vehicles following him since Saturday.

He sipped tea and ate naan with honey at one of his primary cafes—where the server's network had first heard from the informant.

The air grew warmer. It would be another brutally hot day.

He slid the latest folded note from the newspaper into his pocket, praying no one watched with binoculars and saw the subtle movement. He wanted desperately to read the message, but he couldn't take the risk. His strict adherence to proper spy tradecraft had kept him alive all these years.

After another sip of tea, he read more of the newspaper, resisting the desire to hurry. Today was like any other day. He tried to convince himself no one watched him. He wasn't being targeted with a sniper rifle from the many rooftops in the affluent neighborhood, and no one sat in cars behind tinted windows near his SUV down the street, waiting to abduct and torture him.

No, everything was fine. Just another day as a successful Afghan businessman. Nothing to worry about at all.

He finished his tea and bread, paid, and returned to the SUV.

Once behind the tinted windows, he carefully removed the folded note from his pocket and read.

The informant wanted to meet tomorrow morning—much earlier than planned—at a busy cafe in the city.

Mike, with his years in the country and fluent Pashto, would have blended in well at the cafe, negotiated the deal, and been out of the country before anyone knew he was there.

The new man—Thomas—might be okay, as long as he didn't have to speak. His accent would betray him as a foreigner if he had to say more than a few simple words.

Sardar would have to go along—which would not be a problem, as long as no one was actually following him.

"To the office," he told his driver.

As they drove through the congested streets, he desperately thought of a way to break free from any potential surveillance this evening so he could pick up Thomas and Dominic, take them to the rendezvous, do the deal, and escort them back to the airport, all without being seen or shot.

128

THE DESERT

Sunday Night (Pacific Daylight Time)

In her dreams on a night like this, Melissa would have loved being in the desert with Shane.

They could have set out a blanket in the sand and admired the brilliant expanse of stars.

Tonight, though, she struggled to stay calm as Shane rolled Lou out of the back of Shane's rental SUV. The poor guard was still hog-tied, and the older man landed on the ground with a pained grunt.

A second later, it was her turn. At least Shane pulled her along the trunk area instead of rolling her, and half-lifted her down to the ground. It wasn't a soft landing, but it didn't hurt.

"Shane, you don't have to do this," she said, using her most persuasive girlfriend voice. He'd already taken the mini flash drive from her hair clip. "Whatever you have planned, we can—"

"No," he interrupted with a sad laugh. "There's no doing it together at this point."

"You don't have to kill us," she whispered.

Shane sighed, annoyed. "I told you, I'm not going to kill either of you. But I can't have you messing with my plans, either." He arranged them back-to-back on their sides. In the glow of the parking lights, Melissa tried to catch his eye, to convince him not to do whatever he had planned, but he ignored her. She was a slab of meat to be dealt with, not someone he had made love with and promised they'd always be together.

Behind her, Lou struggled to get to his feet. Shane moved around her and must have kicked him—a dull *thud*, followed immediately by a gasp of pain from Lou. "Stop, or I'll have to rethink the plan of leaving you alive. I'm on a deadline here."

Several seconds later, Melissa's bound hands were zip-tied to Lou's, and their ankles were connected, too. But at least they weren't hog-tied anymore.

"If you work together, you should be able to get to your feet," Shane explained as he loomed over them, admiring his handiwork. "Hop, or shuffle your steps. You're about 9 miles from the highway, but there are off-road tours around here all the time. Maybe not so much on a weekday in the summer, though," he muttered, with a trace of regret in his voice. "Take it easy and you have a good chance of living."

He kneeled next to Melissa and gently brushed back a long strand of hair that had come loose from the barrette. "I'm sorry I lied to you, but I couldn't be sure if you'd go along with me if I told you the truth. I did love you, in my own way."

Melissa wanted to argue that using someone to get what you wanted wasn't anything close to love, but she sensed she had an opening. Shane felt something toward her, and she could exploit that now. If she made it out of this alive, she'd need everything she could get to have her revenge.

"What's the truth? I'll tell you if it would have been enough for me to do all this with you. For us."

Shane smiled sadly, his face red in the glow of the taillights. "I'm a reporter, as I said. Originally, I worked here in Las Vegas. I was researching a story about the most powerful people in the city and kept hearing hints of a 'power behind the throne' type of person. One night, I got a lead really drunk, and he gave me Mike Salestri's name, along with a warning to not cross him. That Big Mike had dirt on everyone from Hollywood actors, directors, and producers to local and national politicians. And that a bunch of people owed him favors for helping them out of jams. He was loved, hated, and feared."

Melissa stared up at him. "What about your sister? Was that real?"

Shane shook his head. "The woman who got killed is real. But she's not my sister. I searched for an unsolved murder of someone with my last name and got lucky."

Melissa fought back tears. "All this to write a story?"

Shane laughed. "Not just a story! An exposé that will bring down his empire, and put him and his daughter in jail. Or—thanks to your miniature flash drive," he said, patting his pocket, "I might not write the story, and just use the opportunity to transfer all of his power to me. Or demand payment to unlock their computer server. I haven't decided yet, but tonight I'm leaning toward the 'vast power and endless riches' option." He touched her hair again. "It could have been us. I would have enjoyed blackmailing people with you." Shane leaned closer. "So tell me. If I had been honest with you from the start, would you have betrayed your best friend, risked the wrath of Big Mike, and blackmailed people, bleeding them dry little by little while living a life of luxury with me, happily ever after?"

She tried to fake it, to get him to release her and take her along so she could escape and call Krissy, but Shane read her like a book. "Not so much. Too bad."

He stood. "Gotta go. Good luck. Nice night for a hike. Better hurry—it'll be brutal out here once the sun comes up." He smiled down at her. "It was really fun for a while, Melissa. Thanks for everything."

Melissa struggled with the zip ties as Shane left her behind and climbed into the SUV, but she couldn't break free.

"Let him go," Lou said. The SUV engine turned over, and Shane drove away slowly, avoiding throwing rocks into her face. "We can get out of this, but the more time we have before it gets hot, the better."

As she watched the SUV recede into the desert, mile by mile, Lou was already hard at work doing something behind her, moving his hands and feet, dragging hers along with him.

129

THE FRICTION

Unknown Location
Outside Las Vegas, Nevada

The desert was dark despite the stars. She could sense the openness more so than see it.

Getting to her feet with Lou, tied together like they were, seemed challenging at best. Hopping 9 miles was next to impossible.

They might die out here, exhausted from trying to save themselves, baking to death in the sun and heat.

Despite it all, though, Lou kept moving on the ground behind her.

"What are you doing?" Melissa asked. His struggles were causing the zip ties around each wrist to bite deeply, and there was a trickle of blood from both.

"Removing my shoelace," Lou grunted. "Almost... There. Can you grab that end?"

The shoelace brushed her fingers. She missed it the first time, then snagged it between her middle and ring finger the second time Lou wiggled. "Got it. Now what?"

"Wrap it a time or two around a few fingers so it doesn't slip. I've got the other end, and I wrapped the middle around the zip tie holding our wrists together. We're going to pull back and forth. The friction will melt and weaken the plastic. Ready?"

The plan gave Melissa a surge of hope. She might live through this yet.

"Yes," she said. The shoelace tugged her fingers for a moment. She pulled back once the movement stopped.

It took only a minute to get into a rhythm together. "That's it," Lou said. "Just like that. Slow and steady."

The movement made the ties around her wrists bite deeper, but she ignored the pain. Lou seemed to know what he was doing, and anything was better than hopping 9 miles in the dark.

A few minutes later, Lou grunted. "I think that's good. On three, pull your wrists away from me, toward the small of your back. Let's see if we've done enough. One, two, three!"

She yanked hard, grimacing at the pain…

And the zip tie holding their wrists together snapped.

They were still each bound, and attached at the ankles, but this was progress.

"Undo the shoelace from your fingers for a second," Lou said. "I'll rewrap it around the tie keeping my wrists bound, and we'll do the same thing. Once I'm free, it'll be easy for me to do yours."

Melissa had little sense of time in the darkness, but eventually, she and Lou struggled to their feet, free.

"We're 9 miles from the road, according to that asshole," Lou said. He knelt and threaded the shoelace back through his hiking boot. "No water, food, flashlight, or cell phone. But there's a clear path to follow, and our eyes will adjust to the darkness more and more. We won't get lost. One foot in front of the other. We'll flag down a car or keep walking until we reach civilization, but we need to move. We don't want to be caught out here once the sun comes up and the ground gets hot. Ready?"

"Ready." They started walking, following the path the SUV had taken.

"We've got plenty of time," Lou said from beside her in the dark. "Why don't you tell me the story that led to this lovely nighttime desert hike together? Start at the beginning, don't lie, and leave nothing out." He didn't sound upset or angry—just curious, along with something more. A desire to gather all the information he could, so he could report to Krissy and figure out a solution to the Shane situation. "What was all that about a flash drive?" he asked.

There was no sense holding back. Lou had saved her life, and Krissy had been right all along about Shane conning her.

"Don't worry about the flash drive," Melissa said. "I password-protected it, and the idiot never considered that I was capable of that." She felt like a fool for falling for Shane and his bullshit, but at least she'd done something right. "Anyway," Melissa said as they trudged through the night. "It started when I was on vacation in Mexico."

130

THE BOWLS

58 Desert Song Lane
Henderson, Nevada

Monday Morning (Pacific Daylight Time)

Kristine had known something was wrong the moment Lou's phone had gone to voicemail. While it had been early in the morning, he would have answered if he could.

Kristine had rushed to Melissa's house and parked in the driveway.

The neighborhood was quiet. It was already too hot for jogs or taking dogs on their morning walks.

She knocked on the front door. Friends knocked. Strangers rang the doorbell.

No one answered, and no noise came from within.

The side yard had a gate in the 6-foot-tall block wall, but it was locked. Kristine jumped, placed her hands on the top of the wall, mantled up like she was getting out of a swimming pool, and dropped into the gravel side yard, hoping no one was watching at this early hour and called the police.

She stopped in her tracks as she came around the back of the house.

There were two shattered bowls on the covered back patio, along with what looked like soup that had splashed all over and dried on the concrete.

The sliding door was locked, but Kristine had seen all she needed to.

Melissa and Lou had gone outside for dinner, which was common here in the summer. Few people enjoyed the heat of the day, but being stuck indoors all the time made everyone stir crazy, the same way it tended to during the winter in colder climates. People wanted to get outside, and when the relative coolness of the evening hit, they would venture onto patios to eat, watch TV, or relax before eventually returning inside to sleep in their air-conditioned homes.

Last night, something—or someone—had surprised whoever carried the soup.

And now Melissa and Lou were gone.

Along with Kristine's chances of accessing the computer server in time to transfer the money to the informant.

The only saving grace was that Dominic and Thomas were still in the air and wouldn't arrive in Kabul for a few hours.

But to be ready, she had to find Melissa and get her to the bank—and her safe deposit box—before it closed at 4 p.m.

Kristine picked up one of the patio chairs, gauged its heft, and hoped it would work.

With a mighty swing, she smashed it against the sliding door, shattering the glass.

She kicked out an opening large enough for her to squeeze through without getting cut, slipped inside, and ran through the house.

No one was there.

Lou and Melissa weren't lying dead in the living room.

There was still hope.

Although she found it ominous that Melissa's green backpack was still by the front door where it had been yesterday, after their heart-to-heart talk.

Kristine took a deep breath to get herself under control, opened the door, and calmly walked out. She turned and fiddled with the door as if locking it, then pretended to slip the key into the pocket of her khakis. With her head down, she walked to the car, not hurrying, and trying not to look guilty.

No one stopped her or called out. The neighbors were probably still asleep or going about their normal business of getting ready for work.

As Kristine drove away, she worked out a plan to find Melissa and Lou —assuming they weren't dead already.

131

THE HIGHWAY

Unknown Location
Outside Las Vegas, Nevada

Melissa had watched the sun come up as they reached a road. The desert air warmed quickly. Melissa went from being slightly cool to uncomfortably hot in a quarter mile of empty blacktop.

Now she walked side by side with Lou down the center of the two-lane highway, with her on the left of the yellow centerline and him on the right. If—when—a car came along, they would spread out, taking up both lanes. Unless the driver ran them over or swerved onto the narrow gravel shoulder, the car would have to stop.

Melissa resisted the urge to complain about her blistered feet, empty stomach, or parched throat. Her lips were cracked from dehydration, but Lou was in the same situation. He had it worse—he was at least thirty years older and carried extra pounds around his middle, but he wasn't bitching. Neither would she.

After all, if Shane hadn't had a soft spot for her, they might be dead in a shallow grave right now.

The temperature soared. They put one foot in front of the other. No vehicles came.

There was no shelter from the sun. The tallest desert shrubs were knee high—not nearly enough to provide shade. There were no cacti, power poles, or abandoned buildings. Only miles upon miles of desert and highway.

The world was a populated place. Surely someone would drive by eventually, right?

On the other hand, how far could they walk before one of them dropped?

132

THE SWITCH

Shahr-e-Naw District
Kabul, Afghanistan

Sardar hugged his wife close, relishing the smell of her hair and the feel of her arms wrapped around him. "Go to bed as usual," he whispered. "Leave no extra lights on. Pretend I am here."

It had been many years since he'd snuck out at night to meet Mike. She had supported his efforts to help the American and accepted the risks he took. But that was another time. When the war ended, the American forces had eventually left the country. The Taliban had resumed control, and the mastermind had vanished.

Sardar had confined his spying to the morning stops for tea, dropping off money to fund his network of long-term contacts, and reading the occasional message on his phone or a handwritten note slipped into his morning newspaper at breakfast.

For years, he'd successfully kept Mike informed of suspected Taliban actions, the locations of extremist training camps in Afghanistan, and about terrorists in the region.

Very helpful, and relatively low risk.

Until nine months ago, when the bombings had started around the world—ones that had the look and feel of the mastermind, or so he and Mike believed.

Suddenly, life became more interesting—and dangerous.

And while some messages were sent via the encrypted communications app, money still had to be paid to his network of spies, and several preferred low-tech paper notes to the use of a smartphone and app, especially people who would be in a great deal of hot water if an encrypted communications app was found on their phone.

"You'll be safe?" his wife whispered in his ear, more a gentle reminder than a question.

"Of course."

He hesitated, torn between needing to say a potential final goodbye and not wanting to tempt fate.

If he didn't say what was in his heart—about how much he loved her, how he wouldn't have had the courage to keep going in the hunt for the mastermind without her unwavering support, and a thank you for the wonderful years they had spent together—nothing bad would happen tonight.

He hoped.

But what if he left it all unsaid and something terrible happened?

He held his tongue. If he had lived his life right, she already knew how he felt.

With a final squeeze of his wife's hand, he looked into the living room. His servant perched on the couch, unhappy and uncomfortable, wearing some of Sardar's old clothes. He had agreed to exchange clothing and loan Sardar the old yellow car he drove.

He would spend the night in a spare bedroom.

The live-in security guards weren't happy at Sardar's plan, either, but they'd had their say. They stood in the living room looking like they were trying to think of an argument that would convince him to change his mind.

Sardar gave the three of them a look that he hoped conveyed his gratitude, along with a plea that if he didn't return, they would look out for his wife.

He wouldn't normally ask them to help with a plan like this, but with very skilled—and dangerous—people potentially watching the house, he needed their assistance now.

Sardar checked that the outdoor light was off, stepped out of the house via the back door, and walked slowly across the small courtyard to the servant's tired yellow car, as if he'd finally completed another long, tiring day of work.

Pakistan ISI operator Latif—Lion—had his black SUV facing away from the target's walled compound, half a block up the street. The vehicle was much too comfortable for long stakeouts, with both heated and air-conditioned seats that seemed to cradle his body. While on this assignment, he'd slept soundly inside the vehicle when it was his turn to nap—and fought to stay awake while watching the businessman, cursing the plushness of the seats.

Tonight, as they did when needed, Lion was alone on the streets. Vasim—Bull—had a few hours off. It was early evening. The target, his wife, and their two bodyguards—who lived in a bungalow behind the house—were in for the night, unless the businessman and his wife went somewhere, which was unlikely at the beginning of the week. If that happened, Lion would tail them. His partner was a phone call away; he could leave the comfort of the nearby hotel, where they had a room, and meet him, showered, rested, and rejuvenated, only a few minutes later.

The solid black gate opened at the target's home. In the rearview mirror, Lion confirmed it was the servant's yellow car. The man was leaving a few minutes later than usual, but the timing wasn't different enough to raise Lion's suspicions.

The car turned right, away from him, as it did every night, lurching forward as it left the driveway and entered the flow of traffic.

Lion moved before he had made a conscious decision. Something was off.

He grabbed the black helmet from the passenger seat, jumped out of the vehicle, and rushed the few steps to a newer motorcycle parked directly in front of the SUV. He hit speed dial on his phone before slipping it into his pocket.

"What is it?" Bull asked. He sounded alert, but he had a hint of sleep in his voice. Still, he was all business. Lion wouldn't call to chitchat.

"Take over at the house," Lion said through the helmet's Bluetooth connection. "The servant's car just left, and it felt wrong." He didn't need to say anything more. They'd both been in the business long enough to recognize and honor their intuition.

Lion started the bike, gunned the engine, and pulled into the street. Three cars honked in irritation as he swung around to ride toward the target's house and catch up to the servant's car. With the motorcycle, he could weave in and out of traffic; he should be able to catch up easily.

"It will take five minutes," Bull said, the noises in the background indicating he was already moving.

"We have to risk the gap in coverage."

"Understood. Will you call it in, or should I?"

"You tell them, please," he said, avoiding a car that changed lanes abruptly. "I'm on the bike. It's probably nothing, but…"

"Yes," Bull said. The one word conveyed that it was likely not worth the effort, but that it had to be done, regardless. "Be careful," he added. The hotel room door slammed shut behind Bull, carrying over the phone line.

"You too," Lion said, and disconnected the call.

133

THE SAFE HOUSE

Inter-Services Intelligence Safe House
Jalalabad, Afghanistan

As an ISI field manager, Imran Bhatti was used to the boredom that came with all surveillance missions. He had been confined to this luxury apartment since the start of the operation. The modern twelve-story apartment building had a swimming pool, gym, sauna, and library.

He'd been able to use none of it. He had only the view of the poorer areas of city spread out below him, surrounding this in-fill development. But there was satellite TV, high-speed internet, and a comfortable couch.

He'd been ordered to use two operators—"Lion" and "Bull"—to observe an Afghan businessman named Sardar suspected of being a spy, or spy handler, and report on anything suspicious.

Two other operators—"Hawk" and "Owl"—watched the home of a young courier named Naveed who was suspected of… something. Imran's superiors had shared few details of the operation with him.

The mission timeline was open-ended. Plenty of money and resources were available, including cars, SUVs, and motorcycles, along with expensive hotel rooms as safe houses not far from the targets' homes.

But there weren't enough people to do the job properly. The lack of manpower meant that his latest mission was important enough to waste his time but not essential enough to commit the proper resources to.

Or it was so highly classified, the number of people involved had to be kept to a minimum.

It didn't matter. Imran would sit in air-conditioned comfort, watching football and writing daily reports about the boring habits of a rotund, middle-aged Afghan businessman and a thin, tall late-thirties courier.

Imran muted the television the instant the communications app buzzed on his phone.

"Lion is following the servant's car," Vasim—Bull—reported.

"Why?" Imran asked.

"He had a feeling."

Imran didn't argue or second-guess. The three of them had worked together a few times before; he trusted their instincts. "But he's on comms?"

"Yes. He asked me to call because he's on the motorcycle. He needed it to catch up to the vehicle—and we've been relying on the SUVs a lot."

"Understood. How long was the compound unwatched?" Imran asked his field operative.

"Three minutes."

He considered the gap in coverage. If the target had discovered he was being watched, he could be using the servant's car for a once-monthly meet.

Or the businessman could have used the servant acting differently to draw away the surveillance long enough for him to slip away unnoticed on foot or in his own vehicle.

"He has no way of knowing we are following him," Bull argued. He sounded like he was trying to convince himself, too. "We have been careful. And if he somehow has noticed, he would not guess there was only one unit watching him. This is likely nothing—Lion said so himself."

"I agree," Imran said. But he would still call it in. The ISI was no different than any other organization. It paid to cover your ass. "Stay on the house, and have Lion report when he is able."

"Copy," Bull said before disconnecting.

Imran turned off the television. He had to compose his thoughts before making the call to his superior.

And if past missions were any indication, the operation had gone from boring to exciting—and stressful—in a moment.

134

THE AIRPORT

Kabul International Airport
Kabul, Afghanistan

Bone stifled a yawn as the plane taxied for longer than he thought it would, but he figured they were going to the farthest corner to deplane, where there would be fewer questions asked about the arrival of the jet.

He'd slept surprisingly well on the sixteen-hour flight. No nightmares. No desire for a beer or drink from the plane's well-stocked mini bar. Maybe returning to Afghanistan and finally facing the trauma he'd long pushed down was doing him good.

Whatever the reason, his head was on straight, and he was ready to get in, complete the mission, and get out. He was in fighting form, had a supremely competent—though aging—combat partner by his side, and a clear objective.

Even if many of the operation's details remained sketchy.

The plane finally stopped outside a building that had seen better days. A large fuel truck pulled up immediately, followed a moment later by a beat-up old yellow car that stopped near the front of the plane.

The pilot came from the cockpit and opened the small front door.

"See you soon," he said as Dominic and Bone stepped outside into the warm night air. It was just after 10 p.m., but it was still hot—just like Arizona, Nevada, and the years Bone had spent in this country.

There were no customs formalities. No one asked for their passports, had their hands out for bribes, or gave them a hard time. The area was simply deserted.

———————

Outside the Kabul International Airport

Kabul, Afghanistan

Leaving the motorcycle behind was risky, but Lion couldn't drive it close to the fence around the airport. There were barricades, and it would draw too much attention. He'd left it a few blocks away. Running flat out, he could return to it in less than three minutes.

A high chain-link fence with coils of razor wire surrounded the airport. There was a gap, then another fence with razor wire. Between the two, more rolls of wire covered a thick, 4-foot-tall concrete barricade similar to the ones surrounding the airport that prevented him from bringing the motorcycle closer.

Huddled in the shadows of a building just past the cleared open ground, Lion could see the servant's yellow car.

"The plane comes from America," Imran—their field manager—said via the helmet's Bluetooth speakers.

The plane faced to Lion's right, putting the cabin door on the far side of him. He was on the wrong side of the airport to see well, but this was the best he could do given the circumstances. If he wanted to be able to follow the yellow car again, he couldn't take the time to circle around to the other side of the airport and hope he'd have a better vantage point.

At least he'd been able to relay a description of the airplane, along with its registration number on its tail. Imran had worked his magic or called headquarters to track down the flight details.

Surprisingly, no airport patrols had passed the area. The entire section was deserted except for the fuel truck and yellow car.

"Bribes have been paid," Lion reported. "It is too quiet here."

"Understood."

His daily talks with Imran were always professional, but with this latest development, their conversation took on a more focused and precise tone. The operation had entered the active phase.

"The plane has shut down. A fuel truck and a car have arrived."

"Copy."

"It's the servant's car. It has parked near the front of the plane." Lion paused.

"Is the target getting on the plane?"

"I can't…" Lion had the thinnest sliver of a view to the car. He was too far away, and it was too dim to see who the driver was. "No. No one is exiting the car."

A few moments later, two men walked between the nose of the plane and continued to the car. One sat in the front seat, and the other, who looked younger, though at this distance it was only an impression, climbed awkwardly into the rear of the small car, as if he were too tall to comfortably sit in the back.

Lion spun and ran to the motorcycle at top speed, pushing hard as he reported. "Two men, one tall and younger, I believe, with dark hair and a thick beard. The other one is older, with short-cropped gray hair. Both have military bearings. They emerged from the plane and got into the car."

"You can follow them?" Imran asked.

"Yes," Lion said, gasping for air in the helmet.

"Very well. Follow and stand by for further instructions."

"Copy," Lion said. The bike was in view. He was almost there.

Kabul International Airport
Kabul, Afghanistan

Bone had followed Dominic to the waiting car and climbed into the tiny back passenger side when Dom opted for the front seat, resting the backpack full of US dollars on his lap.

The short, chubby man in the driver's seat put the car in gear. It lurched forward, like he wasn't used to driving it.

"I am Sardar," the driver said in lightly accented English. "Thank you for coming."

Bone chuckled from the back seat. The bastard spoke English. Bone had been played earlier when they'd spoken in Las Vegas.

"Dominic," Dom said.

"Thomas—or Bone," Bone said, adding the nickname.

Sardar slowed as he approached a large chain-link gate at the perimeter of the airport. He flashed his headlights three times. A man emerged from a small hut, barely bigger than a phone booth, unlocked the gate, and rolled it along a track on wobbly wheels.

The guard kept his back to the car and never glanced their way.

"The timeline has been moved up," Sardar said. "And I apologize for the vehicle; I believe I may be under surveillance. This is our servant's car. He's staying the night at my home, and I drove away pretending to be him."

"You're being watched?" Bone asked. "How many people, what types of vehicles—and why?"

"I do not know. It is partly a feeling, and a suspicion. My driver recognized an SUV he thought was following us, but it turned after a short distance. And I have seen a man twice at the coffee shops I frequent."

"I don't like coincidences," Dom said from the front seat.

"Neither do I," Sardar agreed.

He approached an intersection, slowed, and turned right. There were vehicles on the road, but the traffic was light—another reason Sardar had wanted them to arrive later and not during the daytime.

"We will be careful, just in case people have discovered our intentions. I have made arrangements for us to stay at a run-down warehouse until tomorrow morning's meeting," Sardar said. "It is vacant. There is air conditioning and running water. I have some food from home if you're hungry." He gestured to a large cloth bag on the seat next to Bone.

"The source changed the meeting time?" Dom asked. He didn't sound happy.

"Yes. His original message specified later this week. Now, he wants to meet tomorrow morning—8 a.m.—at a busy cafe called Kabuli Coffee, near a small park." He glanced at Dom. "You will not blend in well, even with the clothes I have for you at the warehouse. Bone and I will go first with the red handkerchief he designated as a signal. If all is well, I will have you come. If there are police or Taliban nearby, or it seems unsafe, you can negotiate with the man via my phone, hopefully with line-of-sight from the car, so you can talk somewhat face-to-face." He once again nodded to the bag in the back seat. "There is a phone for each of you, plus ear buds. But I had to promise not to bring weapons onto the airport grounds, so those are in the warehouse."

They approached a roundabout, forcing Sardar to slow again. A few cars exited the circle, going in the other direction.

"If all goes well, I will bring you back to the airport twenty-four hours from now. We will have stopped the latest terrorist attack, and the mastermind will be captured or killed."

"If all goes well," Bone muttered, sure Dom was thinking the same words.

135

THE CONCERN

Inter-Services Intelligence Headquarters
Islamabad, Pakistan

Assistant Director Raza put the speakerphone on mute after Imran, their field officer in Afghanistan, gave his report.

As the director assigned to this operation, Raza would normally have full discretion for the mission in Kabul.

This was not a normal operation, however.

From the start, the personnel on station had been kept to the absolute minimum number necessary, leaving the field operators with a challenging workload.

Four men—two to watch the man suspected of offering money for information on a former ISI officer, and two to watch one of the officer's employees, a courier.

No one had told Raza why the former ISI officer had a bounty on his head, who the officer was, or why Naveed—the courier—needed to be watched.

Not that he'd asked. Moving up in the organization, which he had every intention of continuing to do, meant following orders, keeping questions to himself, and keeping his mouth shut.

Special Project's Officer Hafiz, Raza's superior, sat to his right and slightly behind him in an old, cheap wheelchair that looked like the man had stolen it from a local hospital. The metal footrests were flipped up, which allowed Hafiz to pull himself along using the toes of his white slip-on sneakers, which were definitely not proper dress shoes. Hafiz was past his prime, gaunt and physically spent to the point he had to use at least a cane to walk, and often the wheelchair. But his mind was as sharp as ever, and he knew where the bodies were buried, both figuratively and literally. So he was allowed to wear his old-fashioned, wrinkled clothes and to let his pure white stubble grow for days between shavings.

Tonight, Hafiz had been snoozing in the wheelchair, lightly snoring, head slumped, thin white hair disheveled, when Imran called.

"The businessman may have snuck away from his home," Raza told him as Hafiz blinked himself awake. Raza ran down the rest of the report from their field manager—including the details of the airplane from America, and the two men who had arrived in Kabul who could easily have been spies. "What is going on—and what shall we do?" Raza asked.

Hafiz sighed and leaned close enough for Raza to feel the old man's warm breath on his ear. "The former ISI officer we are protecting is Colonel Tariq."

Tariq was a legend in the ISI: a bomb maker extraordinaire, and a master of logistics. He'd retired to some fanfare a year ago—or as much fanfare as an intensely secret intelligence organization allowed. The colonel had had a long, exceptional career. Although the details were classified above Raza's clearance, there were plenty of whispered rumors: of operations run like clockwork, strategic and tactical plans that helped the country over decades, and hundreds—thousands, maybe—of Americans killed by men he trained to build bombs during the war in Afghanistan, all to help the Taliban, which assisted Pakistan in its fierce rivalry with India.

It said a lot about Tariq that he served his entire career in the ISI instead of leaving once the war in Afghanistan concluded and the Americans left. Tariq had dedicated his life to Pakistan, forgoing a wife, family, and riches to serve his country.

Raza put the pieces together. "Tariq didn't actually retire?"

"Oh, he retired," Hafiz said. "But…"

Raza turned to gauge the man's expression. The crafty old spy's sharp eyes drilled into him, seeming to will him to figure out the puzzle. "He is… available… if we need him?" Raza asked.

When Hafiz's eyebrow lifted a millimeter, Raza continued. "And we need him… soon."

Hafiz said nothing, but leaned back with a pleased look on his face.

"Whoever was on that plane—American operators, we can presume—may be there to help the businessman discover the identity of Colonel Tariq," Raza said, staring at his screen showing the map of Kabul. He turned back to Hafiz. "They cannot be allowed to do that."

Once again, Hafiz said nothing. Perhaps the old man was letting Raza take the fall if the operation went bad. Or maybe Raza was being allowed to do his job without being micromanaged.

Raza went with the second option. "Better to be proactive. I am going to order the operator to eliminate the Americans and the businessman, clean up the scene, and go to ground. The Americans will be forced to admit they sent spies into the country, and the Taliban will be blamed for killing them, all before they learn of Tariq or find him."

He waited three seconds without looking back, and when he heard no objections, he unmuted the phone and spoke to Imran, the field officer.

136

THE APPROVAL

Airport Road
Kabul, Afghanistan

"They are approaching a roundabout," Lion said from three car lengths behind the beat-up yellow car on Airport Road. The motorcycle he rode was fast and in excellent condition, and the helmet was high tech, with integrated speakers and a microphone. "There are no vehicles nearby at the moment—this is a good location. I need an answer."

On the other end of the call, his field officer answered immediately. "Eliminate the target and the two men from the plane."

"Copy. Eliminate all three," Lion said. He'd slept little the previous night, but the exhaustion vanished with the new orders.

He resisted the impulse to gun the motorcycle's engine. Instead, Lion accelerated just enough to catch up to the car as it eased into the next roundabout. There was no traffic; this was the perfect opportunity.

He wished he had the SUV and the automatic rifle in it, but the nine rounds in the Soviet pistol that headquarters had issued would be enough.

He had the element of surprise.

Lion pulled up next to the driver—it was the businessman he'd been watching, not the servant. His hunch had been correct.

Lion drew the weapon and aimed, ready to kill the target and the two soldiers that had arrived in the airplane.

It was the motorcycle that drew Bone's attention. It didn't compare to Patrick's, which Bone had ridden from Salestri senior's house and parked in Dominic's garage. But few bikes were that nice.

Still, the one passing them was powerful and relatively new; the rider obviously took pride in it.

Maybe when this mission was over, Bone could buy an inexpensive bike. The Arizona weather was perfect for touring about ten months of the year. Stephanie could ride behind him, snuggled close, her arms around his body...

"Gun! Gun left!" he yelled before fully comprehending what was happening.

The car swerved right, but Lion got off three rounds before the passenger —the older soldier—yanked the steering wheel.

The car swerved left.

It clipped the motorcycle's front wheel before Lion could turn away, and driving with only one hand, Lion lost control.

He went down.

Lion landed hard on his shoulder. The pistol slipped from his grip. He slid on the pavement as the car continued in front of him. His foot caught something—a crack on the ground, or a pothole—and he rolled. His leg broke with a sharp *snap*.

The car continued to the left as he slid to a stop.

His head rang—it must have hit the ground hard. The helmet had saved his life.

Bone flung himself over the front seat, taking control of the wheel. He struggled to pushed Sardar's limp body to the side, and finally sat in the driver's seat and hit the brake, bring the car to a stop. "Are you hit?" he asked Dominic.

"Yes, dammit," Dom grunted, the pain clear in his voice.

"Is he alive?" Bone asked, leaving Sardar to Dominic for the moment. The priorities were eliminating the threat and escaping.

Behind them, the motorcycle rider was sprawled on the road.

"I don't know," Dom said. He sounded weak. "He's breathing but unconscious."

"Copy." Bone put the car in reverse and shoved hard on the gas pedal. He'd channel Zia from the mission in California and use the only weapon at his disposal.

Ahead of Lion, the car's brake lights went off as the engine revved and it flew back toward him.

He crawled, pulling with his arms as he pushed with his good leg. If he could get to the center of the roundabout, he would be safe behind a large tree enclosed by a low brick wall.

Bone twisted the wheel to account for the motorcycle rider's slow crawl. He avoided the man's head—the helmet offered too much protection.

The front tire rolled over the man's chest. Bone stopped, changed gears, and drove over him again.

"Are the targets eliminated?" the field manager asked from far away.

Lion struggled to answer, to say anything, but the pain was too intense. The darkness closed in on him before he could reply.

A car approached the roundabout from the south, several hundred yards away, but Bone wasn't waiting around. He steered across the roundabout, wracking his memory for the best option. He and Dom had spent a few hours of the flight studying maps of the city and the surrounding area. They didn't get a detailed picture of any specific areas, but he had a general overview of the main roads, landmarks, embassies, top hotels, parks—and hospitals.

He wasn't far from a 24-hour emergency hospital. Straight down Airport Road, a right turn, and he was there.

"Will both of you make it ten minutes, or do we stop for damage control?" he asked Dom, who was ripping his shirt to make a bandage.

"I will. Not sure about him. He's bleeding, but not bad. He might have hit his head on the window when I jerked the wheel, or he could have passed out from the pain. But there's no way you're taking me to the hospital. We're in this country illegally. I'm old, but I'm still a former Navy SEAL. The moment they realize who I am, we're this far away from an international incident. I'll be arrested as a CIA spy. Or the Taliban swoops in and executes me."

Bone floored the gas pedal again, shooting east. "We drop him off, then I have an idea for you. Pass me Mike's phone."

He had the most important call of his life to make.

137

THE HOSPITAL

Kabul, Afghanistan

Bone took the phone from Dom and dialed one-handed while he sped down the road, praying the phone worked in the country the way Kristine said it would.

"Pacific Oasis BBQ & Smokehouse," the young woman answered in San Diego, nearly eight thousand miles away. Bone recognized the voice of Tiffany, Zia's college-age counter worker. She sounded fresh and chipper—they must have just opened for a busy Sunday.

"I need to place a catering order," Bone said, sticking with the tradecraft he and Zia had agreed upon and used during their occasional calls the last several weeks where Bone practiced his Pashto. "It's urgent —I need to have it right away, if possible."

"Of course, sir." Tiffany was all business. They had done this enough times for her to recognize him, and Bone bet she could hear the stress in his voice. "Let me have my manager call you right back. What's the best number to reach you at?" Normally, Bone would give a number he'd looked up for a local business. Zia would ignore it and reach out to Bone's account on the encrypted communications app. Tonight, though, that wouldn't work. Bone didn't have his own phone, or his latest operation burner; he had to break protocol and give Tiffany Mike Salestri's account.

"It's best to reach me online," Bone said, and gave Tiffany the numbered comm account for Mike Salestri. "Please read it back," he said. Tiffany did, nailing it.

"I'll have the manager call immediately," Tiffany said, and disconnected.

Bone steered around a slow-moving car. "How you doing?" he asked Dom.

There was no answer from the passenger seat. Bone risked taking his eye off the road for a second to glance over. His new partner was slumped against the window, unconscious. Sardar lay across him, also out cold. Both looked pale.

The smell of blood filled the car.

Bone changed lanes to pass another car. He was approaching the turn to the hospital and had a difficult choice to make.

He could drop off Sardar. No problem. The doctors would treat him. He would live or die, but either way, he was a local. An Afghan. There would be questions, but nothing that couldn't be explained away. The city was a dangerous place.

Bone fished in the man's pocket and removed his wallet and phone. He'd be treated as a John Doe—or whatever the equivalent placeholder was here. Anyone targeting him by name would be out of luck.

The problem was Dominic. The older man was right. Dropping him off at the hospital was problematic. While it might not create an international incident as he'd said, his presence in the country would present too many uncomfortable questions.

Or he'd be shot, hanged, or his head chopped off, depending on who picked him up and how they felt that day.

But Bone couldn't let the man bleed to death—and his injuries were far too much for Bone to handle himself.

The phone buzzed in Bone's hand. Bone answered, getting right to it. "I need help."

"Of course, my friend," Zia said. "What is wrong? Are you tempted to drink?"

Bone barked out a laugh. Zia asked that every call, but the idea of drowning his troubles with alcohol hadn't entered his mind since Admiral Nalen had given him the mission. "No, it's much worse than that. I'm in your hometown."

"You're here in San Diego? Where? I will come get you."

Bone swerved around a pothole in the road. The turn for the hospital was coming less than a kilometer away. "No. Kabul. Your cousin lives here, right?"

"Wait. How are you in Kabul?"

"I need help, Zia. He's here, right? Would he help me if you asked? I have money."

It took Zia an agonizing second to get his head around what Bone had said, but he got there. "Sorry. Yes. He is there and would be happy to help. No money needed."

"I'll let him decide that. I need a private doctor who doesn't ask questions. My friend has been shot and I can't take him to the hospital."

Zia hesitated again.

Bone was sure the call to his cousin would be interesting, to say the least.

"I understand," Zia finally said. "I owe you my life. I will call my cousin. We will find a way to help."

The well-maintained hospital was several stories tall and surrounded by other shorter buildings. The grounds were surprisingly lush, with trees and bushes everywhere.

A large sign with a red crescent symbol representing emergency medical services pointed the way to a drop-off area. Bone pulled close to the double glass doors of the entrance and jumped out of the car, keeping his head down to avoid getting his face caught by security cameras.

He opened the passenger door. Dom groaned as he half fell out. "Hang in there," Bone whispered. He grabbed Sardar under his arms and yanked backward, dragging the man's bulk out of the car to a gasp of pain from Dominic. He shoved Dom back inside and eased the door shut.

"Help!" Bone yelled in Pashto, hoping his accent didn't give him away, but willing to take the risk to get Sardar help that much sooner. He backed to the doors, which slid open. Cool air greeted him, along with a security guard with an AK-47, who hopped off a stool. The man used a walkie-talkie to call for help.

Sardar looked deathly pale. Blood poured from at least one wound in his upper chest, near his shoulder. Bone stopped dragging Sardar as two male nurses came through the inner set of doors. He bent over as if he had lost his breath, was going to vomit, or both.

"What happened?" one asked.

Bone shook his head, hands on his knees. They'd figure it out.

They asked more questions as another nurse appeared with a wheeled gurney. As soon as they had Sardar on it and pushed him inside, Bone waved his arm like he was asking for a moment and walked slowly out the doors and to the car.

The guard called to him. Bone waved again without looking back, pointed to the car, and hoped it was obvious: He'd be back after parking the car.

He slid into the driver's seat, head still down, and drove away, praying Sardar pulled through.

138

THE CALL

Henderson, Nevada

Kristine cruised the back streets and alleys of Henderson, stopping at every dumpster to look inside for the bodies of Melissa and Lou.

So far, she'd seen only rotten garbage.

She'd done all she could. The alert had gone out via cell phone to her father's network of spies across the southwest.

Her spies, now, though none of them could know about that yet. They believed they were helping Big Mike. So far, no one had any leads on Melissa and Lou, meaning Shane hadn't taken them to a grocery store, convenience store, bar, restaurant, casino, club, hotel, airport, bus depot, or gas station.

It was late morning.

The bank closed at 4 p.m.

When the phone rang only a few minutes after the last call, Kristine had a good feeling.

"Miss Salestri?" the middle-aged woman's voice asked.

"Yes, speaking," Kristine said. Her stomach dropped. The woman on the other end of the line didn't sound like she had a hot tip to share with Mike.

"I'm calling from Boulder City Hospital. We have two of your friends here, Melissa—"

"Are they alive?" Kristine said, interrupting the woman.

"Yes. They're resting and rehydrating, but they were adamant we contact you as soon as possible."

"Rehydrating?"

"Yes. When they were picked up, they were in rough shape. We can't discharge them for a while, but—"

Kristine didn't need the details now. The hospital wasn't far. "I'll be there soon to pick them up," she said, and hung up without waiting for approval.

Unless Melissa was unconscious, the two of them were going to the bank to get the code out of her safe deposit box, then straight to the casino and the Vault.

PART 9

TUESDAY

139

THE LIGHT

Kabul, Afghanistan

Bone drove a few minutes from the hospital to be safe before turning into a side street, then again onto a narrow road with a mixture of residential and commercial buildings, mostly two and three stories tall. He pulled over, blocking a driveway, and checked on Dominic.

The older man bled from a wound to his stomach. Even half unconscious from the pain and loss of blood, he pressed the ripped shirt he'd used as a bandage against the wound.

For a second, Tank's face appeared, replacing the older man's. Bone shook off the flashback and ripped the bottom off his own shirt in what was probably a futile attempt to help. If he'd had a typical med kit, like they'd carried into combat, he would have been able to make a difference. But in a stranger's car in Kabul, there was little he could do.

Dominic gasped when Bone gently pulled his hand aside and pressed the fresh fabric to the wound, putting more pressure on it.

"No regrets, brother," Dom muttered, his eyes still closed. "It's better to go this way. In battle. Right?"

"You're not going to die."

Dom chuckled before gasping again at the pain. "Good job—that's exactly what you're supposed to say." He winced and let out a sob, quickly sucking in air to cover for it. "I've said it myself a time or two."

There was more blood than Bone expected from the wound. He'd seen others shot there—ally and enemy. Some had been fine and lived. Others had died quickly. It depended on what the bullet hit going in, and what it did inside the body.

"Keep pressure on that," he said.

Dominic nodded and opened his eyes. "What did it feel like—dying?"

Bone wanted to lie again and tell the man he'd be fine, to convince him to hold on, but Dom cut him off. "No bullshit. I'll fight—promise. But I have to know."

The car faded. Bone was once again at the ambush, the way he'd been in so many nightmares over the years.

The desert sand scratched his cheek as the pain faded from the multiple gunshot wounds he'd suffered.

The white light drew him in. Safe. Warm. Welcoming.

He snapped back to the car and met Dominic's eyes. "It felt good. My guys…" He choked up and couldn't go on.

Tank's voice echoed in his head. "Give it a minute," Tank had said. "You're almost here."

The rest of the Team had been waiting, ready to welcome him to the afterlife.

"They were there? The ones who had gone before?" Dom asked.

Bone could only nod.

"Well, in that case…" Dom said with a peaceful smile, and closed his eyes again.

"No, come on. Don't you dare give up!"

140

THE RESTAURANT

Shinwari Restaurant
Kabul, Afghanistan

Bone carried Dom inside via the restaurant's back entrance and through the immaculate kitchen to the first table in the dining room.

He grunted as he lowered Dominic onto a table covered with a pristine white linen tablecloth. The older SEAL didn't gasp in pain, which Bone took as a bad sign. But Dom was still breathing—raggedly—and that had to count for something.

"Hold fast, brother. You promised," he whispered in Dom's ear.

A light knock came from the front door of the upscale restaurant. It hadn't been closed very long—the smell of food lingered and made Bone's stomach rumble with hunger.

Zia's cousin—Wali—glanced furtively back at Bone. He was a handsome man, with a close-cropped beard and stylish dark hair. He wore the typical lightweight pants and long tunic common for the area, in dark gray and black, but something about it seemed sharp and classy, like the owner of a successful high-end restaurant was supposed to look.

He was also freaked out at Bone's arrival. But he'd spoken with Zia and agreed to help despite the fear.

"Lights first," Bone told him in Pashto.

Wali moved to his left and switched off the lights, leaving the dining room in darkness except for a faint glow of lights from outside bleeding in around the edges of the thick, golden curtains covering the windows. Bone nodded, and the man twisted a key in the deadbolt. He opened the door just enough for another man, carrying a doctor's bag, to slip through.

The doctor rattled off a long whisper at Wali, who was busy locking the door.

Bone didn't catch all the words—he wasn't as good with the language when the locals spoke so quickly—but what he understood was clear: The doctor was annoyed at being called to the restaurant, but also concerned for his friend.

"We need help," Bone said in Pashto from the table near the kitchen.

The doctor turned toward him as Wali flicked on the lights. He was a few years older than Bone but still under 40, dressed in the traditional *shalwar kameez* like Wali, but his was less fancy and more casual, like he'd grabbed the first thing he could.

In the soft glow of the sophisticated, muted restaurant lighting, the doctor focused on Dominic's bloody body sprawled on the table.

"You should take him to a hospital," the doctor replied in English. He didn't move from his spot near the door.

Bone frowned. Was his accent so terrible that from one short sentence, the man could tell he was an American?

"I can't," Bone answered, reverting to English, too.

"Then he will die. Soon." The doctor turned to Wali and whispered again, speaking too low and fast for Bone to understand what was being said. Wali nodded, chagrinned, but whispered back words he knew. "My cousin," Wali said, followed by the term for an obligation to assist someone as a debt of honor.

That was Bone's cue. He and Zia were forever linked by the bond of warriors. Bone had saved Zia and Lamar's lives, but they had also helped save his. Wali was caught up in a family obligation to help Bone, but the doctor wasn't.

Bone unslung the backpack, reached inside, and brought out three banded stacks of hundreds—thirty thousand dollars. "Money is the key to solving everything," he said in Pashto, quoting the popular sentiment. "Twenty thousand dollars to try to save him," he added in English. "And an extra ten thousand if he survives. A great deal of money for a night of your time—and your discretion."

The doctor wanted to say no—it was as clear as Dom's shallow breathing from the table—but he couldn't take his eyes off the money.

"He's lost too much blood," the doctor said, fighting with himself.

"I'm type O-negative—a universal donor. We can do a direct blood transfusion." The process involved taking Bone's blood and putting it straight into Dominic. It would help Dom, and might allow him to survive, but it would cost Bone—depending on how much blood he gave.

"Forty," the doctor said as he walked across the restaurant, trailed by Wali. "But not for helping him. Solely for the risk to me and my family."

"Forty," Bone agreed. He snagged another bundle of hundreds from the backpack and offered all four to the doctor, who shook his head. "Later." He looked up at the lights and spoke to Wali. "We must move him to the kitchen," the doctor said to Bone. "There is better lighting there."

The doctor handed his bag to Wali, who also took the cash, and picked up Dominic's arms. "Hurry."

They carried Dom through double swinging doors into the kitchen. Wali cleared a long prep counter of cutting boards and a few large pots. Bone and the doctor hoisted Dom onto the metal counter. His head hit harder than Bone wanted, producing a faint *thud*.

Blood immediately spilled from the wound in his stomach onto the stainless steel.

The doctor took his case from Wali, opened it, and removed several items, lining them up along the matching counter across from Dom. "I am Fazel," he said as he hurried to the sink and washed his hands. "You will do exactly as I say, without question."

"I understand," Bone said, scrubbing his hands as soon as Fazel finished.

"Tell me what happened."

"He was shot. Once. Maybe twice, no more."

Doctor Fazel put on gloves and used scissors to cut off Dom's clothes. "Type of gun?"

"A pistol. Semiautomatic. It was…" Bone didn't have a watch—another item he'd left behind at Dom's house. "Thirty minutes ago. Maybe less." He could check the phone, but the doctor didn't seem to care about the time.

"It doesn't look good," the doctor said after a minute of examining the older SEAL. "But I will do what I can. We will take your blood—as much of it as you're willing to risk."

"Take as much as he needs."

"I won't have you both dying," the doctor muttered as he ripped open a package of sterile IV tubing and needles.

The work began under the bright lights of the kitchen. The delicious smell of cumin, cinnamon, and other spices competed with the metallic smell of Dominic's blood.

Bone easily handled the sights and sounds of the doctor working, but Wali only lasted a few minutes before hurrying out the back door to vomit in the alley.

Bone sat on the cold tile floor of the kitchen, slumped against the wall. He felt weak, like he'd run 100 miles without eating or drinking. The room spun until he closed his eyes, controlling his breathing in an attempt to steady his rapid heart rate.

Doctor Fazel grunted tiredly. "There. I have done all I can." He stripped off his gloves and added them to the open plastic trash bag near his feet where he had dropped bloody gauze and Dom's clothes.

Bone struggled to his feet. The prep counter was covered with blood, but Dom's wound was expertly stitched closed. The man's breathing was steady, and some color had returned to his body.

"Thank you," Bone said. He found the four stacks of hundreds on the counter where Wali had left them and gave them to the doctor, who hesitated for a second before shaking his head.

"No. It was my duty."

"Please," Bone said. "For your discretion. I insist."

The doctor hesitated again, longer, until Bone placed the money into his hands.

"He is a fighter," Doctor Fazel said, accepting the money. "He should be in the hospital, but if he makes it through the night, and tomorrow, he will gradually heal. Bed rest. No... exertions." His look said it all. Dom was more fit than 99 percent of men his age, had his gray hair in a typical American military crew cut, and he and Bone couldn't go to the hospital despite Dominic nearly bleeding out atop a counter in a high-end restaurant's kitchen. Not to mention the stacks of hundred-dollar bills in Bone's backpack.

It didn't take someone as intelligent as a doctor to figure out that Dom and Bone were on some type of classified mission.

"You too," the doctor said. "With as much blood as you gave, you should rest for a few days—at least, if possible," he added.

"Don't worry, Doctor. We're not going anywhere," Bone lied.

His face must have given something away. The tiredness hampered his ability to hide his thoughts and feelings. The doctor was polite enough to nod, pretending to believe him. Fazel packed his bag and left through the back door, leaving Bone with Dominic's body, a bunch of bloody kitchen surfaces to clean, and the next steps to plan—all before the 8 a.m. meeting with the informant at Kabuli Coffee.

141

THE GUNS

Shinwari Restaurant
Kabul, Afghanistan

Bone left Dominic on the prep counter but slid white tablecloths under him and covered him with others to keep him warm. If Dom made it through the night, they'd find a place for him to rest after Bone had the meeting with the informant.

A shaken Wali avoided looking at Dom—and the blood—as Bone cleaned and disinfected the counters, floor, and every other nearby surface.

"Thank you for your help," Bone said in Pashto. Wali spoke no English, though Bone could reach out to Zia to translate in a pinch.

Wali nodded and swallowed hard as Bone mopped drying blood off the floor with a clean kitchen towel, which went into the large black trash bag a moment later, completely saturated. He grabbed another neatly folded towel from a stack on the opposite counter and continued, fighting to keep moving. He was doing better than Dom, but the effects of the blood donation had taken a toll.

"We need more…" He didn't know the right word for kitchen towel—it hadn't come up when he learned Pashto on deployment, nor lately when he'd been practicing with Zia. "These," he said, holding up the latest one, already bright red with more of Dom's blood.

Wali gagged and turned away, but at least he didn't run out the back door to vomit again.

"I'm sorry," Bone said. "Also…" He waited until Wali turned partly back toward him without looking at Dom or the blood. "I need guns. A pistol. And an AK-47. And bullets."

Wali shook his head. "I am a chef. I own a restaurant." He rattled off a few sentences. Bone didn't understand all the words, but he caught the gist. The war was over. This was a different time. The city was still dangerous, but guns weren't as common these days—except for with the Taliban.

Bone wanted to offer money, but Wali looked close to going over the edge. Knocking on doors in the middle of the night, trying to buy black market weapons, was too much.

"I understand," Bone said. He'd have to adapt and overcome. "Clothes?" They were about the same size.

Wali looked him up and down. "Yes. I can help."

"And my accent?"

Wali laughed for a second before controlling himself and shaking his head. "Not before morning."

Bone nodded. He'd avoid speaking and hope a local outfit helped him blend in.

Wali spoke again—more words Bone didn't know. As Bone shook his head and continued to clean, Wali demonstrated. First, he pointed at Bone and imitated Bone's posture and walk—exaggerating how Bone stood tall and walked with purpose, like the warrior he was. Wali then pointed at himself before gesturing in a circle—the entire city, or country maybe. He lowered his gaze, staring at the floor a few feet in front of him, and rounded his shoulders. Walking across the small kitchen, he moved with purpose without exactly hurrying. Bone got it. He had to walk and act like a native, alert but keeping to himself, aware of the surroundings but minding his own business.

"I understand," he told Wali. "Where is Kabuli Coffee? Near a small park," he added, repeating what Sardar had said.

Wali nodded. "Not far from here."

Bone had time to finish cleaning the kitchen, update Kristine, and maybe get some food and a short nap.

And he needed the subtle signal Sardar had mentioned the informant would use to find him. "Do you have a red handkerchief?" he asked.

When Wali nodded, Bone hit him with the crucial question. "Do you have two?"

The realization of what he intended dawned in Wali's eyes.

He nodded, terrified but committed.

142

THE PASSWORD

The Vault
Fortuna Magnifico Casino and Resort
Las Vegas, Nevada

Kristine unlocked the door to the Vault and made a note to change the passcode. If Melissa had figured it out, maybe some of the other techs had, too.

"Have a seat," Kristine told Melissa once they stepped inside.

Melissa sipped from her jumbo lime green sport drink—her third since Kristine had picked her up at the hospital—and moved to the desk chair in front of the computer monitors.

They had left a well-stocked Lou the security guard at Melissa's house to manage the emergency repair of the sliding door Kristine had broken, rest, and prepare for what Melissa claimed was Shane's inevitable return.

"Kristine," Melissa said without turning.

Melissa had hit the high points of what had happened at the house and in the desert on the way to the bank, but had fallen asleep on the drive to the casino. They hadn't had a proper talk yet.

"Let's save it for once the computer is unlocked and the job is done, okay?"

Melissa nodded, pulled a notecard from her pocket, and jiggled the computer mouse.

The screen came to life with the password prompt and blinking cursor.

Melissa typed in a long string of letters and numbers from the card she had stored in the safe deposit box and hit the return key.

The password prompt disappeared for a second...

Then returned, with the cursor blinking steadily.

"What...?" Melissa muttered.

Kristine closed her eyes and counted to five to keep from shooting her friend in the back of the head.

When she opened her eyes, Melissa had turned to look at her. "I swear, this is the password!"

"The password Shane gave you—and said would work."

"Oh, no," Melissa whispered. "Krissy—Kristine—I am so, so sorry. I never—"

"Maybe you entered it wrong," Kristine interrupted. She picked up the card. "I'll read. You type. Ready?"

They took it character by character, painfully slowly. Each letter and number disappeared the instant it was typed, replaced by asterisks, which made it difficult to make sure Melissa was typing it correctly.

After the last letter, Melissa pressed the return key.

The password prompt disappeared...

And reappeared.

The cursor blinked, mocking them.

"Is this Shane's handwriting?" Kristine asked, turning the card toward Melissa, who nodded. "It can't be that difficult. A simple replacement cypher—maybe we add a 1 to each number, and use the next letter in the alphabet."

"Or he could have transposed the letters—maybe only the last two," Melissa said.

"Is he clever?"

"I'd say he's careful. But not clever."

Kristine considered for a second. "We'll go one by one, from the simplest to the most complex. We'll work it until we figure it out, but let's start with trying it backward."

Kristine read aloud. Melissa typed.

"Please," Melissa muttered as she hit return.

The password prompt disappeared...

And was replaced by the familiar box asking for a User ID and Password.

They were in.

They switched places. Melissa took the sport drink bottle and slumped into the wingback chair in the corner.

As Kristine logged in to the system, Melissa spoke, her voice quiet. "I'm sorry I believed Shane instead of you. He was just so perfect. Handsome. Funny. Out of my league..." She sighed sadly, cleared her throat, and continued. "I understand if you don't want me around anymore, but I swear—if you give me another chance, I'll never fail you again."

Kristine said nothing. Now that she was sure the computer server worked, she logged off from her user ID, took her father's note from her pocket, and logged in as him.

"I had to tell Shane that Big Mike was dead. But aside from that, no matter what else happens," Melissa added in a whisper, "your secrets are safe with me."

Kristine didn't know if she should take that as a promise—or a threat.

But she had more pressing problems to deal with than her childhood friend who could lead the police to the bodies of her father and brother under a half-finished pool in the backyard of her father's new house.

143

THE CLEANING SUPPLIES

20th Arrondissement

Paris, France

Asad rushed through the night's bus cleaning, doing only the most important tasks, the ones that would be immediately obvious if he skipped them. He practically sprinted through each bus, picking up small pieces of litter and wiping up spills.

At the shift's lunch break—early in the morning—he should have been halfway through the evening's work, but he had done enough to get by.

His real job could now begin.

He walked toward the bus depot's kitchen area only long enough to confirm that the area was filled with workers on their mid-shift break, leaving no one in the main depot area—especially his manager, who definitely enjoyed every second of his mealtime… if not a little more.

Adopting the air of a tired yet dedicated worker, Asad detoured toward the loading area. A pallet of midsize boxes had been delivered late in the evening, at the start of his shift. He'd noted the unusual timing, as had the manager, who had allowed it despite it being long past the normal time for supplies to arrive. Someone had obviously messed up, but it happened in every bureaucracy. It was best just to go along and, when possible, leave it for someone else to fix on another shift, which Asad's manager was very good at.

The clear plastic wrap holding the boxes to the pallet came off with some effort. Asad loaded the boxes onto a bright yellow handcart, moving faster than he might normally but being careful not to look like he was hurrying—more like someone behind in his tasks.

Three trips did the job of moving the boxed "cleaning supplies" across the floor of the cavernous depot and near the buses he cleaned each night, where he stacked the boxes quickly against the wall.

There was no one around to give him a second look.

He carried two of the boxes to the nearest bus, positioned himself next to the rear wheels, and slid each heavy box underneath with his foot.

Asad took one last look around the bus depot, then at his watch. He had time, and no one had left lunch early.

He ducked to the ground and slid under the bus.

This was the riskiest part.

He couldn't be caught now.

He ripped the tape holding the first box closed and removed the large bottle of industrial cleaner. There wasn't much light, but he knew what to expect—and exactly where to go. He had his phone's flashlight feature, if necessary, but preparing and positioning the bombs was all he'd thought about the last several days. He could find the spots in his sleep.

The bottom of the white bottle of "cleaning fluid" twisted off counterclockwise, exactly as promised, revealing the metal inside: a thick, concave copper container, a small cheap mobile phone, and a thumb-sized timer with a gray background and black numbers, all attached with thin, colorful wires.

Asad had to bring the device close to the ground and use the glare from the depot's powerful overhead lights to make out the numbers, which counted down hours, minutes, and seconds.

He did the math in his head.

The bomb would detonate in the middle of the morning.

When all the tourists would be milling around, waiting in lines, or taking pictures.

Late risers would be lingering over coffee at outdoor cafes.

Workers in all types of stores and government buildings would be busy taking care of business.

He shrugged off the guilt that threatened to intrude.

Although he'd been born in France, the people of this city had never treated him as one of their own.

This was his chance not only for revenge but also for money to start a new life elsewhere.

He moved forward under the bus.

It only took a second to power on the phone, peel the backing from the strips of mounting tape attached to the back of the phone and the timer, and press them to the side of the bomb that looked exactly like a bottle of industrial cleaning solution.

Asad then peeled the protective backing from the thicker mounting tape attached to the base of the device, where the bottom of the white container had been, wiped grime off the bus with a cleaning rag, and attached it to the first location he'd been shown on the video chat with his mysterious employer.

He kept pressure on the bomb for fifteen seconds, counting silently, then gave a gentle pull.

It didn't budge. Neither did the timer and phone attached to its side.

Asad repeated the process with the other box.

He took a deep breath and listened. He heard no shoes on the concrete floor, and no talking from coworkers returning to work early.

He gathered the trash, slid from under the first bus, checked his watch again, and picked up the next two boxes before walking to the second bus.

He was right on time.

18th Arrondissement

Paris, France

Six kilometers away, in the 18th arrondissement's bus depot, 24-year-old Jawad finished placing his bombs with plenty of time to spare.

All he wanted to do was leave work early, but that would be suspicious.

Instead, he double-checked the area. He had already broken down the boxes the "cleaning solution" bottles had come in and taken them to the recycling bin.

He'd disposed of the thick pieces of adhesive backing he had torn off the bombs to attach them to the buses.

What was he forgetting?

The cleaning rag in his pocket. It was filthy with grease and grime—

much dirtier than it would have been from simply doing his job of cleaning the interior of the bus.

Jawad folded it carefully, hiding as much of the dirt as possible, and tossed it into the trash. He wouldn't take the risk of adding it to the dirty rag hamper.

Satisfied he'd done all he could, he reluctantly returned to the first of his buses and resumed cleaning, very aware of the bombs ticking away below his feet.

In only a few hours, he'd be free.

And rich.

PART 10

WEDNESDAY

144

THE WAITING

Inter-Services Intelligence Safe House
Jalalabad, Afghanistan

Field manager Imran had moved to the kitchen table hours before. He needed the better lighting, a power outlet for his laptop—and to be closer to the high-end coffee maker.

It had been a long night, and it might be hours before he could sleep again.

The mission had gone horribly wrong.

Lion was likely dead, though Imran couldn't risk confirming it by pulling Bull off his surveillance of the target's house in case it had actually been the servant driving the yellow car and not the businessman.

Nor did Imran know if Lion had successfully eliminated the targets before he lost comms—or died.

The uncertainty bothered him, which he'd passed along to the assistant director in Islamabad, but the man had ordered nothing except for continued surveillance.

Shortly after midnight, Hawk and Owl, the other operators in Afghanistan under Imran's command, had confirmed that their target, the courier named Naveed, had returned home on time the previous evening and spent all night in his apartment.

Imran called Owl for an update. "Where is he now?" Imran asked the moment the man answered.

If the field operator was surprised to hear from him, he covered it well. "He is at the coffee shop. It is part of his normal routine. There have been no deviations."

"You're sure he didn't slip out last night?"

"Positive. Our vantage point allowed us to see both the front door and the back window. At no point did he—or anyone else—exit the apartment, nor did anyone enter."

When Imran said nothing, Owl spoke again, defensively. "We took no breaks—not even for the toilet. I would admit if there had been a gap, but there was none. He has done nothing since he returned three days ago except have his morning coffee, take his mother to the hospital, and buy food. We cannot maintain constant surveillance inside the hospital or in his apartment, but otherwise, he has been in our sight."

"Understood," Imran said, reassuring the operator. "You have done well. Contact me immediately if he deviates from the normal routine."

"I will, and I will pass along the directive to Hawk. He relieves me at noon."

"Understood."

All Imran could do now was wait and hope that the businessman was dead, along with the two men from the private jet, and that the mission wouldn't ruin his promising career.

145

THE MEET

Kabuli Coffee
Kabul, Afghanistan

The yellow car's front seats had been coated with congealing blood, so Bone rode in Wali's tiny older car through the streets of Kabul. He felt like a fool in Wali's drab clothes—a pair of loose-fitting pants and a long tunic, both in gray and black.

Worn black leather shoes at least allowed him to wear thin dark socks. Wali had first offered leather sandals with straps, but one look at Bone's tan line from his running socks stopped him. Bone's legs were dark from the sun, but his feet were too white and noticeable.

Bone had elected not to take a knife from Wali's restaurant, so he was unarmed. The loose tunic would hide a knife, but there was no sheath, and the last thing he wanted was anyone to notice him sitting at a cafe with a knife handle at his waist.

Any fighting would be done old school—hand to hand—though Bone hoped it wouldn't come to that.

At least he was already feeling better after the blood transfusion. His ultra-running training and excellent fitness level seemed to be paying off, making him less tired than he'd thought he would be.

Wali's knuckles were white on the steering wheel, and he was nearly hyperventilating with anxiety. He hadn't complained when they'd realized

Sardar's yellow car couldn't be driven and they had to take his. But acting like this, he'd be more of a liability than an asset.

"Help me with my accent," Bone said. "You are too scared to come along."

Wali gave him a look filled with relief and shame. He took a breath to protest, but Bone stopped him. "I can do it. Just help me speak well enough to order. We can practice now. All is good."

For the next fifteen minutes, Bone mimicked Wali's cadence, accent, and demeanor.

Ordering coffee. Paying the bill. Answering most questions with the easily spoken phrase, "Everything was fine. Thank you."

By the time Wali found a parking spot along the street a block from the cafe, they were both satisfied.

"You wait here," Bone said. "I will return soon. If not..." He offered the man a kind smile. "Forget about me. Help Dominic. Spend the rest of the money." Bone had left behind the backpack with all the American dollars except one packet in his pocket—ten grand—in case of emergency. His other pocket had local currency—coins and bills provided by Wali. He knew what a coffee should cost plus how to order and pay for it.

If Bone didn't make it back, Wali would hide Dominic until the older man could travel; after that, getting home safely was on Dom.

Wali looked stricken. "You will return."

Bone got the distinct impression that while the Afghan hoped Bone wouldn't die this morning, Wali would be happy to never see him again. Wali had done his duty when called upon by his cousin in America, but risking his life, his restaurant, and his family hadn't come easy to him.

"I will return," Bone agreed, more to reassure Wali than because he believed it. So many things could go wrong with this meet. The informant could be a plant from the mastermind designed to lure his enemies into the open to kill them. Or he could double-cross Bone and Kristine, take the money, and flee before sharing information.

Taliban soldiers could wander by, realize an American spy was in their midst, and capture him. Or try. Bone wouldn't go down without a fight.

He removed the local phone provided by Sardar, slipped an earbud in, and used the comms app to place the call that would be his lifeline.

It was during the dinner rush in San Diego, but Zia picked up on the first ring. "I am here, my friend," Zia said. "Lamar, too. We have the map of the city on the computer and are ready to help any way we can."

"Good," Bone said. "Thank you. Hold on."

He used the three-way call feature to patch in Kristine. "I'm ready," the woman said from somewhere in Las Vegas.

Bone nodded to Wali and exited the car.

He walked as Wali had instructed, doing a good job blending in, he hoped. The cafe was just down the one-way street, off a small park. He held the red handkerchief in his hand—the signal the informant would use to find—or target—him.

Bone held back a smile as he felt an old familiar feeling.

He was in the zone.

He was back in action, right where he belonged.

"Let's do this," he whispered under his breath.

146

THE SPOT

Kabuli Coffee
Kabul, Afghanistan

Naveed sat in his usual spot—a small outdoor table farthest from the entrance to the busy cafe. It was near the apartment he shared with his mother, around the corner from the hospital, convenient for her many tests and whatever the latest treatment offered in a futile effort to improve her health.

The coffee was good here, the servers unobtrusive, and the small park nearby provided shade.

He felt a strange sense of calm. A detachment. One way or another, this morning was the end. Soon, he would be dead, or rich.

But no matter what, his time as a proud former member of the ISI and current trusted employee of Colonel Tariq would be over.

If the meet was a trap set up to catch him or other traitors, men hired by Tariq would escort him out of the city, into the tribal area on the border between Afghanistan and Pakistan, near where Tariq had his business and bomb-building warehouse.

There, they would have plenty of privacy to torture him. He would serve as an example for others.

He doubted Colonel Tariq would punish his mother for his sins. She would be allowed to flounder and continue her slow decline. That would be worse than killing her.

If the meeting went well and he lived, however, it would be a new beginning.

A life on the run for himself and his mother.

No more trips around the world, carrying Tariq's messages or negotiating his deals.

The money he was about to receive would buy his mother the medical care she so desperately needed.

That alone was worth this morning's risk.

A man walked through the park toward the cafe, his head down and shoulders slumped. Just another Afghan stopping for tea or coffee on his way to a long day of work...

Except this one clutched a red handkerchief in his right hand.

A quick scan of the park and outdoor seating area of the cafe showed no one else with a red handkerchief. It was 8:00 exactly. The contact was right on time.

It wasn't very hot yet, but Naveed casually reached into his pocket and wiped his forehead and neck with his own red handkerchief before setting it on the table next to his coffee, closest to the empty table to his right.

Bone was focused on his walk and blending in, but he didn't miss the flash of red fabric the man at the table nearest the park used to wipe his face and neck. He looked a few years older than Bone. His beard was closely trimmed, and he had a refined look, though he wore the same type of outfit Bone did—loose pants and long tunic, also in muted colors.

Bone subtly scanned the rest of the men sitting with their coffee, tea, and food, but there were no other red hankies. He slowed and sat in the chair nearest the man he hoped was the informant, but he made no move to contact him. He'd let the man make the first move.

A server promptly appeared. Bone relaxed into the role and ordered coffee exactly as Wali had helped him practice. The server didn't look at him strangely or remark on his accent.

At least one small part of this operation had gone well.

Naveed waited until the man had his coffee. Too late, Naveed realized he should have included some code besides the red handkerchief to establish communication, so he took a risk and began with a basic greeting. He raised the cup to his lips and spoke. "*Salam alaikum.*"

The man behind and to his side hesitated a moment, as any stranger might, before returning the greeting. "*Wa alaikum salam.*"

There was something about the way the stranger spoke…

"You're American?" Naveed whispered in English, struggling to hide his surprise. The man blended in well with his sun-darkened skin, bushy beard, unkempt hair, and world-weary walk.

"My accent is that bad?" the man asked softly in Pashto, but he didn't sound at all surprised. Resigned, if anything.

"Not… horrible," Naveed said, realizing as he did that the man would easily see through his lie.

Naveed leaned back in his chair and took a moment to check the cafe seating area, the park, and the street beyond. Cars passed, and others were parked along the road. He came here every morning he wasn't traveling for Colonel Tariq. Nothing felt off. He was safe and could continue with the conversation.

"I have the information you need," he said, once again raising his cup as he whispered in English.

"I have the money you want," the American said. "Is there a place we can go that is less public?"

"Yes," Naveed said. "Up the street—north. Cross the street, go two blocks, then right at the green building into the narrow alley. Forty meters on the right, look for a broken wooden fence. Go through. There is a vacant lot. We will continue there. I will come after you and make sure you are not followed. But finish your coffee first, and pay."

"Understood," the man said. With the one word, more than anything else, Naveed knew the man was a soldier and not a spy. The type of person who worked with a team—people who could easily abduct him and extract the information they needed without having to pay for it.

The ISI and the CIA had long been adversaries that pretended to trust each other for mutual gain.

The American military, however, had distrusted the Pakistan intelligence service from the start, and discovering that Osama bin Laden had been safely living in Pakistan for years before the Americans found him did nothing to help the relationship.

Naveed's pulse pounded harder. The already risky meeting and exchange of information for money had gone from dangerous to insane. There was no way for the American to know Naveed had been with the ISI, but Naveed had assumed he'd been dealing with a local—even if the Americans were funding the operation.

He thought of his mother alone in the apartment a few blocks away, and wondered if he would see her again.

147

THE TAIL

Kabul, Afghanistan

Wali, though petrified, was proud of what he'd accomplished with the American. From the car, just up the street from the cafe and park, it looked like "Bone," as he called himself, had done well. He had walked to the cafe, found a table, and ordered. No one looked at him strangely. If Wali had not known better, he would have assumed the man was a native of Kabul.

Bone sat for several minutes, drank his coffee leisurely, paid, and walked across the park to the sidewalk. He turned away from the car instead of toward it, however.

The meeting must not have happened, or he had received instructions via the phone call with America to go to a different nearby location.

Should Wali follow him? The original plan called for Wali to wait in the car for an hour before leaving. With Bone walking away, Wali could hope all was well and the dangerous, bizarre ordeal was finally over. Perhaps he would return to the restaurant to find the other American gone as well.

He noted the time. Sixty minutes to wait. After that...

The younger man who had been sitting at the table next to Bone stood and also walked through the park.

No one else would have noticed, but the timing couldn't be a coincidence.

The meeting had happened under Wali's watchful gaze without him noticing, which reassured him. The American—and the young man he met —were professionals.

There was hope none of this craziness would impact his life more than it already had.

Bone crossed the street and disappeared around a corner a few blocks up the road, and the younger man followed.

Fine. They were continuing the meeting elsewhere, out of view of the public. Very smart. At least they hadn't requested his restaurant as the meeting place.

Wali's work was largely done. In less than an hour, he could return to the restaurant, take care of the other American for a few more hours, then finally put this family obligation behind him.

As the younger man turned into the same alley where Bone had gone, a car door opened three vehicles in front of Wali.

A man with a blocky head, dark eyes, and a hard face tinged with concern glanced his way, but he was only making sure there was a break in traffic. He hurried across the one-way street, dodging a car, and rushed up the sidewalk in the direction Bone and the other man had gone.

Someone else had been watching—and was now going after the two men.

Wali's hands shook as he fumbled with his phone. He pressed the button on the new app Zia, in America, had him install—a secure way to communicate. They had set up the plan for emergencies, a contingency plan in case things went horribly wrong.

The call was answered immediately by Lamar. "What is it?"

"They are being followed by a man. He looked..." How could Wali describe the brief impression he'd gotten?

"He looked dangerous," Wali blurted out.

148

THE TANGO

Kabul, Afghanistan

The fence, constructed with junky old boards, was on the right, 40 meters in, exactly where the informant had said it would be. A section of it had been broken off, leaving a gap for a child, skinny man, or motivated larger person to force his bulk through.

Bone poked his head in and scanned the lot. It was filled with trash and broken chunks of concrete from what might once have been a building's foundation. Otherwise, it was deserted and protected from prying eyes.

A perfect place for a clandestine meeting—or an execution.

"The man you met is being followed," Zia said in Bone's ear. His tone was controlled, exactly as if they'd been on a mission back in the day, but his fear was obvious. "One man. He got out of a car in front of Wali."

Bone pulled his head back from the fence opening and double-checked his surroundings. Behind him was a single-story brick home with a buckling metal roof that had seen better days—or maybe that's how it had always looked. The alley continued, curving to the left ahead, but there was nowhere to hide unless he climbed over walls or fences.

"Copy," he said. His only real choices were to run, fight, or wait and hope for the best.

He pushed his way through the wooden fence, breaking off some of the rotten wood along the way.

The long, narrow lot had a similar fence at the opposite end. "How long until the person following my contact reaches the alleyway?" Bone asked as he sprinted across the junk-filled yard, avoiding the larger piles of trash and the bigger pieces of cement.

The reply took forever to work its way from Zia to Lamar, Lamar to Wali, and back. Bone was vaulting over the fence, committed, as Zia spoke to him. "No more than sixty seconds. Probably less. The contact turned the corner a few seconds ago."

"Copy," Bone whispered. The last thing he needed was someone in the neighborhood to hear him speaking English. "Describe his clothing or body—how can I identify him?" Zia translated his question into Pashto for Lamar as Bone spoke, trying to speed the process.

Bone rounded his shoulders again and hurried back to the side street he'd walked up only a few minutes before, trying to strike a balance between acting like a typical Afghan man and getting where he needed to be in time.

As he neared the corner of this alley and the side street, Zia spoke. "Black pants. Black tunic. Muscular. Block head."

The man Zia described hurried past Bone, glancing his way for a second before ignoring him.

Bone slowed, turned the corner, and fell in behind the tango.

Years ago, in combat, Bone would have known exactly what he could and couldn't do in this situation. The rules of engagement would have been spelled out ahead of time in a mission briefing. He and Dominic had discussed the topic on the plane ride over, but neither had guessed they'd be in danger immediately after they landed.

The previous night's situation had been clear. The man on the motorcycle had opened fire on them.

Bone hadn't considered merely driving away last night. The motorcycle rider had to die so Bone could get Dominic and Sardar to safety without fear of the man reporting what had happened.

This morning's situation, though, was less clear. The man in black slowed as he reached the alley while glancing down the narrow lane.

Bone slowed as well, reverting to the walk he'd used to cross the park. Head down, shoulders slumped, trudging along. He felt the man's eyes sweep him again before continuing on.

The disguise worked.

The man turned into the alley.

He could be the informant's wingman, following along to make sure nothing happened to him.

Or he could be someone dangerous, ready to kill the informant and Bone once they were together out of the public's eye.

Bone had to make an immediate, life-or-death decision.

He didn't hesitate. Turning the corner, he rushed forward, silent, the way he had so many times before during his life as a SEAL.

The man glanced back too late.

Bone slammed into him, taking the man to the ground hard.

A second later, Bone locked his arm around the man's neck and squeezed, cutting off the supply of blood to the tango's brain and air to his lungs.

The man was well trained, moving expertly in an attempt to escape the hold.

Had he noticed Bone a few seconds earlier, he might have made it more of a challenge.

He realized that he couldn't escape and reached beneath the long tunic for a weapon.

Too late. His body slumped unconscious before he could draw it.

Bone held tight for another second before loosening his grip. He grabbed the pistol the man had been reaching for and stuck it in his own pocket.

He dragged the potential enemy to the opening for the vacant lot.

The informant stood along the fence on the right, looking concerned.

Bone tightened his grip again, choking the tango to prevent him from coming to, and called in Pashto, doing his best to nail the accent. "Is this man a friend?" He loosened his grip and maneuvered the tango's face into the opening for a few seconds.

After a quick glance around the alley to be sure he was still alone and safe, Bone made eye contact with the informant, who had moved closer to the opening. The man shook his head, fear on his face.

Bone hesitated. The tango began to struggle weakly, his hand once again fumbling under his tunic for the weapon that Bone now had in his pocket.

Someone had already tried to kill Sardar, Dominic, and himself.

Bone was alone in Kabul, Afghanistan, with no one coming to his rescue except Zia's civilian cousin.

A terrorist was plotting a bombing somewhere, and it looked like the man Bone had in a choke hold was trying to stop Bone and the informant from working together to catch the mastermind.

Admiral Nalen was nowhere to be found.

Zia, Lamar, Wali—none of them could tell him what to do. Nor could the informant.

Bone was on his own.

The decision was on him.

With a sharp twist, Bone broke the tango's neck.

149

THE PARTNER

Kabul, Afghanistan

Bone pulled the dead body of the tango through the small opening in the fence, breaking more boards and expanding the hole, but it had to be done.

"Here," the informant whispered in Pashto. He had cleared trash from a dip in the ground.

Bone dragged the tango there and manhandled the body into the space.

Bone reached under the man's tunic and removed the pistol's black leather holster, along with a spare magazine from the man's pocket and a key ring and a cell phone from the other, which he handed to the informant.

"What do I call you?" Bone asked in Pashto, following the man's lead. Someone seeing them hiding a dead body would be bad. But if anyone heard them speaking English, too, all bets were off.

The man hesitated for an instant. Bone saw the lie forming on his lips before he changed his mind. "Naveed," he said, telling the truth—or lying very well.

"I'm Bone."

While he patted the tango down, feeling for other weapons, Naveed tried the man's fingerprint and face scan to open the phone, with no luck.

"No wallet. No identification," Bone whispered just loud enough for Naveed to hear.

"An intelligence agent," Naveed said. "But whose?"

They moved a chunk of concrete near the body and pushed it over the dip in the ground, partly covering the tango. They gathered smaller pieces of concrete, along with trash, and placed them on and near the body, trying to conceal what Bone had done without making it obvious that the pile was hiding a dead man.

"How long?" Bone asked in Pashto, hoping the meaning was clear.

"Long enough. The problem is..." he continued, but Bone lost the thread. He simply didn't have the vocabulary to follow along.

Bone shook his head, but he guessed at what Naveed meant based on the words he caught. "It's his reporting schedule and handler we have to worry about?" he whispered in English.

"Exactly." Naveed gestured, and they moved halfway down the vacant lot. They stood next to a brick fence that backed to a building where they would be less likely to be overheard.

"I would guess him to be an agent of my employer," Naveed said in English, speaking quietly. He hesitated, then seemed to make up his mind. "Who I am willing to betray in exchange for ten million American dollars, as you have been offering."

"Does he seem sincere?" Kristine asked in Bone's ear. The microphone in the earbud had picked up the conversation.

"Yes," Bone said, responding to Kristine before continuing to make it seem like he was answering Naveed. "That is the offer."

"What is your plan for capturing or killing my boss?"

Kristine and Dom had worked out the plan, which Bone had approved. "If he is located in a Western country, the authorities there will be contacted. If he is in Afghanistan or another country in the region—that is much more difficult."

"You are the American government, yes? You can have a team somewhere in a matter of hours. Or a drone, perhaps?"

Bone shook his head. "We are not the government. We are a private enterprise."

"And your team? They are nearby and can help?"

Bone had to smile as he shook his head. He liked the guy. Naveed wanted to get paid and get out, but he also wanted his boss out of the picture, which made sense. Naveed would be in jeopardy until the boss was dead.

"There is no team," Naveed muttered, not asking.

Bone shrugged. "There is. Just not in this country. Listen, I understand.

You need the boss gone for you to be safe. We will pay you half now for his name, location, and the information about the upcoming bombing. You receive the other half once we check the information out." Bone looked him in the eye. "You have my word."

To a Navy SEAL, his word was his bond. Bone meant it—he would move heaven and earth to make sure Naveed got what was coming to him, as long as the guy wasn't running a scam. Bone hoped he conveyed the strength of his commitment with his words and tone.

Naveed nodded slowly. "I accept. The bombing will take place today in Paris. The plan calls for bombs hidden in metro buses to detonate, using shrapnel to kill pedestrians, people in cars, in nearby buildings, and of course the bus passengers. I do not know the exact time, which specific buses, or where the bombers are to be found. However, the terrorists will be young men native to France but of Pakistan or Afghan descent. I am sorry, that is all I know. As for the man behind the attacks, my boss is in Afghanistan. A town called Surobi, less than two hours from here. He—and his entire team, including me—had to relocate from Pakistan. In case we were caught, we couldn't be seen as part of Pakistan intelligence, or associated in any way with our former employer."

"Did you get that?" Bone asked to Kristine, with a finger pointing to his earbud for Naveed to know he was speaking to someone else.

"I have it. I'll put you on speaker with Melissa, my... operations manager," Kristine said. "I have to make some calls."

"Copy," Bone said.

"However..." Naveed said once Bone finished. He nodded toward the pieces of concrete and the mound of trash hiding the tango's body. "There is no time for your team to arrange an attack on my boss. His name is retired Colonel Tariq, formerly of Pakistan's Inter-Services Intelligence agency, though he uses an alias here in Afghanistan. If the man you killed was sent by my boss and he fails to check in, Tariq will be warned and escape. So we will go to Surobi immediately. Together. I will help you kill Colonel Tariq."

150

FIVE MILLION

The Vault
Fortuna Magnifico Casino and Resort
Las Vegas, Nevada

Kristine logged into the bank holding her father's secret stash of money and prepared to wire five million dollars to the numbered account Naveed had specified via Bone.

Melissa sat next to her in the other desk chair, covered the phone lying on the desk with her hand, and whispered in her ear. "Are you sure this is the right thing to do?" Melissa asked. "Five million dollars... Shane just conned me. What if this is a scam, too?'

Kristine finished entering the data and paused for a second to double-check the information. "Then it will be a very expensive lesson." She pressed the "send" button and moved Melissa's hand gently away from the phone. "Half of the money has been sent," she said. "You're on with Melissa now. I'll be back in a minute." Kristine handed the phone to Melissa and switched screens, pulling up the contact management database she and her father had used.

His side of the computer had many more contacts than her version of the database.

Kristine went to the search bar and typed, "France."

Two results popped up. Both had last been updated several years before.

"There's no time," she muttered. She couldn't get bogged down trying to convince some French spy that had once known her father to trust her intel.

Reaching someone she knew—and her father had spoken with recently —put an extra layer of bureaucracy and management in the loop, but...

She searched again.

Gregory Addison's name, cell phone number, and encrypted comms app contact details popped up on her screen.

She grabbed her phone back from Melissa. "Are you okay for a few minutes?" she asked Bone. "I need this line."

"Once we leave the city, we're going to be out of cellular data range to use this app for a while, anyway," Bone said. "But here's where we're going. There's no address—just a rough description, and Tariq's alias."

She made notes while Naveed spoke about the road into the town of ten thousand people between Kabul and Jalalabad.

"Be careful," Naveed called. "If the bombers in Paris are alerted and warn Colonel Tariq..."

"The two of you will be heading into an ambush."

"Exactly," Bone said.

Kristine nodded, not that Bone could see her. "I'll make sure to mention that. Call you back soon. Be safe."

She hung up on him. He was a professional and could take care of himself for a little while. She had to prevent a devastating attack in Paris.

151

THE CONTINGENCY

Kabul, Afghanistan

Naveed drove the dead tango's car toward the alley where the American waited.

This was his chance. He had five million dollars in a Swiss bank account. That would be enough to take his mother to a country with first-rate hospitals, find a cure, and go into hiding.

He checked the rearview mirror. A car had pulled out of its parking place as soon as he had—proof that the American had at least one team member in Kabul with him, in addition to the people he spoke with via a Bluetooth earbud to transfer the money to Naveed's bank in Switzerland.

Ahead on the left was the building where his mother rested in their small apartment. He could lose the tail, pick her up, and vanish.

But Colonel Tariq would win.

Eventually, Tariq would find and kill him for his betrayal.

As risky as helping the American was, going to kill Tariq immediately was safer in the long run.

Naveed pulled over. The American emerged from the alley, walking like an Afghan, and climbed into the car.

Naveed pulled back into traffic. As he approached the apartment building, he made another difficult decision. "See that building?" he asked. He gave the address and apartment number. "Did your friends hear that?"

The man—Bone—shook his head. "No. They're offline handling Paris."

Naveed shrugged. It would have to do. "Tell them before we reach Surobi. If I don't return, I ask that someone help my mother. Give the other half of my money directly to her. She is ill."

"If you don't come back, I'll be dead, too," Bone said. "But I'll make sure they see to it," he said, gesturing to his earbud.

The car following them turned away at the next large street.

"The other car—it does not come along?" Naveed asked.

"No," the American said with a smile, like he'd said something amusing. Then he added, with all seriousness, "We are on our own."

152

THE CONFESSION

The Kabul-Jalalabad Highway
Outside of Kabul, Afghanistan

Traffic was slow on the edge of the city.

Bone had done all he could. Dominic was alive and recovering, according to Zia via Wali.

Kristine's connections were working to thwart the Paris bombing.

And he was in a stolen car with a supposedly trustworthy former ISI spy on an 80-kilometer drive across Afghanistan to kill the bombing mastermind.

Armed with only a Soviet pistol and one spare magazine.

"If there's a police or Taliban checkpoint…" Bone started.

"Let me do the talking," Naveed replied, straight-faced for a moment before trying to hold back a smile.

"My accent is that bad? Tell the truth."

"No," Naveed said, serious again. "But I have been speaking English fluently for years. Do I have an accent?"

"Yes. It's slight, but there."

"Now imagine what it was like when I first started. That is how you sound. Not bad. Just… foreign. Like you are speaking the words for the hundredth time, not the millionth."

In front of them, traffic sped up with nothing to show for the delay. Just like in America.

After a few kilometers of silence, Naveed spoke again. "I have a confession."

Bone glanced his way while subtly moving his hand toward the pistol at his hip.

"I have only been to Colonel Tariq's compound once. I was there at night. It might take some time for me to find it again."

"The longer it takes to find, the more chance there is he will be warned."

"Yes. I am sorry. I thought there would be more time, or that you would have a team that could discover his exact location, and a drone with a missile."

"I wish," Bone muttered. "If he is warned, will Tariq flee or stay and fight?"

"He had many guards when I was there. Loyal former Pakistan Army soldiers. But unless he has materials he cannot replace, I would expect him to flee."

"Where would he go?"

"He would prefer Pakistan, but that is not allowed."

"Why?"

"The deal he made with the leaders of the ISI. He had to assume a new identity—as an Afghan. We all did. And we were not allowed in Pakistan. To ensure no... how do you say..."

"Blowback?"

"Blowback, yes. If any of us were caught, or the mission compromised, we cannot lead back to Pakistan or the ISI."

"So?"

"I do not know where he would run to, but he is an experienced spy. He has an extensive network of loyal contacts and will have at least one safe house nearby, and possibly others. Kabul, perhaps. But I would guess Jalalabad. It is closer to Pakistan, and a more modern city in some ways than Kabul. Safer for him."

"You think we won't get there in time?"

Naveed drove just above the speed limit. A few vehicles sped past, but the majority kept pace with them.

"I think we plan to attack a warehouse guarded by experienced, well-armed men—and there are only two of us, with one weapon."

"Do you have any better ideas?"

Naveed shook his head while keeping his eyes on the road. "No. Do you?"

"No. Not yet," Bone said.

153

THE CITY

Gregory composed himself before entering the conference room. Wyatt and Marcus had been at this for days with little to show for their efforts.

There had been no new bombings.

There was no chatter online, no rumors of an imminent attack.

He had to face facts: There was a good chance that despite their best efforts, they were wrong.

He unlocked the door and slipped inside, locking it behind him.

The room smelled worse than ever, which Gregory hadn't thought was possible. Wyatt must have been eating the frozen burritos he loved so much in here instead of in the small employee kitchen down the hall. Their stench lingered.

The taped-together papers still covered the conference table, but more of the reverse side had been filled in since the last time he'd checked on Wyatt and Marcus.

Both men looked up as he entered. They sat on opposite sides of the huge table, faces drawn, chins resting on their hands as they stared at the lines, arrows, circles, and notes on the paper. They looked exhausted. And like they'd had the same thought—all of this might have been for nothing.

"No progress," Wyatt said before Gregory could ask.

"Paris," Marcus said. "If it were us, we would hit Paris."

"Oh, yeah," Wyatt said, perking up. "That's right. Paris. Tons of security, but if it's the same guy as the other attacks, he'll have thought of something to get around that."

"How would he—or you—do it?" Gregory asked.

"Tourists," Wyatt repeated as he stood. Marcus forced himself up as well.

"They are soft targets," Marcus added. "People walk around all over the city."

"Museums. The Eiffel Tower. The Louvre. Cafes," Wyatt said.

Marcus agreed. "Bombs at a museum—or museums. Another possibility is a small plane packed with explosives flown into the Louvre or the park area near The Eiffel Tower. Lots of people out in the open. But what we're most worried about is car bombs," Marcus said. "Hard to detect, nearly impossible to prevent."

"Paris has excellent defenses for vehicle bombs," Gregory pointed out.

"Not if they're loaded with shrapnel and are blown up on the street instead of trying to ram into a building," Wyatt said, his voice quiet.

The three of them pondered the destruction the scenario would bring.

"Countermeasures?" Gregory asked. "Any way to predict a time and likely locations? Ways to prevent it from happening?"

"We've brainstormed some ideas," Marcus said, pointing at a section of the mind map that had been freshly filled in.

"But really, the best thing would be to figure out who the bomber is and catch him before he strikes," Wyatt said. He gestured with his head for Gregory to move to the side of the room with him while Marcus watched with amusement.

"I know it's against protocol," Wyatt started in a whisper to Gregory. His breath stank of cheap frozen burritos and energy drinks. "But what if Wyatt and I flew to Paris and poked around? Or if not Paris, what about Islamabad, Pakistan. Maybe we could—"

Gregory's phone buzzed in his pocket, the angry, insistent tone of the comms app. He held up a finger to Wyatt, grateful to interrupt the young man's dream of going into the field on a wild goose chase, got the phone out of his pocket, and unlocked it.

The display had only a string of numbers. No name.

Just like his own user ID on the system.

Gregory slid the circle to answer and moved the phone to his ear, but said nothing as he walked toward the door.

"Mr. Addison," the woman's voice said. It wasn't a question. She knew who he was.

Gregory stopped walking. It took him a second, but he placed the voice.

He turned to share a look first with Marcus, then with Wyatt.

"It seems you've taken over for your father, Ms. Salestri. You must have accessed his notes or database to find the contact information I gave him."

"There's a bombing attack planned for Paris later today," the young lady said, getting straight to her point. "I know some, but I don't have all the details. Am I wasting my time calling you first, or is this something you can help with?"

She sounded much more self-assured than the last time they had spoken. Focused.

In fact, she sounded a lot like her father had, back in the day.

Gregory walked to the conference table and gestured for Wyatt to return to the mind map. This might be the break they needed. "Ms. Salestri, that is definitely something I can help with."

154

A JOB WELL DONE

With his shift over, bus cleaner-turned bomber Asad opted to walk home —at least for a few blocks.

He definitely wouldn't be taking his usual bus across town to his small apartment. The buses he had attached the bombs to were now leaving the service depot that supplied many of the buses which traveled to the city's largest tourist attractions.

He wasn't an expert, but the mobile phones attached to each device in addition to the countdown timers could be used to detonate them at any moment.

He wouldn't risk it.

The sun was coming up soon. It was going to be a perfect summer day.

There would be plenty of people outside—pedestrians and shoppers, tourists and locals—for the bombs to kill.

The bombs he had planted.

He felt a pang of guilt, but he pushed it aside. He had done what he needed to do to start a new life.

Stopping at the corner, Asad checked his account balance in the online payment app. He kept his expression neutral, though his joy threatened to break into a smile.

He now had enough money to start over, to be someone more than a custodian.

To get away from France and its bias against him.

Checking the website of the high-speed rail service, he confirmed his train to Marseille was on time and hurried up the street.

He'd take the metro to his small apartment, collect his backpack, and take another metro to the train station.

Less than five hours from now, he'd be in Marseille. Shortly after that, a ferry would take him to Algiers, where he'd have enough money to be anyone.

To do anything.

Within reason. The money would go far, but he couldn't retire to a life of leisure. He'd use it to buy a new identity, then open a small business like a coffee shop or electronics store.

And he'd hire someone else to do the cleaning.

18th Arrondissement

Paris, France

As the sky lightened over the only city he'd ever lived in, Jawad walked home from the bus service depot and checked his phone.

A huge smile filled his face.

He was rich.

He'd never have to clean another bus again.

In three hours, he would board a plane for Turkey.

He'd had it with the French. Though he'd been born here, he'd never felt like he was treated as a native. His skin was too dark, and he was too poor. His immigrant parents had passed away a few years ago, leaving him stuck here.

His cousins in Karachi, who had set him up with the job to place the bombs on the buses, were ready to welcome him "home." They had a small apartment picked out for him.

By tonight, he would be in Pakistan, the land of his ancestors.

Behind him, a light blue bus with white accents pulled onto the street, followed by others, ready to serve the residents and guests of the city.

155

THE FEELING

Inter-Services Intelligence Headquarters
Islamabad, Pakistan

Raza sat in the basement room where he'd worked and slept for the past several days. He stared at a map of Kabul which filled his computer screen. The courier's apartment building was marked with a red pin, along with another at the home of the businessman and probable spy in an upscale neighborhood.

Three yellow pins, two near the apartment and the other by the house, marked the general area where the remaining operators were, according to Imran, the field manager in Jalalabad.

"No word from—who is this one?" Hafiz asked from his wheelchair behind Raza. His breath stank of stale coffee, but Raza was sure his was just as bad.

"His code name is Owl. His partner is Hawk, but not on duty until noon."

Hafiz pointed at the other yellow pin.

"Bull," Raza said. "Still watching the house as ordered."

"Has the target—Sardar, the businessman—gone to work?"

"No. If he had planned to stop for breakfast at a cafe, he would have left by now. If he goes straight to his office, he will leave shortly."

"How often does he go directly to the office?"

"Rarely."

Hafiz grunted and sat back. He was silent for several seconds. Raza wasn't sure if he was waiting for more data or thinking, but as the nominal person in charge of the operation, Raza felt it was up to him to speak next. "I recommend bringing Hawk in immediately to back up Owl watching the courier, or have him help Bull with the house. I believe something has happened."

Hafiz grunted again. Raza took it as permission and called Imran. When the field manager answered, sounding exhausted, Raza had a gut feeling and went with it. "When was the last time you heard from Owl?"

"An hour ago. He will report if there is anything unusual."

Raza considered the answer while he gave his other orders. "Activate Hawk. Put him in a vehicle and have him on standby to backup either Owl or Bull." He made a snap decision. "But first, contact Owl for an update."

He hung up and turned to Hafiz. "Sir, you have more experience than I, but…"

Hafiz nodded grimly. "Yes, I have a bad feeling as well."

Inter-Services Intelligence Safe House
Jalalabad, Afghanistan

Imran finished the remaining coffee, burning his mouth on the latest in the steady supply of caffeine keeping him functioning.

He selected Owl's contact in his app's speed dial function and pressed it.

The phone rang steadily for several seconds before giving him a message that the call had failed to connect.

He dialed again, trying to convince himself that the local cellular internet service here in Jalalabad, or in Kabul where Owl watched Naveed the courier, was to blame.

There was still nothing.

Imran called Hawk, who answered on the first ring, disproving both theories. "You are needed immediately. Take your car and find Owl. He is in his car watching the courier near Kabuli Coffee. Or he was," Imran said. "He is not answering his comms."

"Owl always answers his comms," Hawk said. It sounded like he was already on the move.

"Yes. Hurry."

Imran hung up and reached for the coffee mug before remembering it was empty. He would make another cup—or two—but first he had to report.

He dialed and gave Raza the news. "Hawk is activated. I have sent him to Kabuli Coffee. Owl is off comms."

"Understood," Raza said. "Report the moment you hear from Owl," he said, as if Imran would do anything other than that.

―――――――――

Inter-Services Intelligence Headquarters
Islamabad, Pakistan

"Owl is not answering," Raza said, spinning the desk chair to face his superior. "It could be nothing."

Hafiz snorted.

"Shouldn't we warn Colonel Tariq?" Raza asked for a second time that night—or day, as it had become.

Killing Sardar the suspected spy and the two American operators hadn't worked. The courier was gone. The next thing to do was to reach out and warn Tariq.

Hafiz shook his head. "No. If the courier is gone and another of our operators is no longer communicating, it means the Americans are aware of Tariq now. All of this has to be the Americans and the target, the businessman turned spy," he said, gesturing at the map on the computer. "That is the only logical assumption. Maybe, before the Americans arrived in Kabul, I could have justified a warning. Or if the first operator had succeeded in killing the two men who landed at the Kabul airport. Now, though, it is too risky. If we warn him at this stage and anyone finds out, we will be implicated in his... business."

"What is his business?" Raza blurted out.

Hafiz frowned at the question and didn't answer for several seconds. Finally, he spoke in a quiet voice that was nearly a whisper. "The same as when he worked for us."

"Planning. Logistics," Raza said, leaving the rest unspoken.

Hafiz surprised him by responding. "And?"

"Bomb making."

"Exactly."

The pieces clicked into place for Raza. "The embassy bombing in Egypt?"

Hafiz said nothing.

"And the food court in Turkey? The airport in Spain? They had his style, though not any of his usual methods."

Hafiz didn't confirm Raza's questions, but he didn't deny them, either. "We cannot risk warning him," Hafiz repeated.

"But—he did those on his own, right? He retired. Pakistan did not help, direct, or support him in any way." The country wouldn't have done such a thing.

"That is correct."

Raza was missing something.

An essential piece of the puzzle.

Maybe there was another bombing planned?

Raza worked it out.

If there was an attack that Pakistan was aware of, interested in, and would be pleased about... If it would clearly benefit Pakistan...

That had to be it. There must be another attack coming. And if the world suspected Pakistan had helped with it, or supported the perpetrators, there would be hell to pay.

"We cannot warn Colonel Tariq," Raza agreed, his voice firm. "To do so and get caught would get us blamed for any attack Tariq has in motion. One that would benefit Pakistan—one that would result in death and destruction."

Hafiz met his gaze but said nothing, which Raza took as confirmation his deductions were correct.

The solution was clear now.

They had to cut Tariq loose, distance themselves from him, and paint him as a rogue operator acting completely on his own.

Pakistan could not risk being linked to Tariq. Not if the Americans knew about him and were prepared to capture or kill him, as they were so successful at.

Hafiz stared at the computer screen, ignoring Raza. He chewed his lip and absently rubbed the white stubble on his face. "Give..." He pointed at one of the yellow flags on the map.

"Hawk."

"Yes. Give Hawk five minutes to find his partner. There is a chance a phone battery died, or he has been in a car accident. Something minor. But..."

"Coincidences are never good."

"Correct. Pull Bull from the businessman's house. Send him to Surobi, halfway between Kabul and Jalalabad on the Kabul-Jalalabad Highway. That is where Tariq has his warehouse. Hawk, also, when he fails to find Owl. Have them both make the best time possible. More directions to follow."

"Yes, sir."

Raza hated to ask, but it was his right to know, and it was long past the time for secrets. "You believe the Americans have something to do with the disappearance of Owl? And that they are going to Surobi—for Tariq?"

"Don't you?" Hafiz shot back.

Raza nodded as he turned back to his computer to pass along the orders. Unfortunately, that was exactly what he believed, too.

156

THE WARNING

DGSI (Direction Générale de la Sécurité Intérieure) Headquarters
Levallois-Perret, France

Fewer than 10 kilometers from the Champs-Élysées, the Louvre Museum, and the Musée d'Orsay, the headquarters for the French domestic intelligence agency appeared quiet from the outside.

In an interior room with no windows, Pierre Marchand had just arrived at work. He sat at his desk and prepared to review the previous night's "take"—intelligence gathered from human sources, cyber intelligence, and signal intelligence in an effort to protect the country, its citizens, and an estimated twelve million summer tourists.

As the director of intelligence, it was his job to keep tabs on the rumors, threats, and actual concerns. His day-shift team had also just started work for the day. They handled intelligence in real time, as it arrived—following up, assigning assets to investigate further, or taking action in the event of an immediate threat.

Pierre's desk phone rang as he took a sip of coffee from his commuting cup, finishing up the last of the café allongé his wife made him every morning.

"Yes?"

"I have Gregory Addison, director of America's Central Analysis

Group on the secure line," his executive assistant told him. "You met him—"

"Yes," Pierre said, interrupting her. "Put him through."

He had met Addison at an intelligence conference put on by the Americans a few years before. Addison had been in the business for years, like him, and had impressed Pierre with his professionalism, intelligence, and quiet candor. They'd shared a lunch and had hit it off, but hadn't kept in touch.

Addison would only be calling for a few reasons. One would be to ask for a very serious, under-the-radar favor, the way that top professionals in the business did from time to time when they needed information or assistance.

Another would be to offer intelligence directly, when there wasn't time to go through more formal channels.

"Good morning, Mr. Addison," Pierre said in English. It was past midnight in Washington, DC.

"Good morning, Mr. Marchand," Addison said. He sounded exhausted, but focused. "I have urgent intelligence for you," he said, getting straight to the point. "Unfortunately, it comes from one source only, but I have high confidence there is an imminent threat of an attack on Paris."

Pierre traded the commuter coffee mug for a pen and a sheet of paper. "Can you tell me the source?"

Addison paused for a moment, then answered. "This comes to me from a new—yet trusted—asset. It is not an official notification from Gregory Addison, Director of the Central Analysis Group in the United States, but a tip from one friend to another. And unfortunately, my asset didn't give me as much information as I would have preferred. We took a few minutes to try to confirm the intel, or find a second source, but we weren't able to."

Pierre jotted a note. "I understand. The threat—what is the target?"

"The entire city of Paris. The source claims that bombs planted in, under, or on city buses will be detonated throughout the city, possibly at or near museums and other tourist attractions. Pedestrians would be the primary targets via propelled shrapnel, though the devices are likely strong enough to demolish the buses themselves, along with nearby vehicles and non-fortified or protected buildings."

Pierre made notes while forcing his mind to stay on task and not consider the ramifications of such an attack.

"Timing?"

"Today," Addison said. "I have an analyst who predicts 10:30 a.m., 1:30 p.m., or 5 p.m. in that order of likelihood. That isn't from the intel—it's a model on our end. The bombs could go off at any time, however. The source did not have that information. We don't know if they could detonate all at once or individually, based on GPS, triggered by suicide bombers riding in the buses, observers nearby, or remotely."

"And the confidence level?" Something didn't feel right to Pierre.

"High confidence, as I said."

"But?" Pierre asked. His years in the business had given him a sixth sense to know when an asset, source, employee, or even a friend was holding back.

"It's tricky," Addison said. "It isn't one of our operations. In fact, while I have an analyst who predicted a bombing of this kind—without any concrete details—prior to this it has not been on our radar. But I believe it is solid and worth acting on." He sounded more sure of himself. "I wouldn't be calling otherwise."

"A new source. Unofficial." Pierre didn't like the sound of any of it. If he mobilized the entire city—the police, the soldiers who patrolled sensitive sites, the elite units that handled counterterrorism, and other tactical units to investigate this, and it turned out to be nothing, he'd look like a fool.

If he ignored it, and bombs exploded, wounding and killing people, though, he'd not only look bad, but he'd also have blood on his conscience.

"Take this seriously, Pierre," Addison said, switching to his first name. "I know it sounds sketchy—and there is a chance my source is being played. But I believe it's accurate."

"Thank you for the information, Gregory," Pierre said. "Please be in touch if you have anything more."

"Actually…" Addison said.

"Yes?"

"I have two very perceptive analysts who have been looking into this type of scenario. They have some specific suggestions…"

157

THE WAREHOUSE

Rahbar International Trading Partners
Surobi, Afghanistan

The old forklift rumbled as its driver followed Tariq, who led the way at a measured pace. Two armed guards shadowed him.

The plastic explosives for the next operation had finally arrived.

Local workers moved out of the way as Tariq walked along the aisle in the middle of the warehouse. Long rows of sturdy metal shelves ran lengthwise beside him. Crates, boxes, and pallets of car and motorcycle parts packed the shelves on the left. The shelves on the right contained clothing for men and women, bolts of fabric, and goods made from leather: jackets, bags, and shoes. All in keeping with the legitimate business of importing and exporting goods.

In wide, open spaces between each row of shelves, workers unpacked every imaginable spare part for vehicles, organized them, and repacked them for distribution to local parts stores and repair shops.

Other workers packed leather goods made by local craftsmen for shipment around the world.

Tariq took charge of any special deliveries that arrived, personally escorting them to the rear of the building, away from the main rolling doors where trucks backed in for loading and unloading.

The heat inside the tall building was already growing, and it was only midmorning, though large fans helped keep the temperature tolerable.

A local nodded at Tariq respectfully as he backed out of the way, pausing from his day-to-day work of the import-export business. He studiously looked away from the men walking near Tariq. The locals ignored all the guards, including the ones on the metal walkway that lined the interior of the warehouse 20 feet off the ground, the men who patrolled the grounds outside the building, and the two who stopped each delivery truck before it could enter the compound. The guards were former Pakistan Army soldiers, happy to be paid double what they'd been earning before to leave the service and work for him in Afghanistan. They wore comfortable civilian clothing—long tunics in drab colors over loose pants, and sturdy sandals. Contrasting with the civilian clothes, tan plate carriers with extra magazines for the AK-47s they carried looked out of place.

The locals were well paid, earning much more than they could have elsewhere in the small town. They knew to keep their eyes to themselves and their mouths shut—especially about the occasional special delivery Tariq escorted to the rear of the building. The guards had reported the rumors exchanged by the locals—that Tariq's real work was importing expensive electronics from the West while exporting drugs.

Tariq did nothing to quash the rumor. It served him well.

He led the way around the long, tall metal shelf that ran crosswise and separated the main part of the warehouse from his work area.

On his right, the small office he'd had built was where he planned operations, communicated with his extensive network, and conducted the legitimate import-export business.

On the left, where he led his entourage and the forklift, was his workshop—a rusty full-length orange shipping container.

He stopped near the large door at the end of the container and showed the forklift driver where he wanted the pallet. The man placed it exactly where indicated—gently, though the plastic explosives weren't dangerous until Tariq and his latest protégé worked them into the bombs they would soon become.

The guards knew who he was and what he did—they took no chances, even though the risks were minimal.

The two guards who had escorted him climbed the steep metal stairs leading to their second-floor walkway, and the one driving the forklift backed carefully around the shelves, past the office, and returned the machine to the local workers on the other side of the shelves, leaving Tariq alone with his toys.

A short, thin, nerdy young man with thick glasses hurried over from the shipping container and joined Tariq.

"Is this…" Maaz trailed off, not speaking the words, as if the two of them weren't safe in the back of the warehouse surrounded by highly trained guards. Maaz was the latest in a long line of intelligent men Tariq had taken under his wing. He exuded an air of eager focus.

"Yes, my friend." Tariq enjoyed showing the next generation how to plan and conduct operations, along with how to devise—and disguise—all types of bombs.

Maaz had been a great help already, vetting the two bus depot workers in France and constructing many of the bombs that would wreak havoc across the city later today.

Despite the exciting day in Paris, though, their work was never done. Tariq would call a halt to their work to watch the news of the destruction in a few hours, but until then, they had a job to do.

They would spend several days carefully constructing the bombs needed for the next operation—the mission he had offered his former ISI superiors as an incentive to allow him to retire and go into business for himself. Tariq was looking forward to it more than any other operation of his career.

It would rock India—Pakistan's old adversary—and would finally bring about the settlement of the disputed Kashmir region so long sought by Pakistan. Because of its strategic location and symbol of national identity, it rightly belonged to Pakistan… Though India felt exactly the same.

With one magnificent bombing, Tariq would help his country—and make a great deal of money from a terrorist organization that would gladly take the blame for the attack, as others had for the destruction in Egypt, Turkey, and Spain… plus the bombing in Paris later this morning.

Tariq allowed Maaz to remove the plastic holding the unmarked boxes together on the pallet as he entered the shipping container he used as a workshop.

Maaz already had the small air-conditioning unit running. Tariq settled onto a short stool near his workbench, welcoming the cool air. As he'd gotten older, and softer around the middle, he'd tolerated the heat less.

Maaz grunted with effort as he carried two boxes inside and set them on the floor nearby. "Sir, this is… a lot."

Left unasked was what they would do with so much explosive power.

Tariq smiled. "It is just enough for the hotels and army bases that we will eliminate next month. And"—he pointed at the adorable teddy bear on the workbench—"a special surprise for the shopping malls... and the children of some troublesome military leaders."

Maaz's feral grin proved Tariq had chosen wisely by bringing this one on board. His previous student—Naveed—hadn't been as cutthroat, though his talents at negotiation had served Tariq well.

After the destruction in India next month, Tariq would be free to focus his energies and talents on attacking the United States.

That's where the real money would be.

Extremists would gratefully pay dearly to take credit for a bombing in Washington, DC, or New York City.

"That's enough to start," Tariq said. "Let me show you what I have planned for next month."

His former superiors at the ISI were going to be overjoyed by what happened to India.

158

THE SEDAN

The Kabul-Jalalabad Highway
Outside of Kabul, Afghanistan

Hawk weaved in and out of traffic, risking an accident as he pushed the expensive SUV hard along the highway.

After several kilometers of congestion, where he honked to bully people from his path and drove along the side of the road, he was finally making up time.

Somewhere ahead of him was the man who may have killed his partner.

Hawk would find out what had happened—and get his revenge.

Kilometers from the city, traffic on the open highway moved mostly at the speed limit, aside from Hawk and a few other people in a hurry.

Hawk risked moving into the oncoming lane to pass a slow car.

The next car in front of him—a black luxury sedan that reminded him of the one Owl had been driving—stuck to just over the speed limit.

Hawk glanced at the slow driver before pulling back into the lane in front of the car.

The driver of the sedan was tall and thin, in his late thirties, with a close-cropped beard.

It was his target—Naveed, the courier—driving Owl's car.

Only years of training kept Hawk from slamming on the brakes, letting the car rear-end him, then getting out and killing the driver.

Hawk kept up his speed, pulling away slowly, and checked the rearview mirror.

There was no doubt. The driver was the courier he'd been watching for days.

And there was an Afghan in the passenger seat.

He had to call this in.

His phone on the holder attached to the dash had no bars for internet connectivity. Using the encrypted comms app was out of the question. He had to make the call using the open cellular voice network.

Hawk defaulted to Pashto instead of Urdu or English, as he would have spoken on the comms app. If America's NSA was listening on the open line, or any other of the world's intelligence organizations that sucked up every phone call they could, searching for terrorist threats or keeping tabs on the Taliban, the common language of the area would be less suspicious than any other.

The call connected. Imran would have seen that it came via a cellular call in the open. He grunted a greeting instead of speaking.

"It's me," Hawk said. "I am on the road and have just passed our friend's car. Our other... friend... is driving. With a passenger—an Afghan. I have yet to make his acquaintance."

"What good news!" Imran answered in the same language, continuing the ruse that this was a call about running into some friends. "I'm happy you two have finally found each other. You will stick together?"

"Yes, of course."

"Good. Thanks for calling—that is a relief. I will talk to you soon, I'm sure. Go safely," he said, and hung up.

Hawk slowed to keep from pulling away.

He would find out what had happened to Owl before killing the courier slowly, making him suffer, if he'd had anything to do with Owl's disappearance.

159

THE ORDERS

Inter-Services Intelligence Headquarters
Islamabad, Pakistan

Hafiz used the toe of his slip-on sneaker to push the wheelchair several meters from Raza's computer desk. He needed a moment to think, and space away from the younger man's gaze.

The decision in front of him would be scrutinized and questioned. No matter what happened, some in the upper echelon of the organization would agree with him. Others wouldn't.

But he had been specifically chosen for the assignment because he didn't care what any of them thought. He hadn't much when he was younger, and now that he was well past his retirement years, the opinions of others—even those at the very top—mattered little.

He would do what was best for the country, the ISI, and the men involved.

In that order of priority.

Consequences—and feelings—be damned.

Hafiz had about thirty minutes until the courier and, presumably, one of the Americans, disguised as an Afghan, reached Surobi.

A year ago, in exchange for a promise to bomb India—Pakistan's nemesis—Tariq had received permission to retire from the ISI and go into business for himself.

He had made several promises. First, not to be detected or caught.

But it now appeared he had been discovered and had at least one American operator on his way to Tariq's warehouse in Surobi, Afghanistan.

Second, if discovered, Tariq had promised to go into hiding, or take the fight to the enemy. In the worst case scenario, he would never be taken alive.

Hafiz shook his head. With Americans involved, it was too late to rely on Tariq to do the right thing—and pull it off.

Tariq had broken his promise and gotten caught.

It was time to cut Tariq loose, and make sure it was clear the man was acting on his own without the support of Pakistan or the ISI.

Anything less would be a disaster if the world discovered the ISI had known what Tariq was planning when he retired.

The powers that be would hate the idea of not having a "rogue" Tariq attack India, but Hafiz had been chosen to do what was right.

He had made his decision.

"Listen carefully," he told Raza, and gave the orders.

160

THE DGSI

Command Center
DGSI (Direction Générale de la Sécurité Intérieure) Headquarters
Levallois-Perret, France

The DGSI command center's dim red overhead lighting contrasted with the blue and white light from the many computer monitors that filled the room. Each of the twenty workstations had at least two monitors, and some had four. Across the length of the far wall, large screens stretched side by side, showing live feeds of Paris, Lyon, and major ports, bridges, and tunnels around the country.

Pierre stood on a platform at the rear of the room. As the point person with the most details—limited though they were—the operation was Pierre's to run. He didn't work in this room often. His department mainly gathered clandestine intelligence. If he needed to come to this room to manage a mission, it meant something had gone horribly wrong.

The tall, distinguished director-general of the agency stood behind him and to his right. Pierre had briefed the man as they hurried down the hall to the command center. He had the same attitude as Pierre: Better to look like fools if Gregory Addison's source was wrong than do nothing and risk the lives of the people in the city.

"Ladies and gentlemen," Pierre called. Twenty heads turned his way, every one of them alert and ready to go. No one uninterested in working hard and giving it their all made it to these desks.

"This is not a drill," Pierre said.

The already high level of focus in the room ticked up a notch. People sat up straighter, turned their chairs more his way, and waited expectantly for his next words.

Before today, he would have said that they had enough people to handle any situation thrown at them, but looking at them now, he wasn't so sure.

But it was all he had.

"We have an unconfirmed intelligence tip that one or possibly all of the city buses in Paris have explosive devices in or on them. They will be detonated in high-traffic locations throughout the city today to kill pedestrians and other unprotected individuals near the streets."

France had learned from bombings across the world. All the city's high-profile targets had barricades to prevent vehicle access to sidewalks and plazas. Many routed vehicles away from attractions completely. Few, though, had any defenses against a shrapnel attack where soft targets—people—gathered near the attractions.

"Please pull up the top tourist sites, especially museums, where pedestrians or crowds gather in close proximity to city bus routes," Pierre said, "along with the buses themselves, if we have that real-time data."

He didn't work in the room frequently enough to know who to ask, so telling the entire room would have to do for now.

"Also, overlay the current location of our on-call bomb disposal units, soldiers, and police."

A few seconds after he gave the order, a map appeared on the largest screen in the center of the long wall. One by one, the analysts highlighted points across Paris, starting with the city's many museums. Other locations followed as bus lines that intersected the potential targets appeared. Bus coordinates were layered on a second later.

"The intel was sketchy about the timing of the attack," Pierre continued. "The most likely times for the attack are as early at 10:30 this morning, 1:30 this afternoon, or 5 p.m.—in that order of likelihood, according to…" Pierre paused, realizing he'd spoken himself into a corner.

He glanced back at the director-general, who knew of Gregory Addison's unofficial tip—and the American analysts' recommendations—but the man was no help. He stood there stoically, letting Pierre do the job.

"The source of the intelligence," Pierre finished. "But really, it could come at any time. We also don't know if the bus—or buses—have GPS trackers to explode once they reach pre-programmed locations. There could be suicide bomber terrorists onboard, or spotters watching for the buses to arrive at specific locations. Or they could be designed to detonate all at once, or at various times." He held back his frustration. "We have to figure out what the actual situation is. We have a possible solution, but if anyone has a better idea, you are hereby ordered to speak up. Do you understand?"

He received a chorus of "Yes, sir" responses.

"Good. Let's get this first part done as quickly and quietly as possible. No outward displays of concern or heightened security. We have an advantage in that we are aware of a possible imminent attack. Let's not alert our enemy by revealing that we know about the danger. Also, while we don't want panicking in the streets, we cannot move too slowly and have people die. Not on our watch."

"Not on our watch," the analysts repeated.

"We need to answer several essential questions.

"One: Are there bombs on any, many, or all of our city buses?

"Two: How are they to be detonated, and when? When the buses reach certain destinations? At specified times? Are there spotters on the streets near the targets? Are there suicide bombers aboard?

"Third: We need a plan for disarming one or multiple buses." Two teams of bomb experts were highlighted on the map, both near the center of the city. "Put all bomb disposal units on high alert and quietly bring in any that are off-duty.

"We will only use cell phones or encrypted radios to communicate, in case the terrorists are eavesdropping." Pierre paused. It didn't feel like he'd forgotten anything, so it was time to proceed.

"Now," he told the group. "Here's the plan."

161

THE STUDENT

Rahbar International Trading Partners
Surobi, Afghanistan

The small air conditioner in the shipping container did its job almost too well. The space had cooled off to the point Tariq found the remote control on his workbench and used it to adjust the settings. The unit switched from a dull roar at full blast to a quiet hum.

He remained on his stool, watching Maaz with pride. The young man's nerdy looks were deceiving.

In Tariq's experience, there were two kinds of people. One group handled computers easily. They intuitively knew which buttons to push to make the machines work. It was infuriating to him when he couldn't make the office computer do the simplest things and one of the staff members sat at the desk, clicked the mouse a few times, and produced the legitimate business's profit-and-loss report, or easily found files on the hard drive he believed lost or deleted.

The other group of people was more like him. They dealt with the real world. Fixing a motorcycle or building a cabinet were problems with solutions that came naturally.

Give Tariq a block of plastic explosives, a box of ball bearings, and a target. He would build a devastating device in no time, his hands knowing what to do before his mind formulated the plan.

Maaz seemed to be more in the mechanical camp, though he helped a great deal with the computers, too. He had a knack for grasping the intricacies of bomb making. As Tariq explained what he wanted, step by step, Maaz quickly caught on and did as requested.

He might have been the brightest pupil since the end of the American war in Afghanistan. Brighter even than blue-eyed Zeno, and certainly more careful than Tariq's student who had blown off three fingers while building an IED to kill American soldiers.

This morning, he and Maaz were making quick work of the items needed for the India mission.

Tariq continued with the step-by-step instructions.

Once these bombs were constructed, Maaz would crate them. The legitimate side of the business would ship them to India.

He had recruits ready to plant them where they would do the most damage.

Hundreds across the country—thousands—would die. Including children.

Most importantly, the key holdouts in the government, the ones most opposed to giving up control of the disputed region of Jammu and Kashmir, would be vaporized.

Along with their families.

A worldwide terrorist organization would happily take credit and threaten more destruction if their demands weren't met.

Jammu and Kashmir would soon after return to Pakistan's control.

Tariq's promise to his former employers would be fulfilled.

Millions of dollars would flow into his secret numbered bank accounts.

And he would move on to the next attack.

162

THE DUTY

Inter-Services Intelligence Safe House
Jalalabad, Afghanistan

The fresh coffee was too hot for Imran to drink, no matter how badly he needed it. He set it on the table and paced the length of the kitchen, waiting for the latest word on what he hoped wouldn't be the downfall of his career.

He'd already lost one operator. Lion's death had finally hit the news in Kabul—a motorcycle rider with no identification had been run over repeatedly on a road near the airport. The authorities hadn't yet identified the dead man and had no leads.

The comms app rang.

The phone's screen showed the call to be from Raza at headquarters.

Imran had no updates since reporting that Hawk had caught up to Owl's car and the courier driving it. The call could only be new orders.

Hopefully, Raza was ready to have Hawk pull alongside the car and open fire.

As long as he did a better job than Lion had, and didn't die, the mess of an operation would be nearly over.

All they'd have to do next was find the businessman turned spy, eliminate him, and take out the remaining American—wherever he was.

Imran frowned. There was still a lot to be done. But once he passed along the orders, maybe he could get some sleep.

"New orders," Raza said. Just as Imran had hoped—but Raza's voice sounded odd.

"I'm ready," Imran said.

"Hawk is to make contact with the courier. I suggest waving a white flag to get the car to pull over."

Imran blinked. It had been a long night. He'd obviously missed something. He picked up the mug, blew on the coffee, and burned his mouth and throat gulping it down.

"Please repeat the order," he managed to choke out through the discomfort, hoping the dose of caffeine would kick in quickly enough for his ears and mind to return to proper functioning.

"Hawk will flag down the courier in a non-threatening manner. They will pull over. Hawk will offer his services—and Bull's—in attacking the compound in Surobi."

"I... I understand."

The question was, would Hawk and Bull?

Imran didn't dare question the decision. It came directly from headquarters. If he had any chance of working there someday, there could be no dissent.

"Tell Hawk and Bull to make it happen. The courier and the other person, who we assume is one of the two Americans from the airplane, are to have their full support. The mission is the elimination of retired ISI Colonel Tariq—he is a former officer and bomb maker who has gone rogue—plus any combatants and members of his organization, and the complete destruction of his facilities." Raza paused. "Are these orders a problem for you? Or the operators?"

Colonel Tariq was spoken of highly in the ISI, though there were few mission details. Only that he had been a successful career officer for decades—and was an expert bomb maker.

If Tariq had gone off on his own, he was no longer an asset to his country.

Last night, Imran had been ordered to stop the Americans and the Afghan businessman—and protect Tariq.

When that failed, the Americans must have met with the courier—Naveed—and learned Tariq's location.

Now Tariq had to die.

The lack of manpower for this mission finally made sense.

The fewer people who knew about the operation, the better.

Imran wanted to assure headquarters that following orders and duty to country overcame any desire for revenge, but Hawk and Bull had lost their partners—likely killed at the hands of one or both of the men in the car. Imran had to answer truthfully. "Not for me, sir. But the men... Their partners..."

"I understand," Raza said. "The situation is extremely dangerous for Pakistan and for our agency in particular. They must succeed. Perhaps this will help," he said, and gave Imran a final order.

"Yes, sir. I think that will work."

"Hurry. Make them understand," Raza said, and ended the call.

Imran immediately dialed Hawk. He should be close enough to Surobi by now to have cellular service, allowing them to communicate securely— and openly.

For these orders, that would be essential.

163

THE SWITCH

The Kabul-Jalalabad Highway
Outside of Surobi, Afghanistan

Hawk used the insistent tone of the comms app as an excuse to pull to the side of the road. He pushed the answer button, signaled, and slowed as he moved onto the shoulder of the road.

It was probably overkill. The targets behind him weren't likely to pay much attention to a random vehicle in front of them—or the actions of the driver—but just as the best lie contained an element of truth, good tradecraft made sense in the moment. If they were vigilant, they'd see a man answering a call and pulling to the side of the road to concentrate on it.

It was a subtle way to get behind their vehicle. When the orders came to kill them, he could pass again without raising suspicions—and open fire on the car.

"Yes," Hawk said, using the SUV's hands-free microphone and speaker system.

The courier and the other man in Owl's sedan passed without glancing his way.

"I have new orders," Imran said. Hawk knew from the field manager's tone that he wasn't going to be happy.

He let two other cars go ahead before pulling back into traffic.

"Do not tell me to break off and return to Kabul. I have them in front of me now. I can pull alongside and shoot—"

"No," Imran said, interrupting him. "Understand, these orders come directly from the top."

Hawk gritted his teeth. "Go on, then. Tell me."

"You are to signal them and request they pull over. The suggestion was to use a white flag of surrender."

"Surrender?" This was worse than he thought. Unless… "And then kill them?" It wasn't a bad idea. Dishonorable, yes, but this was a terrible business. He'd done worse.

"No." Imran took a breath. It sounded like he was steeling himself. "Your new orders are to aid the courier and the other man, who is likely an American operator, not an Afghan. They are planning to attack a warehouse of a bomb maker named Tariq. Former ISI. He retired and has gone rogue. You will help in every way possible. The bomb maker must be eliminated, along with all members of his organization, and the entire facility, by any means available. Spare any civilians—if possible."

"You want me to help the men who killed Owl." It wasn't a question.

He briefly considered his tone, which was borderline insubordinate, but he didn't care.

"I don't want you to," Imran said with a sigh. "But it's what you have to do. For the good of the service, and the country." Imran paused. "I will call Bull and give him the same orders. I will vector him to you once you make contact with the courier. Do you have any questions about your orders?"

Hawk shook his head, partly in answer to the question, and partly in disgust. "No, sir."

"Good. Report as soon as you've made contact. And," Imran added, "there is one final order for after you've accomplished your mission." He said it as if it would be a reward for a job well done.

When Imran explained the last part of the operation, much of the tension Hawk had held faded. He loosened his grip on the steering wheel and took a deep breath.

"I understand," he said, ended the call, and looked around the SUV for white material he could use to signal his enemies turned allies.

164

THE OFFER

The Kabul-Jalalabad Highway
Outside of Surobi, Afghanistan

Bone fought off exhaustion by watching the countryside pass by and remembering his past missions in the country.

Night after night, he and the guys choppered into enemy strongholds to capture or kill high-value targets: bomb makers, insurgents, terrorists, murderers—whoever the intel team had determined needed to be interrogated or eliminated.

He had been at the top of his game, as had the other men of the Team.

Yet on that last mission, they'd been ambushed.

Everyone but he had died.

Technically, he'd been dead too, but he had been brought back to life to live and fight another day.

Today.

"The SUV behind us pulled over a few kilometers back," Naveed said. "Now he's passing the vehicles in between us."

Bone casually turned in the seat as if to better chat with Naveed and glanced back.

Sure enough, a black, high-end luxury SUV pulled into the oncoming lane and rocketed forward. Bone didn't wait to confirm the danger of the situation. He pulled the pistol from the holster at his waist and held the weapon low, ready to fire. "Stay at a steady speed, and keep your head back—do not lean forward," he told Naveed.

The SUV's passenger side window slid down.

"Roll down your window—now!" Bone said, raising the pistol and taking aim at the driver...

Who held up a white napkin with his right hand—and waved it at them. His left hand held the steering wheel. There was no weapon in sight.

"Slow down," Bone told Naveed. "It looks like he's... surrendering."

The car slowed as Naveed let off the gas. The SUV's blinker flashed, and the man pulled in front of them.

"It could be the partner of the man you killed," Naveed said. "A trick to kill us."

"Yes, it could," Bone said. "But it doesn't feel like that."

There was some type of park or small forest of tall trees along the road ahead on the left. The SUV braked and signaled the turn. The driver stuck his hand out his window, waved the napkin, and gestured to the entrance.

"Signal and follow him."

"If it's a trap? They could have more people waiting."

There were other cars in the parking lot of what Bone took to be a combination rest stop and park area for the Kabul River on the far side of the trees.

"Better an ambush now when we expect it than later when we don't know it's coming."

Naveed said nothing, but he followed the SUV as it turned, then tailed it as it slowed and drove to an empty part of the parking lot, far from the smooth gravel walking trail leading through the canopy of trees toward the water.

"Don't go straight in," Bone said as Naveed prepared to park. "Go there," he said, pointing farther into the parking lot, "turn around, and park behind the SUV, pointing toward the road." The move would put Bone closest to the SUV and protect Naveed. "If it is an ambush, go back to Kabul, get your mother, and disappear. My people will take care of the bomb maker." He'd been able to have one last call via the comms app before losing internet data connection outside of the city. It might take time, but others would come, pick up the trail, and eventually find and eliminate Tariq—whether he stayed in place or escaped.

Naveed didn't have time to argue. He pulled behind the SUV, blocking it in.

"Stay here," Bone said. He opened the door before the car completely stopped. "Keep the car in gear just in case."

The driver of the SUV stuck both hands out of his window. He held only the white napkin—no weapon.

Bone reached under his long tunic and put the pistol in his pocket, but he didn't let go. He could fire instantly if he had to, straight through the clothing, or take an extra second to draw and shoot if he had time and needed more accuracy.

He moved to the left, conscious of how easy it would be for ambushers to hide in the back seat or the rear of the SUV, but no one popped up and opened fire.

Behind him, Naveed crept the car forward—to better see the showdown, Bone figured.

The driver nodded at Bone, deliberately glanced at Bone's arm and hand in his pocket under the tunic, and spoke in Pashto. "*Salam*. I am here to help you." He had a narrow face with eyes lined by years in the sun, a full dark beard like every man in the area, and a nose that had been broken repeatedly, healing worse each time, it looked like. His eyes were those of a hard man.

A warrior.

A killer.

Bone didn't want to speak and have his accent give him away, so he gestured with his head, knowing the signal was universal—the man should get out of the vehicle.

The killer moved at half speed with exaggerated movements, opening the door and stepping out. "I have a pistol at my waist," he said, still in Pashto.

Bone took that as a good sign—both the man admitting he had a weapon and speaking as if Bone was an Afghan and not an American.

"My orders are to help you kill the bomb maker," the man said in perfect though lightly accented English, ruining Bone's hope that he was still incognito.

For a second, Bone thought about faking confusion, but the game was up—and time was short. Once the authorities in Paris stopped the attack, the bomb maker would hear and go on high alert. They had to get to him first.

"Why should I believe you? And let you help?" Bone asked.

"Tariq is a retired ISI bomb maker working on his own to commit terrorist attacks without Pakistan's approval," the killer said. "He must be stopped. My partner and I will help you. You cannot do it on your own, nor can we." He paused. "It is not my first choice. But I am a soldier, and we follow orders. Yes?"

Bone nodded, wanting to believe him but not completely convinced.

"I am 'Hawk,'" the stranger added. "And I must know. My man whose car you have..." He left the question unspoken.

Bone shook his head slowly, communicating all that needed to be said.

The man's nostrils flared as his eyes narrowed and hands clenched, but he breathed deeply a second later and got himself under control.

"And 'Lion'—a man on a motorcycle?"

"Ah," Bone said with a slight tilt of his head. "He shot our car and my people. I defended us." Bone chose to leave out that the man—Lion—had been hurt and trying to crawl to safety when Bone ran him over.

Twice.

After another pause to process the news, the killer spoke again. "That was then. Our orders have changed."

"Because we found out about Tariq," Bone said, confirming the obvious.

"Yes." Hawk drew himself up, standing at attention, but didn't salute. "We will kill Tariq together, then go our separate ways. Agreed?"

"Yes," Bone said. "A temporary alliance."

Four men against an unknown target were much better than two.

As long as they helped kill Colonel Tariq, Bone would take all the help he could get.

And worry later about what happened afterward.

165

THE TEAM

Outside Surobi, Afghanistan

From a cemetery on a hill, Bone surveyed the area. The Kabul-Jalalabad Highway bisected the large town of Surobi. Several small restaurants, two gas stations, and a pharmacy shared space with a few shops on the main road. Many were painted in bright aqua, blue, and yellow.

The area's main streets split off from the highway and wound through the neighborhoods, while secondary lanes curved, narrowed, and often ended abruptly. Many of them were unpaved.

Houses, apartment buildings, and walled compounds formed a chaotic jumble with no rhyme or reason. Maybe there was a town plan or zoning, but it didn't look like it.

Given the proximity to the Kabul River on the north side of town, though, the area was more lush than much of Afghanistan. Off the highway, on the south side of the town closest to them, there were green fields. Tall trees grew throughout the area, making it look more hospitable than many Afghan towns and cities Bone had visited years before while on active duty.

In the cemetery on a hill near the southwest edge of town, small chunks of rock marked the sites of most graves while more formal—and expensive—pads of concrete showed where wealthier people had been interred.

Bone, Naveed, and the two ISI operators made an unlikely team. They stood in a row, heads bowed as if they were remembering a fallen comrade, but they looked down the hill, across a kilometer of the town, to a long, three-story-tall building.

"That is Tariq's warehouse," Hawk said. A high block wall typical of the region surrounded the building, and there was a sturdy-looking black double gate at the front entrance. It was open, but two armed men guarded it. They stopped a white three-quarter-ton boxy delivery truck as it approached.

"Sloppy," Bone muttered. If he were in charge of security, he would have the guards stationed outside the walls to intercept the truck, identify the driver and the contents, and only signal the gates to be opened if everything checked out.

"We can use their carelessness," the other Pakistani said in English. He was shorter and stockier than Hawk but with the same thick beard and dark hair. He looked less dangerous only because his nose was straight and unbroken, though his eyes and expression were just as cold as Hawk's. He called himself Bull.

"A truck every hour?" Naveed asked.

"Thirty to forty-five minutes to unload and reload," Bone said. "We get into place... there," he said, but didn't point. "The empty lot by the curve of the road. Broken-down car?"

Hawk and Bull nodded. "Obvious, perhaps, but practical," Hawk said. He seemed to be the leader. If there was any lingering resentment over Bone taking out his partner—and Bull's, the one on the motorcycle—it didn't show. "Naveed and I at the car," Hawk continued. "We will have the hood up. You and Hawk come from the trees there."

"Once we take the truck," Bone said, "Naveed and I get in the back. You two drive and talk our way in—or kill the guards quietly. Back into the loading dock as the other trucks have. Then we all come out shooting."

A frontal assault in daylight was a horrible plan, but aside from accessing the rear of the compound, climbing the tall wall, and going in through a back door—assuming there was one—they didn't have any other good options. They couldn't wait until nightfall, didn't know if Tariq stayed on the property or left at the end of the day, and had no way—or time—to gather more intelligence.

Naveed had detailed the layout of the warehouse for them, from the likely number of guards to Tariq's orange shipping container workshop across the back and his office in a freestanding room in the back right corner, where Naveed had met with Tariq once before.

"Tariq surely has a safe room or a secret door to the outside," Naveed said. "But I do not know how he would get over the wall, and there appears to be no way through. There could be a ladder, though, and a rope to lower down the other side, so we should try to get to his office as quickly as possible."

That would be Bone's primary mission. Tariq wasn't likely to pick up an AK and join the fight—he'd run to safety.

The other consideration was that they were dealing with an expert bomb maker with access to plenty of materials. The place could be packed with explosive devices to repel or slow an attacking force. But it was something they'd have to risk.

Hawk first opened the rear of his SUV, then Bull's, and pulled the cover to reveal the spare wheel area.

Hawk removed an AK-74—the newer version of the reliable AK-47—along with an armored plate carrier with extra magazines. He slipped on the plate carrier and handed the rifle to Naveed, then reached in for a smaller version with a folding stock—a compact carbine better suited for the close-quarters combat they were about to engage in.

He kept it for himself.

Bull did the same, putting on his armored plate carrier, keeping the lighter, more compact weapon, and handing the AK-74 to Bone with only a slight hesitation.

Hawk and Bull passed out extra magazines, threaded suppressors onto their pistols, and closed the rear doors. Hawk looked at Bone and Naveed. "Are you ready?"

Bone thought of Stephanie back home. It was after midnight. The bar would be winding down. Henry would be there, along with a few regulars. Steph would have one TV on a sports station, reporting the scores and plays of the day. The other would be on a 24-hour news network. Both would be muted, with the closed captioning getting most of the words right, though at least ten seconds after the announcers spoke them. It took some getting used to.

The odds were against this mission succeeding, but Bone had to try. At least he and Naveed were in better shape with Hawk and Bull. Although they were still outnumbered, they had rifles and carbines instead of only the pistol Bone had taken from the tango in Kabul.

The mastermind—Colonel Tariq—had to be stopped. Mike Salestri had spent a fortune and many years searching for him. Sardar was in a hospital in Kabul—or dead—having dedicated his life to the pursuit of the man, too.

Bone was experienced, well trained, and with two other warriors, plus Naveed, the spy or courier—whatever he was.

"Ready," Bone said.

They climbed into the vehicles and drove down the hill to the town, ready to kill Tariq—or die trying.

166

THE CULTURE

Hôtel La Nuit
Paris, France

Hans had enjoyed his time in Paris, but he found the party scene lacking—and the locals were completely uninterested in a young German college student.

After striking out again at a nightclub and stumbling back to his hotel room alone in the pre-dawn hours, he'd fallen asleep fully clothed.

Or passed out, he wasn't sure.

Either way, he'd forgotten the alarm on his phone set to wake him up in plenty of time for breakfast, a bus to the Eiffel Tower—which he'd saved for his last day of the short vacation—and a packed schedule of visiting several of the smaller museums the city had to offer.

His parents had been impressed he was going to Paris for the culture. If he returned without stories of museums, other than the Louvre, they'd know he had truly only been interested in drinking, dancing, and hooking up.

The museums were also his last hope of meeting someone for a night of fun before going home tomorrow.

Hans fought for consciousness as the beeping alarm continued, finally finding his phone on the floor next to the bed.

He was conscious enough to check the bus schedule.

There. He could sleep another hour, grab the free breakfast in the hotel, and catch a later city bus. It would take him to the Eiffel Tower. He'd arrive at 10:30.

That would be early enough to enjoy the area, get his picture taken in front of the tower, and catch another bus to the first museum.

He reset the alarm on his phone and promptly fell back asleep.

167

THE LOADING DOCK

Outside Rahbar International Trading Partners
Surobi, Afghanistan

The truck they had hijacked bumped slowly up the poorly maintained road. Bone stood in the back holding onto a strap that kept pallets from shifting. A narrow shaft of sunlight came through a crack at the back corner.

The driver was hogtied, gagged, blindfolded, and terrified on the floor at his feet.

Naveed stood at Bone's shoulder, focused, his face set, but Bone could sense the uncertainty radiating from him.

"How much experience do you have with this type of mission?" Bone asked Naveed.

"None. I am a good shot, but I have never assaulted a warehouse—or any other type of building. My missions have been in the shadows as a spy, courier, and negotiator."

"That's what I thought. Stay several steps behind me. Shoot any people I miss or who appear suddenly. Don't try to take the lead." He leaned closer to whisper in his ear, though there was little chance Hawk and Bull in the front could hear them. "And watch our backs. I don't trust them to not shoot us once we've helped them inside."

Naveed nodded. "I agree."

The truck slowed and came to a stop.

Bone barely heard the two quiet *pops* from Hawk's and Bull's silenced pistols.

Would anyone notice the front gate guards dropping to the ground?

A few seconds later, the truck moved forward slowly, then turned and backed up.

No one shot at them.

So far, so good.

"Ready?" Bone asked.

Naveed didn't speak, but he nodded. His breathing was rapid, and his eyes were wide.

"Remember," Bone said, "aim, shoot, move."

The latch on the door clicked as someone on the loading dock opened it.

Naveed turned to Bone. "Remember your promise. If anything happens to me, you take care of my mother," he whispered in Pashto.

Bone wanted to respond, to reassure him, but the door opened at the same time Hawk and Bull stepped out of the truck's cab and started shooting.

It was time to fight.

168

LE GARDIEN DE LA PAIX

The Eiffel Tower Gardens
Paris, France

On duty, Hugo was officially *"Gardien de la Paix* Lavigne"—but Lavigne to his peers, Monsieur Lavigne to any local who read the name tag on his dark-blue uniform with **POLICE** in white lettering across the back, or "Officer *Lav-i-g-knee*" to American tourists who attempted his last name.

He'd proudly worn the uniform of the Paris police for eight years and relished the assignment he'd scored two years earlier. Patrolling the area around the Eiffel Tower, from the hectic main entrance off the street to the slightly quieter gardens to the southeast, meant there was never a dull moment. Tourists got lost or had questions, pickpockets tried to rob them, and there were always a few vendors in the park who "mistakenly" gave the incorrect change, "confusing" the bill denominations of the rich, unaware, or distracted.

Lavigne was constantly busy chatting with tourists and occasionally doing actual police work. Both suited him well—as a big bear of a man, with a thick goatee and blue eyes, people gravitated to him. The conversations, the glares at the petty criminals who dared enter his orbit, the kilometers of walking, all under the looming Eiffel Tower—none of it got old.

He'd finished pointing a group of American tourists toward the nearest public restrooms when his mobile phone rang. He glanced at the screen to see if it was important enough to take while on duty and was surprised to see the main number for his local police station.

"Hello," he said into it, turning his back on a group of tourists who had their cameras out and undoubtedly wanted him to pause in his police duties to take a picture of them, one of the few ways he refused to help. If he took one picture, a line would form, and he'd be doing it for one group after another.

He'd learned that the hard way.

"It's Sophie," the caller said. The station's dispatcher had never called him on his mobile.

Lavigne glanced at his radio, securely attached to his belt, expecting to find it off or broken, but it looked fine.

"What's wrong?" he asked in a low voice, glancing back and shaking his head at the dad of the family waiting patiently for him to finish. The man nodded and turned to his family as Lavigne walked a few steps farther away.

"We have a situation," Sophie said. She sounded stressed—and spooked. "We're keeping it off the radio for now in case they are being monitored."

He turned in a slow circle, phone to his ear. Nothing seemed wrong, and his senses, honed over years of being attuned to the ebb and flow of the sizeable crowds in the area, gave him no warning signs.

"There is a terrorist threat. We are at Attack Alert."

"Understood. What are the orders?"

"Act normal. You are near the intersection of Rue Desaix and Avenue de Suffren?"

"Yes. Closer to the park, but I can be there in a minute." He started toward the intersection, doing his best not to hurry.

"In a moment, you will direct traffic."

"Direct traffic?" The streets were busy, but there was no gridlock, people double-parked to take a quick picture of the looming tower in the distance, or pedestrians clogging the crosswalks.

"Yes. No more questions—I have other calls to make. Direct traffic. All buses—especially city buses—that come to the intersection, no matter what their destination or direction, you will direct northwest up Avenue de Suffren. Clear cars out of their paths, route vehicles anywhere needed, block all traffic necessary without regard to delays, but all buses go northwest. But…" Sophie paused. "Try to make it look like you're not doing it intentionally. Do you understand your orders?"

"I understand."

"You'll know when to start," Sophie said. "And good luck, Lavigne," Sophie whispered before she hung up.

A few seconds later, he reached the intersection.

The day was sunny and warm without being hot. The trees along the sidewalk rustled in a light breeze. It was the type of day that made Paris a wonderful city to live in and visit.

Two empty buses were parked facing west at the bus shelter. Another approached down the block. It would continue straight unless he detoured it.

Lavigne waited and watched. The bus drew closer and stopped near the corner. Six passengers stepped off; two boarded.

What was he to do?

Tires screeched behind him as several cars skidded to a stop.

For a moment, there was silence. A second later, the drivers laid on their horns, but there was nowhere to go.

The stoplights were red in every direction.

Act normal, Sophie had said. He would know when to start.

Lavigne raised a hand at the nearest driver honking. She frowned at him, but stopped as he marched into the intersection.

The buses were the priority, but first he had to clear the lane.

He pointed at the older man stopped with the nose of his car already in the intersection, facing west. Lavigne gestured for him to drive straight through.

The man gave a small wave, carefully looked right and left, and poked his way across the open lanes and west along Rue Desaix.

The woman Lavigne had ordered to stop honking lurched her car forward, the right-hand turn signal blinking.

Lavigne shook his head sharply and gestured for her to go straight through.

The driver shook her head, pointed right, and mouthed something about turning.

Lavigne shook his head again, stepped across the intersection to block her way, and pointed down Rue Desaix again.

She gave a heavy sigh, rolled her eyes, and drove forward, allowing the bus behind her to approach the intersection.

Lavigne stepped back and pointed northwest. The bus driver pointed straight, toward the car with the irate driver, but shrugged when Lavigne shook his head, signaled right, and turned the bus smoothly up Avenue de Suffren.

The other two buses were still parked, idling against the far curb.

Two cars back on Rue Desaix, heading east, another city bus full of passengers waited.

Lavigne got busy, directing the front cars where they wanted to go to quickly get them out of the way of the bus, which he forced to turn left up Avenue de Suffren.

After that, it was a simple matter of directing traffic, keeping the cars moving—and the northwest street as clear as possible.

It reminded him of a video game he'd played when he was younger, moving falling blocks to fill in holes and clear paths for the endless blocks dropping from the top of the screen.

He focused on the puzzle and avoided looking too closely at the buses that, from the fear in Sophie's voice, might be packed with explosives, terrorists, or some other danger than mandated killing the stoplights and snarling traffic for blocks.

169

THE SHELVES

Rahbar International Trading Partners
Surobi, Afghanistan

The man raising the delivery truck's door was dressed like Bone, in loose pants and a long tunic. No plate carrier. No weapon.

As the door reached chest height, Bone stepped forward and kicked him between the legs, dropping him in a heap.

He did the same to another worker standing on the loading dock.

A startled guard at the left side of the loading dock raised his AK. Bone swung that direction, but a red mist flew from the back of the man's head before Bone could pull the trigger.

Bull was a good shot.

Across the floor of the warehouse, on a metal walkway around the interior, several guards shouted and raised their weapons.

Bone aimed and fired. The first one dropped.

Bone rushed forward, firing as he went.

Bullets zipped through the air around him.

Naveed cried out, but Bone had no time to assist him. It was a target-rich environment.

Bone found cover at the near end of one of the tall storage shelves, ducked around, and picked off two guards before returning to cover.

A barrage of fire came from other guards stationed farther away, but the bullets pinged off the metal supports or slammed into the boxes and pallets hiding Bone's body.

Naveed stumbled his way over next to Bone, his arm bleeding. "You okay?" Bone called over Hawk and Bull's measured shots as they took out guards from the relative protection of the front of the building.

Naveed nodded. "A ricochet or a near miss, nothing more," he said. He sounded more surprised than hurt.

"We have to get to the back," Bone said. Time was passing, and staying in one place meant the guards could flank and kill them, even with Hawk and Bull covering them. "We're going to run up this row. The tall shelves will give us some protection from the sides."

Guards were already moving to the catwalk at the end of the building. Bone fired and killed one, though his next bullets missed a second guard as the man ducked to the left. The protection offered by the shelves meant the guards could hide from his fire as well.

"Shoot ahead and to the left," Bone said. "That's your section. It doesn't matter if you hit them—just keep them from aiming well. Ready?" Bone didn't wait for an answer. "Go!"

He aimed up and right, trusting Naveed had enough fortitude and motivation to follow and do his part.

170

THE TIMER

Rahbar International Trading Partners
Surobi, Afghanistan

It didn't take being a spy as long as Tariq had been to know the sound of gunfire from many weapons.

Tariq only hesitated for a second before making his decision and reaching for his watch.

He'd raised a few eyebrows when he'd bought the expensive Swiss motorsport watch years before, but few others had the precision and main feature he needed.

He pushed a button to initiate the preset four-minute countdown timer.

On the small digital screen, the timer started.

Tariq lifted the bottom of the brown pegboard attached to the wall of the shipping container, felt underneath, and found the tiny recessed button, smaller than the head of a nail. Without another thought, he pushed it in. It clicked and remained in place.

He looked up to see Maaz staring at him wide-eyed. While Tariq had never admitted to his student the existence of the many explosives hidden in the walls of the shipping container, his office, and throughout the rest of the warehouse, Maaz was smart enough to guess—and his expression showed he understood what Tariq had just done.

Tariq stood so quickly the stool toppled behind him, but he ignored it.

"We have less than four minutes. Come. I have an escape route in my office."

Relief and gratitude flooded Maaz's face as he followed Tariq.

As they reached the large shipping container door, Tariq pushed it open and faltered, his hand to his chest. "I'm fine," he said before Maaz could ask. "You go ahead. I will be right behind you. Go to the workbench in the center of my office." It was more like a kitchen island in a home, but Tariq used it as a large desk to plan his operations. "The far side has a hidden door leading to an improvised tunnel. Unlock it with a switch under the counter. I will join you as soon as I can."

"Sir, let me—"

"No. Go. I will make it. If not... you will continue my work."

As the tempo of the gunfire picked up, Maaz clapped him on the shoulder and nodded. "I will make the tunnel ready and wait for you."

Tariq nodded, swung open the door, and pushed the student gently on the back. "Hurry now," he said.

Maaz took a breath and stepped through the door.

Tariq smiled, like a predator about to catch his latest meal. There was a chance Maaz would have agreed to his plan, but there was no doubt this way. Tariq would have his human shield without discussion or argument.

Tariq shadowed his student, hiding behind the thinner man's body and the gunfire coming from the front of the warehouse.

171

THE ASSAULT

Rahbar International Trading Partners
Surobi, Afghanistan

Tariq ran to the left of Maaz, wishing he'd picked a heftier student instead of a skinny nerd.

Despite Tariq's bulk, he had little trouble keeping up with Maaz, who had only given him a glance of surprise before rushing straight toward the door of the office.

They had a clear path and were protected for the moment by the high row of storage shelves that reached toward the ceiling of the tall warehouse. But the shelves, set perpendicularly to the others in the main part of the building, ended 20 meters before the door to the office—an oversight that Tariq vowed wouldn't be repeated if he made it out of this alive.

Tariq placed his hand firmly on Maaz's shoulder as they approached the end of the shelves. This was the most dangerous stretch, and he didn't want the young man getting ahead of him.

Bone fired as he rushed forward, worried less about the accuracy of his shots and more with keeping the guards' heads—and rifles—down.

He killed at least two guards, and the volume of fire directed at him decreased. From the sound of it, Hawk and Bull had abandoned their cover at the loading dock and were assaulting up the left and right sides of the warehouse, keeping most of the remaining guards occupied.

Bone fired again, wounding a guard on the catwalk.

Behind him, Naveed cried out. "There!"

A young, thin man ran across the opening between shelves positioned across the warehouse, perpendicular to the others.

Behind him, an older, heavyset man kept pace, his hand on the younger man's shoulder, using him as a human shield.

Tariq.

With his balding head, rotund belly, and short legs, Tariq looked like a bulldog, only uglier and meaner.

Bone stopped, aimed, and fired as the pair reached the door to a free-standing office in the back right corner.

The younger man stumbled and dropped to his knee.

Before Bone could fire again, a bullet flew close enough to his head to brush back his hair.

He switched his aim to a guard shooting at him from the catwalk directly ahead and dropped him with two shots.

By the time he aimed back at the first target, the thin man was kneeling at the door to the office, pounding to be let in.

Bone killed him with a shot to the head and dumped the remainder of the clip into the door as he ran forward, desperate to get inside the office before Tariq escaped out whatever secret passage Naveed had claimed he would have.

Tariq hugged the floor as Maaz's pleas stopped abruptly and bullets penetrated the door.

He didn't dare reach up to pull the wooden security bar into place as an added measure to delay the attackers.

The lock would have to do.

He crawled under the gunfire to the far side of the island work area in the center of the room.

When the gunfire paused, he reached up and pressed the hidden button underneath the island's countertop.

With a click, the side panel of the island popped open. A dark tunnel sloped down before leveling out a meter below.

Tariq slipped into the small tunnel and pulled the panel closed behind him.

He didn't wait for his eyes to adjust. There wasn't much time left.

Instead, he crawled down the tunnel, head low and shoulders nearly scraping the ceiling.

"Cover me!" Bone yelled to Naveed.

He sprinted to the doorway. Behind him, Naveed opened fire, squeezing off shots in a steady cadence.

Bone reached the doorway and hesitated. This would be the perfect place for a bomb maker to have a booby trap.

A burst of gunfire from the catwalk above made him turn and kill a guard from below who had been targeting Naveed.

Toward the middle of the warehouse on both sides, it sounded like Hawk and Bull were engaged in heavy firefights.

Part of Bone wanted to help his new teammates, but that wasn't the mission. They were experienced operators. They could take care of themselves.

Naveed, on the other hand...

"Naveed, I've got you covered. Come to me—now!" Bone called. He fired steadily up at the catwalk, right and left, though their sectors looked clear of the enemy.

The magazine ran dry before Naveed made it. Bone let the AK dangle on its sling and switched to the pistol, continuing with the suppressing fire, only pausing to switch magazines.

Naveed ran to the office door, gasping for breath. "I'm out of ammunition," Naveed choked out.

"Down!" Bone yelled.

A guard ran at them from the front of the warehouse, firing as he came. Bone shot the guard... and another right behind him, and two others who must have come from a back room as a quick reaction force, or who had finally worked their way down from the catwalk.

Killing them took the remaining bullets for the pistol.

Bone wrestled with wasting time and the risk of running to the nearest dead guard for ammunition versus pursuing Tariq. He opted for finishing the mission, stood, and tested the doorknob.

Locked.

What were the odds the bomb maker had activated a trap on the door while Bone had been shooting at him?

Slim—Bone hoped.

He kicked once, again, and a third time before the door cracked enough to force it open.

With Naveed on his heels, Bone rushed into the room.

It looked like any other office, with a cluttered desk facing the wall in the back corner of the room. A laptop computer sat closed on top, along with an old phone. Two black, four-drawer filing cabinets were next to the desk.

In the center of the room was a rectangular island used as a workstation. There were large sheets of blueprints, or maybe schematics, atop the counter.

Otherwise, the room was empty.

Tariq had vanished.

Bone closed the door and flipped down a wood bar attached to the wall to hold it closed.

If Tariq had a hiding place inside, they were now locked in together.

172

AVENUE DE SUFFREN

Avenue de Suffren
Paris, France

For bus driver Léon Escoffier, the day was going from bad to worse. Last night, his next-door neighbors had yet another argument, which kept him awake late.

This morning, he hadn't tightened the lid on his commuter cup, and he'd spilled two-thirds of the coffee he badly needed.

Not good, especially on one of the busiest tourist days of the year. When he'd driven along the Champs-Élysées earlier, more people than usual had been eating pastries in the cafes and strolling the avenue, taking pictures and enjoying the morning.

Now, the traffic lights were malfunctioning throughout the city, according to the alert he'd received via the real-time communication Service Management System in the bus.

He was off route, going where a stocky policeman had directed him.

It was going to be a long day.

At least the weather was perfect—sunny, a cool breeze, not too humid. Pedestrians were everywhere. The tourists were out in force. Locals and summer visitors lingered over morning coffee and croissants, packing the sidewalk cafes. Joggers enjoyed the shady streets, young and old walked dogs and greeted each other or were glued to their phones. From his cushioned, spring-mounted seat, he loved every inch of the city he had called home all his life.

A block behind him, another city bus followed. It was far off route, too.

There must be a problem with the roads. Dispatch, working with the police, were rerouting them all.

A few hundred meters ahead, a young policewoman stood in the middle of the street. Two cars sat in the center of the intersection. One had rammed the other in the side. She looked up, made eye contact with him, and gestured for him to slow with clear, crisp arm and hand motions.

Horns blared, but the policewoman refused to allow anyone to pass.

Gardien de la Paix Renée Ducasse was a year away from a promotion that would have her working the area directly underneath the Eiffel Tower, but for now she was stuck 200 meters away, without a clear view of the mass of tourists.

If she stood in just the right spot on the far sidewalk, and craned her neck, she could see the Eiffel Tower looming over the eight-story apartment buildings lining the streets.

Ducasse dealt with lost tourists two hundred sixty-four steps from the famed attraction, as well as the tired, hungry, and thirsty leaving the area, looking desperately for a decent, hopefully affordable place to eat a sit-down meal that wouldn't treat them like the tourists they were.

Ducasse invariably directed them to the cafe on the corner, which had good food, decent service, and a kind owner who checked on her every afternoon. He charged a premium, but he didn't gouge the tourists any more than other places farther away.

Across the street, an elderly man approached large black gates blocking the back entrance to a stadium. Hurrying as much as his age allowed, he fumbled with a large keyring attached to his belt, selected a key, and unlocked a sturdy padlock securing a hefty chain.

Ducasse shoved down her nervousness and addressed the drivers of the two cars that had crashed together when the traffic lights went haywire, before she'd gotten to the intersection. Her trainers at the police academy had drilled into her head that how she conducted herself would be how she was perceived. She set her face, squinted, and stood ramrod straight.

"You two," she told the drivers of the cars. "Move your vehicles out of the intersection and over there," she said, pointing to an open stretch of street with a no parking zone.

"But he—" one started.

The other spoke over him. "No, he ran the red light and—"

She cut them off with a glare. "Move your vehicles right now. I will deal with you both shortly." They hesitated. She took a breath. "Go!" She pointed at the curb. They obeyed.

She turned in a slow circle. The traffic was backed up in three directions. Drivers honked their horns impatiently. Up the street, next to the blue and white bus in the right lane, several people had stepped out of their vehicles to see what had caused the holdup.

As the crashed cars edged out of the intersection, she once again made eye contact with the driver of the first bus to reach her corner. She'd received the most basic instructions from her dispatcher via her personal mobile phone, but she didn't know if the bus drivers had been alerted to the danger.

Probably not, she decided. The driver looked calm, ready to follow whatever directions she ordered.

She nodded at the man and used her arms to direct him to turn left, drive onto the sidewalk, over the knee-high metal vehicle barricades that were lowering into the ground as she watched, through the recently opened double gates, and onto the football stadium grounds.

The driver's eyebrows came together in confusion, and his head tilted to the side.

"There?" he mouthed.

Ducasse nodded once, all business, and repeated her hand gestures.

With their eyes locked across the intersection, they shared a moment, one worker to another.

The man's eyes widened, and Ducasse nodded again and gestured with more urgency. The bus moved forward.

The next bus was slowing as the first one bumped over the curb, past the barricades now flush with the sidewalk, and onto the running track ringing the football field. The old stadium worker pointed the way onto the grass.

Ducasse repeated the gesture for the next bus driver, who followed the first without question, though his eyes also met hers, and lingered before he nodded in understanding.

For the moment, the street to the southeast was clear. She turned north, gestured, and got the vehicles moving.

Drivers pointed east and west called to her, but she ignored them. They weren't the priority.

When the bus that had been stuck up the road neared the intersection, she slowed it and convinced the driver to make the challenging sharp turn into the stadium. He joined the other two, front to rear, still filled with passengers.

She finally could clear the cars to the east and west, directing them all south—far from the area.

Ducasse hadn't been told exactly what was happening, but whatever it was, the fewer people around the buses in the stadium, the better.

173

THE OFFICE

Rahbar International Trading Partners
Surobi, Afghanistan

Tariq's office had no windows.

Bone checked under the desk for a trapdoor.

Naveed rocked the file cabinets away from the wall next to him.

There was nothing.

Bone moved along the exterior wall, feeling for a seam hiding a door to the rear of the building.

Naveed did the same in the other direction.

"Anything?" Bone asked.

"No."

Bone looked up. Could the man have climbed a rope or a ladder and disappeared onto the roof of the standalone office without them seeing?

"We would have noticed," Naveed said, reading his mind.

They both looked at the island in the center of the room at the same time.

Bone started on the side near the door, feeling for an opening or a latch.

On Naveed's side, a *click* broke the silence.

Naveed looked up, smiled, and pointed at his feet.

The end panel of the island had popped open a few inches.

Bone peered into the opening. He held the pistol in front of him in case Tariq was hiding just inside—he wouldn't know Bone was out of bullets.

There was no one, only the rough opening of an improvised escape route just wide enough for a single person to crawl through—it was too low to walk or even crouch. There were rough frames of vertical wood studs supporting wider boards across the top, but they were much farther apart than Bone thought was safe.

It would be hands and knees into the blackness of the makeshift tunnel after Tariq, who was likely armed.

Naveed slowly crouched to enter the opening, but Bone stopped him. "No," Bone said. "I'll go. This is a job for an operator, not a spy."

Naveed stood, looking relieved.

A burst of automatic gunfire came from the other side of the office door, followed a moment later by a single shot. Hawk or Bull mopping up.

He nodded to Naveed. "Give me a minute, then follow. There are still holdouts up here. We'll exfil through the tunnel and meet up with the other two at the vehicles."

Bone didn't repeat his concern that Hawk and Bull might have been ordered to kill the two of them once the mission had been accomplished.

Bone got down on his hands and knees, his useless pistol holstered, and crawled downward, into the blackness.

Naveed watched the American head into the tunnel, more relieved than he'd let on.

Not much in the world scared him. He had faced down sociopaths and psychopaths, and had chosen to work for Colonel Tariq and facilitate payment for killing unarmed, innocent civilians.

His hands were far from clean.

But he'd always been claustrophobic. Not horribly so—he could force himself to tune out the terror for seconds at a time in an emergency. Going into the tunnel was a far better option than trying to exit through the warehouse, where guards still fought Hawk and Bull—who likely had orders to eliminate him and the American as soon as they confirmed Tariq was dead.

Bone had easily taken the bait when Naveed offered to go into the tunnel first. No American would allow someone like him to take the lead on their operation, especially with the final responsibility of killing Tariq in the tunnel.

As Bone's feet disappeared down the steep, rough slope into the tunnel, Naveed crouched at the entrance, ready to force himself to enter.

If the American was killed in a shootout with Colonel Tariq, so be it.

But no matter what, Tariq had to die, even if it meant Naveed facing his fear and going into the tunnel barehanded to finish him off should the American not accomplish the mission.

174

THE STADIUM

La Liberté Stadium
Paris, France

The baggy, dark-blue coveralls and day-glow yellow-green high-visibility vest made Bernard feel like a fool, but disguises were occasionally part of the job.

The higher-ups wanted them to look as much like actual bus repair workers as possible, and he followed orders. They were concerned that there may be spotters or suicide bombers on board with orders to detonate the devices immediately if they had been discovered.

The longer Bernard and the others could continue with even a semi-plausible ruse, the better.

He'd much rather be with his bomb-disposal unit partner, Rita, but she claimed he'd be a more convincing mechanic than her, so he'd ended up on the bus instead of under it to convince the passengers there was a mechanical issue with the vehicle.

"I'm sorry," he said, addressing the passengers in the first bus. Most of the seats were filled with tourists—he'd have to repeat the announcement in English.

If there was a spotter or trigger man aboard who didn't believe the story about their fake mechanical inspection, at least he and Rita would go out with a bang.

"There has been an emergency safety recall on brake parts in use by several of our city buses," he continued. "We will check this bus and either allow you to continue or move you to another bus without the issue."

Bernard repeated the announcement in decent English but couldn't help the few tourists who looked at him blankly. They'd figure it out soon enough—if they all lived.

"No one leaves the bus yet," Bernard muttered to the driver, who sat with his hands still holding the large steering wheel.

"I understand," the driver said, and Bernard believed he did. Completely.

Sometimes, people just had a feel for the truth.

***

The grass of the football field smelled nice and was a welcome change from crawling under vehicles on the street like she usually had to do. Despite the baggy coveralls and safety vest slowing her, Rita found the bombs before Bernard finished his announcements.

There were two devices mounted to the bus, disguised as bottles of cleaning solution for some reason. Each had a countdown timer and a basic mobile phone wired to it.

"Don't bother," she muttered to Bernard as she scooted out from under the bus. He'd been about to slide under to join her.

"At least it didn't blow up," he muttered softly, so no one aboard the bus could hear. "Yet."

"That's something," Rita said, standing. "No onboard suicide bomber or spotter."

"On this one. Or at least any that have authority to blow the bus early."

"True," she said. "Two devices. I'll call this one in while you check the next one?"

He nodded and walked to the next bus, holding up his hand to the driver to communicate everyone should stay inside. Rita walked to the official city bus maintenance van they'd parked nearby and used her mobile phone to call in. While she wanted to snip wires and disarm the bombs, her priority had to be reporting the issue. Only when headquarters knew the situation could she save the people on the bus.

And though she'd like to evacuate this bus immediately, and the rest that were coming her way, there was a chance that the terrorists had another contingency plan for the bombs being discovered. A person with an explosives-packed vest standing in the middle of a crowd of evacuated passengers could wreak havoc—and kill hundreds.

"Two bombs under Bus RATP 4042," she reported to headquarters. "Detonated by mobile phone and/or countdown timer, it looks like. No GPS is visible, and no one on the buses have triggered them as of yet. The devices appear to be designed to blast shrapnel or ball bearings outward to both the left and right sides of the bus, though the bus and passengers would be destroyed, too."

At the south end of the field, two more buses made their way onto the grass, followed by a small newer car. A white and brown springer spaniel dog sat in the front passenger seat, panting eagerly. The bomb detector dog to check for suicide bombers hiding among the passengers had arrived.

175

THE MOP-UP

Rahbar International Trading Partners
Surobi, Afghanistan

Most of the guards were dead.

At least, Hawk hoped so. They had to be—he was almost out of ammunition, and he had killed more men this morning than he had in any other operation.

Without the element of surprise, and launching the assault at the end of the lunch hour, he and Bull wouldn't have made it.

He reached the rear of the warehouse at the same time as his comrade.

They didn't speak.

Bull gestured to the door, eyes raised. Hawk nodded. The American and the courier had to be inside.

The locked office door behind Naveed shook as someone tried to open it.

"It's us," Hawk called in a loud whisper. A burst of gunfire from farther away was answered with one from the other side of the thick plywood walls. "Let us in—there are still a few guards. They're flanking us."

The American's feet had disappeared into the darkness of the main part of the tunnel.

"Hold on," Naveed called over his shoulder.

Gunfire ripped through the door in his direction.

A round grazed his arm—the same one that had been hit by a ricochet earlier—and he tumbled onto his rear.

Another burst of gunfire tore away the wood around the sturdy brace holding the door closed.

One of them—Hawk or Bull—kicked the door. It splintered but didn't give.

Whether there were guards flanking the two operators or not didn't matter.

The mopping up Naveed had been worried about was starting…

With him.

176

THE NUMBERS

Command Center
DGSI (Direction Générale de la Sécurité Intérieure) Headquarters
Levallois-Perret, France

"How long on the countdown timers on the devices?" Pierre asked from the raised command platform at the rear of the dimly lit room.

He must have been on a speakerphone because the bomb disposal technician answered immediately. "They are set to detonate in twenty-three minutes, sir—at 10:30."

"Understood. You're checking the other bus now?"

"My partner is, sir. We also have a third bus here, and two others just arrived."

"Copy," Pierre said. "You may evacuate the buses as the passengers are checked for explosives. Continue, please, and thank you for your work."

Pierre turned to the analysts. "We'll quickly send out final instructions via text to the police, bomb disposal units—everyone, then shut the cellular networks down. That will at least buy us some time and ensure the terrorists cannot detonate the bombs remotely."

He shook his head. "But we have too small of a sample size to know how many buses are affected," he muttered to himself, though the director-general, still at his post behind him and to the right, must have overheard.

"What depot services those buses?" the DG asked the analysts. "The same one for all of them at the stadium?"

"Yes, sir," an analyst said after a moment of checking.

"How many buses left that depot today?" Pierre asked.

The same analyst clicked her keyboard a moment before responding. "I will check with them directly, sir, but around two hundred on an average day."

"Two hundred," the director-general muttered.

"There is a second bus depot, near the 20th arrondissement, that services many of the other buses that pass the major tourist attractions," the analysts said. "They have about the same number each day—two hundred."

"We need to check buses from that depot," Pierre said.

"It is already happening, sir," another analyst called out. "The first bus will be in a park in"—he checked his screen—"five minutes."

"That's too long," Pierre said. "And we don't have enough bomb disposal units. Four hundred potential buses?"

"And that is if only those two depots are involved," one of the analysts toward the back said.

"We can't get them all," the director-general said.

"Not all of them can have bombs," Pierre said. "Can they?"

The analysts focused on their screens. No one wanted to argue—or agree.

The director-general shook his head. "We can't take that chance."

"No," Pierre said. "Show me where the buses will be when the countdown timer reaches zero. 10:30, correct?"

"Yes, sir. One moment." The screen changed to show the real-time location of the buses on the streets. It flickered, and their locations changed from blue to red.

"At 10:30…" the analyst said, but trailed off.

There were so many tourist attractions in the city, and so many buses…

"There are too many, sir."

Most of the buses were already being directed to local parks by the police. Had they been allowed to continue on their routes, there would have been dozens—hundreds—of buses near, next to, or in front of museums, parks, and apartment buildings at 10:30, along with cafes, businesses, plazas, shopping areas, monuments, and government buildings.

Pierre's plan for picking out the most likely threats by location at 10:30 wouldn't work.

"What are the orders, sir?" one of the analysts asked.

Pierre stared off into space, frantically forming a last-ditch plan he wasn't sure could work in the time they had.

177

THE REVENGE

The Tunnel under Rahbar International Trading Partners
Surobi, Afghanistan

The faint sound of gunfire drifted down the tunnel to Tariq.

He had a ways to go, and his body wasn't dealing well with crawling over the uneven ground and less-than-straight tunnel. Rocks kept jabbing his palms and knees, and he'd bumped his head twice on sections of the tunnel where the men he'd had dig it had been too lazy to maintain the height he'd demanded.

Too bad he couldn't kill them again.

He stopped to catch his breath.

With a sudden jolt, he realized that he'd gotten old and out of shape.

He put the thought aside. By his best guess, he was under the wall of the compound. Another few minutes of crawling, and the tunnel should slope upward to the exit.

But what if the men who had haphazardly dug the tunnel hadn't completed it before he'd met them outside of town, shot them, and dumped their bodies in the river?

He kicked himself for not sending someone through to check. Maaz could have been trusted with his secret.

The luminous hands of the watch glowed in the darkness, but the digital countdown timer had no backlight. Tariq wanted to rest, to wait, but he had to hurry. It was faster to crawl without the mobile phone flashlight. His warehouse had been attacked, which meant someone might be aware of the buses in Paris.

He would make it to the surface and dial a phone number.

Bombs in Paris would explode earlier than their timers were programmed for.

Ignoring the pain from the stab of yet another sharp rock into his kneecap, he hurried on.

Turning around in the narrow tunnel was difficult, but Bone had done it. Someone was firing at the door to the office, and Naveed had cried out in pain.

The light coming from the office showed Bone the way.

He fought away a flashback as he crawled.

The light ahead was real.

It wasn't the pure white, all-enveloping glow of the afterlife, of Bone's vision as he'd died after the ambush years ago.

"Took you long enough, brother," Tank said in the tunnel, his tone quiet and kind.

Bone kept crawling. The part of him that had been trained to never quit moved one hand forward, then a knee. The other hand. The other knee. Over and over, as fast as he could.

He had to get to the light.

"Once more," Hawk said. He balanced on one foot, reared the other back, and kicked with all his strength.

The flat of his boot hit the door square, just to the side of the splintered wood attached to some sort of strut holding it closed.

The door cracked the rest of the way, and he was finally able to open it.

Bull was in first, his AK up and ready to kill Naveed, the American, and Tariq—if they weren't already dead.

Hawk flowed into the room after him, clearing his sector.

The room was empty.

Bone pulled the secret door the rest of the way closed as the office door smashed open. The tunnel turned pitch black.

He huddled against the wall next to Naveed, whom he had climbed over, and put a hand over the man's mouth for a second until he got a nod of understanding.

Any sound now would reveal their location.

Hawk and Bull would shoot them, pull their bodies from the tunnel behind the secret door, find and kill Tariq, and get away clean, their mission accomplished.

Bone and Naveed would be found by the authorities.

With any luck, they'd be unable to identify Bone.

If not, the international incident Dominic had worried about would be his to deal with.

America would be put in an uncomfortable position of having to explain why a former Navy SEAL had been shot in a warehouse in a small Afghan town with a couple dozen dead guards in the building with him.

He felt bad for Admiral Nalen.

So much for an off-the-books, clandestine operation.

At least there wouldn't be a trail back to Nalen and whoever gave him orders. They could easily deny any knowledge of him.

Steph would play ball. Nalen could convince her to tell anyone who asked that Bone had taken a freelance contract to… Whatever. They'd make up a story. He didn't have to worry about it.

On the other side of the secret door, Hawk and Bull cleared the room. Their hesitant steps mimicked his and Naveed's when they entered the office to find Tariq gone.

Were these two smart enough to realize there had to be a trapdoor leading to a hiding place?

And to find it?

In the darkness, Bone closed his eyes.

If they found the door, at least the end would come quickly. Hawk or Bull would take their revenge and dump round after round into him.

The bright white light would come again.

He'd be yanked forward to the afterlife.

Tank would be there, along with Bossman, Baldy, Sneaky, Biscuit, Iron, and Dizzy.

Dying wouldn't be all that bad.

The footsteps stopped.

Close.

There was a click as the release button was pushed.

Hawk and Bull pulled the door open, looking down at Bone with satisfied, sadistic grins.

Bone screened Naveed's body with his own, a last-second instinct to protect.

To save.

In the distance, instead of Tank's voice, Bone heard an insistent beeping. Like an alarm, maybe.

When the countdown timer on his watch beeped, Tariq stopped crawling, dropped flat, and covered his head.

The tunnel should hold. It was deep enough, but he had wired enough explosives to demolish the warehouse twice over and eliminate the computer, every piece of paper, and all the bomb-making materials.

Along with everyone inside, alive or dead.

Nothing would be left to incriminate him or implicate Pakistan and the ISI.

A raging fire would consume the rubble.

No bodies would be recovered.

He would be presumed dead by the ISI—along with whoever had betrayed him, and those who were attacking the warehouse—and could start fresh with a new passport and identity.

Scale up from scratch.

He wouldn't be able to rely on his old contacts, but it wouldn't matter.

He'd go to Europe, or America, and become a one-man force of destruction against the West.

He grinned in the darkness, already looking forward to the challenges.

Bone used his body to screen Naveed's from the two men and looked up to the floor level, locking eyes with Hawk and Bull holding AKs pointed at Bone's chest.

"This is for Owl," Hawk said.

"And for Lion," Bull whispered.

Bone refused to close his eyes. He wanted to see the end coming.

It would be quick this time.

Standing above him at ground level, Hawk and Bull vanished in a cloud of bloody vapor.

The overwhelming sound of an explosion followed an instant later.

Bone's body rocked backward—along with Naveed—propelled the rest of the way down the slope of the tunnel by the powerful blast.

Bone's eyes closed and he faded away.

Above Bone, at the tunnel opening, a fire raged.

The view disappeared inch by inch.

He was being pulled farther into the darkness of the tunnel.

With a rumble and shake, the view disappeared completely as a portion of the ceiling behind him collapsed.

178

THE WIRE CUTTERS

La Liberté Stadium
Paris, France

Beneath the bus, Rita clenched the flashlight with her teeth, pointing it at the first bomb. Her hand held the wire cutters, ready to snip.

She had checked the device multiple times for booby traps and found none.

Cutting the wires would remove the timing device and phone from the system, preventing the explosives from being triggered. The bomb would remain dangerous, but they could deal with removing it from the bus later, once they'd disarmed as many as they could in the time remaining.

"The passengers are away and safe," the driver said from less than a meter away, standing next to the bus. His voice was shaky with fear, but he was doing his part. The bomb-sniffing K-9 hadn't discovered any explosives in the passengers' backpacks or on their bodies, and no one had detonated the devices as they exited the bus.

"Get out of here," she called to the driver. "And thank you."

There was hope this could work out after all—as long as the bomb didn't explode when she...

Rita snipped the wires for the timer, and the mobile phone, too.

Nothing blew up.

The phone and timer went into the front pocket of the coveralls.

She'd known it was safe, but she closed her eyes in silent prayer anyway.

She scooted to the far side of the bus, ready to repeat the process. There were a lot of buses in the stadium, with more due to arrive in the next twenty minutes.

A few more snips with the wire cutter, and the other timer and mobile phone joined the first two in her pocket.

Rita slid from under the bus, rose to her feet, and sprinted to the next one in the long line.

"There are no bombs on this one," Bernard said from under the bus. The driver was close enough for Bernard to reach out and touch her shoe. "Use the alert system. Send your bus number and the code word for no danger: **BleuCiel**."

The older driver muttered a prayer of thanks as she hurried to send the good news that not all buses from the depot had bombs attached.

Bernard scooted from under the bus and ran to the next one in the line as three more turned into the stadium.

If many more came, there wouldn't be room for them all.

He reversed course and ran to the driver sitting in the front seat, eyes closed and hands clasped in prayer. "Excuse me, but I need your help. Move your bus, and tell the other drivers whose buses have been cleared —directly, no radio. Park around the edges of the field. If we don't get all the bombs, your buses will absorb the brunt of the damage. Maybe it will save lives outside of the stadium. And send that idea along to the rest of the drivers."

He waited long enough for her nod of understanding, then ran to the next uncleared bus.

They had nineteen minutes left—assuming all the buses were on the same detonation schedule.

179

THE GARDENS

Tuileries Garden
Paris, France

With his bad leg, it was hard for Jacques to hurry, but while he might have been 75 years old, he wasn't done with life yet. And though he didn't speak to the tourists much—or the locals, for that matter—as a groundskeeper, he fielded the occasional question about the garden.

Ordering people around, however, was a different story. That was always done by the police. But as a former captain in the army, he'd lead men in the Lebanese Civil War as a peacekeeper. He could handle a family of tourists in khaki cargo shorts, baseball caps on backward, and black slip-on sandals with white calf-high socks.

Americans. Obviously.

"Excuse me," Jacques said, pronouncing the words carefully. "The park is closing for a…" He hesitated. The text message from the parks department—before the cellular network went offline—had said to use the threat of a gas leak as the official excuse for closing the park, but for the life of him, he couldn't come up with the word for "leak" in English.

The pause allowed the American father, tall and fit like he spent hours a week in a gym, with red hair and a close-cropped beard in the way of all the young men these days—to jump in. His three boys looked up solemnly at him while the blond wife held the baby—a girl. "What do you mean the park is closing?" he asked. He held his hand up to shade his eyes, which he wouldn't have had to do if the cap were on correctly. "How do you close a park on a beautiful day?" He looked up at the clear blue sky. "It's—"

"Leak," Jacques blurted out as the word popped into his mind. "There is a gas leak. Danger. Please, exit there," he said, pointing toward the nearest park exit.

"A gas leak? In a park? That doesn't make any sense. I really don't understand how—"

His wife cut him off with a hand to his arm. "Charlie," was all she said in an even voice, along with a nod to the far end of the park, several hundred meters away. A bus drove—fast—up one of the wide packed-gravel pedestrian walkways between the pristine green lawns. Three more followed close, while another turned into one of the few vehicle entrances to the park. Police and men in gray coveralls with safety vests stood waiting for them in the distance.

"Come on, kids," the mother said. She took one of the small boys by the hand. The youngest held his arms out to his father, who scooped him up. "We'll ride the Ferris wheel later. Mama needs a chocolate croissant or some ice cream. Anyone else want a treat first?"

She pulled them toward the exit as the father muttered, "Oh, shit," and hurried after them.

"*Merde,* indeed," Jacques said, and limped as fast as he could toward a nanny sitting on a bench, one hand absently pushing and pulling a baby carriage while she focused her attention on a mobile phone, holding it up and frowning as if it was no longer working.

He'd clear the park as quickly as his leg would allow, and only then get himself to safety.

180

TIMING

Tuileries Garden
Paris, France

"City buses may have had faulty brake lines installed over the weekend," the bus driver had told the passengers minutes before. "All buses are to be inspected as soon as possible, which is why we are deviating from our normal route. You will exit the bus and walk to a waiting area on the far end of the park. Workers will direct you. If the buses are safe—as we hope —you will be allowed to reboard. If not, vouchers for the metro, taxis, or rideshares will be provided. Thank you for your understanding."

Valentin listened, but he didn't pay the announcement much attention. He enjoyed taking the bus. It showed him the city and allowed him to picture it the way it had been in his youth. He could have gone to the local park near his small apartment, but something about the grandeur of the Tuileries Garden appealed to him.

He had all day—a bus problem didn't bother him.

But the more he considered the situation, the less it made sense. The bus had sped up, not slowed down. If there was a brake problem, they should have moved as slowly as possible.

And the driver's voice... She seemed like she was made of stern stuff. Drivers had to be. They dealt with traffic, tourists, the changing weather. A stressful job.

What had her so shaken up?

When the bus edged through a narrow entrance onto the park grounds and accelerated again, he knew there was a serious problem that had nothing to do with brake lines.

Martin had worked with the bomb squad for years. Today wasn't the first time he'd been called in, ruining his day off. Right now, his relaxing plans didn't matter. Nothing did except the buses arriving at the park.

He slid from under the latest bus. This one had no bombs.

An earlier one had, though. Those were the first he'd disarmed since IEDs during the Afghanistan war.

He hurried to the next bus, confirmed the passengers had been evacuated, and dropped to the ground to crawl under it.

The process was simple. Martin and the rest of the bomb disposal units that had been on duty or able to make it to where they were needed in time flung themselves under each bus. As quickly as they could, they found the bombs—if any—and assessed them to be sure they were the same as reported: a simple timer and a small mobile phone attached to a device that looked like a bottle of cleaning solution. They seemed designed to propel shrapnel through the thin side of the bus and into whatever the bus was next to when they went off.

A few snips of the wires, scoot to the other side of the bus, and repeat the process.

A quick look underneath the rest of it to make sure they hadn't missed anything.

Then out from under and to the next one in line.

All in a day's work.

Most of the buses had no bombs. But they had to check every one.

And the time was nearly up.

At what point did he stop and run for safety, ignoring the many buses lined up that they hadn't gotten to?

"Get out!" the driver called as the bus skidded to a stop on the gravel walkway of the famous park. The passengers stood hesitantly. They had been due to arrive in front of a plaza by the Louvre soon. They now had a long walk ahead of them. Despite the panic in the driver's voice, and the line of buses they were behind in the middle of the Tuileries Garden, of all places, several were reluctant to disembark.

Or maybe they didn't understand French. That was certainly possible.

"There may be bombs under the bus!" the driver said, standing to address them. She waited at the front, next to her chair, though she clearly wanted to exit first.

French speakers reacted immediately. They rushed into the aisle and hurried toward the door.

Other passengers remained seated or stood by their seats, confused.

Valentin had learned English as a child, but it had been years since any of the words were accessible to him. French and English weren't that different, though. He'd do what he could. "Danger!" he called from his place in the back. Several faces turned his way. English speakers. "Evacuation. Haste! Rapid!"

His words—or maybe the look on his face and that of the driver—got the rest of them moving.

181

THE TUNNEL

The Tunnel
Surobi, Afghanistan

Naveed choked on the dust in the air of the tunnel as he fought off panic.

The walls were not closing in.

They were the same narrow, confining, deep-under-the-earth walls they had been while he dragged the American.

Except for the collapsed section behind them. It wasn't the same at all.

But he refused to think about that.

He would curl up into a ball and sob if he did.

Instead, he held the burner phone with one hand, its flashlight feature lighting the way, kept his head low, fought the pain in his arm, and crawled, pulling the stunned American operator again.

"Stop," Bone said, coughing. "I'm awake."

Naveed released the man's hand and collapsed. Between the claustrophobia and the pain in his arm from the ricochet wound and gunshot, he was struggling.

"What happened?" Bone whispered.

"An explosion threw us down the tunnel," Naveed said. "Then the ceiling collapsed."

"Thank you for saving my life."

"You're welcome. But perhaps it is too early for that sentiment. We have to find a way out."

"And catch up to Colonel Tariq."

Naveed closed his eyes. He'd allowed himself to leave the Tariq problem for later, but Bone was right. Not only did they have to continue through the tunnel—he shoved the thought of being underground aside as soon as it came up—they needed to complete the original mission.

"How is your arm?" Bone asked, moving closer. He took the phone and aimed the light at the wound. "Looks okay," he muttered, answering his own question. "You'll live."

He would. For now.

Trapped underground…

With the person who they had to find and kill somewhere far ahead of them.

Tariq woke to sand and pebbles falling onto the top of his balding head. They were small, but hurt when they landed. He felt the part of his skull that his hands hadn't been able to cover. It came away wet with blood. A rock must have fallen and knocked him out.

He coughed hard and spat dirt from his mouth.

Dust filled the air, but he was alive.

Behind him, on the surface, the warehouse would be destroyed, and the remains engulfed in flame by now.

His eyes were open—he was sure of it—but he could see nothing.

He pulled his mobile phone from his pocket. It would make crawling down the tunnel slower, but he could take the time to light his way now that the warehouse had exploded.

But he still had to escape—and detonate the bombs in Paris as soon as he reached the surface.

182

FIFTEEN MINUTES

Command Center
DGSI (Direction Générale de la Sécurité Intérieure) Headquarters
Levallois-Perret, France

There was little chance one thousand city buses had bombs on them, but Pierre had no way of knowing which ones were rolling improvised explosive devices and which ones were safe.

The computer monitors spanning the wall of the command center showed live video of the city's major tourist attractions, along with popular shopping and dining areas.

Tourists waited in lines to enter. Others milled around, taking pictures. At every location, from the museums to monuments, crowds gathered. It was a record-setting year for visitors, and the perfect weather had brought tourists out for coffee and croissants, followed by walking tours and museum visits.

Other screens switched to traffic cameras showing angry, confused, or frightened drivers standing near their pulled-over vehicles as buses sped past them and made sharp turns not usually seen from vehicles that large, all hurried along by police standing in the middle of intersections, directing traffic, clearing paths, and holding chaos at bay.

Pierre had ordered a corner of one monitor to display a countdown timer.

All the bombs they'd disarmed so far had the same detonation time programmed into their timers. He was counting on any they hadn't found to be the same.

The red digital clock counted down another second.

They had fifteen minutes left.

"Open all museums and other tourist attractions to the public immediately," Pierre said. "No tickets. No lines—except for expedited security. Get people inside the doors quickly—before 10:30. Clear the plazas, the cafes, the sidewalks. Don't hold back any longer—no more subtlety. And have the police do everything they can to protect people from the few buses that haven't made it to the parks."

He left unsaid his concern that there could be bombs in private vehicles.

The entire city might have car bombs driven by fanatics, all waiting to detonate along with the buses at 10:30.

But at least there had been no suicide bombers, or spotters ready to detonate the bombs when the buses detoured from their usual routes.

One of the screens showed the real-time tracking system. Most of the buses had already been routed to the nearest parks.

Pierre's orders, combined with the intel analysts' expert communication and the many anti-terrorism drills the city had run over the past few years, had combined to produce an exceptionally well-run operation.

The police and soldiers in the streets acted quickly.

Bus drivers followed the commands given to them without question.

Groundskeepers cleared the city's parks where the buses had parked, from the smallest neighborhood green spaces packed with trees to the largest gardens.

Bomb disposal units wasted no time getting into position and inspecting the buses as they arrived.

Not many buses were left on the roads—but there were a few stuck in gridlock traffic, one with a broken communications system, and three others that were close to parks but not moving fast enough to make it.

A single bus exploding would kill dozens. Hundreds, even, depending on the location.

"Not on my watch," he muttered again. "At the five-minute mark, all buses are to discharge their passengers whether they are in a park or not," he called. "The areas around all buses are to be evacuated." Five minutes should be enough time. Pierre would take the chance and hope there wasn't a single spotter or suicide bomber in the city.

"And get police, firefighters—someone—on board that bus with the broken radio and tell them what's going on!"

183

THE MISGIVINGS

The Tunnel
Surobi, Afghanistan

Bone shoved aside the misgivings he felt about still being alive—again.

It obviously wasn't his time yet.

He had to be at least a meter below the surface. Braces—vertical wood struts—were attached to wider boards running horizontally, supporting the dirt ceiling. They were infrequent, not regularly spaced as Bone thought made the most sense.

He had his phone out, having given Naveed's back, though both were off for the moment. Tariq had to be far ahead, but better safe than sorry.

He sensed discomfort—fear, maybe—from Naveed. The man's wounds didn't look bad enough to be the cause of it, so it had to be something else.

He was about to ask when a faint sound came from ahead of them in the tunnel.

A deep cough, repeated several times.

If this were any other mission, Bone would have at least one weapon left.

At the end of the ambush years ago that had killed his Teammates, after expending all of his ammo and using his last-resort throwing star to distract the enemy, he'd still had a knife to rely on.

Now, though, stuck in the narrow tunnel with what had to be his enemy ahead of them, he had only his bare hands.

They would be enough.

Naveed had heard the coughing, too. He hadn't moved a muscle since.

Bone pressed his hand firmly down on the man's non-injured shoulder, hoping he got the message: Stay here. Don't move.

Once Naveed relaxed, Bone let go and put one hand out, setting it carefully on the ground. He moved his knee next, slipping past Naveed, then his other hand and other knee.

He moved as quietly as he could without wasting time, balancing his desire to creep up on an armed Tariq with the need to reach the man before he made it to surface.

184

PARIS

Champs-Élysées
Paris, France

Grant had planned the marriage proposal with precision.

He'd worn loose shorts to hide the shape of the velvet box in his cargo shorts and kept his left hand casually in his pocket—he'd read about Paris's pickpockets.

Hanna had wanted to drink coffee and have pastries at "the best pastry shop in Paris," on the Champs-Élysées. It wasn't the most romantic place to propose. Certainly not better than the Eiffel Tower, or some of the many other sites they'd see on this trip before they climbed too far up the corporate ladder.

But Hanna had confided in him, late one night snuggled together in her apartment's full-size bed, that she'd had the dream since she was a little kid. Someday, she had promised herself, she would sit at this specific cafe —she'd seen it on TV—outside on a beautiful day, drink coffee, sample pastries, and celebrate a life worth living.

So here they were.

Grant had barely touched his coffee. His hands were shaking too much with nerves. He debated holding off on the proposal. He could always ask later. Cars were honking their horns in the gridlocked traffic just a few feet from their sidewalk table. Several people were standing next to their cars, doors open, talking with one another about the holdup.

It was definitely not the quiet, romantic scene he had envisioned.

Vehicles in the right lane inched forward while cars in the left lane forced their way over in an effort to move ahead.

A city bus idled next to the pastry shop. As Hanna broke off a piece of one of several different flavors of croissants on their table, it pulled ahead a few inches before stopping again. The driver, a guy about Grant's age—early thirties—looked terrified. Maybe it was his first day on the job.

"Are you okay?" Hanna asked, her mouth full of croissant. She didn't look too concerned—she was focused on the food.

Had he made a mistake? Was she ready for a proposal?

She was perfect. She had a heart so big it made him count his blessings every time she smiled.

Enough was enough. This was it. The spot was a fine place to propose. She'd say yes.

She had to, right?

"Hanna?" He blushed and smiled, knowing how scared he must look.

His heart pounded. This was it. The moment that would change his life forever.

Grant pushed the chair back and slipped off it, lowering to one knee.

Hanna gulped down the last of the croissant, and her eyes widened. "Oh my goodness," she whispered.

But she was ignoring him and looking over his shoulder.

His mind translated the words yelled from behind him, the four years of high school French paying off. "Everyone move away from the bus! Hurry! Danger!"

Along the street, the bus doors opened. He didn't catch the entire message the young bus driver yelled, but his mind translated the meaning.

There was a bomb on the bus.

Hanna grabbed half of a croissant with one hand, took his hand with the other, and dragged him up the street, toward the Arc de Triomphe and away from the bus disgorging its panicked riders.

Tuileries Garden
Paris, France

The baseball cap Charlie wore backward did nothing to keep the sun out of his eyes, but he refused to spin it around and have the brim do its job. He wanted to look cool—he was in Paris, after all.

He would have been happy taking the kids to a theme park in Florida, even in the summer. The boys were old enough to enjoy the gentler rides at the amusement park.

They were much too young to appreciate anything France had to offer besides chocolate, ice cream, and croissants.

The trip to Paris had been Leslie's idea.

The hotel was expensive and small. They were doing a ton of walking, and while the weather in Paris had been cooler and less humid than it would have been in Orlando, everyone spoke French. He knew they would, of course, but he thought everyone understood English these days. Leslie studied French and could get her point across at the restaurants and shops, but he was at a loss. He was sunburned, tired, and had to carry the youngest boy nearly every step of the way. Half the time, he had the oldest riding piggyback, the youngest on one hip, and the middle one on the other.

Leslie got to carry their daughter—the lightest one.

At least he was getting his workouts in.

And now the damn garden was closed? For a gas leak?

And who drives buses into a park during a gas leak emergency?

Leslie rushed ahead, pulling the older boys along with a discussion about ice cream flavors.

"What's really going on?" he asked her in the muted tone they used when trying to keep the kids from paying attention to their grownup conversations.

"My guess is some kind of terrorism," she muttered over her shoulder.

Charlie made eye contact with his wife, and suddenly the stress of four kids, the too-small hotel room, and expensive…. everything… dropped away, and he was afraid for them all.

"What's tear scissom?" the oldest asked. "Like scissors?"

"I want 'nilla ice cream," the youngest boy cried from Charlie's hip.

"Chocolate is best," the next oldest said.

"Mint chip is best," the eldest argued, thankfully dropping his line of questioning.

A police officer beckoned to them and several others as they exited the garden. He called something in rapid-fire French and escorted them across the strangely deserted road along the park. An older man stood in the doorway of one of the magnificent buildings—a doorman.

"They want us to go inside," Leslie called back to him.

Charlie didn't ask why. The fear on the faces of the men, women, and children around him was enough to keep him moving.

The building was spectacular. Thick red carpet runners over hardwood floors on the ground level gave way eventually to a huge, shaded courtyard. The doorman gave up his fast walk and ran across the open area, pulling a key from a ring on his belt as he went.

From behind them, the policeman yelled something, and everyone who spoke French—including Leslie—dropped to the ground, so Charlie did too.

"I love you," Leslie whispered next to him.

"I love you too," he answered.

They gathered the confused and now crying kids, shielded them with their bodies, and waited.

A second later, the ground shook, and the world exploded.

185

THE DECISION

The Tunnel
Surobi, Afghanistan

Tariq directed the flashlight forward. He couldn't see the upward slope of the tunnel. He must not have gone as far from the warehouse as he thought, hence the chunk of tunnel falling on his head and knocking him out.

Or the idiot tunnel diggers had gone much farther beyond the walls of the compound than he'd ordered.

He coughed again, and crawled forward, once again cursing the men who carved out the tunnel for not making the floor smoother, the roof higher, and the path more direct.

The light from Tariq's flashlight made it easier for Bone to move when the bomb maker did. The older man made no effort to be quiet, crawling noisily and cursing under his breath whenever a stone dug into his palms or knees.

Saving the American, dragging his body through the tunnel, had been the distraction Naveed had needed to keep his mind off the dirt above and the walls closing in around him.

With Bone gone ahead after Tariq, Naveed was left alone with his phobia.

For a minute—or a second, or an hour, he couldn't be sure—the memory of his mother and the hope for her healing kept his mind occupied.

It didn't last.

The shakes came first. His hands trembled, then the rest of his body.

The tears came next, though he refused to sob out loud.

A second—or an hour, or a day—later, he tipped over onto his side, no longer in control of his body as his mind deserted him.

Bone matched Tariq's moves, palm by palm, knee by knee, gaining on him by stretching forward and covering more ground per crawl.

He was within reach. Bone stretched out his hand to grab Tariq's leg—

Tariq's foot snapped back. It caught Bone between the eyes and on the bridge of his nose, making his eyes water.

The fight was on.

Tariq's head whipped around, locking eyes with Bone. The man bared his teeth and growled as he turned in the confined space, dropping the phone and reaching to his waist.

Bone launched himself forward. If Tariq drew a pistol, Bone would die.

He swatted away the man's hand as they crashed together.

The phone, face down in the dirt, provided just enough illumination for Bone to see the fistful of sand Tariq grabbed to fling at him, and he closed his eyes before it landed.

The colonel fought like a tiger, or a cornered rat. He punched. Bone blocked and connected with his own shot to the man's face.

Bone had the upper hand. He was thirty years younger and a front-line, direct-action operator, not a behind-the-scenes bomb maker.

Bone closed on the man, getting his arms around Tariq's body and his legs around Tariq's waist, going for a choke hold, but Tariq bucked and kicked one of the support beams on the ceiling of the tunnel.

Sand trickled from the ceiling... then chunks of dirt and small rocks crashed down.

Just ahead of them, the ceiling caved in. Dust filled the air.

Tariq wiggled in Bone's grasp and kicked the wall, hard, causing more sand to tumble down.

Tariq must have realized he couldn't win. In the tight confines of the narrow tunnel, he was only inches away from the wall and a few feet below the ceiling. Without Bone incapacitating him entirely, Tariq could easily lash out.

He rolled despite Bone's best attempt to hold him in place, and kicked the wall again—hard. More of the ceiling collapsed around them. Bone had to end it now, or Tariq would bury them both alive.

Bone grappled, finally succeeding in slipping an arm around the bomb maker's neck. His other hand grabbed his own bicep and squeezed his arms together. Tariq struggled, kicking for the ceiling, but Bone held fast, preventing him from connecting.

After a few seconds, Tariq stopped kicking—and switched to frantically tapping his hand on Bone's leg in submission.

For an instant, Bone considered releasing the man. He had given up. Surrendered.

But they were in an underground tunnel Tariq had made, leading away from the warehouse where he had built bombs and shipped them around the world to murder innocent men, women, and children.

Along with the IEDs he may have manufactured and used to kill and maim allied warriors during the war years—and he had trained other men to do the same.

Tariq was pure evil.

And while he might have valuable intelligence, or proof that Pakistan's ISI had in fact supported him, he didn't deserve to live.

Admiral Nalen had chosen Bone to do what he thought was best. To get involved and not stop until the mission was completed.

Bone kept the pressure on the bomb maker's carotid arteries. "For everyone who died because of you," he whispered in the man's ear.

A moment later, the man went slack. Seconds passed, but Bone didn't move. He felt the moment Tariq's life ended...

And broke the man's neck, just to be sure.

186

THE DAMAGE REPORT

Command Center
DGSI (Direction Générale de la Sécurité Intérieure) Headquarters
Levallois-Perret, France

The large monitors displayed the views across the city.

Pierre, the director-general, and the analysts watched the screens flick from one location to another.

"Damage report," Pierre called once he found his voice. "Casualties?"

"It's too early, sir," an analyst called.

"Count the buses," Pierre said. "And show me the stadium and the garden." Those locations were where nearly all of the buses from the two depots suspected of being the sources of the bombs had been vectored.

The large center screen showed the football stadium. Through smoke and dust, a horrific picture emerged.

Several of the analysts gasped.

"Steady, people," Pierre said, though it took all he had to force his voice to remain calm.

The football field and running track had been packed with buses.

They were now a smoldering ruin.

An analyst pulled up a view of the Tuileries Garden.

Near the back of a long line of buses, two were totally demolished.

The buses to their right, in another row, were shredded—the shrapnel from the bombs had cut straight through them. On the far side of those two, and to the left of the ones that had exploded, trees had been sliced apart at waist level.

"Show me the streets near those areas," Pierre ordered.

A few seconds later, the screens switched to security camera views from intersections near the stadium and garden.

Several windows were blown out of a cafe on the corner near the stadium, but the wall of the building was clear—it hadn't been hit by shrapnel.

Near the park, the street looked peaceful. No bodies bled on the sidewalk.

No one sat slumped in destroyed cars.

"Most buses are offline, sir, but I don't think many exploded. The ones that did demolished others that were used as protective barricades. Also, there was a bus parked alongside the roadway by the Seine. A driver vectored there when he couldn't make it to a park. He likely saved the Musée d'Orsay—or at least any pedestrians still outside near it. So far, none of the reports are mentioning casualties."

"Did any buses blow up in the streets?"

Thirty seconds passed. Pierre was about to ask again when a different analyst answered. "No, sir. There were a few that were stuck in traffic and didn't make it to a safe spot. None of them exploded."

Pierre didn't hesitate. "Vector the nearest bomb disposal units to buses on the streets. Expand the evacuation near them, just in case. There could still be danger."

Analysts relayed his orders as he let out the breath he'd been holding.

The director-general clapped him on the shoulder. "Well done, Pierre," he said. "Make sure you thank your American friend for me, please.

"And good job, everyone," the DG said, addressing the room. "Your professionalism and calm under pressure exemplify what we strive for." He turned and exited the command center. Pierre would have to join him shortly—there were bound to be plenty of questions from the politicians. Why hadn't they known about the threat earlier? Who was behind it? Why had it happened?

With any luck, one or two might take a moment away from trying to place blame and offer their gratitude for saving hundreds or thousands of lives—but Pierre wouldn't count on it.

187

THE ACCENT

The Tunnel
Surobi, Afghanistan

Bone used the light on Tariq's phone to inspect the tunnel.

It wasn't as bad as he thought.

After a few minutes of grabbing armfuls of dirt and pulling them out of the way, he created an opening large enough to wiggle through.

They could escape after all.

———

"Naveed? Naveed—can you hear me?" Bone shook the man, who looked and felt alive, but something was horribly wrong. Naveed was on his side, not passed out but...

Catatonic.

"Come on, buddy. Let's get you out of here."

Bone had seen the same expression twice, both during the brief time after the ambush when he'd taught the next generation of SEALs at BUD/S in Coronado, California.

Candidates occasionally believed they could overcome a deep-seated fear or phobia. Other times, a man might not know he was terrified of sharks, or freezing to death in the cold water of the Pacific Ocean, or sliding face-first down a steep rope on the obstacle course.

When facing the fear, many pushed through and learned the lesson of training—the mind was a useful tool, but it often played it too safe. At times, it had to be ignored or overcome. SEALs decided what to do and did it, the body or mind's prejudices, beliefs, or programming be damned.

Many of the men in BUD/S, however, couldn't transcend their bodies and minds. In the face of exhaustion, fear, or phobia, they allowed their limiting beliefs to dictate what they couldn't do and gave up instead of pushing through.

Two candidates had come face to face with their fears—known or unknown—and instead of quitting the program, had pushed...

And gone so far, their minds had checked out on their behalf, refusing to continue.

They'd had the same vacant, slack-jawed stare as on Naveed's face in the tunnel.

The ceiling was too low for Bone to carry him, so Bone took the man's good arm and pulled.

Bone put his shoulder to the wooden square at the top of the tunnel and pushed. One great heave shifted heavy dirt, and the entryway slid to one side a few inches, allowing daylight to shine into the tunnel.

Another push opened up a large enough gap for Bone to crawl out into a deserted lot of packed dirt and a lone tall tree, dragging Naveed behind him.

"Hey, look," he told Naveed. "Sunshine. We're out of there. You're safe. Come on back."

Naveed stared at the ground, only upright because of Bone's help.

"Come back," Bone said in Pashto. "You must help me with my terrible accent."

Naveed blinked several times. A minute later, he glanced back at the hole to the tunnel. His entire body shuddered.

"You're okay now," Bone told him in English. "We're done with that. Never again. Mission accomplished."

Naveed nodded, still not speaking.

Bone left him for a moment to crawl back into the tunnel.

A few careful kicks to one of the wooden supports caused sand to trinkle down.

A harder kick triggered a collapse. Dirt and sand crashed down, filling the tunnel and blocking access.

Bone crawled out, replaced the wooden cover, and scattered dirt to once again hide the exit.

Finally, Bone helped a blinking Naveed to his feet and supported him as they took small, hesitant steps. It was slow, but easier and less of a spectacle than picking him up and carrying him.

Bone expected fire trucks, sirens, and ambulances, but in the harsh afternoon sunlight, the fire raging on the other side of the tall compound walls behind them burned out of control.

They neared one of the narrow back streets. Their car should be a few blocks ahead and around a corner.

"Just act normal, all right?" Bone told Naveed. With his arm around Naveed's shoulder, avoiding the upper arm, where blood still trickled from the two wounds, they shuffled toward the car.

A skinny old man walked along the road toward them, switching his gaze from the fire to Bone and Naveed.

"Is everything okay?" the man asked in Pashto. His voice was raspy. "Do you need help? Water?"

Bone shook his head and answered in Pashto without thinking, exactly how he'd practiced with Wali. "Everything is fine. Thank you."

The man nodded and continued on, passing them.

Several seconds later, Naveed's body shuddered again. He stood straighter, no longer needing Bone's help to walk. "Your accent," Naveed said, his voice almost as dry as the old man's.

Bone glanced back at the local man. Had he raised an alarm? Pointed at the two of them walking away, telling people that an American was in their midst?

The man stopped near two others standing in front of a house, but they continued to watch the compound burn behind the tall walls.

"Well done. You sounded like an Afghan," Naveed said.

188

THE FAILURE

Yemeni Independence Brigade Headquarters
Aden, Yemen

Ali Al-Haddad fumed. The huge main room of his headquarters was packed with his men, from the lowest soldier to his top advisors, along with people from other militant groups he'd planned on impressing today.

Three large high-definition televisions were arranged around the room, each displaying a different 24-hour news network. Across from the sofa sectional, a projector threw the image of the most widely watched news channel across the entire wall, ready to show the results of "his" attack in Paris.

He'd kept the plan—and the millions he'd paid in advance—from his people, only hinting at it once the guests had arrived.

Now, as he watched the reports of what looked like a failed terrorist attack, his plan was falling apart before his eyes.

And before the eyes of his followers, comrades, and regional competitors in the lucrative world of criminality and freedom fighting.

"What is this?" a cocky voice called from across the room. His main rival from another militant group in the region smirked at him. Ali had planned to use today's events as proof of the Yemeni Independence Brigade's reach and power, but Paris hadn't blown up as expected—or as he'd been promised.

"A failed attack, they are calling it," the man said. "Pathetic." He shook his head in disgust and headed for the exit.

Ali burned with shame. For a moment, he considered ordering his guards to shoot the competitor, along with anyone who dared show contempt for Ali's efforts. But he allowed the man to leave, along with the other guests as they realized the party was over.

No one celebrates a failure.

Ali slumped on the couch and contemplated what he could do. Attacking Europe or America was far beyond his reach, but there was always something that could be blown up, even if it was closer to home. It might take years, but he would have his glory.

189

THE DRIVE

Outside Surobi, Afghanistan

Bone directed them to the cemetery on the small rise overlooking the city. Naveed was coherent enough to drive, but he was lost in thought, content to follow Bone's instructions.

The short trip was made in silence as Bone contemplated the operation. He'd killed Tariq, along with several guards, and survived.

His training—both to become a SEAL and the more recent intense work he'd done to hone his skills—had paid off.

But it had been a close thing.

"If it wasn't for Hawk and Bull..." Bone muttered as they reached the cemetery and Naveed parked the car. Below them in the distance, flames still poured from the warehouse.

Locals had formed a bucket brigade to toss water on nearby structures, but no one bothered to try to extinguish the warehouse fire. Without professional equipment, which it looked like the small town didn't have, they could only let it burn.

"The majority of the warehouse guards focused on Hawk and Bull," Bone continued. "The plate carriers they wore, their better weapons, and how they attacked along the sides of the building allowed us to go straight up the middle."

"They were the distraction we needed," Naveed said.

Before they left the cellular data coverage of the town and drove to Kabul, Bone used the comms app to call Kristine back in Las Vegas. He put in an earbud so Naveed couldn't overhear. They'd saved each other's lives during the operation, but the less the man knew, the better.

"It's done," he said when Kristine answered. "One hundred percent confirmed. Tariq is dead, and his bomb-making facilities are destroyed."

Kristine let out a loud sigh of relief. "Thank you," she said.

"How's—" He was about to use Dominic's name, but thought better of it. "My partner?" he said instead.

"He's conscious and on the mend. So is Sardar. His wife is with him in the hospital. Sardar has a warehouse ready. I can vector you in. Dom's already there, along with one of Sardar's men. Sardar and I will arrange an exfil—probably Friday or Saturday."

"Fine." It would give Dom a few more days to heal. "We can leave whenever you two work it out."

"Okay, I'll send you the address and directions—you're mobile?"

Bone glanced at Naveed, who stared at the burning compound. "Yes. No problem." He would have Naveed drop him off near Sardar's warehouse, but far enough away to not compromise security.

"Great. We'll get you out of there soon. Well done, Bone."

"Team effort," Bone said. "Speaking of which…"

"I'll wire the second part of the money now," Kristine said.

"She's wiring the rest of your money now," Bone told Naveed. "What happened in Paris?" he asked Kristine.

"A few bombs exploded, but no lives lost thanks to our intel. A complete success. Make sure you thank Naveed—he helped save hundreds of lives. Thousands, maybe."

"Copy that," Bone said, and hung up.

"Thanks to you," he told Naveed, "hundreds or thousands of innocent lives were saved in Paris."

Tension dropped from Naveed's body, but he said nothing, only stared at the black smoke filling the sky above the compound. "You okay?" Bone asked him.

The man only nodded.

"First time in a real combat situation," Bone said.

Naveed nodded again.

"And first kill?"

"Yes. Also the last," Naveed whispered. "I was a spy. A courier. Not a killer."

They sat together, staring at the compound.

"Why did you do it?" Bone asked. "Why tell us about Tariq?"

"I should say it was because he wanted to kill more and more innocent people, but the truth is I did it for the money. Tariq promised we'd be rich, but he kept making excuses. His costs were high preparing for the next operation, and the next. The supplies, the guards. I set up the deals—I can guess how much he earned. But nothing came my way." Naveed turned to Bone. "Why did you save me? Twice?"

"No man left behind," Bone said, and turned the question around. "Why did you save me?"

"You are an honorable man," Naveed said.

They exchanged a look, both nodding their thanks to the other.

"What's next for you?" Bone asked.

"I have a safe house for my mother and I until we leave the country. Then, with the money from you, I will get the best doctors to discover what is causing her symptoms."

"Will the ISI come after you?"

Naveed tore his eyes from the compound to glance at Bone. "No, I do not believe so. With Tariq gone, they will likely allow me to live. I am their proof that Tariq was not associated with ISI or the government. That he did it all on his own. And I am not a threat to them the way he was."

"They need you."

"Exactly. I hope." Naveed returned his gaze to the compound. "And you? What is next?"

Bone smiled tiredly. "Home."

190

THE REPORTER

Conference Room 1
Central Analysis Group Headquarters
Alexandria, Virginia

Wyatt picked up a can of energy drink from the table, but it was empty.

With the immediate crisis over, however, he probably shouldn't have more caffeine anyway. It was nearly time for him to go home and get some sleep.

He'd switched the big monitor on the wall to the 24-hour news station, currently reporting nonstop from Paris.

A reporter stood with the Arc de Triomphe in the background, looking like she was fighting to hide her excitement and appear professionally detached.

"Officials claim the explosions that rocked a park near the Louvre Museum, a stadium near the Eiffel Tower, and a small roadway along the Seine may have been from a gas leak, but I interviewed two American tourists who have a different take on the events. This was what they had to say."

The image cut to a young woman and young man. "I speak a little French," the woman said while her friend—maybe a boyfriend, Wyatt thought—stood next to her. He had his hand in his pocket and looked more frustrated than flustered. And something else… Stricken, maybe.

"The police had us run away from a bus," the woman said. "And the bus driver distinctly said something about a bomb. Right?" She turned to the friend, who nodded.

The screen switched back to the live shot of the reporter. "So far, there are no reports of casualties from the explosions—whatever their cause. We'll update you with news as we get it. Back to you in the studio, Kathleen," the reporter said.

Gregory muted the television as the scene changed to a woman sitting at a news desk. A map of Paris appeared onscreen over her shoulder with small flame icons on it.

"If only they knew," Wyatt muttered.

"It's our job to not only keep people safe," Gregory said, leaning back in his chair, "but—sometimes—to make sure they don't know the danger they were in."

"Who decides?" Marcus asked. He probably meant it rhetorically, but Gregory answered.

"Not us." Gregory stood and extended his hand toward Wyatt.

Wyatt scrambled to his feet and shook.

"Excellent job," Gregory said. He turned to Marcus, shook, and told him the same. He turned toward the conference table with the patchwork mind map covering it. "Your analysis and suggestions saved lives today. Well done. Now, both of you go home. Get some sleep." He turned back to Wyatt. "Take a few days off—that's an order."

Gregory left the conference room, followed by Marcus, who gave Wyatt a thumbs-up.

Wyatt reluctantly folded the mind map papers, careful as always. With the Paris bombing thwarted, he should have three months until the next attack—assuming he was right, and there was a connection between the bombings in Egypt, Turkey, Spain, and now France.

Maybe a shower, some decent food, and a few days away from the office would give him a fresh perspective before he dove back into the data, looking for the terrorists truly responsible for the attacks.

191

A SUMMER DAY

Tuileries Garden
Paris, France

Groundskeeper Jacques sat up from the concrete base of the statue of a Roman woman he had hidden behind. When he'd realized his bad leg wouldn't allow him to make it out of the park in time for whatever was going to happen, he'd curled into a ball and prepared to die.

But it seemed he was to live another day. Aside from the ringing in his ears and the smoke and dust hurting his eyes, he was fine.

Nearby, trees were shredded. The rose bushes were destroyed. Buses burned in the distance.

In slow motion, the statue above him wobbled and then fell to the side, where it broke into pieces.

His beloved park was wounded, but it would rise again.

Charlie licked his thumb and used it to wipe a smudge of chocolate ice cream from around his son's mouth. The pre-lunch dessert had made the kids hyper for fifteen minutes but had erased their tears from the noise of the explosion and the terror of lying on the courtyard ground with their parents covering their small bodies.

The baby had fallen asleep as they'd been escorted from the luxury condo building and down the street, away from the middle of the park, where they'd been walking earlier.

The park looked like someone had taken a chainsaw to the trees. Buses smoldered as firefighters directed water on them.

If not for that old guy...

They'd found a place for ice cream two blocks off the main street, an outdoor table to sit at, and after the kids finished arguing yet again about which flavor tasted best and dancing around like the annoyingly adorable tiny creatures they were, the three boys had slumped against them, drowsy from the day's excitement.

Charlie tore his gaze away from the scene and reached out for Leslie's hand. "Thanks for getting us away from there."

She nodded. "Next year, we're going to Orlando," she told him, and squeezed his hand.

La Liberté Stadium
Paris, France

Bus driver Léon Escoffier surveyed the remains of his bus and wished again he'd had his full allotment of coffee that morning.

The vehicle, which he'd moved to the running track of the stadium after the bombs underneath had been disarmed, was completely destroyed.

Most of the buses in the stadium were, though it looked like only a few had actually exploded on their own. The rest were shredded from shrapnel. A few others had blown up and burned when their gas tanks caught on fire.

The other drivers stood around near him at the entrance to the stadium.

They had done their part. And saved lives. But whoever had the idea to get the buses off the roads was the true hero.

Rita and Bernard surveyed the destruction from the upper tier of the stadium seats, where they'd climbed to get an overview.

"We missed a few," Bernard muttered.

"No. We ran out of time."

They had checked many buses and disarmed fourteen before being forced to run to safety.

But they had done their jobs well given the time they had.

Once the burning buses cooled, they would be back underneath them, double-checking the remains for unexploded ordinance.

Just in case.

Gardien de la Paix Renée Ducasse gratefully accepted an espresso from the owner of the cafe. In the stadium across the street, smoke poured from the buses she had sent there.

Her feet crunched on the broken glass from the cafe's windows, which had shattered from the nearby blast.

Renée's hands shook at the thought of how close she had come to death.

"The way you directed traffic…" the owner whispered to her so the tourists standing nearby couldn't hear. "And brought everyone into my kitchen…"

He had followed her instructions without question, getting the tourists out of their seats and onto the floor of the long narrow kitchen at the back of his restaurant.

Together, they had saved lives.

"Thank you," he said, kissed both her cheeks, and left to take care of his customers.

Tuileries Garden
Paris, France

Valentin stood with the tourists across the park from his bus.

It hadn't exploded, though others had.

A man in coveralls pulled a flashlight from his pocket and marched toward the bus and crawled underneath.

A short time later, he crawled out and moved to the next one to repeat the process.

Valentin found a bench facing the correct direction and slowly lowered himself. The Tuileries Garden had been decimated, and buses burned, but the sun was shining, and there was what could only be a bomb disposal technician inspecting a long line of buses.

This was a fine place to spend the rest of the day.

Hôtel La Nuit
Paris, France

Hans woke to his alarm for the second time.

He'd partied much too hard the night before.

But he was determined to see the last of the Paris sights on his list before returning to Germany the next morning. Maybe he'd meet someone at a museum, since he'd struck out repeatedly at the bars and nightclubs of the city.

He grabbed a hotel breakfast of Gruyère cheese—delicious—and extremely undercooked eggs, the way the French preferred them—ate quickly, and exited the hotel.

No one else was at the bus stop, which he counted as a good omen. He wouldn't be crammed in with a bunch of other tourists.

But after thirty minutes of waiting, he grew annoyed, then disgusted. The Paris bus system was supposedly on par with Berlin's or Frankfurt's, yet three scheduled buses had failed to arrive.

With a sigh, he started walking, vowing to go to Spain next summer and lie on the beach all day, drinking beer.

He'd had enough of culture.

The Eiffel Tower Gardens
Paris, France

In the first hour after the explosion in the stadium a few blocks to the west, *Gardien de la Paix* Lavigne could only describe the mood in the area as haunted.

The tourists moved hesitantly, looking around in trepidation as if another ground-shaking explosion could happen any moment.

By the second hour, as more of them checked their phones and asked him what had happened—"Gas leak. No danger," he told everyone—

things got back to normal. People enjoyed the day, took pictures of the Eiffel Tower looming above them, and only occasionally glanced west to the wispy smoke rising above the buildings a few blocks away.

Lavigne provided directions, overtly shadowed the obvious pickpockets and criminals who wandered by, forcing them to move on, and apologetically refused the requests to take pictures for people.

Just another summer day in Paris.

192

THE CAREER

Surobi, Afghanistan

The sky was growing dark by the time Imran made it to Surobi and questioned a man sitting near an empty lot next to the burned compound.

"Two men came from there," he said in answer to Imran's question. "Both tall, but one thinner. Dusty."

"Dusty?"

"Dirty," the man said. "Like they had been digging. And the one was scared. Had been, but he was calming down."

"Both Afghans?" Imran asked. "Locals?"

The man shook his head. "Not locals. From the city, maybe," the man said. "He spoke like a city boy."

It sounded like the courier and the American. No one would call Hawk or Bull "boys"—they were hard men—and neither was tall.

"But only those two? You saw no others?" Imran asked. The area smelled of ash—and death. Bodies had certainly burned inside the warehouse.

And as long as one of them had been Colonel Tariq, so be it.

The skinny man shook his head and gladly took the money Imran offered to thank him for his time.

Imran made his way through the narrow, winding streets, but he found no one else who knew more about the fire earlier in the day, or who had seen survivors fleeing.

He eventually came upon two black luxury SUVs tucked into pullouts along the main road to the compound. The key fobs were on the front driver's side tires.

Once he reported in, headquarters would dispatch operators to retrieve them.

There could be no clues left behind that could tie Pakistan and the ISI to the area.

Imran returned to his own SUV. It was time for his report.

"Two men survived," Imran told Raza. "From the description, one was the courier and the other the American, though the locals claimed he was an Afghan. The compound is destroyed—burned to the ground. Nothing remains but ash and metal shelves warped from the heat. There will be no bodies found. Maybe teeth, but only if someone puts a great deal of effort into the salvage. An unfortunate accident at an import-export business, the locals are calling it. Two of our SUVs are parked nearby, but there is no sign of our men."

There was a pause on the other end of the line. Raza was receiving orders from whoever was actually in charge.

Imran was resigned to his fate. All four of his operators were dead. The mission—at least as initially envisioned—was a failure.

His once-promising career was over. He'd be pulled from field operations—which was what he wanted—but instead of a promotion to headquarters, he'd be stuck in a dead-end position in a far-off basement and given menial tasks.

His shoulders slumped. His next orders might be for him to shuttle the SUVs back to Islamabad. He'd be reduced to a driver. An errand boy.

A nobody.

"You have done well with a difficult assignment," Raza finally said.

Imran blinked, not believing his ears. He whipped his head around, checking the growing darkness. A compliment like that was what they would offer a man about to be shot in the head by a cleanup crew, but there was nobody around.

"We will send a team for the vehicles," Raza continued. "Return to Jalalabad, get some sleep, then sanitize your safe house. Report to headquarters tomorrow. You will be working with me—a small promotion. You won't be in the field any longer, but I believe you will find your new position both challenging and rewarding."

Imran fought his tiredness and disbelief. There was a final question he needed answered.

The last piece of the operation he should handle before finishing the assignment.

"What of the courier? And the American?" he asked. "For continuity, I should manage—"

"They are no longer your concern," Raza said. His voice left no room for discussion. "I will see you tomorrow afternoon."

The call disconnected.

Imran had done his best. Not every mission could succeed.

He put the SUV in gear, flipped on the lights, and navigated to the highway.

The mission was over.

Inter-Services Intelligence Headquarters
Islamabad, Pakistan

Raza spun his chair to face Hafiz, who slumped tiredly in the wheelchair. The old man had flipped down the metal footrests at some point, and had his slip-on sneakers supported off the ground.

The two had been together for days, only separated for trips to the restroom attached to the basement office, but Raza didn't know the man any better than the moment they'd met.

"A promotion for him?" Raza asked. The news had been as much a surprise to him as it had been to Imran.

"Sooner or later, this was likely to happen," the old man said. His voice had grown more gravelly over the past days. "Tariq was too much of a wild card. That is why I was put in charge of monitoring him. We were faced with an impossible situation. You and Imran are to be commended for your efforts."

Raza nodded his thanks and hesitated.

"Ask your questions," Hafiz said. He sat up straighter and stretched his back.

"Did you know the courier would betray him?"

"I did not, but I thought it possible. I guessed Tariq would be greedy— and he did not know about the courier's mother being ill. It was only a matter of time."

Raza considered the situation. "And now? The courier? The Americans? The businessman spy, if he is still alive?"

Hafiz slipped his feet from the footrests, kicked them up, and used his toes to turn around and propel him toward the office door.

"Let them live," he said over his shoulder.

PART 11

SATURDAY

193

JUSTICE

El Madania, Algeria

Thankfully, the white delivery van was air-conditioned. Though it was early, the day was already far hotter in this area of Algiers than Paris would be today.

The panel van idled on the street near their target's rented room. He had yet to emerge this morning.

Yesterday, he'd been on his way to a local tea and breakfast shop by now, but there had been too many people on the street for the men to do their job.

They were undercover, wearing locally purchased track pants and T-shirts. They only left the van after the target had retired to his room for the night.

But had he somehow noticed them the day before?

And snuck away overnight?

"Here he comes," the leader said from the front seat. He'd been in the DGSE—the Direction Générale de la Sécurité Extérieure, France's version of America's CIA—for fifteen years. His three men were just as experienced. They'd worked together often on operations of this type.

They would not—could not—fail.

"No one is on the street," the second in command said from the passenger seat. "We're good to go."

The target left his building and approached along the sidewalk.

"Ten seconds," the leader said.

The two in the back of the van crouched at the door. Ready.

One had his hand on the handle, prepared to turn it and slide the door open. In his free hand, he had a thick black hood.

The other had a stun gun.

"All clear. We're on. Five seconds."

They all counted silently.

At zero, the man in back opened the door.

The other one stepped out, bumped into the target, and zapped him.

He caught the target before he could fall and "helped" him into the van.

The hood went over the target's head, the men in back slammed the door closed, and the leader drove smoothly away. It was a short ride to the coast and the fishing boat waiting to take them back to France.

One second, former bus cleaner Asad was heading to the nearby tea shop for breakfast.

For the past few days, Asad had been living his dream. Algeria was everything he had hoped.

Nothing much had come from what he'd done in Paris. A few buses had exploded, but no one had been injured.

When his name and picture weren't in the news, Asad had figured he was fine—though he had still purchased new identity papers.

But now, he could barely breathe. His hands were cuffed behind his back, a thick cloth hood was over his head and tight around his neck, and he bounced on the warm metal floor of a van as it hit pothole after pothole in the lower middle-class neighborhood where he had rented a room.

Somehow, the authorities had found him.

He was going back to France to face a life in prison.

Karachi, Pakistan

The traffic in the city was out of control compared with Paris, but Jawad loved every inch of his ancestral homeland. Here, people looked and acted like him, and strangers didn't stare; he was just another face in the crowd.

To his cousins, he was a hero for attaching the bombs to the buses in Paris, though the results had been less spectacular than they all had hoped. But he had done his part—and was treated well because of it.

The money he'd earned helped, too. Jawad had been happy to take his cousins out for meals. He was on his way to meet them today. A new kebab restaurant had opened recently, owned by the best friend of one of his cousins. They'd been looking forward to eating there.

Jawad waited for a break in the heavy traffic, then hurried across, avoiding two scooters and several cars.

The street congestion and lack of respect for traffic laws worked in the old French spy's favor.

The white compact car's air conditioner wasn't cold, but it didn't matter. He was used to uncomfortable jobs.

He'd been trailing the young man for several blocks today, waiting for an opportunity that hadn't presented itself yesterday.

His superiors had decided that attempting an extraction in Pakistan was too politically risky.

But both of the two men who had planted bombs on the buses had to face justice.

So the mission came to him.

He had little intel to go on—not the young man's routine or favorite places, just the kid's picture from the security badge at the Paris city bus depot and the address where he was staying.

"Jawad," he muttered, shaking his head as the man darted into traffic.

This was the moment the spy had been waiting for.

He gunned the engine, racing for a break in traffic—or so it would seem to anyone watching.

At the last second, he cranked the wheel hard right and nailed the young man standing in the street, waiting for him to pass.

The kid—Jawad—flew several meters before landing on his shoulder and head.

Satisfied that his part was done, the spy accelerated and left the scene. One kilometer away, he had a second car waiting on a side street.

He'd make the switch and be out of the country in a few hours, and safely home in France in time for a late dinner and a glass of wine.

If Jawad survived, he'd be in the hospital. That would be another operator's problem. There was a special detail trained for hospital assassinations.

And if the kid was already dead, it was another job well done.

194

THE PRESIDENTS

The President's Weight Room—The White House
Washington, DC

Gregory entered the weight room wearing new workout shorts, a nice T-shirt, and his good sneakers. He wouldn't be embarrassed in front of the former president again by old clothes, though he doubted he would get much of a workout this morning.

He'd only give his report, which he had agonized over for the past few days.

President Heringten stood near the top of the bench press as former President Vernon Westerlin worked out. "Very well done, Vernon. I'm impressed."

Heringten guided the bar—this time with two of the room's smallest weights on it, one per side—to the bench press racks, then handed Westerlin a small white towel.

"Been working out at home since the last time we saw each other," the older man said, wiping his face as he sat up.

"It definitely shows." Heringten turned to Gregory with an amused twinkle in his eyes. "Ah, here's the man of the hour. Welcome, Mr. Addison."

"Mr. President," Gregory said to Heringten, followed by the same to Westerlin.

"What do you have for us, son?" the former president said in his Southern twang. "Was my friend Rutherfield murdered?"

Gregory nodded. As Wyatt had initially guessed and Kristine had reported, Rutherfield had been murdered by Big Mike's son, along with Frandren. Not that Gregory was going to give the former president any of the details.

"Yes, Mr. President. After an initial investigation, it appears to be the case. Unofficially, that is."

"Unofficially?"

"Yes, Mr. President."

The two presidents stared at him, waiting, but Gregory held his tongue.

"Care to elaborate?" President Westerlin finally asked.

"No, sir."

Gregory didn't want to be difficult, but he wouldn't tell the former president where the investigation into Rutherfield's death had led unless President Heringten specifically ordered him to. If it weren't for Admiral Nalen's retired SEAL—Bone—and Gregory's own outreach to Mike Salestri, he wouldn't even have been able to tell Westerlin that much.

The less Gregory said, the better.

For all of them.

Heringten cleared his throat, which Westerlin must have taken as a signal to move on.

"Can you tell me this—was justice served?" Westerlin asked in a low, quiet drawl.

"Yes, Mr. President. It was," Gregory said, his voice firm and sure.

Rutherfield's killer—Mike's son, Patrick—was dead. It hadn't been Gregory's doing, but justice was done.

They stared at each other. Gregory refused to budge.

"No details?"

"No, sir." Gregory had already been through a similar process with his wife, who had wanted to know why she'd sheltered in the White House for a week—not that she'd minded meeting and having dinners with the president and first lady. Gregory had avoided discussing what exactly his job was, and whether they would be in similar danger in the future. If he could successfully hold out against her questions, an aging former president wouldn't be a problem.

"I'm to take your word for it?" Westerlin asked.

"Yes, Mr. President."

Westerlin raised his eyebrow, looking like he wasn't sure whether to rip into him or laugh it off.

"Mr. Addison is exceedingly good at his job, Vernon," President Heringten said when the tension grew thick.

The former president said nothing for several more seconds, but neither Gregory nor President Heringten spoke.

Westerlin nodded. "Very well, Mr. Addison. Thank you. I owe you one."

Gregory offered the older president a tight smile. "Not at all, Mr. President."

"Thank you, Mr. Addison," President Heringten said, dismissing him.

"Thank you, Mr. President," Gregory said, and left.

He'd have to get a workout in at the office.

195

THE DIAGNOSIS

Al Ain City Hospital
Al Ain, United Arab Emirates

The fourth largest city in the UAE had excellent medical facilities, especially for people with deep pockets.

After many expensive tests, the doctors had good news.

Naveed sat in a comfortable chair in his mother's private room. Sunlight poured through a large window, though the air conditioning kept the temperature pleasant. His mother opened her eyes as the doctor and a nurse entered.

After short pleasantries and a check of his mother's vital signs, the doctor stood by the bed and smiled. "The tests indicate you have a rare disease that is very difficult to diagnose. But now that we know what is happening, you're going to be fine," she told Naveed's mother.

Naveed kept tears from flowing with difficulty, but his mother didn't hold back. She took the doctor's hand and kept thanking her.

"Mom, let go," Naveed said. "She has work to do."

Eventually, the doctor left after explaining the treatment plan they'd start today.

His mother turned to him, tired again but happier than he'd seen her in months.

"What did you do to make this happen?" she asked.

She had questioned him repeatedly the past few days, but he'd been able to put her off. From the look on her face, though, he could not avoid the question any longer.

"I…" He trailed off.

How could he explain what he'd done? From leaving the ISI to work with Colonel Tariq in hopes of earning enough money for today's successful results, to betraying the man for the same reason.

The innocent people he'd had a hand in killing as Tariq's courier.

The guards he had shot in Tariq's warehouse.

The two ISI operators, his own countrymen, who had died in the warehouse—right before they had meant to kill him and the American.

Pulling the American to safety—and the man killing Tariq before saving Naveed's life by getting him out of the claustrophobic tunnel.

"I did what I had to," he finally said, but his mother was already asleep, a smile on her face.

196

THE FAVOR

Operations Room
Fortuna Magnifico Casino and Resort
Las Vegas, Nevada

Kristine stood next to the door to the Vault as her team filed into the operations room and took their seats, looking at her expectantly.

A week ago, speaking in front of them might have made her nervous.

But after all she'd been through, this part was easy.

It was tonight's Saturday dinner that would be a challenge.

There had been too much happening to think about calling off the party, and now it was too late.

Kristine cleared her throat and began her speech. "Thank you all for coming in a bit early, and especially for handling the computer glitch on Monday. I hope you all enjoyed your day off." When the computers weren't working Monday, Kristine had sent the crew home—with pay.

"I have an announcement," she continued. "You may have noticed that Big Mike hasn't been down here in a while. Patrick, either. They have had the opportunity of a lifetime, and have taken a sabbatical. They're traveling for a while, and I'll be in charge until they return."

The lie came easily—and would give her plenty of time to plan for their retirement or unfortunate demise. She'd figure something out.

The men and women who handled the day-to-day operations of the organization took the news in stride. No one acted suspicious.

"It's a sudden change, but everything happened so quickly. Mike said he knew we were all up for the challenge, so we'll do our best, and nail it."

When Kristine gestured to her, Melissa stood at her workstation. "I'm promoting Melissa to be my operations manager. We'll be looking for trustworthy candidates to take her old job. If any of you have recommendations, please see her."

Kristine checked her watch. There was plenty of time, and she had an idea about the dinner. "We have a big night planned. Let's get to it."

The techs turned to their workstations and got busy. Kristine unlocked the Vault door and held it open for Melissa, who walked in hesitantly. "Are you sure about this?" she asked once the door shut.

"You were conned. It was a misunderstanding," Kristine said. "I trust you."

The room was filled with the smell of fresh flowers from a large bouquet that overwhelmed the computer desk. The note from the singer-turned-actor MacKenzie Minrael simply said, "Thank you! XXXOOO"

"Log in, pull up the contact management database, and look up MacKenzie Minrael's cell phone number," Kristine told Melissa. Kristine couldn't stomach taking one of her father's chairs yet, so she stood behind the desk chair as Melissa assumed Kristine's old position and got to work.

Melissa removed the office cell phone from its signal-blocking case and dialed the number.

When the singer answered, Kristine was ready. "Hi, MacKenzie. This is Kristine from Las Vegas—we spoke a few weeks ago?"

"Hi, Kristine! Yes, of course I remember our chat." She really was a talented actress—MacKenzie sounded like Kristine was her long-lost best friend she hadn't heard from in much too long.

"Big Mike wanted to call himself, but he's on a sabbatical. He left me in charge. We rarely publicize it, but I'm his daughter." Kristine hated to play the family card, but she needed all the pull she could get. "We wanted to congratulate you. Great job nailing the audition. We're so excited to see your movie debut. And thanks for the flowers. They're exquisite."

"Thank you, Kristine—and please pass along my undying gratitude to Big Mike. I couldn't have done it without you guys."

"That's sweet of you to say. You did the heavy lifting—we only made the introductions."

MacKenzie laughed, a throaty chuckle that the public would love when she became a movie star. "You're too modest. Corey Langfore practically begged me to take the part. You did more than put in a word for me—you made it happen. I'm in your debt. Forever."

Kristine let it go without comment, wondering what sort of arm-twisting Dominic had done to Langfore that Mike hadn't told her about. When he and Thomas flew in later tonight, she'd have to ask about that.

And whether he would do the same for her, if needed.

"Well, now that you mention it, I wondered if I could impose upon you for a favor," Kristine asked. She'd try the soft approach first. If that didn't work, she would have to play hardball. Not only did the singer owe Mike —and now Kristine—but they'd found some pictures on her phone she was sure the woman would rather stay private.

There was the slightest hesitation from MacKenzie, but she sounded sincere when she spoke. "Name it," she said.

"Last minute notice, but Big Mike has his traditional Saturday night dinner scheduled for tonight, and he's already left on his trip. I have to host, but I'm a major wallflower. I could use a wingman. Or in this case, a wingwoman. What do you say? I can have a jet ready to fly you in as soon as you can get to the airport. You're less than an hour away. Want to mix and mingle with the CEOs of three high-flying tech companies, two superstar football players, and—this might interest you—an up-and-coming fashion designer? And everyone's partners, of course. Could you help Big Mike and me out?"

"It's like the lunch I had with Mike—only bigger? More of a party?"

"Exactly. You back me up, help me host."

"Hell yes!" MacKenzie said. Kristine had to hold the phone away from her ear to lessen the sound as MacKenzie yelled, "Vegas, baby!"

After working out the details, they hung up. The party would be a lot easier with MacKenzie there.

Finally, Kristine sat in her father's favorite wingback chair in the corner and opened the secure comms app.

Gregory Addison needed to know a few things about what had happened in Afghanistan. She owed it to him.

She'd send him one last message.

197

THE WALK

58 Desert Song Lane
Henderson, Nevada

Shane struggled to contain his anger as he walked along the suburban sidewalk. He'd waited until almost midnight to avoid the post-sunset dog walkers and joggers. At this time of night, Melissa's neighborhood was deserted. The houses were dark, and the night was quiet.

He adjusted the baseball cap he'd bought at the airport, pulling it lower over his face. Too many people had security cameras these days. It wouldn't do to get caught on one tonight. Although he didn't plan on killing Melissa, he was prepared to hurt her.

Badly.

He'd do anything necessary to get the mini flash drive's password. If he couldn't access the data stored on it, everything he'd worked for would have been for nothing.

And if things went too far tonight…

Well, as long as he got the password and made it out of the country before the police caught him, so be it. He was done messing around.

He'd agonized over the password prompt for days, guessing what Melissa would have entered. She had surprised him by encrypting the device. That hadn't been part of the plan. She hadn't even mentioned it.

On some level, maybe she knew all along he was conning her.

He only wished he'd been able to pull off his initial deceit a little longer—and had thought to check the drive before dumping her and the guard in the desert.

At least she had lived.

If she hadn't survived, he'd be out of luck.

He had to smile, though. He'd pulled his own switch by reversing the order of the long alphanumeric password to unlock the ransomware.

The look on everyone's faces when they weren't able to get into the computer server, even with the password he'd left with Melissa, would have been something to see.

In a pinch, he was willing to trade passwords. It wasn't ideal, but he'd do it if he had no other option.

Shane cut across Melissa's front yard, planted his hands on the top of the side fence, and vaulted over, exactly as he had the first time.

He pulled the stun gun out of his pocket, flicked off the safety, and snuck along the side yard. Melissa had come home from work later than usual, but the house was dark. She had to be sleeping soundly upstairs by now.

The lock on the back patio door was child's play with the lock pick gun. Anyone could have broken in.

Melissa hadn't gotten smart. There was no dowel or additional latch keeping the door closed.

Shane slipped inside, closed the door quietly behind him, and stood still, allowing his eyes to adjust to the dark.

Electricity jolted through his body, filling it with searing pain. His muscles contracted as he froze in place. It felt like the hand of a giant was squeezing the life out of him.

He panicked but couldn't move, couldn't fight, couldn't scream.

He hadn't realized how horrible it was to be zapped.

"Let's see how you like it," a man's voice said next to him.

Shane was dimly aware of padded cuffs being attached to his wrists and ankles.

A distant part of his mind told him this was a bad sign. Padded cuffs wouldn't leave marks on his body like plastic zip ties could.

Hands roughly searched him, found the small flash drive, and removed it from his pocket. The stun gun, lock pick gun, and his phone were taken, too.

Shane was picked up and carried to the garage. An older car was parked next to Melissa's. He must have been here all along.

The man carrying him grunted with the effort. It had to be the old guard Shane had zapped and dumped in the desert with Melissa.

Shane was dropped into the trunk, and the car started.

They drove and drove.

Much later, the trunk opened.

Shane was zapped again, longer this time, until his mind nearly shattered with the pain, fear, and agony.

He was dimly aware of being dropped to the ground.

His shoes and socks were removed.

Then the old guard cut his clothes off.

Shane tried to fight, but he had no strength. Not after so much electricity had coursed through him.

Finally, the cuffs were unbuckled.

"I doubt you'll live," the man's voice said. Definitely the man from several days before. "But if you do, don't come back. Don't get in contact with Melissa. Don't mess with us. Disappear and consider yourself lucky. Because if we ever see or hear from you again, I'll bury you out here. Alive. Understand?"

The man didn't wait for an answer. He drove off, leaving Shane staring up at the stars, naked and traumatized, with no idea of where he was.

As soon as he could, he got to his feet and looked around.

He couldn't hear the car, and there were no taillights.

Hilly desert stretched out in every direction.

The stars were no help. He'd never learned how to navigate by them.

A long way off, there was a glow in the sky that could be the lights of Las Vegas, but he wasn't sure. And walking directly toward the city wouldn't be smart.

He felt on the ground for tire tracks, found what he hoped were them, and started walking.

Every step hurt his bare feet.

They would be bloody in less than a mile.

And after the sun came up, the ground would be much too hot to walk on.

He kept walking. There was nothing else he could do.

What the hell had he been thinking?

He should never have crossed Big Mike.

198

THE SCROLL

Conference Room 1
Central Analysis Group Headquarters
Alexandria, Virginia

Wyatt was back at work, fresh from sleeping ten hours in his own bed. A few more days like that and he'd be back to his old self in no time.

He removed the folded quilt of papers from his desk safe, grabbed his laptop, and claimed the huge table in conference room 1 for his mind map.

The tape holding the pages together was as brittle as ever. He wasn't sure how many times he could fold and unfold it before the paper and the tape ripped beyond repair.

Maybe he should stop going home for a while. Sleeping on the carpet under the table during the crisis had been rather comfortable—except for not knowing where he was and slamming his head into the underside of the table when he awoke.

He pulled up video footage from the Paris bombing, along with reports from France's DGSI.

There had to be something here to help put the puzzle together—and prevent the next attack.

If the terrorist behind the bombings kept to his schedule, Wyatt had fewer than three months to figure out the next target.

Gregory had been helping his wife clean up after dinner when his phone buzzed with the angry tone of an encrypted message coming in.

After the week they'd had, Shari understood more than ever what the sound meant.

He left for the office a few minutes later. He couldn't allow Wyatt to waste time on his latest obsession.

There were other threats that needed his focus.

Wyatt took in his creation. The scrawled notations, lines, arrows, and sticky notes, including a yellow one off to the side—his best guess so far.

Pakistan ISI officer? Retired?

Weeks of effort, four international bombings, and nothing more than that to show for it.

If there were only a way to infiltrate the ISI.

He went to the conference room window and tilted the white blinds hiding him from the bullpen where the analysts had their cubicles.

Haley Albright's cube was at the far end.

Empty.

Of course—it was Saturday night. Unless there was a threat to the country, she'd be doing whatever she did on the weekends.

But come Monday morning, he'd have a talk with her.

She had resources he didn't—he'd pieced that together from the things she'd said while training him.

Maybe she could help. Send a direct-action operator to Pakistan to bribe an ISI human resources person to reveal who had retired from the service a year or two earlier.

It was a long shot, but...

Gregory walked by the window and nodded at him. A few seconds later, Gregory entered and locked the door behind him.

"I thought I'd find you here," he said. He wore jeans and a sweatshirt, not a suit, as he would have worn if this had been a normal work day.

Wyatt said nothing. Gregory popping by the office dressed like this meant something had come up, but not an emergency.

As they walked to the table, Gregory slipped his phone from a pocket and entered two separate passwords. Standing over the mind map, Gregory read a message. "The person responsible for the Paris bombing—and Egypt, Turkey, and Spain—was Colonel Tariq, a retired Pakistan ISI officer known for his logistical abilities, vast network, and bomb-making expertise. He allowed terrorist groups to pay him to take credit for his attacks."

Gregory reached to the side of the paper and picked up Wyatt's sticky note with his carefully printed headline: *Pakistan ISI officer? Retired?*

He held it up for a second before ceremoniously placing it in the center of the mind map, where all the lines from other notes led to the empty center square.

Gregory read from his phone again. "Tariq is confirmed dead, and his bomb-making facilities were destroyed. The ISI did not condone nor support the attacks—Tariq had gone rogue."

Gregory swiped the message away and returned the phone to his pocket. "I thought you should know."

Wyatt struggled for words, finally blurting out the first thing that came to mind. "Are you sure?"

"Yes."

"Wait." He glanced at Gregory's pocket. "Who…?"

Gregory's face was blank. Wyatt wouldn't get any details from him.

"Did we…?" Wyatt asked, trailing off as he realized the inappropriateness of the question.

"No," Gregory said, his voice firm. "If there were operators present, it wasn't us or any of our allies."

"Then how…?"

Gregory didn't bother to answer. "You were right," Gregory said, gesturing at the sticky notes filled with cramped writing, the many arrows and lines connecting them, all leading to the bright yellow note in the center of it all with *Pakistan ISI officer? Retired?* printed on it. They stood side by side, staring at the paper quilt. "Well done, Wyatt," Gregory said. "You would have gotten the full story sooner rather than later. I have no doubt."

Wyatt accepted the compliment but wasn't sure it would have worked out as Gregory said.

"I guess that's it then." Wyatt said. He tried to hold back a sigh and failed. "What about all this?" He gestured at the mind map—the creation he'd obsessed over for weeks.

Gregory offered a sad smile. "Shred it, then put it in the burn bag."

Wyatt couldn't hold back a pained sound of grief, frustration, and agony at the thought. It was time to let go of the project. To leave it behind. His shoulders slumped. "Yes, sir."

Gregory walked to the door and unlocked it before turning. "Find the next threat. Solve the puzzle. Protect the country."

Wyatt thought of the endless stream of data waiting for him. The hints and clues. The connections no one else could find—except maybe Haley. A new challenge awaited.

"Yes, sir!" he called as Gregory closed the door behind him.

Wyatt was back in his cubicle, the mind map shredded into tiny pieces of confetti and stuffed into a burn bag, ready to be turned to ash.

He perched on the edge of his chair, elbows on his desk, chin resting on his clasped fingers, eyes inches from his twin computer monitors.

It had been weeks since he'd last watched the reports from the country's intelligence agencies on his screen. When he'd first joined the Central Analysis Group, he'd reconfigured the display from primarily search-focused to a ceaseless scroll of headlines and top-secret report titles marching down the monitor.

It was nearly impossible to keep up with the listings, but he let his mind go, absorbing the incredible amount of intel coming into the system.

There were tidbits out there.

Clues to upcoming attacks.

Information that would lead to terrorists and extremists who wanted to harm the United States—and the world.

Pieces that, when put together, revealed threats, plots, and dangers.

All he had to do was recognize which tidbits were important…

And use them to save lives.

199

THE ARRIVAL

Henderson Executive Airport
Henderson, Nevada

The small airport east of Las Vegas wasn't set up to receive international flights, and was usually closed at this time of the night, but Kristine hadn't let that stop her. The director of operations was in Big Mike's database as a binge gambler Mike had bailed out twice already. He'd been clean for a while, but had recently picked up the habit again. He stood in the dark next to her on the tarmac, looking nervous and uncomfortable.

"The plane doesn't have any guns, drugs, or terrorists, right?" he asked. "I'm way out on a limb here. It's the middle of the night. I had to call in the air traffic controller and the chief of security and promise them both they wouldn't get in any trouble over this." He leaned closer to her so he could whisper. "The security chief is in the terminal, watching. He might come out and demand to inspect the plane."

"That's fine," Kristine said. "There's nothing illegal going on." Except for bringing Dominic and Thomas back to the United States, straight from Afghanistan, without going through customs or passport control. "Mike is helping out a friend—an NGO."

"What's an NGO?"

"Non-governmental organization. A charity, basically. In this case, one that helps rural areas of Afghanistan. These guys were helping build roads, dig wells, that sort of thing. The Taliban shot one of them." She turned to the airport manager. "We're bringing him back here to get better medical care. His daughter lives in Las Vegas."

All lies, but blaming the Taliban was a great story for the manager to tell the other people he'd had to loop into her scheme.

"We can search the plane? And inspect the IDs of the passengers?" The operations director sounded shocked that it would be that easy.

"Yes. Whatever you need to do."

"And then I'm square with Big Mike? He's going to wipe out my latest debts?"

"Your people will be taken care of," Kristine said. She held up two business-size envelopes thick with cash. The man eyed them hungrily. "But about your compensation..." In the distance, an airplane lined up on final approach, its lights winking in the dark sky.

At some point, Kristine would have to formally take over from Mike. For now, she would rely on his reputation—and start to include herself in the process. "We'll take care of your markers, but there's no cash for you." The operations director deflated. "And as much as we appreciate your help tonight, I have a warning."

"A warning?"

She fixed him with her best drop-dead gaze, hoping she was channeling her father's likeness. "No more gambling. You were doing well there for quite a while. Get back to meetings or therapy or whatever you have to do. If we catch you gambling again..."

The man waited expectantly, but she didn't continue.

"What?"

"Think of the worst thing imaginable. That's what Big Mike said to tell you." She'd heard her father use that line before.

From the man's reaction, it worked.

"Never again," he said, and she believed him.

"Bring out your security guy," Kristine told him. "We've got nothing to hide."

Bone sat in the back seat of Kristine's sedan after helping Dominic sit in the front. The older man hated needing help, but settling into the low vehicle clearly hurt.

They'd both slept most of the sixteen-hour flight, aside from a few minutes of after-action report from Bone, and Dominic complaining about being on the sidelines for the battle.

As Kristine drove them off the airport grounds, Dominic cleared his throat. "First off," Dom said, "I want to apologize to you, Kristine." He turned to Bone. "And to you."

Bone raised his hand to protest, but Dominic glared at him. "I never meant for you to take on the entire mission by yourself." He turned back to Kristine. "He did an outstanding job—and I should have been with him."

Bone waited to make sure he was finished, then jumped in before Kristine could. "You saved my life, and Sardar's. You kept the mission going. It's always a team effort, right?"

Dom nodded, grumpy but conceding the point.

"The operation was successful. And everyone came home alive—if a little worse for wear," Kristine said.

"Now that we have that out of the way," she said, and pulled the car onto a side street a few miles from the airport, "we have a call to make." She fiddled with her cell phone.

The sound of the call connecting came over the car's high-end speaker system. She snapped her fingers twice, paused two seconds, then snapped them once again.

"Hello, everyone," Sardar said. He sounded alert, but tired.

"Hello," Kristine said, and gave a nod to Bone and Dominic, who repeated the greeting.

"I won't keep you," Sardar said. "But I wanted to extend my thanks." He paused as his voice cracked. He cleared his throat and continued. "The man Mike and I have hunted for years is dead, thanks to you."

"Thanks to all of us," Bone said, jumping in. "The operation wouldn't have succeeded without you and Mike pursuing the leads all this time." He turned to Kristine in the front seat. "Or you keeping it together when Patrick…" He trailed off.

Kristine looked down and nodded.

"And especially you, kid," Dom said to Bone.

"And my contacts here in the states—along with their relatives," Bone said. He would pay a visit to Zia and Lamar. They deserved his thanks.

"We all played a part," Sardar said. "But Mike and I had to. The rest of you—"

"Had our duty just as much as you," Kristine said.

There was silence for a second until Sardar spoke again. "Mike would be grateful and very proud of you all. Especially you, Kristine."

They shared a moment of silence.

"To Mike," Kristine whispered.

"To Mike," they repeated.

After a pause, Sardar sniffed and cleared his throat. "Until we meet again," he said, followed by a click of the call disconnecting.

200

THE REQUEST

Interstate 40
Kingman, Arizona

It was late—or early, really, when Bone pulled into the rest area along the interstate and parked. He kept the car running. It was too hot to not have the air conditioner on, though it was still dark out.

He'd reached out to Steph at the bar before it closed to let her know he was coming home, but he had one more call to make.

A quick online search on his reclaimed burner phone brought up Donald Everett's home phone number—thankfully, he still had a landline.

Bone dialed, but no one answered. The call went to voicemail.

It took four more tries before a groggy and annoyed Everett answered the phone. "Hello?"

"It's your friend from last Saturday morning," Bone said. "The groundskeeper from the edge of the cliff."

Everett sucked in a breath but said nothing.

That had woken him up.

"I have good news," Bone said. "The danger has passed."

"What—how…?"

"I can't give you details. You understand that from your old life, right?"

"What do you mean? I... I worked at the Department of Transportation."

Bone hoped Everett had been a better liar when he'd been a spy—or when he hadn't been woken from a sound sleep—because he didn't sound convincing this morning.

"Sure. Well, someone at the 'Department of Transportation' must have been looking out for you, because they wanted you safe. Now you are. Believe me or not, but it's been handled. The man who pushed you is gone for good. And no one else is coming after you."

"How do you...?" Everett paused for a second as it all clicked. "Oh."

Bone let the man think he had been responsible for taking out his would-be killer. Bone's actions had made a difference even though he hadn't pulled the trigger.

"Yeah. You're fine now. Get up. Go golfing. And watch that slice."

Bone hung up, opened the burner phone, removed the SIM card, and snapped it in half. He would smash the phone and dispose of the pieces along the way home.

Whether Everett the weasel believed him or not, Bone had done his part.

———

71 Ocotillo Street
Sands, Arizona

Bone took a long hot shower—his first in... he couldn't remember how many days.

The long drive home from Las Vegas had given him plenty of time to process the mission.

He—and the makeshift team that had come together—had prevented hundreds of deaths in Paris and succeeded in killing a notorious bomb maker turned freelance terrorist.

He toweled off and wiped a small circle in the bathroom's mirror.

He looked like hell.

The sleep he'd gotten on the flight from Afghanistan hadn't been nearly enough to catch up.

But he was alive.

And sober.

The big question was, now what?

He had several more weeks until the new school year started.

Bone stared at himself in the mirror. His eyes were a faded black and blue from Tariq's kick to his face in the tunnel fight.

But he looked past the bruising and the bushy beard, searching his soul.

Could he go back to work as a teacher in small-town Arizona?

Wear tan chinos and button-down short-sleeve shirts five days a week?

Wait on standby for Admiral Nalen to maybe drop by with another mission?

And do his best to not drink—one day at a time?

His contemplation was broken by a sharp knock on the door. Stephanie was here.

"Come in, Steph. I'll be right out—I just finished showering." He hurried into his bedroom, made sure the door was closed, and got dressed.

"Thanks for calling," Steph called. "I was a little worried about you. I brought coffee and breakfast burritos."

A minute later, Bone stepped into the living room. Steph had breakfast arranged on his coffee table. She sat forward on the couch, obviously impatient to dig in. Her short hair was still dyed hot pink. "Finally," she said. "I'm starved." She looked up at him. "Wow."

Steph met him in the middle of the room, but not for the hug he'd dreamed of. She was intent on studying his nose and eyes.

"Impressive bruising. Let me guess—I should see the other guy?"

For a second, Bone was back in the partially collapsed tunnel, choking Tariq to death before snapping his neck.

He shook off the memory.

"Too soon?" Steph asked quietly. Her fingertips brushed his face below his eyes. He fought to keep from flinching—or leaning in for a kiss.

Instead, he chuckled to diffuse the tension of the moment.

"No," Bone said. "Not at all. I was doing yoga and fell over. Landed face-first. Lesson learned."

She didn't move away from him. Her nearness made it difficult to keep up the ridiculous lie. He felt like she could see into his soul—and the memory of the men he'd killed, along with the lives he'd saved.

"Yoga, huh?" she asked after a second when he hadn't changed his story.

Bone nodded and offered a smile he hoped looked charming but probably seemed gruesome with his black and blue bruises. "You said something about breakfast?"

Steph still wouldn't move.

Was he supposed to kiss her?

It didn't feel like that's what she wanted, but she was staring intently into his eyes.

She had something on her mind.

Usually, SEALs take charge. Action is almost always better than inaction.

But in this moment, it felt like the best thing to do was wait.

Bone stared down at Steph while she worked through something.

Eventually, she decided. She leaned close to whisper in his ear.

"I want in," Steph said in her frank, no-bullshit way. "Whatever you've been up to, I want to be a part of it."

She leaned back and waited for his answer.

Admiral Nalen had been clear: Bone couldn't tell Stephanie about the missions.

But what if…?

No.

When those lower down the chain of command decided which orders to follow exactly, which to interpret, and which they could safely ignore, the system broke down.

"I can't help you," Bone said. He wouldn't lie to her and deny the existence of what he'd been up to. She was too smart to believe that. But he couldn't involve her.

Orders were orders.

Steph smiled as she turned away.

"We'll see," he thought he heard her mutter, but it might have been his imagination.

"Ready for breakfast?" she asked, and he wondered what the hell he'd do next time when—if—Admiral Nalen showed up with another mission.

201

AUTHOR'S NOTE

Thank you so much for reading. I hope you enjoyed the book.

For a free short story about one of Bone's early missions, scroll to the last page.

For information about my other series (*A Team of One, A Team of Two,* etc.), please keep reading.

But first, if you're interested in seeing book three of the Covert Asset series, starring Thomas "Bone" Marks, where thousands of lives are at risk and Stephanie gets involved in the mission, please let me know:

- Leave a 4 or 5 star ranking for this book
- Write a short review. Something like, "I loved the story and hope the series continues!" would be perfect.
- Drop me a line via email or on social media (see below for contact information).

I'm at a crossroads and am trying to decide whether to continue Thomas's story or start a different spinoff series. (The "Team of" series is continuing—there's no doubt about that!)

If *Target: Redacted* and/or *Target: Unknown* are the first of my books you've read, please check out my other series starting with book one:

A Team of One

New York City faces a fate worse than death, the president suspects a traitor in the government, and an intelligence analyst discovers a diabolical plot.

Former Navy SEAL "Axe" Southmark is enticed out of retirement to help the analyst and the president. But does he have what it takes to save the world?

As a Navy SEAL, Axe was trained to never give up. But after fifteen years on the front lines, it was time to let younger, faster men take the reins.

When he's enlisted to help the president's niece search for both a terrorist on the loose and a traitor in the government, he doesn't hesitate.

It's what he does: protects the vulnerable and hunts bad guys.

With New York City threatened by a virtuoso bomber, there's plenty of both to be done.

Will they be able to stop a madman before it's too late? And is there more to the plot than meets the eye?

Find out in this wild ride of a story.

If you like the adventures of Mitch Rapp, Scot Harvath, Jack Ryan, and Court Gentry, you'll enjoy "Axe" Southmark.

Type this short link into your internet browser to view on Amazon: https://geni.us/Team

---

Finally, please note: in *Target: Unknown*, I used the names of some real places but fictionalize many details.

I also take inspiration from areas but change names and some features to improve the story.

My apologies if you live in or are acquainted with one of the places and think, "Wait, that's not right." You're correct.

License was also taken in describing technology, equipment, weapons, tactics, and military capabilities.

Where location details, distances, or technical issues conflicted with the story, I prioritized the story.

Also:

- **Get a free Thomas "Bone" Marks short story by signing up for my newsletter.**
- **Go to: https://www.authorbradlee.com/story**
- Once again, if you enjoyed the book, please leave a five-star or written review. It helps new readers discover the book and makes it possible for me to continue bringing you stories.
- I'm active on social media, sharing photos and writing progress updates. I also occasionally ask for input on character names, plot points, or reader preferences as I'm writing, so follow me and help out. Find me here:
- Facebook: https://www.facebook.com/AuthorBradLee
- Instagram: https://www.instagram.com/bradleeauthor/
- You can email me here: bradlee@authorbradlee.com
- Finally, please join me in thanking Beth, Nicole, Mac, and Crystal for their help. The book is far better because of them.